James H. Graff, James Grant

The Adventures of Rob Roy

James H. Graff, James Grant

The Adventures of Rob Roy

ISBN/EAN: 9783337341534

Printed in Europe, USA, Canada, Australia, Japan

Cover: Foto ©Andreas Hilbeck / pixelio.de

More available books at **www.hansebooks.com**

THE

ADVENTURES OF ROB ROY.

BY

JAMES GRANT, ESQ.

AUTHOR OF "JACK MANLY," "DICK RODNEY," "SECOND TO NONE,"
ETC. ETC.

LONDON:

GEORGE ROUTLEDGE AND SONS,

THE BROADWAY, LUDGATE;

NEW YORK: 416, BROOME STREET.

LIST OF ILLUSTRATIONS.

CONTENTS.

viii CONTENTS.

ADVENTURES OF ROB ROY.

—◆—

CHAPTER I.

COLIN AND OINA.

THE sun of a September evening — we need not
say in what year—was shining down a wild and
lonely glen, a few miles eastward from the head of
Loch Lomond, where a boy and a girl sat on the
slope of the green hill-side, watching a herd of
fifteen red-eyed, small, and shaggy black cattle,
with curly fronts and long sharp horns, that were
browsing mid-leg deep amid the long-leaved fern.
The place was one of stern and solemn grandeur.

Leaping from ledge to ledge, and foaming between
the grey and time-worn rocks, a mountain torrent,
red and fierce, swept down the steep slope of the
narrow glen, now disappearing in deep corries,
that were covered by dwarf birch, hazel, and alder
trees, and elsewhere emerging in mist and spray,
white as the thistle's beard, till it reached the lake
which reposed under the shadows of the vast Ben
Lomond, whose summits were hidden in grey mist.

Ben Lawers, which towers above the source of the Tay, and Ben More, that looks down on the Dochart with its floating isle, are there; but the king of these is Ben Lomond, a name which means in English " the hill of the lake full of isles," for four-and-twenty stud the loch below ; and the bare scalp of that mighty mountain rises to the height of 3,300 feet above the water.   There the wild winds that came in sudden gusts down the glens, furrowed up the bosom of the loch, causing its waters to ripple on the silent shore, and on its verdant isles, with a weird and solemn sound.

But here where our story opens, the shrill note of the curlew, as he suddenly sprang aloft from the thick soft heather, made one start ; while the rush of the many white watercourses that poured over the whinstone rocks, and woke the silence, was sharp and hissing.   The setting sun shed a flood of purple light along the steep-sided glen, making the heather seem absolutely crimson.

The boy and girl, Colin Bane, the son of a widow, and Oina MacAleister, belonged to the clachan, or village—the smoking chimneys of which alone indicated its locality—about three miles off; for the walls of the little cottages so closely resembled the grey rocks of the glen, and their roofs, thatched with heather, blended so nearly with the mountain-side, that, except for the forty little columns of white vapour that ascended into the clear evening sky, there was nothing else to indicate a human habitation.

Neither of these young people was above twelve years old; but the boy was tall, lithe, and manly for his age. His dark grey eyes were keen and sharp as those of the wiry otter terrier that sat beside him; and his bare legs, which his tattered kilt revealed from the knee, showed that he was handsome as well as strong—so strong, that he was already entitled to wear a man's bonnet, as a proof that he could lift and fling the " stone of strength," —the test of manhood, which lay beside the door of Rob Roy's house, as beside that of every Highland chieftain, to test the muscle of his growing followers; for previous to being able to poise and hurl the *Clachneart*, a boy wore his hair simply tied with a thong.

A jacket of deerskin, fastened by wooden buttons and loops of thong; a pouch or sporan composed of a polecat's skin, with its face for a flap ; and a skene dhu (or black knife) stuck in a waist-belt, completed the attire of Colin.

His pretty companion, who sat with her little bare feet paddling in a pool of water that gurgled from a rock, was enveloped in a short plaid of red tartan, fastened under her chin by a little silver brooch, and her thick brown hair, which she had wreathed with blue bells and golden broom, fell in masses on her shoulders.

But the faces of this boy and girl were thoughtful, keen, and anxious in expression; for they were children of a long-oppressed, outlawed, and broken tribe, the MacGregors, or Clan Alpine. Still, as they tended the cattle, they sang merrily; for when reaping in the fields, or rowing on the lochs, casting the shuttle at the loom, or marching in the ranks to battle, in those days the Scottish Highlander always sang.

Ever and anon the boy and girl would pause and utter a joyous shout, when a large brown salmon leaped amid a shower of diamonds from the rough stream that tore through the glen; or when a sharp-nosed fox, a shaggy otter, or a red polecat came stealthily out of the gorse and whins to drink of it; for as yet they had no other visitors, and saw not those who were secretly approaching.

Colin, who had started up to cast a stone at a wild swan, and pursue it a little way, returned breath-less; but nevertheless, producing a chanter of hard black wood, mounted with ivory rings, from his girdle, in which it had been stuck, he said,—
"Come, Oina—Mianna Bhaird a thuair aois—sing, and I shall play."

"It is a song of many verses, and is too long," replied the girl.

"Long! There are only two-and-thirty verses, and mother says that old Paul Crubach can remember as many more."

Colin commenced the air at once upon his chanter, and without further hesitation the girl began one of the old songs which are half sung and half recited, in a manner peculiar to the Highlands.

I have no intention of afflicting my readers with all the said song in Gaelic; but it ran somewhat in this fashion (a friend has translated it for me), and the girl, as she sang sweetly, splashed the sparkling water with her tiny feet :—

> Lay us gently by the stream
>   That wanders through our grassy meads ;
> And thou, O sun ! with kindly beam,
>   Light up the bower that o'er us spreads.
>
> Here softly on the grass we'll sit,
>   Where flowerets bloom and breezes sigh ;
> Our feet laved in the gentle tide
>   That, slowly gliding, murmurs by.
>
> Let roses bright and primrose fair
>   With sweet perfume and lovely hues,
> Around us woo the ambient air,
>   And breathe upon the falling dews.

Intent upon themselves and their simple occupation, and singing thus in the fulness of their young hearts to the objects of Nature, the boy and girl saw not those who were coming up the glen, creeping on their hands and feet, with keen eyes and open ears.

> Place by my hand (with harp and shell),
>   So long our solace and our pride,
> The shield that often roll'd the swell
>   Of battle from our father's side !
>
> Let Ossian blind and tuneful Dall
>   Strike from their harps a solemn sound,
> And open wide their airy hall—
>   No bard will here, at eve, be found !

So closed the song, and at that moment a cry burst from Oina, while Colin sprang up with a hand on his knife, for suddenly there arose out of the long tossing leaves of the braken, or fern, the dark whins and matted gorse, amid which the cattle grazed, about twenty well-armed and fierce-looking Highlanders, whose tattered attire, green tartans, and wild bearing, all proclaimed them to be strangers and foes, who had come intent on spoil and hostility.

CHAPTER II.

THE CATERANS.

WITH her eyes dilated by terror, and her usually ruddy cheeks blanched and pale, the girl clung to her companion, who stood resolutely between her and those who had come so suddenly upon them. Barking furiously, the otter terrier erected his shaggy back and also shrunk close to the side of Colin.

These unwelcome visitors were all armed with basket-hilted swords, dirks, and pistols. He who seemed the leader bore a long *tuagh*, or Lochaber axe, the head of which is adapted for the triple purpose of cutting, thrusting, or hooking an enemy. They all wore waistcoats and hose of untanned deerskin, rough, shaggy, and tied with thongs. Their kilts and plaids were of tattered green tartan, and all wore woollen shirts of dark red dyes. Only a few had bonnets; but in these they wore a tuft of deer-grass, the badge of the Mac-Kenzies. This, however, did not deceive the boy or girl, who knew them to be MacRaes, who followed the banner of Lord Seaforth.

The leader, a giant in stature, but fleet of foot and active as a roebuck, was a dark-visaged and savage-looking man, with eyebrows that met over his nose, and were shaggy as the moustache that curled round his fierce mouth, to mingle with his beard. His belted plaid was fastened by an antique silver brooch covered with twisted snakes, and silver tassels adorned his sporan, which was of otter-skin covered with white spots; and hence such skins are said in Scotland to belong to the king of the otters.

"Keep your cur quiet, boy," said this formidable-looking fellow, " or I must put a bullet into him. Go on with your song, my girl, and don't be alarmed; we shall not harm you."

"He is Duncan nan Creagh!" said Colin.

"And our cattle will be taken," sobbed Oina.

Indeed, while the boy and girl spoke their fears in whispers, the gillies, or followers of Duncan of the Forays, as he was named, ran round the cattle in a circle, driving them together, by holloing and striking them with cudgels or the flat sides of their claymores—occasionally using the point, to spur on the more lazy or refractory. Undaunted by the number of the caterans, Colin began to shout shrilly and wildly for succour; but aid was far off, and the echoes of the rocks alone replied.

"Silence!" exclaimed Duncan MacRae, fiercely, "or I shall fling you into the pool, with a big stone at your neck!"

The boy bravely brandished his skene, and dipping his bonnet in the rivulet, as a defence for his left hand, said,—

"Beware, you false cateran; these cattle are from the lands of Finlarig; and Finlarig belongs to Breadalbane."

The tall cateran grinned, and replied,—

"Ay; but the beasties belong to the Mac-Gregors——"

"From whom all men may take their prey," added another.

"True, MacAulay, and were they Breadalbane's own, every hoof and horn should be mine, even though he were here, with all the Clan Diarmed of the Boar at his back. Hear you that, my little man? But the Griogarich—wheeugh!"

And the tall cateran snapped his fingers with contempt and grinned savagely, as he made a whistling sound.

This action, and the slighting manner in which his clan was spoken of, made Colin tremble with rage. His ruddy cheek grew pale with emotion, and his eyes flashed with light.

In pursuing a sturdy little bullock, one of the MacRaes dropped a pistol. Quick as lightning, young Colin sprang forward, possessed himself of

it, and fired full at the head of Duncan nan Creagh!
The latter reeled, for the ball had pierced his
bonnet, and grazed the scalp of his head, causing
the blood to trickle over his sombre visage. Then,
before he could recover himself, the fearless boy
hurled the empty pistol, which was one of the heavy
steel *tacks* still worn with the Highland dress, at
the cateran's head, which it narrowly missed.

Oina and he now turned to seek safety in flight;
but the MacRae caught him by the hook of his long
poleaxe, and fearing further violence, the brave
Colin clung to his right arm with fierce energy.
Duncan tried to shake him off; but in vain. At
last, he fiercely *bit* the hand of the poor boy, who
relinquished his hold with a scream of pain.

At that moment the savage fellow exclaimed,—

" Wasp of a MacGregor, *that* will take the sting
out of you," and cut down Colin, by a single stroke
of his ponderous axe, severing his right (some say
his left) arm from his body.

Without a moan, Colin fell on the heather in a
pool of blood.

" Quick, lads, quick ! " exclaimed the remorseless
Duncan; " drive on the prey; the MacGregors will
soon scent the blood and be on our track."

At some distance from the bleeding and dying
boy, Oina sank upon the ground, screaming wildly,
and covering her face with her hands and hair.

"What shall we do with the girl?" said one;
" she will soon reach and rouse all the clachan."

" Take her with us," suggested another.

" Oich—oich ! that would be kidnapping."

" But she is only a MacGregor's daughter," said a third.

" And you shall soon be tracked by one Mac-Gregor, who will revenge us," exclaimed the girl, whom excess of terror now endued with courage.

" Oich ! and who may he be ? " asked Duncan nan Creagh, mockingly.

" Rob Roy of Inversnaid."

" The Red MacGregor—is that all ? "

" All ! Conn Ceud Catha was a boy when compared to him, as you shall soon find, false thief of a MacRae."

" A swim in the linn will be good for one of your temper," said the tall Cateran, as he took up the girl, and regardless of her shrieks, rushing to where the torrent that flowed towards Loch Lomond poured over a brow of rock forming a cascade that plunged into a deep pool below, he tossed her in, without ruth or pity.

In falling, Oina caught the stem of a tough willow, and clung to it with all the tenacity a deadly fear could inspire. The rush of the foaming torrent was in her tingling ears, and its snowy spray covered her face, her dress, and floating hair, as she swung over it. She closed her eyes and dared not look; but her lips prayed for mercy in an inaudible manner, for the power of speech had left her. And now, with her weight, the willow bent so low that at last her feet and ankles dipped in the rushing water ; while with a pitiless frown, the

wild MacRae—for so this tribe was named, from
their fierce, lawless, and predatory habits—surveyed her from the bank above. Then saying,
" Oich—oich, but the Griogarich are folk that are
hard to kill," by a slash of his long axe he severed
the willow, and with a faint shriek Oina vanished
into the cascade that foamed beneath !

Duncan nan Creagh then hastened to overtake
his gillies, who by this time had driven the cattle
across the stream, which they forded in the old
Scottish fashion, with their swords in their teeth,
and grasping each other's hands to stem the current,
which, otherwise, must have swept them away
singly, as it came up to their armpits.

They then wrung the water from their plaids, and
driving the cattle at full speed by point and flat of
sword, hurried up a gloomy and lonely ravine, and
soon disappeared, where the sombre evening
shadows were deepening over the vast mountain
solitude.

Well did they know that the vengeful Mac-
Gregors, whom some aver to be the Children
of the Mist, would soon be on their track, following them with blade and bullet, hound and
horn.

The poor boy soon expired, but the girl was not
destined to perish. She was swept by the torrent
round an angle of the rocks, towards a pool, where
a young man was fishing.

He saw her body whirling in the flood, and without a moment of hesitation, cast aside his bonnet

and plaid, his rod and dirk, and plunging in, soon
caught her in his arms.

Being powerfully athletic, he stemmed the fierce
brown torrent, which ran like a flooded millrace,
bearing along with it stones, clay, and dwarf trees,
the spoil of the hills that look down on Loch
Dochart; and, after a severe struggle, he reached
the bank and laid the girl on the grass.

"Oina!" he exclaimed, with deep commiseration,
on removing the masses of wet brown hair from her
pallid face, for he recognized her to be the child of
his own foster-brother.

She was pale, cold, severely bruised by being
tossed from rock to rock, and lay there to all
appearance dead. He placed a hand on her heart;
he opened and patted her clenched fingers; he
placed his warm ruddy cheek to her cold face, and
his ear to her mouth, to ascertain whether or not
she breathed.

Then taking her up in his arms as if she had been
an infant, he wrapped his plaid around her, and
with rapid strides, hastened towards the smoke,
which curled greyly against the now darkened sky,
and indicated where the clachan or village stood.

This man was Robert MacGregor of Inversnaid
and Craigrostan, otherwise known as Rob Roy, or
the Red, from the colour of his hair, and who, by
the proscription of his entire clan, had been compelled by law to add the name of Campbell to his
own, for reasons which will afterwards be given to
the reader.

CHAPTER III.

THE ALARM.

HE soon reached Inversnaid, which lay about three miles distant.

At first he walked but slowly, comparatively speaking, as he believed the girl to be quite dead; but the motion of her limbs, as he proceeded, having caused the blood to circulate, he perceived with joy that she still lived, and then he increased his pace to a run, which soon brought him to the cottage of her father, Callam MacAleister (*i.e.*, the son of the arrowmaker), to whose care he consigned her; and the bed of the little sufferer was rapidly surrounded by all the commiserating gossips and wise-women of the clachan.

No doctors were required by the hardy men of these secluded districts. Their wives and daughters knew well how to salve a sore; to bind up a slash from an axe or sword; to place lint on a bullet-hole, or on a stab from a dirk; while valerian, all-heal, liver-wort, and wild carrot, bruised in a quaichful of whisky, formed the entire *materia medica* of the matron of a family. So men lived till patriarchal years, strong, active, and fearless as mountain-bulls; for sickness was unknown among them.

Of these female family physicians, Rob's wife,

the Lady of Inversnaid, was the queen in her time and locality.

Inversnaid is a small hamlet on the estate of the same name which formed the patrimony of Rob Roy. It lies two miles eastward from Loch Lomond, on the bank of a small stream, which falls into the great sheet of water, from a lesser, named Loch Arklet, a place of gloomy aspect.

Northward, on the side of the latter, is a deep and wild cavern, which sheltered Robert Bruce after the battle of Dalree, in Strathfillan; and on more than one occasion, in time of peril, it became a place of concealment for our hero.

As MacGregor approached his own house—a large and square two-storied mansion, the walls of which were rough-cast with white lime, and which, though thatched with heather, had an air of comfort and consequence in that locality,—a wild cry, that pierced the still air of the evening, made him pause and turn round with his right hand on the hilt of his dirk.

Alarmed by the protracted absence of the boy, Fairhaired Colin, his widowed mother had sought the glen where the foray had been. The last red gleam of the sunset had faded upward from the summit of Ben Lomond, and the dark woods and deep glens about its base were buried in all the obscurity of night, till the moon arose, and then the mountain-stream, and the pools amid the moss and heather, glittered in its silver sheen.

The cattle had disappeared as well as their

young watchers, and the heart of the widow became
filled with vague alarm.

Now a mournful cry came at times upon the
wind of the valley, and made her blood curdle.
Was it the voice of a spirit of the air, or of a water-
cow, that had come down the stream from the loch?
Again and again it fell upon her ear, till at last she
recognized it to be the howling of her son's companion and favourite, the little otter terrier; and
she rushed forward to discover the dog, which was
concealed by some tufts of broom.

The sweet perfume of the bog-myrtle was filling
the atmosphere as the dew fell on its leaves; and
now, deep down in the glen, where the soil had
never been stirred, where the heather grew thick
and soft, and where the yellow broom shed " its
tassels on the lea," the poor woman found her son,
her only child, lying dead, and covered with blood.

His right hand still grasped his skene dhu, and
near him lay the chanter, to the notes of which
Oina had sung, and a black, ravenous glede soared
away from the spot as she approached.

At first, his white and ghastly face, his fixed and
glazed eyes, struck terror on the mother's soul,
and she shrunk back—shrunk from the babe she
had borne, the child she had nursed; then she cast
herself in wild despair beside the body—in such
despair as had never filled her heart since the
Grahames of Montrose had hanged her husband,
Ian Banc, on the old yew-tree of Kincardine, for
the crime of being a—MacGregor.

Then enducd by frenzy with superhuman strength, she snatched up the dead boy, and bore him in her arms, sending shriek after shriek before her, as she rushed through the glen and across the moorland, towards the clachan of Inversnaid.

It was her cry that Rob Roy heard, as he paused at his own threshold, and turning away, he hastened to meet her, just as she sank at the door of her cottage.

The whole population of the clachan was speedily alarmed, and the wailing of the women mingled with the deep-muttered vengeance of the men, as they began to arm, and looked to Rob Roy for orders and instructions.

CHAPTER IV.

THE HOLY STEEL.

THE inhabitants of the little hamlet were soon assembled in and around the hut of the widow of Ian Banc.

The latter had been a brave man, sacrificed in their fcud with the Grahames, after the battle of Killycrankie, where he had served under Viscount Dundee. He was long remembered on the Braes of Balquhidder, as an expert swordsman, a hardy deer-stalker, and a careful drover of cattle for the English and Lowland markets, where he had been wont to march after his herds, with his sword at his side, and a target slung on his back, as was then the custom of the Highlanders to go to fair and market.

A few lines will describe the residence of his widow.

It was a somewhat spacious hovel, built without mortar, of turf and stone, taken from the river's bed, or from the adjacent moorland. It had a little window on each side, and these were wont to be opened alternately, according to the part from which the wind blew, to give light and air, opened by simply taking out the *wisp* of fern which was stuffed into the aperture in lieu of glass and shutters.

A fire of turf and bog-fir blazed on the centre of the clay floor; and here, in this poor dwelling, the widow lived, amid smoke sufficient to suffocate her (had she not been used to it from her infancy), together with her slaughtered boy, her Fairhaired Colin, and a brood of hens, whose roost was among the rafters; a cow, two large dogs, and a sheep or so in winter, though sheep were little cared for in the Highlands then.

A few deer hams, and quantities of fishing gear, hung from the rafters, amid which the smoke curled towards an old herring cask, that was inserted in the thatched roof to form a chimney.

Fresh fir-cones and bogwood were cast upon the fire by order of Rob Roy; and now the ruddy blaze lit up a wild and striking scene. Near the centre of the hut, on a rudely-formed deal table, lay the dead body of poor Colin Bane MacGregor, the golden hair from whence he took his sobriquet all matted with purple blood; but a white sheet was now spread over the mangled form, which lay stiff and at full length in rigid angularity, with a platter of salt upon its breast, and sprigs of rosemary strewed crosswise over it.

At the feet of the dead, on her knees, knelt the sorrowing mother, with her grizzled hair dishevelled, and her face buried in her tremulous fingers, through which the tears were streaming, as she rocked her body to and fro.

Fully armed, three Highlanders of formidable aspect and stately bearing stood at the head of the corpse. These were Rob Roy, Callam Mac-Aleister (his foster-brother and henchman), with Greumoch MacGregor, one of his most active and resolute followers. Each leant upon a brass-mounted and long-barrelled Spanish musket.

Grouped round were a band of hardy and weather-beaten men, in rough Highland dresses of home-spun and home-dyed tartan, all hushed into silence, with their keen grey eyes bent darkly on the corpse, or on each other, and with their brows knit as their hearts glowed for vengeance on the unknown perpetrator of this outrage; for as yet no information could be gathered from the half-drowned Oina.

Outside the door were the women of the clachan with their heads muffled in plaids, kerchiefs, and curchies, wailing as only the Celts of Scotland and Ireland wail, in a weird, wild cadence, muttering vengeance too, and suggesting to each other who might be the author of this new item to the terrible catalogue of wrongs that had been perpetrated on the MacGregors since the battle of Glenfruin had been fought, about a hundred years before.

And all this was seen by the red light of the bogwood fire, in the wavering gleams of which, as they played upon the winding-sheet, the corpse seemed always as if about to start and arise.

"Ochon, ochon, ochric!" wailed the mother of Colin, as she swayed herself to and fro; "the drops of the blessed dew that God sends on earth are resting on the cold cheek of my fair son this night; and they are not more pure than he was; but I knew he was doomed never to see the leaves of autumn fall!"

"How?" asked several, bending forward to listen.

"He drew the black-lot, when the cake was broken in Greumoch's bonnet on Beltane eve."

"Never say so, widow," said MacGregor; "think only that the lad died as became his father's son, boldly defending his own; God rest him!"

Here all bowed their heads, and many made the sign of the cross.

"A slash with an axe has slain him," resumed Rob Roy; "a sword would never cut so deep; but the brave boy has defended himself, for his skene is yet grasped in his better hand, so let it go to the grave with him."

Mutterings of grim approval went through the group.

"To you, Red Rob, I look for vengeance—for vengeance on the murderers!" cried the mother wildly, as she stretched her hands towards the chieftain.

"And vengeance you shall have, Jean; by the faith of our fathers, you shall!" replied Rob Roy. "I have little doubt that the same hand which slew Fair Colin, cast Callam's daughter into the river; but time will show."

"We have the cattle to recover too," said several; "let us to the hills — to the hills! The creagh (spoil) cannot be far off yet."

"What! are the cattle carried off?" asked Rob, with a darkening frown.

"The cattle I bought at Fil-ma-chessaig—that blessed 21st of March, at the fair of Callender—ay, every hoof and horn," said Greumoch.

"Well, the blackest mail we ever levied will I lay on these caterans, and the reddest blood we have shed shall be theirs, Jean! But there are other wounds here," continued Rob, as he turned down the winding-sheet; "look at the poor child's hand: it has been *bitten!*"

"Bitten as if by a wolf!" screamed the mother, with growing horror.

"Nay, bitten by a man who has lost every alternate tooth in his lower jaw, and by that mark shall we know him!"

"Where? among the Buchanans or Colquhouns ? " dcmanded scvcral, while the cxcitement grew apace.

"Among neither," exclaimed a harsh and croaking voice.

" Why—why ? " asked the crowd.

" For 'tis Duncan nan Creagh who did this; Duncan Mhor, from Kintail na Bogh."

" Who spoke ? " said Rob Roy, peering through the smoke which obscured the atmosphere of the hut.

" I, Phail Crubach," replied a decrepit old man, for whom all now made way, with a strangely mingled bearing of respect and aversion ; for this visitor was supposed to have the double gift of prophecy and the second sight.

Phail Crubach, or lame Paul MacGrcgor, was the keeper of a Holy Well near the church of Balquhidder. He had been educated in youth at the Scottish Collcge of Douay ; but on becoming partly insane, he returned to his native place, and became the custodian of a spring which St. Fillan had blessed in the times of old. Near this well he lived in a hut, which was an object of terror to thc peasantry, as it was almost entirely lined and patched with fragments of old coffins from the adjacent churchyard.

At the door of this strange dwelling (on which was a rusty coffin-plate as an ornament) he usually sat and watched the well and the narrow highway, ready to afford any wayfarer a draught from the spring, for which he received a small remuneration, either in coin or food—such as meal, cheese, butter, and a bit of venison, which any man might then have for the shooting thereof.

He was clad in a coat and breeches of deerskin; he was wasted in form, wan in visage, and had red hazel eyes, that glared brightly through the long masses of white hair that overhung his wrinkled forehead.

Supporting himself on a knotty stick, which had a cross on its upper end, he hobbled forward through the shrinking crowd.

"How know you, Paul, that Duncan Mhor Mac-Rae, from Kintail-of-the-cows, did this?" asked Rob Roy.

"Even by the words you have spoken, had I not better evidence," replied the strange old man.

"Explain yourself, Paul; we have no time for trifling now," said Rob, softly.

"Duncan nan Creagh lost each alternate tooth in his lower jaw when fighting with Colin's father, at the fair of Callender, in the year that the field of Rin Ruari was stricken. They came to dirk and claymore about the price of a Clydesdale cow, and Ian Banc smote Duncan on the mouth with the hilt of his sword, and forced him to swallow a mouthful of his own teeth; and a bitter mouthful he found them."

"Dioul! well?"

"Since then he has been well-nigh a toothless man; but if you would overtake the creagh, lose no time, for I saw the spoil and the spoilers not two hours since."

"You saw them?" exclaimed all, bending forward.

"Yes, I," said Paul, brandishing his pilgrim-staff; "and not quite two hours ago."

"Where?" asked Red MacGregor.

"Crossing the Dochart, and taking the road towards Glenfalloch."

"Which—the military road?"

"No; Duncan nan Creagh knows better than to do that," said Paul, shaking his white locks; "they took the old Fingalian drove-road, right across the mountains towards the north-west."

"'Tis well, kinsman," said Rob Roy, sternly and gravely; "now, men of Clan Alpine, swear with me on the bare dirk, by the soul of Ciar Mhor, to revenge the murder of this boy, our kinsman's son, and then away to the hills—even the hills of Kintail, if need be!"

On this being said, every man unsheathed the long Highland dirk which hung at his right side, and passed round the dead body by the course of the sun, from east to west; for it was the custom in the Highlands to approach the grave thus, prior to laying the dead within it; thus to conduct the bride to the altar and to her home: it is a remnant of fire-worship, and, singularly enough, the wine-decanters and the whisky-bottle are to this hour sent round the dinner-table in Scotland, *deisalways*, from left to right, the last remnant of a superstition that is old as the days of the Druids.

Then Rob Roy, MacAleister, Greumoch, even old

Paul Crubach, and every man present, laid his left hand on the cold head of the fair-haired Colin, and holding his bare dirk aloft, with outstretched arm, swore solemnly, by the souls of their fathers who slept on Inchcailloch, by their own souls, and by the memory of every wrong endured by the Clan of MacGregor since the field of Glenfruin was won by their swords, never to seek rest or repose, altar or shelter, till they had tracked out the spoilers, and avenged to the utmost the murder of the widow's only son.

Then each man pressed the bare blade to his lips, and this—the most solemn oath of the Scottish Highlanders—was named swearing on *the Holy Steel;* and he who broke that terrible vow, or wilfully failed in the task to which he had dedicated body and soul, was liable to be slain, even by his nearest kinsman, as a mansworn coward. The usual length of these Highland dirks is about sixteen inches in the blade; so that a stab may be given three inches *beyond* the elbow, and their hilts are always covered with twisted knot-work, perhaps the last remnant of serpent-worship in Europe.

" Now be it dirk and claymore !" exclaimed Rob Roy. " Do men still think to outrage us because we are a broken and a landless clan? If so, we shall teach them who outlawed the race of Alpine, that if it is lawful to kill a MacGregor, it is also lawful to slay a MacRae, or a Colquhoun, like a faulty hound; so let us to the hills at once, and track the creagh! Meet me at the door of my own house in ten minutes, every man who holds dear the cry for vengeance on our enemies."

"We cannot overtake them to-night," said Greumoch; "for the Colquhouns of Luss have sunk the ferry-boat, or stolen it to Rossdhu; so let us cross the Loch-hean to-morrow"

"Dioul! this counsel is not like yours, Greumoch."

"By dawn the ford of the Dochart will be passable," replied the clansman.

"To-night; I say to-night!" exclaimed Rob, passionately.

"To-night!" reiterated all present, brandishing their swords; "to-night be it, or never!"

"We will take the ford as we find it," said Callam MacAleister; "if they passed it, so may *we*."

"Never let us put off till to-morrow that which we can do or begin to do to-day," said Rob Roy. "*Yesterday* passes into eternity fast enough; and, Greumoch, it is a bitter reflection to a man, that yesterday was a *lost* day—a day that never can be overtaken. All men's hands are against us; but I have sworn, by the Grey Stone of MacGregor, that vengeance shall yet be ours!"

"*Ard choille*, and away!" shouted Greumoch, waving his bonnet, yielding to the general impulse.

Within a few minutes he, with MacAleister, Alaster Roy MacGregor, and sixteen other picked men of the hamlet, mustered at the door of Rob Roy's mansion. Each had on his belted plaid, which means the kilt, with the loose end of the web fastened by a brooch to the left shoulder as a mantle. Each had slung on his back a round target of bull's hide, stretched over fir-boards, and thickly studded with brass knobs; and each was fully armed, with a basket-hilted sword, a long dirk, and claw-butted pistols. Their bullets were carried in pouches, and their powder in horns, slung under the right arm.

The bright moon that lit up the little street of the Highland hamlet, glittered on their weapons, and shone on their weather-beaten faces, which expressed dark anger, eagerness, and determination to overtake the perpetrators of the late outrage.

They spoke little, but, after the manner of their countrymen, hummed or whistled in a surly fashion, the sure precursor of a squabble among Highlanders; and busied themselves with the flints and priming of their pistols, or the thongs which tied their cuarans or home-made shoes, the sole and upper of which are in one piece, and worn like the Roman sandal. Armed like the rest, the Red MacGregor soon came forth, and was greeted by a murmur of applause. "Good wife—Helen," he exclaimed, "it is ill marching with a fasting stomach; bring forth cakes and the kebboc, with a dram of usquebaugh; for the lads must have their deoch an doruis ere we start."

With a short plaid folded over her head and shoulders, his wife, a young and pretty woman, appeared at the door, accompanied by two female servants, having oat-cakes, cheese, a bottle, glasses, and quaichs (*i.e.,* little wooden cups) on an oval mahogany teaboard.

Doffing his bonnet to the black-eyed Dame of Inversnaid, each man took a dram of whisky and a morsel of bread and cheese; more as a ceremony, it seemed, than because it was necessary.

Little Coll MacGregor, then Rob's only child, was held up for his father to kiss. "Now, fare-ye-well, Bird Helen," said he; "ere we return, I will have laid the wolf's head on the heather;" and with his followers, he left the hamlet at a quick pace.

The wife of Rob Roy looked after them for a moment, as their tartans waved, and their bright arms flashed in the moonlight; then her eye glanced down the glen, where the burn wound in silver sheen towards Loch Lomond, and with a single pious hope for her husband's safety, she quietly shut the door, which was well secured by triple locks and bars of iron, and which had, more-over, two loopholes on each side, to fire muskets through. When not required for defence, these apertures were closed within, by a plug of wood. To her, the daughter of a proscribed race, the wife of a levier of black-mail, reared as she had been in the land of swordsmen, among fierce and predatory clans, the departure of her husband on such a mission was not a matter for much anxiety, and yet this pursuit of the MacRaes was the first important exploit of Rob Roy which appears in history.

CHAPTER V.

THE RED MACGREGOR.

"History," says a noble author, "is a romance which is believed; romance, a history which is *not* believed." Hence so much that is fabulous surrounds the name of Rob Roy, that, like Macbeth, his real history and character become almost lost; but I shall endeavour to tell the reader who and what he actually was. Rob Roy MacGregor, otherwise compelled by law (for reasons which shall be given elsewhere) to call himself *Campbell*, was in his twenty-fifth year at the time our story opens.

He was the second son of Lieutenant-Colonel Donald MacGregor, of Glengyle, in Perthshire, who commanded a regiment of infantry in the Scottish army of King James II. of England and VII. of Scotland. His mother was a daughter of Campbell of Glenfalloch, a powerful Highland chieftain, nearly related to the House of Breadalbane; consequently his birth was neither obscure nor ignoble. His elder brother was named John, and he had two sisters. His patrimony was the small estate of Inversnaid, near the head of Loch Lomond, and, through his mother, he had a right to a wild territory of rock and forest, named Craig-Royston, on the eastern shore of that beautiful loch, under the shadow of vast mountains; but, in virtue of the arbitrary Act of the Scottish Parliament, which abolished the name of MacGregor, he was always designated, in legal documents, Robert Campbell, of Inversnaid.

After the bloody clan-battle of Glenfruin, which led to the proscription of the whole of his surname, "few of the MacGregors were permitted to die a natural death," says the historian of the clan.* " As an inducement to murder, a reward was given for every head of a MacGregor that was conveyed to Edinburgh, and presented to the Council; and those who died a natural death were interred by their friends, quietly and expeditiously, as even the receptacles of the dead were not held sacred. When the grave of a MacGregor was discovered, it was common for the villains employed in this trade of slaughter, to dig him up, and mutilate the remains, by cutting off the head, to be sold to the Government, which seemed to delight in such traffic."

The historian proceeds to narrate that the chief purveyor of such goods was a certain petty Laird of Glenlochy, named Duncan Campbell, but more usually known as Duncan *nan Cean*—i. e., " of the heads."

It chanced one night that Lieutenant-Colonel MacGregor (the father of Rob Roy), accompanied by three soldiers of his surname, was passing near the ruins of the old castle of Cardross (wherein

* Dr. MacLeay.

Robert Bruce breathed his last, and which were then visible, a little to the westward of the Leven, in Dumbartonshire), when, in a narrow pathway, they met a man leading a horse, on each side of which a pannier was swung.

The path was rough, as well as narrow, and on meeting four armed men suddenly in the dark, the man shrunk from the bridle of his horse, which reared, and caused the contents of the panniers to make a strange noise among the straw in which they were packed.

"Be not alarmed, good fellow," said Glengyle; "we are not thieves, but soldiers in the King's service. What have you in the panniers?"

The man hesitated, and endeavoured to pass on.

"Speak!" said the Colonel, whose suspicions became aroused; "is it plunder?"

"Heaven forbid—I am an elder of the kirk, sir."

"What then?"

"Heads for the Lords of Council at Edinburgh," replied the stranger, gathering courage.

"Heads of whom?"

"The King's enemies."

"Mean you gipsies, or westland Whigs?"

"Nay; of the clan Gregor."

"He is Duncan nan Cean! He is Duncan of the Heads!" exclaimed Glengyle, with ferocious joy, as he drew his sword. "Villain, I have sought thee long, and now *thy* head shall keep them company!" and, by a single stroke, he, in an instant, decapitated him. The panniers were examined by his followers, who, with rage and horror, found therein several ghastly heads, packed in straw. These they immediately buried in a secret place, and resumed their way before dawn.

Rob Roy's father received the tribute called black-mail, for protecting, in arms, all who were unwilling or unable to protect themselves. This tribute was, in every sense, a legal tax, which the justices of the peace, in the counties along the Highland border, enforced upon the heritors and householders. We know not when the Laird of Glengyle died; but, on one occasion, he led three hundred of his clan against the Macphersons, who had given offence to his friend, the Earl of Moray, and, in marching through the forest of Gaich, he slew the deer, and the forester of Cluny, who had resented their passage.

Red Robert, his second son, was about the middle height, but had a frame possessed of vast strength and great powers of endurance and activity. His shoulders were broad, his chest ample, and his arms were so long that it was commonly said he could garter his hose, below the knee, without stooping. This, no doubt, is exaggeration; but ho possessed

A wondrous length and strength of arm,

which gave him great advantage in combats with the broadsword. Of these he is said to have fought no less than *twenty-two*.

Even in boyhood he excelled in the use of the

claymore and all other weapons; for this he was, no doubt, indebted to the tutelage of his father, old Donald of Glengyle, who had handled his sword in the wars of the Covenanters and Cavaliers.

No man was ever known to *wrench* anything from Rob's hands; and so great was his muscular power that he would twist a horse's shoe, and drive his dirk, to the hilt, through a two-inch deal board; and on more than one occasion he has seized a mountain stag by the antlers, and held it fast, as if it had been a little kid. He never, save once, refused a challenge. This was when a peasant, named Donald Bane, drew a sword upon him.

" Beware, fellow," said Rob; " I never fight a duel but with a gentleman."

His character was open and generous, and it was ever his proudest boast that " he had never been known to turn his back *either on a friend or a foe !* "

His lands were frequently wasted, and his cattle carried off, by bands of caterans from the mountains of Ross-shire and Sutherland; hence, for his own protection, he was compelled to maintain a party of well-armed and resolute followers, who, like himself, acquired great experience in war, with habits of daring.

With an open and manly countenance, his features, in youth, are said to have been pleasing and cheerful in expression; but, by the course of life upon which unjust laws and adverse fortune hurried him, they gradually acquired that grave, and even morose, aspect, which we find depicted in the portrait of him possessed by Buchanan of Arden; the brows are knit, the eyes stern, and the firm lips compressed. He has a moustache, well twisted up, and a short curly beard, neither of which were then worn in England, or the Scottish Lowlands. He wears a round, blue bonnet, with a black cockade, and has his weather-beaten neck without collar or cravat.*

His hair, from the colour of which he obtained his sobriquet of Roy (a corruption of *ruadh*, or red), was of a dark, ruddy hue, with short frizzly locks, which he wore without powder—a foolish fashion that was seldom found among the Highlanders, who usually tied their hair in a club behind. The circumstance that MacGregor was named *Red* Robert, to distinguish him from others, is sufficient to show how false is the popular error which bestows hair of that colour upon every Highlander.

" In his conflicts," says Sir Walter Scott, in the introduction to the novel which bears our hero's name, " Rob Roy avoided every appearance of cruelty; and it is not averred that he was *ever* the means of unnecessary bloodshed, or the actor of any deed that could lead the way to it. Like Robin Hood of England, he was a *kind and gentle* robber, and, while he took from the rich, was liberal in

* Two other portraits of Rob Roy are in existence. One belongs to the Antiquarian Museum at Edinburgh ; the other to the Duke of Argyle, and it had a narrow escape from the fire which consumed the castle of Roseneath in 1802.

relieving the poor. This might be policy; but the universal tradition of the country speaks of it to have arisen from a better motive. All whom I have conversed with — and in my youth I have seen some who knew Rob Roy personally—gave him the character of *a humane and benevolent man.*"

As yet, however, he was neither a robber nor an outlaw; but simply a Highland country gentleman, a chieftain of a broken clan, living under the protection of his mother's name and kindred; farming his little estate of Inversnaid; dealing in cattle, then the chief wealth of our northern mountains; and, being of a warlike disposition, occupying himself as the collector of black-mail—the local tax then paid by proprietors, whose estates lay south of the Highland frontier, to certain warlike chiefs and chieftains, northward of that line, for the armed protection of their lands and goods from the irruption of such caterans as those MacRaes, who had stolen the cattle from Inversnaid, and of whom we left Rob and his men in hot pursuit.

And it was the collection of this duty, *black-mail,* which, in 1729, ultimately led to the embodiment of the Black Watch, or 42nd Highland Regiment; and it was continued to be levied by certain chieftains so lately as the middle of the *last* century— certainly until 1743. At the time we have introduced him to our readers Rob had been married for some time, to a daughter of MacGregor, the Laird of Comar.

Far from being the fighting amazon and fierce

virago whom Sir Walter Scott has portrayed, Helen Mary, the goodwife of Inversnaid, was a kind, gentle, and motherly woman, who never flourished abroad with breast-plate, bonnet, and broadsword, as we see her on the stage, when opposing the bayonets of the redcoats; but who attended to her frugal household, her spinning, baking, and brewing; and who wore the simple kerchief and *tonnac,* or short plaid, which, until the close of the last century, formed the usual female costume in the Highlands; and never, save once, and then on a trifling occasion, did she act a stern and resolute part, in an episode to be narrated in its place.

The reader must bear in mind that Rob Roy was not a chief at the head of a clan, but merely the second son of a chieftain (the *second* rank) at the head of a branch of the Clan Alpine, called the line of Dugald Ciar Mhor (or Dugald with the mouse-coloured hair), and the men of this branch adhered to him, as being his immediate kinsmen and tenants.

Deeply in the heart of Rob Roy MacGregor rankled the story of the wrongs and oppression to which his clan had been subjected by the Scottish Government—wrongs which, after the accession of William III., were rather increased than diminished; and thus he burned for an opportunity of avenging them at the point of his sword, on their chief enemies, the Grahames of Montrose, the Colquhouns of Luss, and others; and ere long

an ample opportunity came.   But meanwhile let us
return from this necessary digression, lest Duncan
of the Forays escape with his spoil.

———◆◇◆———

CHAPTER VI.

THE PURSUIT.

THE inroads of the Highlanders were generally
made upon the Lowlanders, whom they still view as
intruders and aliens ; but since the proscription of
the MacGregors, every man might outrage *them*,
under protection of law, and " lift " their cattle, if
he could do so ; and a knowledge of this increased
the wrath and resentment of Rob Roy and his
followers as they hastened after the MacRaes ;
though why people of *that* name, whose home was
in Kintail, should have come so far to molest the
MacGregors, no one can explain.   In the bright
moonlight the pursuers soon reached the place from
which the creagh or spoil had been taken, the same
where this history opened, and where the widow's
son had been so cruelly slain.

There the MacGregor's sleuth-hound paused and
howled, where Colin's bonnet and the chanter, with
which he had accompanied Oina's song, lay on the
heather, and again he uttered a low prolonged howl
on snuffing the odour that came from a patch of

heath, the darkness of which might make one shudder.

It was the crusted blood of the poor boy's death-wound which still lay there. "Callam, lead the dog across the stream," said Rob; "he must find the scent on the other side; let him but once snuff their footmarks, and then woe to the MacRaes!"

MacAleister, the henchman, dragged the fierce dog, by its leash, across the stream. It was a bloodhound of the oldest and purest breed, being all of a deep tan colour with black spots, about two feet four inches high, with strong limbs, a wide chest, broad savage muzzle, and pendulous upper lip.

Crossing the stream hand in hand, with their pistols in their teeth, to keep the flints and priming dry, the MacGregors reached the opposite bank, while the dog ran to and fro, till he suddenly uttered a growl. He had found a man's bonnet.

"Paul Crubach was right—here is the badge of Seaforth!" said Greumoch MacGregor, tearing a tuft of deer's-grass from the bonnet, and trampling upon it with vindictive hate.

"And there are the cattle-marks," added Rob Roy, who had been scrutinizing the grass and heath by the light of the moon; "cast loose the dog, Callam—the caterans can have gone up the glen but a little way yet."

The henchman let slip the leash, and the hound, without hesitation, placed his nose near the grass, and, uttering from time to time low growls of satis-

faction, proceeded up the glen at a trot, which gave
Rob and his armed companions, active though they
were, some trouble to keep pace with him.

All traces of habitation were soon left behind, as
the pursuers and their questing bloodhound pene-
trated among the dusky mountains, entering on a
wild and silent region of sterile magnificence, above
which towered the double cone of Ben More.

On they went, through the lengthened expanse of
a glen that lay between two chains of barren hills,
at the base of which a river, rushing among fragments of detached rock, foaming over precipices
and plunging into deep dark pools, swept onward
to mingle its waters with the Dochart. The dog
went forward unerringly.

The hoof-marks of the hastily-driven cattle were
occasionally seen among the ferns, the crushed
leaves, the bruised stems and twigs of the wild
bushes; but for a time these traces were lost when
they entered on a great expanse of deep soft
heather, broken only here and there by a pool of
boggy water, which shone whitely in the light of
the waning moon: it was a tract of vast extent,
and all of a dun, dark hue.

Afar off, in the distance, rose the hills of Glenorchy; and now, being somewhat wearied by the
long and arduous pursuit, Rob Roy and his men
sat down beside one of those great grey stones
which stud the Scottish hills and moorlands, mark-
ing either the site of a Druid's altar, an old battle-
field, or a forgotten warrior's grave. On consulting

his watch, Rob found the hour was midnight, and that they had travelled about twenty miles, over a road of unparalleled difficulty.

A dram from Greumoch's hunting-bottle revived them a little, and then MacAleister led the blood-hound in a circuit round the stone to find the scent again. These great tracts of heather are frequently to be met with in Scotland, and concerning them a singular tradition lingers in the Highlands.

It is said that the Pictish race were celebrated for brewing a pleasant beverage from the heather blossom, and that they usually cultivated great tracts of level muir for this purpose, carefully freeing them of stones.

On the extinction of their monarchy, and the fabled extirpation of the whole race by Kenneth II., King of the Scots, after the battle of the Tay, two Picts became his prisoners, a father and his son, who alone knew the *secret* of manufacturing this beverage.

Urged by promises of liberal reward, continues the tradition, the father consented to reveal it, on condition that first they slew his son, whom a Scottish warrior thereupon shot through the heart with an arrow.

"Now," said the stern Pict, "do your worst; for never will I be prevailed upon to disclose a secret known to myself alone."

A second arrow whistled through his heart, and the secret perished with him.

It was on one of these moorland spots that the

MacGregors halted. The eye could detect no living object in the distance, and the wind brought no sound to the ear, as by the great grey stone in the wilderness Rob and his men sat listening intently, and frequently with their ears close to the ground, conversing the while in their native Gaelic, which, though strange in sound and barbarous to English ears, is, like the Welsh, a strong, nervous, and poetical language, expressing the emotions of the human heart almost better than any other in Europe. His followers were beginning to lose heart; and fears that Colin's death might be unavenged and the cattle lost were freely expressed.

"Remember the oath we have sworn, and neither will come to pass," said Rob, with stern confidence. "By the soul of Ciar Mhor, and by all the bones that lie in the Island of the Cell, our swords shall cross theirs before another sunset, or my name is not MacGregor!"

"Four of the cattle are brown beasties of my own," observed Greumoch; "and if they should be lost, and Breadalbane does not see me righted, by St. Colme, I'll bring off the Spanish ram and the eight score of black-faced Galloways that are now in his park at Beallach, though every Campbell in Glenorchy puts his sword to the grindstone for it!"

"And I will back you, Greumoch, though Breadalbane is my own kinsman," said Rob Roy.

"We are Campbells by day, oich! oich!" said Greumoch, in a tone of singularly bitter irony,

which drew muttered oaths from his companions;
" but by night——"

" We are MacGregors like our fathers, and again
the sons of Alpine ! " said Rob, starting to his feet.
" 'S Rioghal mo dhream ! Forward, lads ! Mac-
Aleister shouts to us—the bloodhound has again
got the scent."

The chieftain was right—the noble dog had discovered the trail; and once more the pursuit was
resumed in a direction due north-west. As day
broke, the distant hill-tops became yellow, and the
wild moor gradually lightened around them. Rob
and his followers had just doffed their bonnets, in
reverence to the rising sun—a superstitious act, old
as the days of Baal and the Druids—when a *fox*
suddenly crossed their path.

" Shoot, MacAleister, shoot ! " exclaimed a dozen
voices in an excited manner, for the son of the
arrow-maker was the best marksman on the shores
of Loch Lomond.

" But the creagh — the caterans ! " he urged,
while unslinging his long Spanish gun.

" They cannot hear the shot, and, even if they
did, the fox must not escape."

MacAleister took aim and fired. Then a cheer
of satisfaction burst from the MacGregors, as the
fox rolled over, feet uppermost, dead, about two
hundred yards off; and the pursuit was resumed
with fresh alacrity, as it was then a common Celtic
belief, that to meet an armed man, when proceeding on a hostile expedition, portended success;

but to have your path crossed by a four-footed animal without killing it, or by a woman without drawing blood from her forehead, ensured defeat and flight.

Roused by the report of the musket from their lair among the green feathery bracken, more than. one red roebuck started up and fled towards the desert of Rannoch, on the skirts of which the MacGregors were now entering; and closely following the footsteps of the hound, they drew near the hills that bordered the vast sea of bog and heather.

" Halt! " cried Rob Roy; " do you see *that?*— it is another omen."

As he spoke, a black carnivorous raven daringly soused down upon a poor little lamb that was cropping a patch of grass near its dam, and, in a second, picked out his eyes.   As the lamb bleated loudly, the mountain bird next seized and tore its tongue, but a shot from MacGregor's steel pistol killed them both.

" It foretells good fortune," said he, " and that we shall soon pounce on the MacRaes, even as the raven pounced on the lamb."

Greumoch proposed that they should light a fire of dry heather-root and broil a collop from the dead lamb; but Rob Roy, as he re-loaded and primed his pistol, now detected a faint column of blue smoke that rose at the edge of the moor; and, after breakfasting on a little meal and water, he ordered all to advance, but cautiously, towards it.

' We shall have our collop after we have punished the caterans, Greumoch," said he, good-naturedly. "You remember what the Earl of Mar said after the battle of Inverlochy, when supping cold crowdy out of his own cuaran with the blade of his dagger?"

" ' That hunger is ever the best cook.' "

"Yes; so now, lads, forward again; and remember the widow's son."

The appearance of some cattle grazing near the smoke made the unwearied pursuers certain that those they sought were not far off; but, after drawing stealthily nearer, they discovered that the fire was lighted to cook the food of a family of gipsies, or itinerant tinkers, who were about to take to flight on seeing Rob and his armed band approach. On the former calling aloud that they came thither as friends, the eldest of the wanderers turned to hear what their visitors required of them.

MacGregor inquired if they had seen anything of the spoilers.

"They passed us towards the hills, with twenty head of cattle, only two hours ago," replied the gipsy, "and, by the smoke that is now rising from yonder corrie, I am assured that there they have made a halt."

"Good!" said MacGregor, with grim satisfaction. "What is your name, friend?"

"Andrew Gemmil."

"You are a Southland man?"

"Yes," replied the wanderer, doffing his bonnet

with reverence, for the aspect and bearing of Rob
Roy awed and oppressed him.

" From whence ? "

" Moffat-dale. I will show you a track in the
hills that will lead you to the corrie unseen."

Rob promised the old gipsy two Scottish crowns,
and two silver buttons from his coat, if this service
were done. Dividing his band into two, he led
one party straight up the face of the hill, on their
hands and knees; the other, under Greumoch,
guided by Gemmil, the gipsy, made a *détour*, for
the purpose of entering the corrie or deep ravine
on another point, and thus cutting off the retreat
of the marauders.

———◆———

CHAPTER VII.

HAND TO HAND.

THE autumn morning stole in loveliness over the
purple heather of the vast moor of Rannoch; the
blue hills of Glenorchy, that rose in the distance,
were brightened by the rising sun, and their
grey mists were floating away on the skirt of the
hollow wind.

The dark fir woods which then shrouded the base
of that great spiral cone, the Black Mountain,
tossed their branches in the breeze that swept
through Glencoe—the Celtic " Vale of Tears "—
Dutch William's Vale of *Blood!* A blue stream

poured down the mountain-side, past an old grey-lettered stone, whose carvings told of the deeds of other times. Many are these battle-stones over all the Highland hills, for—in foreign or domestic strife—every foot of the soil has been soaked in the blood of brave men.

Creeping on their hands and bare knees, like stalkers stealing on a herd of deer, Rob and his men advanced up the mountain slope, dragging their swords and Spanish guns after them.

The gipsy who acted as their guide was in front. Thus they continued to ascend for three hundred yards, and soon the sound of voices and of laughter was heard. Then came the unmistakeable odour of broiled meat, and in a few minutes Rob Roy, on peering over a ledge of rock, that was fringed by the red heather, could perceive the party they were in search of and their spoil.

Seated round a large fire of dry bog-roots, on the embers of which they were broiling a road-collop as it was named, were the twenty caterans, conversing merrily, making rough jests on the MacGregors, and passing their leathern flasks (containing usquebaugh, no doubt) from hand to hand, in a spirit of right good fellowship. All wore the green Mac-Rae tartan, and conspicuous among them was Duncan nan Creagh; near whom lay his long pole-axe and brass-studded shield, on which was painted a hand holding a sword, the crest of his surname, —for this unscrupulous marauder was not without pretensions to gentle blood.

His ferocious aspect was greatly enhanced by his large and irregular teeth, which were visible when he laughed.

"I was right," said Rob in a whisper to his henchman, who always stuck close to him as his shadow; "'twas his fangs that left a death-mark in the flesh of Colin Bane, the widow's son."

MacAleister levelled the barrel of his long gun through the heather full at Duncan's head.

"Hold," said MacGregor, half laughing and half angry; "I shall meet Duncan in open fight; but take your will of the rest, thou son of the arrow-maker!"

The deep corrie or hollow wherein the caterans lurked was shaped like a basin or crater, but was open at one end. At the other, or inner end, were all the cattle; so Rob's plans were soon taken. He knew that the conflict would be a severe one, for the men of this tribe were so fierce and tumultuary that they were, as we have stated, named the *Wild MacRaes*; but the clan almost disappeared from the West Highlands, when, a few years after, 600 of them enlisted in the Seaforth Fencibles, or old 78th Regiment.

Greumoch, with the rest of his party, now appeared creeping softly along the other side of the opening, where they set up the shout of *Ard Choille!* This is the war-cry of Clan Alpine, and a volley from five or six muskets formed the sequel to it, and speedily altered the aspect of the carousing party; for the whole MacGregors rushed on them in front and flank, with swords drawn, and heads stooped behind their targets.

With a thousand reverberations the jagged rocks gave back the sharp report of the muskets and pistols. A yell rose from the hollow, and in a moment the MacRaes, three of whom were bleeding from bullet-wounds, were up and ready with sword, dirk, and target. Hand to hand they all met in close and deadly strife, the long claymores whirling, flashing, and ringing on each other, or striking sparks of fire from the long pike with which the centre of every target was armed.

Swaying his pole-axe, the gigantic Duncan nan Creagh kept the sloping side of the corrie against all who came near him, hurling every assailant down by the ponderous blows he dealt on their shields, till Rob Roy hewed a passage towards him, just as MacAleister, by a fortunate shot from his gun, broke the shaft of the cateran's axe, on which he cast away the fragment and drew his sword. While he and Rob eyed each other for a minute, each doubtful where to strike or where to thrust, so admirably were both skilled in the use of their sword and shield, the strong cateran, who was a head taller than his muscular assailant, laughed grimly, and said,—" We have drawn the first blood in this feud, Robert Campbell : so it is vain to attack us."

" Coward ! the first blood was drawn from the heart of a poor boy," replied Rob, sternly ; " and remember that, though I may be Campbell at the cross of Glasgow, or at the fair of Callender—yea, or at the gallows of Crieff, if it came to that—HERE, upon the free hillside, I am no Campbell, but a MacGregor, as my father was before me, thou dog and son of a dog!"

Again the tall robber laughed loudly, and said with pride, as he parried a thrust,—"Beware, Red MacGregor—I am a MacRae!"

"And wherefore should I beware of that?" asked Rob, delivering another thrust which the cateran received by a circular parry, that made both their arms tingle to the shoulder-blade.

"It was said of the first of our name—*Bhai Mac-ragh-aigh*—that he was the son of Good Fortune, and his spirit is with us to-day."

"We shall soon see whether it is so, though I believe that his spirit is in a warmer place than the Braes of Rannoch," retorted Rob, pressing vigorously up the rough stony side of the corrie, his great length of arm giving him, when thrusting, a superiority over his antagonist, whose blade he met constantly by his target and claymore, so that he seemed invulnerable.

A wound in the sword-arm now deprived Mac-Gregor of all patience. He flung his target full at his enemy's head, and grasping with both hands his claymore—the same claymore with which his father, the Colonel, slew Duncan of the Heads—he showered blow after blow upon MacRae, whose target soon fell in fragments from his wearied arm; and the moment that protection was gone, Rob closed in, and thrust his sword through and through him !

Writhing his huge frame convulsively forward on the blade, MacRae made a terrible effort to get the victor within reach of the dirk that was chained to his left hand, but suddenly uttering a shriek which ended in a heavy sob, he sank down, to all appearance lifeless, with the blood gushing from his lips and nostrils.

This put an end to the fray, for all his followers fled down the hill-side, pursued by the MacGregors —all save one, a man of powerful form and ferocious aspect, who was naked to the waist, and had his kilt girdled round him by a belt of untanned bullhide.

This Celtic savage, whose name was Aulay Mac-Aulay, flung himself upon MacAleister, who had stumbled and fallen. Seizing the henchman by the throat with his teeth, he grasped Greumoch Mac-Gregor by the right foot, and with a fragment of his sword, which had been broken, endeavoured to despatch them both.

MacAleister strove vainly to release himself, and Greumoch struck MacAulay again and again on the head with his steel pistol clubbed ; but finding that he might as well have hammered on a log of wood, he snatched a pistol from the belt of one who lay dead close by, and shot the marauder through the lower part of the head. He yelled and rolled away, biting the heather, and wallowing in blood; and from this wild man of the mountains—for, in truth,

E

MacAulay was nothing better—that great literary foe of the Celtic race, the brilliant historian of England, was lineally descended.

Six of the MacRaes were left slain in or near the corrie, and several of those who escaped were severely wounded.

Alaster Roy and three other MacGregors were wounded, and one was killed by a musket shot. The cut on Rob's arm was deep, and, for a time, required all the medical skill of Helen to heal it.

It was thus that he avenged the foray of the MacRaes, and recovered the cattle, which he restored to their proper owners, who were poor cotters, to whom the loss would have been a severe one. All the weapons, ornaments, and spoil of the vanquished he gave to the widow whose son had been slain. On the coat of one they found a complete set of silver buttons, as large as pistol shot. Such buttons were frequently worn, even by the poorer classes, in the Highlands in those days, and came by inheritance through many generations. They were meant to serve as ornaments when living, and as the means of providing a decent funeral, if the owner fell in battle, or died far from the home of his kindred.

Rob Roy received considerable praise for this exploit, the scene of which was long marked by a cairn, and Mr. Stirling, of Carden, and many other gentlemen, whose estates lay near the Highland frontier, and who had been neglecting to pay their

black-mail, now sent the tax in all haste to Iuvers-
naid.

It was usually said of Rob that his sword was
like the sword of Fingal, which was never required
to give a *second blow ;* but Duncan nan Creagh was
not slain, for such men were hard to kill. He was
borne away by his followers, who returned on the
departure of the MacGregors, and bound up his
wounds; so Duncan lived to fight at the battles of
Sheriffmuir and Glenshiel.

CHAPTER VIII.

THE BATTLE OF GLENFRUIN.

THE preceding chapter will sufficiently have indicated
that the clan of MacGregor was in a state of hostility with nearly all their neighbours, and that it
proved a source of disquiet to Government.

We will now proceed to relate how this state
of matters came to pass, and an explanation is the
more necessary as it will serve to show the *secret
spring* of many of Rob Roy's hostile actions,—why
he took up arms against the Government, and how,
from being a gentleman farmer and levier of black-
mail, he gradually became a rebel, an outlaw, and
yet a patriot, with a price set upon his head. The
clan and surname of MacGregor are descended from

Alpine MacAchai, who was crowned King of Scotland in 787, hence their motto, *" 'S Rioghal mo dhream,"*—" My race is royal !" They are named the Clan Alpine, and from their antiquity comes the old Scottish proverb :—

> The woods, the waters and Clan Alpine,
> Are the oldest things in Albyn.

Long before charters or parchments were known in the North, their possessions were great ; for they held lands in Glendochart, Strathfillan, Glenorchy, Balquhidder, Breadalbane, and Rannoch, and, until 1490, Taymouth, too, was theirs. They had four strong castles: Kilchurn, which crowns an insular rock in Loch Awe, Finlarig, and Ballach, at the east end of Loch Tay ; an old fortress on an isle in Loch Dochart, and many minor towers.

But when the kings of Scotland sought to introduce into the Highlands the same feudal system which existed in England, and in their Lowland territories, and endeavoured to subvert the Celtic or patriarchal law by substituting Crown charters, which made chiefs into barons, who, in their *single person*, thus became lords of all the land in which their clan had previously a *joint* right and share,—a right old as the days of the first settlers on British soil,—a bloody strife ensued between those who accepted such charters and those who refused and despised them.

Feuds and local wars began, and all who resisted the King were termed broken clans, and to be thus stigmatized was tantamount to a denunciation of outlawry. By their sturdy adherence to the system of their forefathers, the Clan Alpine soon became eminently obnoxious to James VI., the meanest monarch that ever occupied a European throne; the more so, that in 1602, a long and bitter quarrel between them and the Colquhouns of Luss (who had murdered two wandering MacGregors) came to a terrible issue in a place called Glenfruin. Its name signifies the Glen of Sorrow, and it is a deep vale intersected by the Fruin, and overlooked by ridges of dark heathy mountains, that are more than eighteen hundred feet in height.

Here, then, on the 9th of February Sir Humphry Colquhoun, of Luss, at the head of a great force of horse and foot, composed of his own clan, the Grahames, and the burghers of Dumbarton, under Tobias Smollet, their provost,—met Alaster Roy MacGregor of Glenstrae, who had only four hundred swordsmen; but his superior bravery and skill soon decided the disastrous conflict.

Glenstrae divided his little force into two parties. Reserving two hundred to himself, he gave two hundred to his brother Ian MacGregor, with orders to make a long circuit, and attack Luss in the rear.

This manœuvre was most successfully executed, and a dreadful hand-to-hand conflict ensued in the narrow vale. The Clan Gregor cast aside their shields, and plying their sharp claymores, with both hands clenched in the iron hilts, assailed both horse and foot in front and rear, threw them into confusion, and swept them in rout and dismay down Glenfruin towards Loch Lomond.

Two hundred Buchanans and Colquhouns were slain on the field, and though many of the Clan Alpine were wounded in their furious charge, it is remarkable that only Ian MacGregor and another of the clan were slain.

They lie buried on the field, under a large block, which is named "The Grey Stone of MacGregor."

A little rivulet near it is still named "the stream of ghosts;" for there Fletcher of Cameron, a follower of the Clan Alpine, is said to have slaughtered a number of clerical scholars, who had come from Dumbarton to see the battle; and it is still believed that if a MacGregor crosses it after sunset he will be scared by dreadful spectres. Yet, to preserve these boys from bullets and arrows in the hour of battle, it is alleged that Alaster of Glenstrae humanely enclosed them in a little church, the thatched roof of which was fired accidentally by the wadding of a musket, and they all perished in the flames. Others say they were all dirked by Dugald Ciar Mhor, from whom Rob Roy was lineally descended, and that he slew them like sheep, at a large stone, from which the blood can never be effaced.

Being mounted on a powerful horse, Sir Humphry Colquhoun, minus sword and helmet, escaped from the field, and fled to the castle of Bannochar, where he was afterwards slain, when concealed in one of the vaults, *not* by MacGregors, but by some of the MacFarlanes, though the blame of the deed was unjustly thrown on the former.

To James VI., his successor and friends made a doleful report of the battle, in their own fashion, and there came before that monarch, at Stirling, a strange procession of eleven score of women, bearing each, upon a spear, a bloody shirt, purporting to be that of a husband or kinsman slain in Glenfruin.

These females had been mostly hired at so much per head, in Glasgow, for the pageant, and the blood on the woollen shirts was that of a cow, bled expressly for the purpose; but this melo-dramatic exhibition was singularly successful.

James was so incensed that, without further inquiry, he issued letters of fire and sword against the MacGregors; and then the Colquhouns, the Buchanans, the Camerons, and the Clan Ronald joined with others, in a species of crusade, to crush them. They were hunted throughout the land, like wild animals, but could never be suppressed; for, whenever a MacGregor fell, the sword of another appeared to avenge him.

Captured by treachery, Alaster of Glenstrae, the gallant victor of Glenfruin, was ignominiously hanged, at the cross of Edinburgh, with all his nearest kinsmen, the sole honour awarded to him being a loftier gibbet than the rest.

By an Act of the Scottish Legislature, the surname of MacGregor was abolished, and they were

compelled to adopt others. Some called themselves
Gregory and Gregorson, and some Mallet, of whom
the grandfather of the poet of that name was one.
Many took the name of Grahame, but many more
allied themselves with the powerful House of
Argyle, taking the surname of "the Great Clan;"
hence, a hundred years after the grass had grown
above the graves of the dead in Glenfruin, we find
Rob Roy designating himself *Campbell*, the name
of his mother !

The same Act ordained that none of the race of
Alpine should have in their possession any other
weapon than a pointless knife, wherewith to cut
their food; yet, in defiance of the Act, the Clan
Gregor went armed to the teeth as usual.

Bloodhounds were employed to track them in their
retreats; and their very children were abstracted,
and brought up in hatred of the blood they
inherited. But the Celtic nature was soon averse
to such modes of suppressing a warlike and time-
honoured clan; and the Camerons alone maintained
the war against the MacGregors, who, on being
joined by the MacPhersons, met them in battle in
Brae Lochaber, and gave one-half of them a lesson
in charity, by cutting the other to pieces.

After the battle of Glenfruin, seven MacGregors,
who were pursued by a body of Colquhouns, came
over the mountains of Glencoe and Glenorchy, down
by the lone and lovely shore of Lochiel and the
birchen woods that border on the wild waters of the
Spean, till they found a brief shelter in the farm-

house of Tirindrish, which was then occupied by a Cameron.

Alarmed by the approach of the Colquhouns, they fled again, and took shelter in a cavern, which the Cameron, actuated either by treachery or timidity, pointed out to the pursuers. The toil-worn fugitives were attacked with sword and pistol. Six were slain, and lie buried, where some pines, the badge of their clan, were lately planted, in memory of the event. The seventh fled to a little distance, but was overtaken, beheaded, and buried beside a stream, where a friend of the author lately found his skull, which the water had laid bare, by washing away the bank, in which the other bones lie yet embedded.

After their slaughter, the Colquhouns went back to Luss; but the farmhouse of Tirindrish was now said to be haunted from time to time by a headless figure. The Cameron became alarmed, and brought thither a *Taischatr*, or seer, who saw it also—the dim outline of a shadowy and bare-legged Highlander, without a head, but with a remarkable swelling on the right knee, a disease of which the treacherous farmer had long complained; and hence the seer intimated that the figure represented *himself!*

It proved but the shadow of a coming event; for soon after a party of MacGregors, true to the old Celtic instinct of revenge, came to Tirindrish, and, to punish the Cameron for having discovered the cavern to the Colquhouns, struck off his head, by

order of Dugald Ciar Mhor. The place where the
six fugitives perished is still named the MacGregor's
Cave, and a cairn was built there by the Mac-
Donalds in memory of the event.

Hundreds of such episodes followed the battle of
Glenfruin; and more fully to suppress the fated
surname, no minister of the church could, at
baptism, give the name of Gregor to a child, under
pain of banishment and deprivation; and the heads
of the Clan Alpine became a marketable commodity
under King William III., as the story of Duncan
nan Cean remains to testify.

Yet in spite of all these savage laws the clan
grew and flourished in the fastnesses of the Highlands, and in the battles of Montrose their shout of
Ard Choille was heard farthest amid the ranks of
the routed Covenanters. Hence the spirit of their
Gathering—

> The moon's on the lake, and the mist's on the bay,
> And the clan *has a name* that is *nameless* by day—
> Then gather, gather, gather, Grigalach !
>
> *   *   *   *   *   *
>
> While there's leaves on the forest, or foam on the river,
> MacGregor, despite them, shall flourish for ever !
> Then gather, gather, gather, Grigalach !

Hence in 1645 they could muster a thousand
swordsmen; a hundred years later seven hundred
swordsmen, and when the Highland regiment of
Clan Alpine was raised by the chief in 1799, one

thousand two hundred and thirty of the clan and their kindred enlisted to fight for George III.

So little do tyranny and oppression avail in the end! They served but to bind Clan Alpine together like bands of steel; but they were never restored to their ancient rights, surname, or liberty, till an Act of the British Parliament was passed in their favour, *only twenty-four* years before the regiment was embodied.

The wrongs of his name and kindred made a deep impression on Rob Roy, and he thirsted for an opportunity of seeing them righted, either by the restoration of the House of Stuart, or by the destruction of their more immediate oppressors.

He knew and writhed under the unjust laws by which the whole clan, for the deeds of a few, so long ago as the field of Glenfruin, were stigmatized as cut-throats and traitors, and by which they were nominally disarmed—the deepest disgrace that could be inflicted upon a Highlander; by which they were degraded in name and station, and only permitted to live as Campbells, Grahames, or Drummonds—a landless and broken race.

In his soul he longed for an opportunity of avenging all this on the King and Parliament, and for becoming a champion of the old Scottish patriarchal system, and opposing the new, which made feudal lords of Celtic chiefs, with power of gallows and dungeon, over free men—but these were visions wild and vain!

Proud of the past, however vague, the Red Mac-

Gregor, like all his Celtic countrymen, believed in the words of the bard, that—

> Ere ever Ossian raised his song,
>   To tell of Fingal's fame ;
> Ere ever from their sunny clime
>   The Roman eagles came :
>
> The hills had given to heroes birth,
>   Brave e'en amid the brave ;
> Who taught, above tyrannic dust,
>   The thistle tufts to wave !

And this belief in a lofty and warlike ancestry has ever been the Highlander's greatest incentive to moral character and heroic bearing.

CHAPTER IX.

THE DEVASTATION OF KIPPEN.

IN the days of Rob Roy there were no police, troops, or garrisons in his part of the Highlands, and no law was recognized save that of the sword.

William III. had recently been placed on the throne, and he exasperated the MacGregors by restoring all the oppressive Acts passed against them—Acts which had been cancelled for a time by Charles II. Thus they were again compelled to assume other names than their own, or forfeit land, arms, and all means of livelihood. The memory of William of Orange is still abhorred by the Highlanders. He was a king whose cowardice lost the battle of Steinkirke, and by whose behest torture was last judicially used, on Neville Payne, an Englishman, in a Scottish court of law. He introduced flogging into the army, keelhauling into the navy; "and he," says Sir William Napier, "is the *only* general on record to whom attaches the detestable distinction of sporting with men's lives by wholesale; and who fought the battle of St. Denis with the Peace of Nimeguen in his pocket, because he would not deny himself a *safe* lesson in his trade;" and he it was who, by his own sign manual, condemned the whole inhabitants of a Scottish valley to be slaughtered in their beds at midnight, and this was *after* he had *ratified* the Treaty of Achalader!

Hatred of this king and of those who adhered to him determined Rob Roy to punish some of the Whigs in his neighbourhood, and remembering how active the Buchanans had made themselves since the days of Glenfruin, he resolved to fall upon them.

Assembling about two hundred men, and attended by MacAleister and Greumoch, he marched from Inversnaid towards Kippen, giving out that he went "in the name of King James VII. to plunder the rebel Whigs." After a fifteen miles' march, they halted for the first night on the

northern shore of the Loch of Monteith, amid the
thick groves of oak, chestnut, and ancient plane-
trees which flourish there. They shot some deer,
lighted fires, and proceeded to cook and regale
themselves on the venison, with all the greater
relish that it belonged to their hereditary enemies
the Grahames of Monteith; and after posting sentinels, they passed the night in carousing, and singing those long songs still so common in the
Highlands, where the air and the theme have been
carried down, from the days perhaps of the Druids,
who, when seeking to cultivate the people by music
and poetry, framed their songs with long choruses
in which all could join.

And now, under the rustling leaves of the old
forest, the MacGregors, wrapped in their red tartan
plaids, sat round the glowing watch-fires, and made
the dingles echo, as they sang one of the ballads of
the female bard of Scarba—Mary, the daughter of
Red Alister. Two hours before daybreak they
were all on the march again, and eight miles or so
further brought them, in the early dusk of the
autumn morning, to Kippen. This village lies
within ten miles of the guns of Stirling Castle, and
for centuries it had belonged to the Buchanans.
Here the fertile valley through which the Forth
flows was studded with prosperous farms and handsome country seats, surrounded by luxuriant crops
in some places, by the stubble-fields in others—a
rural scene, amid which the rocky bluff of the
Abbeycraig and the wooded summit of Craigforth

start up boldly and abruptly, with their faces to the
west ; and Rob Roy took care to choose the time of
his invasion when most of the crops were stored in
the barn, and when the cattle and sheep were
gathered in pen and fold.

On the approach of the MacGregors, the old
castle of Ardfinlay (of which no trace now remains)
and the tower of Arnprior were abandoned by the
Buchanans, without a shot being fired, while the
village of Kippen was evacuated by its inhabitants,
who fled towards Stirling, with whatever they could
carry. Carts and horses were now seized by the
MacGregors, and loaded with grain, food, furniture,
and whatever they could lay their hands upon. The
cattle, horses, and sheep were collected in herds
and flocks ; and after sweeping the parish, Rob's
men were about to depart for Inversnaid, with
pipes playing triumphantly in front, when a body of
men, armed with muskets and bayonets, swords
and pikes, appeared with drums beating, ready to
oppose them, about an hour after sunrise.

These men had been hastily collected and armed
by Sir James Livingstone, a gentleman who had
served in foreign wars, and who was resolved that
Rob Roy should not harry the district without a
blow being struck in its defence. On the open
ground known as the Moor of Kippen, they came
in sight of each other.

Rob halted his men with the spoil they had
collected, and resolutely advanced to the front,
attended by his henchman, by Greumoch, Alaster

Roy, and a few others on whom he most relied. By his bearing and the richness of his weapons, as well as by his ruddy-coloured hair and beard, and the two eagle feathers in his blue bonnet, Sir James Livingstone recognized the Laird of Inversnaid, and he also came forward from his line, attended by a faithful servant, who was well armed.

Under his ample red coat, which was open, Sir James wore a cuirass of polished steel; his hat was cocked up by gold cord, and his full, white periwig flowed over his shoulders. Under the cuirass he wore a buff waistcoat, which reached nearly to his knees; he had his sword drawn in his right hand, and carried a brace of loaded pistols in his girdle, to which they hung by steel hooks.

"Have I the honour of addressing MacGregor of Inversnaid?" said he, politely lifting his hat when within ten paces of Rob Roy, who replied sternly—

"I am MacGregor. Had you styled me by another name than that which my father left me, I would have killed you on the instant. And you——"

"I am Sir James Livingstone. I have nothing to do with the laws which seek the suppression of your name and the destruction of your clan, save that I reprobate them; but I demand by what right you have broken the King's peace, and come hither in arms to plunder a peaceful district?"

"For three sufficient causes," replied Rob; "first, I have the old Highland right by which we can at any time make a warlike inroad on our enemies,

which the Buchanans of Kippen and Arnprior have
been since that black day in Glenfruin; secondly,
I break the peace of him you name a king because
I deem him a Dutch usurper; and thirdly, I take
from cowards that which they have not the heart to
defend."

"I regret to hear all this," replied Sir James,
persuasively, "for there will be much blood shed,
MacGregor, if you do not yield up the spoil your
people have collected."

"Yield it—to whom?" asked MacGregor, loftily.

"To me."

"Little care we for bloodshed," said the other,
bitterly; "your foreign kings and Lowland laws
have made Clan Alpine like the Arabs of the desert,
whose hands are against all men, because the hands
of all men are uplifted against them. Yet I, personally, have no wish to slay any of your people.
You are a gentleman and a soldier, whose character
I value and honour; thus, if you choose, I will fight
with you here, hand to hand, with target and claymore, in front of our men, and the spoil shall belong
to him who draws the *first blood*."

"Agreed," replied Sir James, sternly; "but,
though expert enough in the use of the sword, I am
unused to such a defence as the target."

"That shall be no hindrance," said Rob, as he
handed to MacAleister his round shield, which was
composed of triple bull's-hide, stretched over wood,
covered with antique brass bosses, and had a long
spike of steel screwed into its centre.

The friends of Sir James now crowded around him, and bade him be wary, and remember the vast strength of Rob Roy; the great skill he possessed, the weight of his sword, and the advantage his length of arm gave him over others. These warnings were not without effect on Sir James, who was too brave to be without prudence. He came forward, and, lifting his little three-cocked hat, the edge of which was bound with feathers, like those of all the officers who served in King William's wars, he said,—

"I agree to meet you, MacGregor, as a gentleman, on the distinct understanding that the entire spoil shall remain with him who is fortunate enough to draw the first blood; but, as being the person challenged, I claim the right to choose my weapon, and for many reasons prefer the pistol."

"Be it so," replied Rob, laughing, as Sir James divested himself of his glittering cuirass : "I am not an old trooper like you, yet am a good marksman nevertheless."

"Are your pistols loaded ?"

"The pistols of a MacGregor are seldom otherwise, in these times," said Rob, as his countenance darkened; "and yours?"

"Are loaded, too."

"Shall we fire together, or toss up for the first shot ?" asked MacGregor.

"We will toss for the first shot, if you please," replied Livingstone, who, aware that he was a deadly marksman, and had fought several duels in

France and Flanders with terrible success, had no fears as to the result, if the lot fell to him.

"Then, Sir James, toss for me, but remain where you are," said MacGregor, with indifference.

"And you will take my word for the coin—for the result!" exclaimed Livingstone, with something of admiration in his tone and face.

"Had I doubted your word, I would not fight with you. On equal terms I meet none but gentlemen."

A servant of Sir James, a man in livery, armed with a musket, now came hastily forward to suggest some trickery, which his master repelled with scorn —even with anger.

He threw up the coin—a crown piece; it glittered in the air, and then fell on the grass.

"A head!" said MacGregor.

"I regret to say it is *not* a head," replied Sir James, touching his hat, while his cheek flushed with triumph: "so I have won the first shot!"

A shout of anger burst from the MacGregors on hearing this; but Livingstone's followers waved their bonnets and clapped their hands in exultation.

It was strange, the scene which took place on that morning, on the wide moor of Kippen. On one side the grim band of armed MacGregors, in their red tartans, with drawn swords, Lochaber axes, and long muskets, guarding the whole spoil of the parish, and keeping together the herds of lowing cattle and tethered horses, laden with bags of grain, bedding, and household utensils,

On the other, the well-armed retainers of Sir James Livingstone, cross-belted and armed with pike and musket; and midway between, the striking and picturesque figures of the two combatants, who were to decide the affray, standing about twelve paces apart, with a pistol in each hand.

CHAPTER X.

THE DUEL.

SIR JAMES drew up his tall and soldier-like figure to its full height, and buttoning to the throat his long-skirted scarlet coat, the breast of which was covered with broad bars of silver lace, he fixed his keen dark eyes steadily on the figure of Rob Roy. He then levelled a pistol at the full length of his right arm, and every eye was bent upon the muzzle from which death was expected to issue.

Rob's coat was of rough, home-made, brown stuff, destitute of lace or ornament; but his great belted plaid of scarlet tartan filled up the eye. His pistols were bright as silver, and came from the famous workshop established at Doune, so long ago as 1646, by Thomas Cadell. A silver chain suspended his splendidly carved powder-horn, and his dirk and broadsword were elaborately mounted with silver. Sir James covered him with his pistol and fired!

A shout of rage and dismay burst from the Mac-Gregors, as Rob's bonnet was turned round on his head, and, cut by the bullet, one of his eagle feathers floated away on the breeze.

"That was a good shot, Sir James," said Rob, smiling, as he replaced his bonnet; "an inch lower, and there would have been one MacGregor less in the world to persecute. Under favour, sir, it is now *my* turn."

Raising one of the claw-butted, steel, Highland pistols, he cocked and levelled it straight at the head of Livingstone, whose eye never quailed, and whose gallant spirit never flinched. Then suddenly lowering the weapon, he said, "One cannot always be a hero like Fingal, but one may always be a gentleman. I am, as you know, Sir James, a deadly shot, and at this moment could kill you without reloading. I have no desire to slay men unnecessarily—brave men like you, who may live to serve their mother, Scotland, least of all! In short, I wish to spare you; but as the creagh must belong to him who sheds the first blood, I must send this bullet either through your head or your hand. If you prefer the latter, please to hold it up."

Scarcely knowing what he did, Sir James held up his left hand. Rob fired, and his bullet whistled through the palm of the upheld hand, which was instantly covered with blood, when Livingstone uttered an exclamation of pain and suddenly lowered his arm.

"We now part on the first blood drawn—your

own terms, Livingstone. To the hills, lads!"
exclaimed MacGregor; "to the hills with the gear
of the Dutch king's rebel Whigs!"

A yell of triumph from the MacGregors rent
the sky, the pipes struck up "The Battle of Glenfruin," and the whole cavalcade moved off towards
the mountains. But the matter did not end here,
for as Rob tarried a moment, to take a more
courteous farewell of his adversary, and to bind up
his wounded hand, Livingstone's liveried valet
levelled a pistol at his head. Fortunately it flashed
in the pan; and MacAleister, who was close by, shot
him dead with his musket!

"Only one man, a servant to Sir James Livingstone, was killed on this occasion," says the
statistical account; "and this depredation was
remembered by the fathers of several persons still
living, and is known as the 'Her'ship of Kippen.'"

It does not appear that any means were taken to
recover the cattle and goods thus carried to the
fastnesses of the MacGregors; but at this time the
whole Highlands, from the German to the Atlantic
Ocean, were full of those scenes of war and plunder
which succeeded the victory of the loyal clans at
Killycrankie, and the fall of their idol, the gallant
Dundee.

CHAPTER XI.

ROB GOES TO ENGLAND.

ALL hope of restoring the exiled House of Stuart having ceased for a time, Rob Roy, for some years subsequent to the establishment of the Revolution, lived quietly on his estate of Inversnaid; only assuming the sword to protect himself, his neighbours, or those whose properties lay south of the Highland frontier, and who paid the usual tax of black-mail for that security of life and goods which he and others afforded them. He dealt largely in cattle, and speculated so fortunately, that before the year 1707 he had cleared the lands of Craigrostan from certain bonds held over them by James, Marquis of Montrose; and he generously relieved the estate of Glengyle, the property of his nephew, Gregor MacGregor, famous in Scottish history as *Glun dhu*, or the Black-knee, from similar incumbrances of a heavy kind; and being, by law, the guardian, or, as it is termed in Scotland, the tutor of Glengyle, Rob had great influence over the whole clan, though nameless, broken, and scattered.

Rob and his gillies, clad in their red tartans, and armed with sword, dirk, and pistol, and with a target slung on the left shoulder, each carrying, moreover, a heavy cudgel, driving some thousand head of cattle, with pipers playing in front, to the fair of Callender, or the Trysts of Falkirk, which were then held on the Reddingrig Moor, and had been so since 1701, presented an appearance so animated, and an aspect so formidable, that few cared to meddle with the Red MacGregor and his followers.

Affrays were frequent at those fairs, and, indeed, everywhere else in Scotland: political and religious differences made men rancorous, and arms were readily resorted to. It was not until 1727 that the Provost of Edinburgh prohibited wearing of pistols and daggers openly in the streets of the city, for brawls had become incessant.

"It may well be supposed that in those days no Lowland, and much less English drovers, *ventured into the Highlands,*" says Scott. "The cattle, which were the staple commodity of the mountains, were escorted down to the fairs by a party of Highlanders, with all their arms rattling about them, and who dealt, however, in all honour and faith with their southern customers. A fray, indeed, would sometimes arise, when the Lowland men, chiefly Borderers, who had to supply the English market, used to dip their bonnets in the next brook, and wrapping them round their hands, oppose the cudgels to the naked broadsword, which had not always the superiority. I have heard from aged persons who had been in such affrays, that the Highlanders used remarkably fair play, never using the point of the sword, far less their pistols or daggers; so that a slash or two, or a broken head, was easily accommodated; and as the trade was of benefit to both parties, trifling skirmishes were not allowed to interrupt its harmony."

King William having restored all the severe laws against the clan, Rob was compelled to resume the name of Campbell, when in 1703, his nephew, Gregor Glun Dhu, who was likewise compelled to call himself James Graham, was married to Mary Hamilton of Bardowie, in the November of that year, and our hero signed their contract as " Robert Campbell of Inversnaid."

While he was acquiring wealth and popularity of a local and peaceful kind by his frequent visits to the Borders, his wife, Helen Mary, managed his household at Inversnaid, and earned the reputation of being a thrifty, active, and careful housewife. Gentle in manner, and gently bred, she could play the old Highland harp with great skill, as she had been taught by Rori Dall, or Blind Roderick, who was bard to MacLeod of that Ilk, and was, moreover, the *last* harper of the Hebrides.

A Highland housewife had plenty of occupation in those days. The corn was then dressed in an ancient fashion by the women. The straw was fired, that the heat might parch the grain, which, though blackened, was gathered into the handmills, or querns, and ground into meal or flour, just as the Israelites ground theirs of old. They had also the management of the sheep. No flocks were then kept in the Highlands; but every family had from the Hebrides a few sheep of a small breed, which

were never permitted to range the mountain, but
were carefully housed at night.

In the household of Inversnaid the spinning-
wheels were never idle; hence there was plenty of
industry and comfort, but few luxuries. All the
furniture was of black oak, or Scottish pine; the
only piece of mahogany being an oval teaboard, a
portion of Helen's "plenishing," when she left her
father's house at Comar. On ordinary days her
dress was linsey-woolsey and a tartan plaid; and
though dignified with the title of *lady* in Gaelic, as
being the wife of a chieftain, and on certain occasions, such as birthdays or anniversaries (the
Gowrie conspiracy, the Restoration, or the imagi-
nary succession of James VIII.), wearing silk and
fine lace, they were all made up at home, for in
those sequestered regions the name and business of
a milliner were unknown. Of their five sons, only
four had as yet been born,—Coll, Ronald, Hamish,
and Duncan.

We are now rapidly approaching those events
which scattered Helen's happy household, and
drove her brave and trusty, generous and humane
husband "to the hillside, to become a broken
man," branded as an outlaw and traitor, with a
price upon his head. King James VII. was dead,
and his son, though in exile, had assumed the title
of James III. of England and VIII. of Scotland.

In 1707 the English endeavoured to *force* the
Scots into a union; and, as a preliminary, very
unwisely seized all their merchant ships that were

in southern ports. On this Scotland prepared for war by strengthening her garrisons, and proposing to raise sixty thousand infantry; so England resorted to other means, and by bribery achieved the measure so long desired. Thus that which was hitherto a weak and federal union, became a powerful and combined one; each country, however, retaining its own church and laws.

Before this great treaty was complete, the Scottish Government restricted the importation of cattle into England; but free intercourse being one of the happy results of the Union, various persons speculated in this traffic. Among others, Rob Roy engaged in a joint adventure with James, Marquis of Montrose, who had received a sum of money for his Union vote, and in the month *preceding* that measure had been created a duke, with the office of Lord Privy Seal for Scotland.

"The capital to be advanced," says Dr. Browne, in his "History of the Highlands," "was fixed at ten thousand merks *each*, and Rob Roy was to purchase cattle therewith, and drive them to England for sale."

The Duke's money he received from his factor or chamberlain, John Grahame of Killearn, partly in cash and partly in bills of exchange, drawn through the Bank of Scotland on Grahame of Gorthy. He soon collected a vast herd, and leaving his trusty henchman and foster-brother, MacAleister, in charge of his household, departed for Carlisle.

The system of fosterage, which consisted in the

mutual exchange of children for the purpose of being nursed and bred, was a custom peculiar to the Scots and Irish, who were wont to allege that there was no love or faith in the world like that which existed between foster-brethren; so Rob departed in confidence on his important mission with a herd worth twenty thousand Scottish merks.

Prior to his leaving Inversnaid, Paul Crubach had come there, and sprinkled all the cattle with water from his holy well. On such occasions he was always provided with certain flint arrow-heads, which he had found where a battle had been fought, long, long ago. These *elfshots* he duly dipped in the water of his well, and then sprinkled it over the herd to prevent any spell an evil eye, or another elfshot, might cast upon them before they reached the great market at "Merry Carlisle."

CHAPTER XII.

THE GIPSIES.

THE trade of cattle-dealing was liable at that time, as at every other, to sudden depressions and mis-calculations; thus, on his arrival at Carlisle, Rob Roy—unfortunately for the success of the joint speculation in which he was engaged—found the southern markets, where Highland cattle had been so long in great demand, completely overstocked.

Many other speculators were now in the field. The prices fell lower than they had ever been before, and he was compelled to dispose of the whole stock of cattle far below prime cost. As his herds diminished, he gradually sent all his drovers and gillies home to the Highlands. The last he despatched was Greumoch MacGregor, with whom he entrusted a letter (dated from an hostelry in Castle Street, where he lodged) addressed to the Duke of Montrose, detailing their mutual loss.

When the last cow was sold, Rob secured the money which remained for the Duke and himself in his sporan, as the pouch worn in front of the kilt is named. It was made of the skin of an otter, shot by himself in the Dochart, and was adorned by its face and claws, and closed by a curious steel clasp.

With his pistols carefully primed and loaded (as the roads were then infested by footpads, mounted highwaymen, and gipsies), he left Carlisle by the Scottish gate, and in very low spirits took his homeward way, mounted on a stout little Highland horse.

Carlisle was then, and for long after, girt by walls and towers as a defence against the Scots, whom the English could scarcely view yet as fellow-subjects.

Without any occurrence he travelled about forty-five miles, and on the evening of the second day found himself entering Moffatdale, a deep and pastoral valley, which is overshadowed by mountains of great height, at the foot of which the Evan and the Annan unite their waters in one. The sun-

light had faded from the green summits of the Moffat
Alps—of Hartfell and Queensberry, and the deep
shady valleys were growing dark. The night-hawk
was winging its way towards the lonely banks of Loch
Skene; the shrill whistle of the curlew as he rose
from among the green waving fern or purple heather
bells, and the coo of the sweet cushat dove in the
birchen thicket, were alone breaking the silence,
when Rob Roy drew his bridle near the village of
Moffat to consider where he should quarter himself
for the night.

He was in a strange place, and had about him
more money than he cared to lose. There were
several ruins of old peel-houses, towers, and cattle-
sheilings on the hills, and in one of these a hardy
Highlander could sleep comfortably enough when
rolled in his plaid; but there was no necessity for
faring so roughly.

A meteor which shot across the darkening sky,
near the spire of a distant village church, made
Rob thoughtful; for it is an old Celtic superstition,
that when a falling star is seen by any one near a
burying-ground, it portends that death is near. At
the moment he paused a cry of distress pierced the
air. He listened intently and instinctively, and
drawing forth a pistol, glanced at the flint and
priming, to be prepared for any emergency. Again
the cry reached him, and it seemed to be uttered
by a female in distress. Urging his strong and
active Highland garron in the direction from whence
the cries came, he entered a deep and savage dell

named Gartpool Linn, where he beheld a very startling sight.

A large and gnarled tree spread its broad branches like a leafy arch above this dell, and beneath them the last red gleam of the western sky shone full into the hollow. There an officer and a party of soldiers were deliberately preparing to hang four peasants on the lower limb of the old chestnut. At the foot of the latter, on her knees, with hair dishevelled and disordered dress, there knelt a young girl, who was alternately bewailing the fate of the four victims, and imploring mercy for them; and, from what she said, they proved to be her father and three brothers.

In the oldest peasant MacGregor almost immediately recognized Andrew Gemmil, the gipsy wanderer who had acted as his guide when he followed Duncan nan Creagh to the Braes of Rannoch. Being single-handed, ignorant of the crime of which the prisoners were accused, and finding himself before eighteen soldiers and an officer, who were all fully armed, and who by their jack-boots, buff breeches, and blue coats, evidently belonged to a Border militia regiment, Rob Roy stood by for some time in bewilderment, and soon saw the four unfortunates flung in succession off a ladder, and all swinging and writhing in the agonies of death between him and the ruddy western sky.

The officer now commanded his men to seize the girl, who had cast herself with her face on the grass, that she might shut out the dreadful scene; he added they were to bind her hands and feet together, and then throw her head foremost into the stream, which then swept in full flood through this savage ravine, and was all the more fierce and deep that heavy rains had fallen of late. Rob's blood began to boil. He thought, perhaps, upon the words of Ossian :—" Within this bosom is a voice—it comes not to other ears—that bids Ossian succour the helpless in their hour of need."

Four soldiers tied her hands and feet, and were about to obey the order of the officer, when Rob, exasperated by such unmanly cruelty, commanded them in a loud voice to pause, and then he demanded sternly, " Why do you treat a helpless female in a manner so barbarous ? "

Perceiving that he was plainly attired in a rough coat of Galloway frieze, with a tartan plaid thrown over his left shoulder, and a broad blue bonnet drawn down close to his eyes, and perhaps unaware that he had a good sword by his side and pistols at his girdle, the officer replied haughtily,—

" Sir, you had better begone about your own business, whatever it may be, less we add *you* to the goodly company who await the crows on that branch, if you dare to interrupt those who act in the Queen's name and under her authority."

" Miscreant ! " exclaimed Rob, " the good Queen Anne never gave you warrant for such deeds as these."

" Then the Lords of her Council do—so it matters not to me."

"Who are these people?" asked Rob, firmly.

"Enemies of Church and State," replied the officer, "and therefore they must suffer. Throw in the woman!"

"Hold, I command you!" exclaimed MacGregor, with a voice like a trumpet, and leaping from his saddle, he unsheathed his claymore. The fury and indignation which filled his heart added such strength to his muscular arm, that in an incredibly short time he had tossed eight of the soldiers into the stream, and rescued the girl, waving his bare blade in a circle between her and the rest, who dared not advance. Confounded by the audacity of the man, by his sudden onslaught, and the whole catastrophe, the officer remained for a moment gazing alternately at the bold intercessor, and at his men, who were struggling, shouting, swearing, and scrambling to the river bank as they best could. With a slash of his skene dhu Rob cut the cords which bound the girl's hands and feet, and bade her "begone and God-speed."

By this time the officer had rallied his energies, and drawing his sword, attacked Rob, who instantly ran him through the body, on which the soldiers, believing that some large force of assailants was at hand, fled without firing a shot, and left him in possession of the field.

He then cut down those who had just been executed. All were motionless and still; but not all dead, for ere long one who had been last thrown off the ladder showed signs of life, and began to revive.

Rob committed him and the girl, his sister, to the care of the peasantry, some of whom were now assembled. He did more, for he carefully bound up the wound of the officer, who was borne away to the village; and then MacGregor, not knowing how the matter might end, or of *what* the persons rescued were accused, put some money into the hands of the half-dead girl, and remounting his horse, galloped through Moffatdale as fast as its heels could bear him.

The author who relates this adventure of Rob Roy, terms the persons who were executed "fanatics;" but it is much more probable that they were all Border gipsies, against whom there were then, and for long after, laws in existence even as severe as those which oppressed the Clan Gregor.

CHAPTER XIII.

INVERSNAID PILLAGED.

On receipt of Rob Roy's letter, containing intelligence that the cattle speculation had been a failure, and that their money was nearly lost, his Grace the Duke of Montrose burst into a very undignified fit of indignation, and instantly summoned his chamberlain, John Grahame of Killearn, who was a remote relation of his own, and in every sense a devoted and unscrupulous follower.

Poor Greumoch, whose rough and weather-beaten exterior, with homespun Highland dress, with a target slung on his back, all combined to gain him but little favour with Montrose's pampered valets, was speedily bowed out by them, and had the door shut in his face, notwithstanding the eagle's feather in his bonnet, which evinced his claim, when on the mountain side, to be considered a gentleman.

Then the angry duke laid the letter of Rob before his chamberlain, who in the Scottish fashion was simply named always by the title of his property.

"Well, Killearn," said Montrose, grimly; "here is a braw business! Ten thousand merks nearly have been made away with by this Highland limmer, and am I to be at the loss of them?"

"Assuredly not, your grace — assuredly not," replied Killearn. "Rob has property; there are both Inversnaid and Craigrostan."

"Craigrostan—bah! it is only a tract of grey rock and red heather, where even the deer can scarcely find shelter," replied the duke, contemptuously.

"But Inversnaid has a comfortable house, with steading, barn, and byre, forbye garden and meadow ground."

"Then, by heaven, I shall take Inversnaid,

though all that bear the surname of MacGregor were on the hills to oppose me!" exclaimed the duke, passionately.

Killearn seemed uneasy as the duke made this outburst, and he twisted his well-powdered wig to and fro, as if the heat of it oppressed him. He was a dapper little personage, who was always accurately attired in a square-skirted coat, having immense cuffs and pocket flaps, a long-bodied vest and small clothes all of black velvet. His cravat, wig, and ruffles were always white as snow; he did not approve of swords, and never wore one, though for more than sixty years after this time every gentleman in Scotland did.

In one huge pocket he carried a silver snuff-box, and in the other a small thick breeches Bible, which he produced on every occasion; for he was one of those religious pretenders of whom Scotland has always produced a plentiful crop.

To describe his face would be difficult; but it expressed a singular combination of suavity, secret ferocity, cunning, and meanness. Montrose was the chief of his name; hence Killearn regarded him as a demigod, and all the more so because he was a duke, and one who paid him well.

So between them it was arranged, that as Rob Roy was absent—luckily for their scheme—possession, in the meantime, should be taken of all the moveables in his house and on his estate; that a warrant for his apprehension should be procured, and a reward offered for his capture by advertisements in the Edinburgh newspapers. Such lawless and arbitrary proceedings were as easily managed as proposed in those days.

"Take a well-armed party of my own people with you," said the duke; "Rob has many enemies in Dumbarton and the Lennox, who have long been resenting his collection of black-mail, and you will find plenty of hands willing enough to aid you in driving his men farther into the hills. There is Stirling of Carden will help you if required; and I dare say MacDougal's Dragoons could be marched up Loch Lomond side, with the Buchanans of Kippen; and," he added, with a sour smile, "perhaps the Laird of Luss may move in the matter, if he has not forgotten the battle of Glenfruin, and the blood that yet stains the floor of a certain vault in the castle of Bannochar. See to this, Killearn, and bring me news when all is arranged."

Killearn was somewhat aghast on hearing this rapid sketch of a campaign in which he was to figure as leader. He had no desire to head an armed raid into the MacGregors' country if he could avoid it; but he resolved to proceed in regular form of law; and in the duke's name he did so, with marvellous rapidity.

All Rob Roy's farm stock and furniture, and ultimately his house and estates, Inversnaid and Craigrostan, were unjustifiably made objects for arrest and sale; and while he was lingering in Glasgow, endeavouring to raise money to repay the duke, the "warrant of distress," as it would be

called in England, was enforced with great strict-
ness and even barbarity.

Another account of these proceedings would make
it appear that Rob was compelled to assign his possessions in mortgage to the Duke of Montrose,
under a solemn promise that they should revert to
him when he could restore the money lost in the
transaction at Carlisle; that afterwards, when his
finances improved, he offered the sum for which the
two little properties were held in hand; but Montrose and Killearn replied that, besides the principal,
there was now interest thereon, and various other
expenses, so that much time would be required to
make up a statement of the whole sum, and that,
in "this equivocal manner, he was amused, and
ultimately *deprived of all his property.*" Whatever
their proceedings were, of the *latter fact* there is
no doubt.

With a band of well-armed followers to support
the officers of the law, Killearn appeared at the
house of Inversnaid, when, fortunately for himself
and for those who accompanied him, the men of
the village were absent—some with the cattle on
the mountains, others cutting peat in the bogs;
some fishing in the loch, and others hunting in
the woods.

Rob's crops of barley, rye, peas, and small black
oats were all stored in his granary; and stacks of
dark brown peats, drawn from the bog on sledges
for winter fuel, were piled before the door. The
young women of the village were busy carrying

manure to the fields in conical baskets, for now the little wooden ploughs were at work on the upland slopes; and the old people sat at their doors, knitting, spinning, or basking in the autumn sun, that poured his yellow glory down the rugged glen, where the voices of the children rang merrily, for a band of bare-headed and bare-legged urchins were having a boisterous and gleeful game, with clubs and balls, in the middle of the clachan, when, to the terror of all, John Grahame of Killearn appeared with his followers.

He had come up Loch Lomond, with one or two large boats, armed with brass swivel-guns, accompanied by several of the Buchanans, and, as some say, by Stirling of Carden, who hated Rob Roy, and dreaded him too, as he had long and unjustly withheld the tax of black-mail.

With all his duplicity and cunning, Killearn must have been a bold fellow in attempting to enforce, in those days of dirks and broadswords—and more especially in the country of Rob Roy—the same harsh measures which similar factors carry out so successfully among the now unarmed population of the North; spreading desolation through Rossshire, Sutherland, and Breadalbane. Yet, anomalous as it may appear, he did so. It is said that on the night before this visit, Rob's staghounds howled in a melancholy and ominous manner, for the old grey Highland dog possesses a sagacity so remarkable, and an attachment so strong for his master, that the people believe he can forc-see approaching evil and death with the eyes of a seer.

Of the interview which took place between Mr. Grahame and Helen MacGregor, only traditional accounts have been preserved; but all who have written on the subject assert that he forcibly entered the house of Inversnaid, and roughly and summarily expelled her, with her four children and all her servants; and that his bearing was harsh, brutal, and unjustifiable.

"Grahame of Killearn," says the "History of Stirlingshire," "over-zealous in his master's service, had recourse to a mode of expulsion inconsistent with the rights of humanity, by insulting Mrs. Campbell in her husband's absence."

The furniture, crops, farm-stock, food, clothing, and everything were carried off to be sold at Glasgow or Dumbarton, and the door of the empty house was closed upon the now homeless family. The poor huts of Greumoch, Alaster Roy, and their more immediate followers, were burned or levelled, that they too might be without shelter; and re-embarking, after achieving these outrageous proceedings, Killearn, with all his plunder, spread his sails, and proceeded down Loch Lomond with all speed.

More than once the long Spanish gun of Rob's foster-brother covered the dapper figure of the duke's chamberlain; but Greumoch arrested the weapon, and bade him tarry in his vengeance till the Red MacGregor returned.

On beholding the total ruin of her household, Helen MacGregor is said to have cast her plaid around her little boys, as they shrunk to her side, and exclaimed, in a piercing voice, "Oh! St. Mary, now with the archangels, look here!" For a time she abandoned herself to the wildest grief; then, when thoughts more fierce and bitter came, she wiped away her tears, and registered a terrible vow for vengeance on their oppressors.

"It is certain," says Scott, "that she felt extreme anguish on being expelled from the banks of Loch Lomond, and gave vent to her feelings in a fine piece of pipe music, which she composed, and which is still well known by the name of 'Rob Roy's Lament.'"

One of the children was sickly and feeble, and thus they were all thrust forth upon the mountain side, in the last days of autumn, when a Highland winter, with all its severities, was at hand, and when the forest of pine—the badge of their name— would be their only shelter; so Helen longed for the return of her husband, and for the vengeance that was sure to follow!

CHAPTER XIV.

ROB AND THE DUKE.

IGNORANT of what had passed—that the fire on his hearth was extinguished—and that his household had been driven forth like beasts of prey—Rob Roy, after failing to procure in Glasgow a sum requisite to gratify the avarice of Montrose, appeared one afternoon at the residence of the latter, the castle of Mugdock, which is nine miles distant from Glasgow, and is situated in Strathblane.

The valets muttered among themselves of what their titled master had done, and marvelled what might be the object of this visit from MacGregor; the latter, especially since his inroad into Kippen, had been somewhat used to be treated with a respect that was not unmingled with fear, so the sudden interest his appearance excited was unnoticed by him, as he was ushered into the library.

The castle of Mugdock, now a ruin, was then a regularly fortified tower. It is of great antiquity, and was protected on the east and north by the water of a lake, which was drawn round it in the manner of a fosse.

The central keep or donjon was surrounded by a barbican, built so as to form an obtuse angle with the latter, so that a cross shower of missiles would protect the arched gateway from any besiegers who might assail it, for *defence* was the first principle of Scottish architecture in the olden time.

Through the grated windows of the library poor Rob. gazed wistfully down Strathblane, "the vale of the warm river," as it is named in the figurative language of his native country. He could see the wooded landscape stretching to the westward far away, the gentle uplands, the pine thickets, the shining lochlets and the winding stream ; the insulated cone of Dumgoaic, covered to its summit with waving foliage, and in the distance, closing the familiar view, the vast outline of Ben Lomond, that overshadowed its lake of the Twenty-four Isles, and looked down on Inversnaid, where, as he fondly believed, Helen, their little ones, MacAleister, and the household awaited his return !

Alas ! how little he knew of all that had happened there within the last few weeks ; and as little dared his titled host to tell him.

A step fell on his ear, as a person in high-heeled riding-boots, with gilt maroquin gambadoes and gold spurs, trod on the polished oak floor. Rob turned, and found himself face to face with the chief of "the gallant Grahams," the Duke of Montrose.

The latter was not a little startled on finding himself, during such a crisis in their affairs, confronted by a man of such known resolution as the Red MacGregor, so he blushed redly to the roots of his ample periwig.

He wore the square-cut coat with buckram skirts and the long-flapped waistcoat of Queen Anne's reign. These were of dark blue silk, covered with gold embroidery, and he looked every way the great-grandson of the High Cavalier Marquis, whose portrait, by Anthony Vandycke, in wig and armour, with sword and scarlet baton, hung upon the wall—the same great Montrose who had been so cruelly butchered by the Covenanters in 1650.

As the duke entered, he had in his hand a newspaper, which he hastily crushed and concealed in his pocket, changing colour as he did so, for that identical paper was the *Edinburgh Evening Courant*, containing the advertisement offering a reward for Rob's seizure, dead or alive, a copy of which Grahame of Killearn had just sent to Mugdock by a special messenger.

Though armed with sword, dirk, and pistols, the bearing of Rob Roy assured the startled duke in an instant that his visit was not hostile, and that he was ignorant, or as yet happily unconscious, of the wreck of his peace and honour, the destruction of his property, and the desolation of his home; so Montrose bowed courteously with a courtier's greeting.

"I salute you, gentleman," said Rob, as in Gaelic there are no terms descriptive of rank. The duke, whose right hand was still buried in his pocket, clutching the paper, as if he dreaded that it would fly out and unfold itself, held forth the other; but Rob drew back with a lofty air of offended dignity, saying,—

"My father's son would not take the *left* hand of a king—nay, not even of him who is far away in France; God save and send him safely to his own again! And so, duke, why should I take *yours?*"

"Please yourself, MacGregor," replied the duke, with chilling *hauteur;* "but remember that I have good reason to be offended."

"Offended!" echoed Rob, with surprise.

"You have used me ill."

"You got my letter from Carlisle by the hand of my most trusted kinsman, Greumoch?" asked Rob, hastily.

"A gillie—a drover," sneered Montrose.

"A *duinewassal* of the Clan Alpine, James Grahame, name him as you will," said Rob Roy, becoming flushed with anger.

"What is all this to me?" asked Montrose, haughtily.

"Dioul!" exclaimed Rob, passionately; "did you not get my letter?"

"I did."

"Then it fully explained all."

"It explained that being undersold in the southern markets, or something to that effect, you had parted with our cattle below prime cost."

"Far below it, as I can assure your grace."

"Well, MacGregor Campbell?"

"'Sdeath! MacGregor only!" interrupted Rob,

whose fury was fast rising, and he stamped his foot on the floor.

"I decline to bear my share in this loss, and have insisted upon repayment of the *whole sum* originally subscribed, with the interest due thereon."

"You have insisted?" repeated Rob.

"The affair is in the hand of my chamberlain," said the duke, evasively. "I am not now to learn the tricks of Highland drovers, and how your band of landless reivers and broken sorners, who drove those cattle south, are likely to serve me." The Duke made this offensive speech for the express purpose of working himself, and Rob too, into a passion.

"Montrose," said the latter, sternly; "those whom you stigmatize as landless reivers and broken sorners are better men than ever inherited your blood, duke now though you be! And if this is the way you mean to treat me, by the Grey Stone in Glenfruin, and by the souls of those who died there, I shall not consider it *my* interest to pay *your* interest, nor my interest either to pay even the principal!"

"Dare you say this to me?" exclaimed the duke, flushing with real anger; "to me, under my own roof-tree?"

MacGregor laughed, and patted the basket-hilt of his sword, put on his bonnet, and arose, saying, "I would say something more if you stood on the open heather, under the canopy of heaven. But now let us understand each other; big words never scared

MacGregor, and they are not likely to do so now. I have but £200 to offer you, and yours it should have been had you acted justly or generously; but now——"

" You will keep it, of course ? "

" Ay, every God's-penny, and lay it out in the king's service."

" What king ? "

" Can *you* ask ? " exclaimed Rob, with a glance of surprise, that was blended almost with ferocity. " I mean King James VIII. of Scotland. Queen Anne is ill, so men told me in the south; the day is not far distant when the flag will hang half-hoisted on the walls of Carlisle; and the first news that the Hanoverian Elector has landed in England will make the Highland hills bristle with broadswords— yea, bristle like a stubble-field! The heather will be on fire from Strathspey to Inverary, and this £200, Montrose, the sum exactly for which, as men say, you sold your country, when bribed to make the Union, I shall lay out in the service of him who has sworn to break it. Ochon! the ills that are coming upon us are a pregnant example of the folly of a people allowing their fatherland to be the property of kings! Thus, ours succeeded to the kingdom of England, just as they might have done to a farm or a barony; but England being the richer and the greater, they soon forgot the old house in which their good forefathers lived and died. And now, Montrose, learn from this hour that MacGregor is your enemy ! "

The duke, who was too high-spirited to brook being bearded in his own house, raised his hand to the bell to summon his servants, but paused on seeing the stern frown that gathered on Mac-Gregor's face, and that his right hand was on the pistol in his girdle.

With a mock reverence Rob left his presence, reached the barbican, mounted his horse, and was soon galloping down Strathblane towards the banks of the Enrich.

The duke's first intention was to have him overtaken by a mounted party and made prisoner; but he speedily dismissed the idea, for to waylay one who had just left his own threshold would cover his name with disgrace and reprobation throughout the north; and, moreover, the castle of Mugdock was uncomfortably near the Highland frontier.

" No, no," he muttered; " 'twere better that he should fall into other hands than mine, and find his way from thence to the castle of Dumbarton, or the *kindly* gallows of Crieff," for so the Highlanders ironically termed that formidable gibbet on which so many a sturdy cateran has taken his last farewell of the sun.

CHAPTER XV.

DESOLATION.

FULL of his own thoughts, which were fiery and bitter, and feeling fully resolved to challenge Montrose to a combat, according to the laws of honour and of arms, Rob rode fast along the eastern shore of Loch Lomond : but darkness had set in before he drew near Inversnaid.

Then his heart began to swell with other and kindlier emotions as he pictured his home and his household—his wife and their fairhaired children welcoming him back; and already their voices seemed to sound in his ears, and their smiling faces to come before him.

The moon had risen, and shed its light upon that lovely lake of many isles, on the vast shadowy masses of Ben Lomond and its wondrous scenery, through which the rugged pathway wound, over-hung in some places by gloomy pines, by impending rocks, or the feathery sprays of the silver birch.

With scorn and defiance of Montrose, certain emotions of pride and security swelled the heart of MacGregor, as he rode on ; for again he was at home—in the home of the swordsman and shepherd —the abode of the wolf and the eagle, where yet, in the garb of old Gaul—

H

The hunter of deer and the warrior trod,
To his hills that encircle the sea.

From some points Loch Lomond resembled a great
river, lying between lofty mountains, its bosom
dotted with isles that are covered with trees, dark
brushwood, or moss of emerald green. Bold head-
lands of rock seemed to jut forth in the water,
which shone in the moonlight like a sheet of silver,
and hills that were covered with wood filled up the
background.

And there, in the moonlight, lay the loveliest of
all Loch Lomond's green and woody isles, the Mac-
Gregors' burying-place—the Place of Sleep, Inchcailloch, or the Isle of Nuns, with its ruined chapel
and all its solemn trees.

The Red MacGregor gazed on it wistfully, for
there had all the dead of his persecuted clan been
gathered, generation after generation, ever since
the days of Donngheal, the son of King Alpin;
and now he whipped his lagging horse, and ere
long reached the narrow track which led to his
home at Inversnaid.

The stillness began to surprise him—no cattle
lowed on the hills, no dog barked or bayed to the
moon as she waded through the fleecy clouds, and
one or two cottages, whose inmates he knew, seemed
to have fallen in or been levelled.

A strange foreboding of evil stole into his
breast.

At last his own house, with its whitewashed walls
and its roof thatched with heather, rose before him

in the glen ; but no smoke curled from its chimneys—no light appeared in any of its windows, and all was solemnly and oppressively still in the homestead around it—still and silent as the islet of the dead that lay in the shining lake below.

Dismounting, he led his horse by the bridle, and was about to approach the door, when three Highlanders appeared suddenly before him : one carried a gun, and was fully armed ; the other two bore a dead deer, which was slung by the feet from the branch of a tree that rested on their shoulders.

He with the gun came boldly forward, and demanded " who went there ? "

" The Red MacGregor," replied Rob, in Gaelic.

" Inversnaid!" exclaimed the three men, joyously ; and, dropping the deer, they almost embraced him, for they proved to be Greumoch and two other MacGregors, who were among his most trusted and valued followers.

" What does all this mean ? " he exclaimed ; " why is my house shut, and where are the people ? "

" Ask Montrose ! " said Greumoch, fiercely.

" Montrose ! I left him but a few hours ago in Strathblano," replied Rob.

" And he told you nothing ? "

" Only that I owed him money, and that this money he would have—every penny. But speak quickly—Helen, the boys—what has happened ? "

The resentment of Rob Roy was deep, fierce, and bitter when he found that his house and homestead had been swept of everything, and that nothing remained for him and his family but an abode in the woods or on the mountain side; and he uttered a terrible vow for vengeance on Killearn and on the duke his master.

Ponderous locks now secured the door of his own house against him. These Greumoch's gun might soon have blown to pieces, and thus he might have forced an entrance; or he might have repaired to the house of his nephew at Glengyle. But Rob did neither; he simply desired Greumoch to conduct him to Helen, who now had found shelter in a little cottage—a veritable hut—in a glen at some distance; and the first boding sound that reached his ear as he approached it was the melancholy wail of the bagpipe, as Alpine, the family piper, played Helen's *Lament*, which we believe has never been committed to paper, but has been handed down from one generation to another.

The presence of his wife and children (one of the latter sick and ailing, too), instead of soothing Rob Roy, added fuel to the flame that burned within him; and the alternate grief and energy of Helen spurred his longing for vengeance on those who had so foully wronged him.

Next, his followers crowded around him, detailing their losses and insults, grasping significantly the hilts of their swords and dirks, and gradually lashing each other into greater fury, for hitherto they had lacked but a leader, and now that Rob had returned they expected him to march them at once against the Grahams, or whoever might come in their way. But Rob Roy had greater aims in view than the mere gratification of private revenge; so he resolved to be patient for a time.

"And when that time comes, Helen," said he, with solemn energy, "I will lay the Lennox in flames, and harry Mugdock to its groundstone. There is not a house or homestead, a castle or village, but I shall lay in ashes, between this and the Trongate of Glasgow, unless my hopes and measures fail me."

Helen answered only by her tears, and pressed her sick baby closer to her breast.

"Woe to you, Killearn," said Greumoch, while feeling the edge of his polcaxe; "if you fall into my hands you shall have a short life!"

Next morning Rob placed Helen on a strong Highland garron, and slung the children in two panniers on the back of the horse he had ridden from Glasgow. Greumoch, MacAleister, and others shouldered their long Spanish muskets, the pipers struck up "MacGregors' March," and in this fashion the family of Inversnaid departed to seek a wilder part of the country, where, rent free, they might dwell amid the hills.

Rob retired twelve Scottish (or twenty English) miles further into the Highlands, but he still remained upon what he considered his own territory; and there, building what was termed a creel-house, resolved to live in open war with, and defiance of, the Duke of Montrose, who, by a regular form of

law, had now become, for a time, legal proprietor of
Inversnaid and Craigrostan!

In the wilds of Glendochart Rob began to frame
daring political schemes, which the protection
afforded to him by his kinsman, Sir John Campbell, of Glenorchy, now Earl of Breadalbane,
enabled him to mature, and arms were collected
and hidden in secret places, and men were prepared
for the coming strife.

Aware that the Paper Court of Dunedin (as the
Highlanders disdainfully term the College of Justice
at Edinburgh) was not a place where a Celt—
especially a MacGregor — was likely to obtain
equity, when opposed to a powerful duke who
supported the Whigs, whose government Rob
abhorred—he resolved to set all law at defiance,
and, like a true Scot of the olden time, to confide
in his sword alone.

In addition to the seizure of all he possessed on
earth, the advertisements which appeared, again
and again, in the columns of the " Edinburgh
Evening Courant," stung him to the soul; for
therein he was stigmatized as a fraudulent bankrupt, an outlaw, and robber—as if it was sought to
make him one, for the express purpose of destroying
him.   One runs as follows :—

"All magistrates and officers of his Majesty's
forces are entreated to seize upon Rob Roy, and
the money which he carries with him, until the
persons concerned in the money may be heard

against him ; and that notice be given, when he is apprehended, to the keepers of the Exchange Coffee-house at Edinburgh, and the keeper of the Coffee-house at Glasgow, where the parties concerned will be advertised, and the seizers shall be very reasonably rewarded for their pains." (*Edinburgh Courant*, No. 1,058.)

" Now, Helen," said he, trampling the paper under foot, and then casting it into the bogwood fire that blazed on the floor of their cabin, " by the soul o' Ciar Mhor, our foes shall find that the days of Glenfruin are come again! Henceforward, all is at end between us and the Lowlanders, and we shall devote ourselves to war and death ! "

When Craigrostan, the last of his patrimony, was taken from him, MacGregor was so exasperated (to quote Browne's " Highland History ") " that he declared perpetual war against the duke, and resolved that in future he should supply himself with cattle from his grace's estates, a resolution which he literally kept, and for THIRTY years he carried off the duke's flocks with impunity, and disposed of them publicly in different parts of the country."

The historian adds that these cattle generally belonged to the duke's tenants, who were thus impoverished and unable to pay their rents. He also levied, at the point of the sword, contributions in meal and money, but never until it had first been delivered by the poor tenants to the duke's storekeeper, to whom he always delivered a receipt

for the quantity he carried off. At settling tho
money rents, he frequently attended with a strong
band of chosen men, and giving receipts in due
form, pocketed the rents of Montrose, who soon
began to repent, in bitterness, that he had ever
molested Rob Roy.

CHAPTER XVI.

ROB TAKES THE TOWER OF CARDEN.

THE hills abounded with red deer, the moors and
forests with other game — the lochs and rivers
teemed with fish—the pastures of the Grahmes
were full of cattle; thus, Rob and his outlawed
followers lived sumptuously in their mountain fastnesses, whither none, as yet, dared to follow them.

Montrose and Killearn were, at that time, beyond
Rob's reach; so on Archibald Stirling, of Carden,
who had long withheld his tribute of black-mail for
service and protection rendered, fell the first burst
of his indignation.

It was on a day in the harvest of 1710, that he
marched about two hundred and fifty men, in hostp
array, with pipes playing, through the parish f
Kippen, after passing through the wild glens tha
lie at the feet of Benmore and Benledi.

This force suddenly appeared before the castle c
Carden, which stood on an eminence or island

formed by what was then a loch, but the bed of which is now a rich green meadow, and its name signifies "Caer-dun," or, the fort on the height. No vestige of this castle remains now; though so lately as 1760 a portion of the great tower was standing.

Archibald Stirling was a high cavalier, who, two years before, had been indicted for treason, for having drunk the health of James VIII. at the cross of Dunkeld, accompanied by the Stirlings of Keir and Kippendavie, while swords were flourished, trumpets sounded, and muskets fired.

On the occasion of Rob's visit, Stirling and his lady were both from home, with many of their servants. No inroad was expected from any quarter, and, as the drawbridge was down, the MacGregors, who had been prepared to take the place by storm, quietly took possession of the gates, spread themselves over the whole house, and the contents of the cellars and pantries were quickly investigated.

When the family returned, about sunset, they found the gates shut, the bridge drawn up, and the windows and bartizan full of grim-looking Mac-Gregors, in their red tartans, and bristling with swords, axes, and long guns; while Rob's favourite piper, Alpine, strode to and fro on the roof, playing his invariable air of defiance, "The Battle of Glenfruin."

Outwitted and alarmed, the laird tied a white handkerchief to the point of his sword, and dismounting from the saddle, behind which his terrified lady rode upon a pillion, he advanced to the outer edge of the moat, and waved thrice his impromptu flag of truce. On this the pibroch ceased, and Rob Roy, with bonnet and feather, broadsword and target, appeared at a window of the hall.

"What is the meaning of all this, MacGregor?" asked the laird, sternly; "wherefore do I find your people here, and my own gates shut against me?"

"Carden, remember the black-mail!" replied the outlaw, with equal sternness. "You have long withheld the reward of that protection I once afforded you; and you must yield it now, or see your house burned to the groundstone."

"I will not yield you a shilling—nay, not a farthing of it. I am able to protect myself against all reivers and thieves whatsoever."

"Our being *in*, and your being *out*, at present, cannot look very like it," said MacGregor, laughing; "and here shall we stay, Carden——"

"Till I rouse the Lennox on you, or get a party of troops from Dumbarton. Remember that Mac-Dougal's dragoons are lying at Kylsyth!" exclaimed Carden, furiously, as he turned towards his horse.

"Hold!" cried Rob, sternly, and the appearance of MacAleister's gun, levelled from the tower-head, made Carden pause; then a scream burst from his wife, when perceiving that Rob held from the window their youngest child, which he had taken from the cradle, as she feared with some cruel intention—perhaps to cast it into the lake! Her husband had the same dread, for he grew deadly pale.

"MacGregor, hold!" he exclaimed; "hold, for Heaven's sake, and spare my child!"

"Who spared mine, when you and Killearn came like wolves in my absence, and made my household desolate? Though my youngest-born was sick and ailing, you stood coldly by, while it and its mother were driven forth, from my house at Inversnaid, like the dam and cubs of a wolf; so if I am the wretch that you and others seek to make me, wherefore should I not dash this youngling at your feet, or cast it into the loch?"

For a moment both father and mother were speechless with terror and anxiety; but Rob was too humane to torment them thus. He laughed, kissed and toyed with the poor child, whose plump fingers played with his rough, red beard, and then he resigned it to the nurse, who was well-nigh scared out of her senses.

"MacGregor," cried the Laird of Carden, "unbar the gate, and lower the bridge, and you shall have your black-mail, every penny, with all arrears."

"'Tis well, Carden; now you speak like a reasonable man, and shall be alike welcome to your own rooftree, and to share with me a glass of wine from your own cellar. Admit the laird, Greumoch," he added to that personage, who had charge of the bridge and gate. He then hurried down, and after courteously assisting the lady to alight from her pillion, he conducted her into the castle, where he soon received the tax, granted a receipt for it in legal form, and drawing off his men, marched under cloud of night, and with all speed, towards the mountains.

Since the battle of Glenfruin, and its subsequent severities, the MacGregors had been a scattered clan; but they now began to flock to Rob Roy in such numbers that he soon found himself at the head of five hundred swordsmen.

As the representative of Glengyle, his influence over them was very great, and they all regarded him as the man ordained by Heaven to avenge their injuries on the Lowlanders; for a wrong done to one member of a clan was a wrong done to all, as they were all kinsmen, and related by blood.

Habituated to war and the use of arms, to a love of each other and of their chief, a clan was endued with what an historian terms the two most active principles of human nature—attachment to one's friends and hatred of their enemies.

" Thus," says Sir John Dalrymple, " the humblest of a clan, knowing himself to be as well born as the head of it, revered in his chief his own honour; loved in his clan his own blood; complained not of the difference of station into which fortune had thrown him, and respected himself. The chief in return bestowed a protection founded equally on gratitude and the consciousness of his own interest. Hence the Highlanders, whom *more savage* nations called *savage,* carried in the outward expression of their manners the politeness of courts without their vices, and in their bosoms the highest point of honour without its follies."*

Notwithstanding the reward offered for his apprehension, Rob Roy was often rash enough to venture from his fastness alone, and into the very territories of his enemies, for he had become openly an adherent of the exiled House of Stuart, and deep schemes were on foot for maturing the plans of an insurrection ; and the conduct of many of these intrigues was committed to his care.

On one of these missions he found himself belated one night near the village of Arnpryor, in the district of Kippen, to which he had paid more than one hostile visit, and where, consequently, he was exposed to many dangers.

Nevertheless, he repaired to the village alehouse, and found a gentleman named Henry Cunninghame, the Laird of Boquhan, seated by the fire over a bottle of claret, which cost only tenpence per mutchkin, and was then a favourite beverage with all ranks in Scotland. He at once recognized MacGregor, and they entered into conversation ; but some remarks which he made, either on the affairs of the exiled king, or those of MacGregor, exasperated the latter, who sprang up with a hand on his sword, in token of defiance and quarrel. Boquhan was unarmed. MacGregor could have supplied him

* " Memoirs of Great Britain."

with pistols; but being the challenged party he preferred the sword, in the use of which few in Scotland equalled and none excelled him.

The goodwife of the tavern, fearing a brawl, averred that she had not a single weapon in her house; so the laird despatched a messenger to his residence for a sword, which his wife refused to send him, knowing well it was required for a duel or a brawl; so daylight broke, and found them still loth to part in anger, and still waiting for a weapon.

It chanced then that Boquhan espied an old and rusty rapier in a corner, which had hitherto escaped his notice. He at once possessed himself of it; Rob unsheathed his claymore; the tables and chairs were thrust aside, and the combat began with great fury.

It is stated that MacGregor soon discovered that he had no ordinary antagonist in Henry Cunninghame; and having no particular animosity to him, and remembering, perhaps, how perilous to his own clan his death, or even a severe wound, would prove at that particular crisis, after a dozen passes or so, he lowered the point of his sword, and said,—

" Enough of this, Boquhan; I find you are brave as you are expert, and I yield to you." So he sheathed his sword, and they parted good friends; but Rob's enemies in the Lennox magnified his prudence into a humiliating defeat.

CHAPTER XVII.

THE JACOBITE BOND.

Rob Roy and those who adhered to him found themselves tolerably safe in the land of the Campbells—the more so as his mother was a daughter of that powerful clan which had been at enmity with the house of Montrose since the wars of the Covenant, since the slaughter of the Campbells at Inverlochy by the Great Marquis, and since the invasion of Lorn by his cavaliers. Fortunately for Rob Roy, the mutual hate between the Dukes of Argyll and Montrose was still as hot as ever.

The death of Queen Anne and the accession of George I. soon brought political matters to a crisis in Scotland, where the Jacobites had remained quiet enough under the rule of a sovereign who was a Stuart, and under none else could the union of the two kingdoms ever have been achieved.

But now, a rising for her brother to succeed as James VIII. of Scotland and III. of England was resolved on, and a great meeting of Jacobite leaders took place in Breadalbane. The better to mask their intentions from Government, it was entitled a hunting match, though among the secluded hills of the Scottish Highlands such a precaution seemed somewhat unnecessary.

The chiefs and chieftains—among the latter was

Rob Roy—who assembled on the occasion, soon ascertained each other's sentiments and the number of men they could bring into the field; and ulterior plans were soon resolved upon, while a previously prepared *bond*, for their mutual faith to each other and to the exiled king, was produced, and thereunto each man appended his signature.

By some inexcusable neglect on the part of a gentleman who became its custodian, this important paper fell into the hands of Captain Campbell of Glenlyon (an officer whose name was unfortunately involved deeply in the Massacre of Glencoe), who was then stationed in the garrison of Fort William, near Lochiel.

Glenlyon retained the bond, and finding that among the names appended thereto were those of many who were his own immediate friends and relations, he did not, for a time, mention its tenor or even its existence; but the horror with which he was regarded in Scotland, as the tool of King William in the midnight slaughter of the Macdonalds, had spread even among his own kinsmen; and thus, when the Jacobite chiefs became aware that a man of a character so unscrupulous held a document that might give all their heads to the block and their estates to fire and sword, they became naturally anxious and alarmed, and a hundred futile plans were formed for its recovery or destruction.

The Earl of Mar, the chief of the Jacobite leaders, turned to Rob Roy, who, although he had affixed his name to the bond as " Robert MacGregor of Inversnaid and Craigrostan," cared not a rush personally about the matter, as he despised alike the new king and his government; but on being urged by others, whose fortunes were less desperate, he resolved to undertake its recovery or perish in the attempt.

To this he was urged by Sir James Livingstone, who had been despatched to him by the Earl of Mar, and who was the same gentleman he had wounded after the devastation of Kippen.

Disguising himself, he relinquished the picturesque garb of the mountains for a rocquelaure, boots, and breeches, and rode to Fort William, which is a strongly-built and regular fortress, situated near the base of Ben Nevis, and at the extremity of Lochiel.

Notwithstanding the peril in which he placed himself, for the advertisements of the "Courant" still, from time to time, offered a reward for him dead or alive, Rob contrived to pass the gates and sentinels unnoticed or unquestioned, and obtained an interview with Captain Campbell of Glenlyon, who recognized him immediately, but dared neither to discover nor detain him, as Rob was a near relation of his own.

His visitor inquired about the bond which had been signed at the pretended hunting-match, and, to his rage and indignation, he discovered, after long evasion, that Glenlyon, in revenge for the contemptuous manner in which he was spoken of by the Jacobites, had placed the document in the hands of the governor of the garrison!

The latter was Sir John Hill, a brave and resolute old Whig officer, who had been placed there so far back as the days of Charles II., and had retained his command during all the changes of the long and stormy period that intervened — in fact, strange as it may appear, he was one of the *last* soldiers of Oliver Cromwell.

" And so this bond, which binds so many of us in life and death to King James, is in possession of Colonel Hill? " said Rob, with visible uneasiness.

" Yes," replied Glenlyon, with a malignant expression in his light grey eyes; "and it shall be forwarded in due time to the Secretary of State for the information of His Majesty and the Privy Council."

" Humph—His Majesty! " repeated Rob, with scorn in his eye and tone ; " will it be sent soon? "

" Why do *you* ask, my friend? " inquired the captain.

" Because," replied Rob, with a smile, " as *my* name is appended to it, I should like, with your leave, kinsman, to get a little further into the hills, as I know that the Lords of the Privy Council take some interest in my movements."

"Kinsman Rob, situated as you and the MacGregors are, it will not make much difference now. But in three days the bond will be sent from this to the Governor of Dumbarton in charge of Captain Huske."

" Does he belong to Argyle's regiment ? "

" No ; the South British Fusiliers."

" He will require a pretty strong party to march with through the glens."

" He will have the usual escort," replied Glenlyon, carelessly ; for he did not remark the red flash of triumph that sparkled in the eyes of Rob Roy, as he took his leave, and lost no time in travelling over the mountains, and reaching his now humble home.

Knowing that Captain Huske and his party must pass through the last-named valley, Rob summoned MacAleister, Greumoch, Alaster Roy, his oldest son Coll—who could now shoulder a musket, and was a strong and active boy—with fifty other MacGregors, all men on whom he could depend, who had been his comrades in every expedition of importance, and whom he knew would stand by him truly " to the last of their blood and their breath ;" accompanied by these he took up a position in a place which commanded a view of the whole glen, and remained there night and day waiting for his prey.

The grey smoke of the clachan of Killin was visible in the distance from Rob's bivouac ; and on the other hand lay Loch Dochart, amid whose lonely waters the scaup-duck, the water-rail, and the ring-ouzel float, and where the long-legged heron wades in search of the spotted trout.

Moated by these waters is an isle containing the ruins of a castle, the ancient residence of the knights of Lochawe. Masses of trees almost shroud it now ; but once, in the days of its strength and pride, it was stormed by the MacGregors during a moon-light night, in a keen and frosty winter, when the loch was sheeted with ice. Constructing large fascines of timber to shield them from arrows and other missiles, they pushed those screens before them, and on reaching the outer wall, soon became masters of the place.

There, too, is a floating isle, formed by the in-tertwisting of roots and water-plants. Often it is seen to float like a ship before the wind, with the bewildered cattle which have ventured on it from the shore, for its grass is rich and verdant.

With tales of past achievements and songs, passing the whisky-bottle round the while, Rob and his followers saw the third day drawing to a close, before Alaster Roy, who had been scouting down the glen, came in haste to announce that a red English soldier was in sight! This proved to be the advanced file of Captain Huske's party.

CHAPTER XVIII.

THE DESPATCHES CAPTURED.

THE summits of the hills, behind which the sun was setting, were dark and sombre, while a ruddy purple hue tinged those on which his light was falling.

Concealing themselves among some tufts of high fern and dwarf alder-trees, the MacGregors watched the advance of those whom they deemed the chief tools of their tormentors—the unsuspecting soldiers of the line.

The brightly-burnished musket-barrels of the men, and the pikes then carried by the officer and his sergeant, were seen to flash and glitter as they advanced through the deep hollow, along which the narrow foot-track wound; and soon the bright red of their square-skirted coats, and their white cross-belts, breeches, and gaiters appeared in strong relief upon the dun heather of the glen.

Rob counted that there was an officer, a sergeant, and twenty rank and file. From his ambush he could with ease have shot down the whole party, had he been cruelly disposed; but, that even his enemies might not be taken unprepared, he ordered young Coll, MacAleister, and the rest to keep out of sight, but to start up at a given signal; and then, rising from his hiding-place, he advanced alone towards the marching soldiers.

The appearance of a fully-armed Highlander, with sword, dirk, pistols, and target, excited no comment then; for, on Rob drawing near, the officer coldly returned his salute, and the sergeant inquired " how far it was from thence to the head of Loch Lomond ? "

" About twenty miles, if you pass through Glen-falloch." The soldiers, who were a mixed party of the 15th Foot and the South British Fusiliers.

muttered something which sounded very like oaths. In those days an officer's escort accompanied every Government letter or message through the Highlands, as smaller parties were liable to be cut off.

"It will be mirk midnight before you get half way through the glen," resumed Rob, with a mocking smile; "and people say that Glenfalloch is haunted."

"By what?" asked the officer, who wore a Ramillie wig, a three-cornered hat, and red rocquelaure.

"Spirits."

"Indeed — whisky, I suppose?" said the sergeant, laughing.

"Loud voices are heard talking in the air overhead, when nothing can be seen but the sailing clouds."

"Voices!" exclaimed Captain Huske.

"Yes, as if one hill-top was talking to the other."

"Bah! I can bid our drummer beat the 'Point of War.' I warrant he'll scare away all your Highland goblins, even Rob Roy himself, whom I wish was as near me as you are."

"You have had him near enough once before," said MacGregor, gravely, as he suddenly recognized the officer, though some time had elapsed since they last met.

"Hah—when?"

"In Moffatdale, where he gave you a lesson in humanity, and in good manners, too."

"Zounds, sirrah, what do you mean?" asked

Captain Huske, cocking his hat fiercely over his right eye, and stepping forward a pace.

"Simply, that he ran you through the body, as he is quite prepared to do again, if you do not instantly yield up your packet of despatches!"

The officer sprang back, threw off his rocquelaure, and brought his pike to the charge; Rob parried the thrust by his claymore, but he uttered a shrill whistle on seeing the soldiers fixing their bayonets and cocking their muskets.

"Shoot down the Highland dog!" cried Captain Huske, choking with passion; but his soldiers paused, for a yell now pierced the welkin, and fifty MacGregors, armed with sword and target, and each with the badge of his forbidden clan in his bonnet— a sprig of the mountain pine—rushed down with a shout of "Ard choille! ard choille! 'Srioghal mo dhream!" Perceiving that he was outnumbered, the officer withdrew his pike, and by outstretched sword-arm Rob kept back his own people, who glared over their shields at the unfortunate party of soldiers, who thought their doom was sealed, and that a hopeless and bloody struggle was about to ensue.

"Are you all robbers?" asked the officer, fiercely.

"No more than your citizens of London or Carlisle may be," replied MacGregor. "You might be shot by a cowardly footpad on Hounslow Heath—ay, or London Bridge, or in the High Street of Edinburgh: but who there would stop a band of armed soldiers as I this day stop you? Here, in front of your men, sir, I will fight you, with sword and pistol, or with sword and dirk; whichever please you."

"Neither please me—I am a king's officer, and may not risk my life, like a roadside bully, thus," said the captain, haughtily. "Am I right in supposing that you are the outlaw Rob Roy, for whose capture a high reward is offered?"

" You are right; I am the Laird of Inversnaid, and instantly require your despatches."

" For what purpose?"

" The service of his Majesty, King James VIII., whom God preserve!" replied MacGregor, lifting his bonnet with reverence.

" I must either give up my life and the despatches together, or the despatches alone," said the officer, bewildered and exasperated.

" What you may do is nothing to me."

" But there is one of vast importance."

" The very one I wish, captain; so surrender it at once, or I shall cut you and your men into collops for the fox and the raven." Captain Huske opened the breast-pocket of his regimentals, and unwillingly gave to Rob a large sealed packet, addressed, " To the most noble Prince, James, Duke of Montrose, Secretary of State for Scotland. On His Majesty's Service."

Rob's eyes sparkled with resentment on seeing the name of his enemy; but he tore open the envelope, and taking out the well-known bond of the Highland chiefs, restored the packet to the English officer.

He then offered him and his men a dram each, and marched off into the darkening mountains, leaving the captain to proceed towards Dumbarton, or return to Colonel Hill at Fort William, whichever suited his orders or his fancy.

By this bold exploit Rob preserved secret the plans of the forthcoming insurrection, and saved from the scaffold, captivity, or exile, many brave nobles and gentlemen, whom otherwise the merciless Government of George I. would have seized and destroyed in detail.

CHAPTER XIX.

ABERUCHAIL.

PRIOR to the great Rising of the Clans in 1715, Rob Roy was engaged as usual in several small skirmishes and frays, in which his skill and strategy as a leader were prominent; and he gained yet more the reputation of being the protector of the poor against the rich, and of the defenceless against those who would oppress them.

In spite of the Duke of Montrose, he had re-established himself again at Craigrostan, from whence he never went abroad attended by less than twenty or thirty well-armed men, including his henchman and Greumoch.

These were his *Leine Chrios,* or body-guard.

Some of the Grahames of Montrose, and others who were obnoxious to himself or to the cause of the exiled king, he confined occasionally in a place which is still named Rob Roy's prison.

This is a mural rock, the eyry of the osprey or water-eagle, which rises to the height of thirty feet on the north-eastern shore of Loch Lomond, about four miles from Rowardennan.

Slung by ropes, he occasionally lowered them from the summit, and after permitting them to swing in mid-air for a time, would give them a severe ducking in the loch below and compel them to shout—

" God save King James VIII."

They were then permitted to depart amid the laughter of his followers ; and it must be borne in mind that this was very gentle treatment when compared with that to which the MacGregors were subjected when captured by the same people.

As the old Highland proprietors or heads of septs held their lands in virtue of an occupancy coeval with the first settlement of the tribes in Scotland, and consequently disdained to hold possession by virtue of a *sheepskin* rather than by their sword-blades, in later years, a system of suppressing the smaller lairds by force of arms had long been pursued with success by the house of Argyle in the west.

A powerful landowner of that name, who had

recently been created a baronet, seized at the point of the sword a small estate in Glendochart, and expelled the proprietor with all his family and kindred.

MacGregor, who could not permit an act of such injustice to pass unpunished, sent Greumoch with forty men to the Braes of Glenorchy, with orders to "bring this oppressor of the poor a prisoner before him."

It was in the sweet season of spring, when the lapwing came to the bowers of silver birch and the green plover winged its way over the purple heather, when the MacGregors departed on this expedition; and being aware of the place and time when their prey would probably pass, they concealed themselves among the bleak granite rocks of Ben Cruachin, a vast mountain, the red furrowed sides of which—furrowed by a thousand watercourses—rise above Loch Awe, and terminate in a sharp cone.

Here stood the wall of a ruined chapel, founded of old by a MacGregor chief, and through it a well, deemed holy, flowed into a stone basin, under an old yew-tree. To the stem was chained an iron ladle, by which the thirsty pilgrim or wayfarer might drink, and at the bottom of the basin lay little copper Scottish coins which had been dropped therein as offerings, while knots of ribbons, rags, and trifles decorated the boughs of the aged yew.

"A place of good omen!" said Greumoch, looking around him; "for here it was that Clan

Alpine won the lands of Glenorchy, when there were no paper courts in Dunedin, or redcoats in Dumbarton."

It chanced that on a day in summer, King David I., of Scotland, was hunting with Malcolm MacGregor, the eighth chief of Clan Alpine, on the side of Cruachin, when a wild boar, of marvellous strength, size, and ferocity, appeared in a rugged defile. It at once assailed the monarch, whose hunting-spear broke and left him at its mercy; but instead of rushing forward, the boar retired to whet its tusks against the rocks, so Malcolm craved the king's permission to attack it.

" E'en do," said the king; " but spaire nocht!"

" *Eadhon dean agus na caomhain!* " shouted MacGregor, translating the king's lowland Scottish into Gaelic, as he tore up a young tree by the roots, and kept the boar at bay until he could close with it and bury his long dagger in its throat. At the third stab he slew it.

To reward his courage, David granted him the lands of Glenorchy, and, in remembrance of the day, added to his arms *argent*, an oak-tree uprooted *vert*, across a claymore *azure*, which every Mac-Gregor may bear to this day.

But now the Campbells were lords of Glenorchy, and just as Greumoch had ended this legend of the clan, which no doubt all his hearers knew before, the great personage they were in search of rode into the defile, when he was surrounded, and his retainers were scattered in a moment.

On finding himself a prisoner, and knowing well to whom, the baronet proposed a ransom; but bribes were offered and threats uttered in vain to Greumoch, who ordered the prisoner to be tied up in a long plaid, which was slung over the shoulders of Alaster Roy and another tall gilly; and thus by turns, with two bearers at a time, he was conveyed for about fourteen miles to a place called Tyndrum, where he was brought before Rob Roy.

This village is at the head of Strathfillan in Breadalbane, on the western military road.

Rob upbraided the prisoner with his cruelty and oppression, and threatened to toss him over the rock into Loch Lomond, with a stone in his plaid, if he did not restore the lands in Glendochart to their original owner.

Paper was produced, a document was drawn up and signed, by the tenor of which he and his heirs renounced them formally and for ever.

He now hoped to be allowed to depart; but there arose a cry of,—

"To the well! to the well! give him a dip in the Holy Pool of St. Fillan!"

It was Paul Crubach who spoke.

"Be it so," said Rob; "if the water has not lost its virtue, a dip therein may improve the Campbell's spirit of honour, and prevent him from robbing the poor again."

In spite of his earnest entreaties, the MacGregors bore their prisoner, who feared they were about to drown him, to the well of St. Fillan. The whole

population of the village followed, and lame Paul
hobbled in front, chuckling and laughing, while his
eyes flashed with insane delight, his long grizzled
hair streaming in elf-locks on the wind, as with one
hand he brandished his wooden cross, and with the
other tolled vehemently the ancient bell of St.
Fillan, which in those days always stood upon a
gravestone in the churchyard.

After permitting his men to duck the prisoner
soundly, Rob procured a horse, and sent him homeward with a safe escort under his son Coll; but
though these indignities were too great to be
forgotten, in followers Rob was too strong now
to be captured, even by the Campbells of Argyle.

For the forthcoming revolt money was requisite,
and Campbell of Aberuchail, taking advantage of
Rob Roy's outlawry, had long withheld his tribute
of black-mail, so, before returning to Craigrostan,
our hero resolved on levying it, and marching from
Tyndrum at the head of his followers, appeared
before the mansion of Aberuchail, the proprietors
of which had been baronets since 1627.

Having heard that the MacGregors had been
seen in motion in the neighbourhood, all the cattle
had been hastily collected in a dense herd within
the outer walls of Aberuchail tower, around which
there grew a fine wood of oak-trees that for ages
had cast their shadows on the Ruchail, which means
the *red-stream*.

A strong gate, loopholed for musketry, and surmounted by a coat of arms with the motto, *Victoriam*

coronat Christus, was closed and secured as the MacGregors approached, and all was still within, save the lowing and bellowing of the cattle, so closely penned within the barbican.

Rob Roy thundered with his sword-hilt on the outer gate, in which an eyelet-hole was opened, and thereat the porter's face appeared, with an expression of anxiety and alarm, which was no way lessened when he found himself front to front with the keen eyes, the ruddy beard, and sunburned visage of the Red MacGregor, whom he knew instinctively.

" Is the laird at home? " asked the resolute visitor.

" Yes," stammered the gate-ward.

" Why does he not come in person when he knows who are here? " was the haughty query.

" He is at dinner."

" What! Is this Highland manners, to close your gates at meal-time, when other men open theirs wide, that all men may enter? Is this the way your master rewards those who protect him from thieving MacNabs and broken men of the Lennox? "

" Sir James Livingstone, Sir Humphrey of Luss, and several gentlemen are at dinner with him, and I dare not disturb them," urged the porter, whose orders were to keep out Rob at all hazards.

" Gentlemen! " repeated Rob. " Whigs, probably, plotting treason against King James. Tell your master that the Red MacGregor of Inversnaid is here, without, where it is not his wont to be kept, awaiting his arrears of black-mail, and that he *shall* see him, even if the King of Scotland and the Hanoverian Elector, too, were at table with him!"

After a time, the gate-ward returned, trembling, to say that "his master knew no such persons as either the King, the Elector, or the Laird of Inversnaid."

"By the grave of Cior Mhor, Aberuchail shall repent of this false whiggery!" exclaimed Rob, as he took a horn from his belt, and blew a blast so loud and shrill that the whole house and the woods around it rang with echoes.

Then anew the cattle bellowed, and the porter shut the eyelet-hole and fled, lest he might be pistolled.

Four pipers now struck up the "Battle of Glenfruin;" the MacGregors uttered a shout, and assailing the gate soon forced it; for the *clach neart* —the putting-stone of strength—which lay beside it, was dashed like a cannon-ball upon its planks by the most powerful of the band, till the barrier crumbled to pieces before them; after which they proceeded with drawn swords to goad and drive off the cattle.

On this, the baronet of Aberuchail came hastily to the door of the tower, and taking Rob Roy by the hand, made many apologies for what he alleged to be the stupidity of the porter, and led his unwelcome visitor into the house, where, however, neither Livingstone nor Luss appeared.

Then he handed him the "black-mail," for which

MacGregor gave his receipt; they drank a bottle of claret together, and separated, to all appearance, good friends. The cattle were all left in the parks, and the MacGregors marched back to Craigrostan.

But does it not seem strange that when Pope was writing at Twickenham, when Addison and Steele were contributing to the *Spectator*, and when Betterton was acting at Old Drury Lane, this wild work was being done among the Highland hills?

CHAPTER XX.

ROB ROY RETREATS.

IN January, 1714, Rob commanded 500 men among the gathering of 2,000 Highlanders who, on the 28th of that month, fully armed on all points, attended the great funeral of Campbell of Lochnell. At their head were a pair of standards, belonging to the Earl of Breadalbane, preceded by thirteen pipers; for, in fact, this great Celtic funeral was in reality a Jacobite meeting—the dead body having been kept unburied for nearly a month, that an assemblage of Cavalier chiefs might take place, to consider and arrange during the march to the interment and the feast that followed it, the measures to be taken for a rising in favour of the Stuarts.

After maintaining, as already related, a vexatious
predatory warfare against Montrose, who long since
repented bitterly his injustice to the unfortunate
Rob Roy, the MacGregors assembled in such numbers under the latter that they began to threaten
the Western Lowlands, towards the lower end of
Loch Lomond, from whence, marching into Monteith and the Lennox, they disarmed all whom their
leader deemed inimical to the cause of James VIII.

To have complete command of the great sheet of
water which lay before his rocky home, Rob seized
every boat upon it, and had them drawn overland
to Inversnaid, for the purpose of attacking or
cutting off a strong body of West country Whigs,
who were in arms for King George, and who were
marching towards Loch Lomond; for so greatly
were the operations of Rob dreaded that the
people of Dumbarton supposed he might come
upon them in the night to storm the castle and
plunder the town.

Exasperated on finding that he had pounced on
all their boats, the Whigs resolved to make a bold
dash for their recovery.

The volunteers of Paisley, Renfrew, and Kilmar-
nock, were mustered and armed from the Royal
arsenal in the castle of Dumbarton. A body of
seamen from the ships of war then lying in the
Clyde towed them up the river in long-boats and
launches, and on entering Loch Lomond the whole
force proceeded by land and water against Rob
Roy and the MacGregors.

These forces acted under the orders of Lieu-tenant-General Lord Cadogan, colonel of the 4th Foot, who had arrived that year in Scotland. At night they halted at Luss, the stronghold of the Colquhouns, the hereditary foemen of Clan Alpine, where they were joined by Sir Humphry Colquhoun, chief of his name (and fifth in succession of him who fled from Glenfruin), with his son-in-law, James Grant of Pluscardine, who brought some forty or fifty men of his clan—" stately fellows," says Rae, in his history of the affair, "in their short hose and belted plaids (*i.e.* kilts), armed each with a well-fixed gun on his shoulder, a handsome target with a sharp-pointed steel about half an ell in length screwed into the navel of it, slung on his left arm, a sturdy claymore by his side, and a pistol or two with a dirk and knife in his belt."

The man-of-war boats, which were armed with brass swivel-guns, took all on board, and then they crossed the loch.

From the high land above Craigrostan Mac-Gregor saw the advance of this force, which was too strong for him to contend against alone; and a stirring sight it must have been, on that beautiful sheet of water—the large boats, full of men in gay scarlet uniforms, their bright arms flashing in the sun; and it would seem, that thinking to scare the Highlanders, they beat incessantly on their drums, while the seamen maintained a constant discharge from their swivel-guns, the reports of which were multiplied among the steep mountains by a thousand echoes, as the whole expedition swept in shore towards Craigrostan.

Rob and his men, who were concealed among the rocks, the heather, and tall braken, high up on the mountain slope, could scarcely be restrained from rushing to the beach and making an attack when they saw the family banner of Sir Humphry, a saltire engrailed sable, crested with a red hart's head, and his followers in their tartan, which is blue striped with red; and each man wore the badge of his name, a tuft of bear-berry in his bonnet.

The union-jack that floated in the stern of each boat seemed but a foreign flag to MacGregor, for never had it waved on these waters before, and the red-coated volunteers he viewed simply as invaders and enemies; yet their strength was too great for him to hope a victory if he opposed them.

"Oich, oich !" muttered MacAleister, and others, as James Grant's boats, with his men in red tartans, appeared; "here come Pluscardine and his kail-eaters"—for being the people who first cultivated that vegetable in the north, they were named "the kail-eating Grants."

As the men began to leap ashore, with fixed bayonets, and form into companies, young Coll MacGregor could no longer restrain his ardour and impatience, and levelled his gun over the rocks, crying—

"A nis ! a nis ! a nis !" (now, now, now !) "E'en do and spaire nocht !"

"Hold, son of mine!" exclaimed his father, grasping his arm like a vice; "boy, would you destroy us all, and, it may be, with us King James's cause too? Let us await our time, and be assured it will come anon."

And so, seeing that a conflict would be useless, he prudently drew off his men to Strathfillan, where the Jacobite clans were forming a camp, prior to their joining the Earl of Mar; while the invaders of Craigrostan committed to the flames several thatched dwelling-houses, and the smoke of the conflagration, as it rolled along the mountain-slopes, added to the wrath and mortification of Rob and his men, as they retreated up the side of Loch Lomond.

While one party of volunteers pushed on the work of destruction, others searched for the missing boats, which they found far inland, at Inversnaid, and drew from thence to the water. Those which were useless they staved, or sunk, the rest were all conveyed to Dumbarton, where they were safely moored under the guns of the castle. And so ended the first expedition against Rob Roy, a history of which—as if it had been a campaign in a foreign land—was published soon after, in the form of a pamphlet.

Summonses were now issued by Government to all nobles and gentlemen, either in arms or who were suspected of being about to arm, including John, Earl of Mar, and fifty-two others, one of whom is designated as "Robert Roy, *alias* MacGregor."

CHAPTER XXI.

JOINS KING JAMES.

THE brave Earl of Mar had now unfurled the standard of the exiled king at Braemar, as lieutenant-general of his forces, and after sending the "cross of fire" through the Highlands, in a few days he found himself at the head of ten thousand men, and half the peers of Scotland, with all those chiefs and gentlemen who had signed the Bond of Union, which Rob Roy had so luckily taken from Captain Huske, in Glendochart.

Mar's standard was of blue silk; it bore a thistle and the words No Union.

The Duke of Argyle, anxious to evince his attachment to the House of Hanover, hastened from London, to put himself at the head of his own clan, tenants, vassals, and all the troops then in Scotland — and a motley force they were, of English, Dutch, Switzers, and Lowland volunteers.

That branch of the Clan Alpine which is named the race of Dugald Ciar Mhor, was not commanded by Rob Roy at this momentous crisis, but by his young nephew, Gregor MacGregor, of Glengyle, who was lineal head of the house. Thus Rob served under him. Glengyle is best remembered in Scotland by his patronymic of *Glun Dhu,* or "Black-knee," from the remarkable spot, which his kilt rendered visible, on his left knee.

He was but a youth when the insurrection of 1715 took place, so there can be little doubt that, on most occasions, he would act under the eye and advice of a captain so skilful and bold as his uncle.

On the latter joining the insurgent camp in Braemar, he was at once despatched by the earl to Aberdeen, to raise in arms the descendants of 300 MacGregors, who had been forcibly conveyed there in 1624 by James Stewart, Earl of Murray, to fight in the feuds in which he became involved with the Grants, MacIntoshes, and others. In this mission Rob was pretty successful, for the popularity of his name, among his own clan and others made him an excellent recruiting officer at this crisis; and so little did he value the Whig Government and their proclamations that he walked openly about the streets of the Granite City, and on more than one occasion dined with Professor James Gregory, who was by descent a MacGregor, but had thus altered his name to elude the Act which proscribed it

He joined the Earl of Mar in time to be present with his clan at the great battle of Sheriffmuir, where the insurgents met the king's forces led by the Duke o' Argyle, who was then lieutenant-general, knight of the garter, and commander-in-chief of the troops in Scotland.

It is no part of our plan to give any history of

that indecisive battle, which was severe and bloody
to both parties.   Both armies wheeled upon their
centres, and each routed the other's left wing, so
that it is impossible to say with whom lay the
victory.

On that day, Rob Roy, who commanded a body
of MacGregors and MacPhersons, was accused of
unwillingness to engage. His enemies went further,
and asserted that, not wishing to offend his patrons
the powerful Duke of Argyle and Earl of Breadalbane, save for whom he would have been crushed
long ago by the Duke of Montrose, he remained
almost aloof from the action. Lack of interest in
King James's cause, or lack of courage could not
be laid to his charge; yet on this great day the
conduct of Rob Roy was incomprehensible.

Scott relates in his History, that when ordered
to charge by one of Mar's *aides-de-camp*, he
replied—

"If the earl cannot win the field without me *now*,
he cannot win it with me."

From this it may be supposed that he considered
the decisive moment past, and wished to spare his
men; but, it is said, that on hearing this answer, a
brave man of the Clan Vurich, named Alaster Mac-
Pherson, cast his plaid on the ground, drew his
claymore, and called to the MacPhersons—

"Advance—advance !—follow *me !*

"Halt, Alaster," said Rob, interposing; "were
this a question about a drove of sheep you might
know something; but as the matter concerns the

leading of armed men, you must allow *me* to judge."

"Were the question about the foraying of a drove of Glen Eigas stots, the question with you, Rob, would not be who should be last, but who should be *first*," was the stinging retort of MacPherson.

This nearly produced a quarrel between them; already their brows were knitted and their swords menaced each other, even while shells were bursting and shot of every kind were tearing up the turf about them; but finding the inexpedience of coming to blows when under the fire of an enemy, they gave each other a grim smile, and exchanged their snuff-mulls in token of amity, yet many of their men now joined the MacLeans, who at this moment made a tremendous charge upon the regulars.

The appearance of this clan in the field, numbering 800 swordsmen, is a memorable instance of the power of the *patriarchal* system over the *feudal*.

The chief had lived for years a banished loyalist in France, and their lands in Mull had been gifted to the House of Argyle; yet, in opposition to the latter, the whole fighting force of the clan were in the field against the duke, their legal landlord, and under their long-exiled chief, the venerable Sir John MacLean, fought valiantly.

With the best born, the best armed, and the bravest of the Clan Gillian in front, he led them on three ranks deep.

"Gentlemen," he exclaimed, "this is the day we have long wished for. Yonder stands Argyle for King George: *here* stands MacLean for King

James! God bless him! Charge, gentlemen, charge!"

And with a wild yell, in which their pibroch mingled, the clan rushed on, and the levelled bayonets of the soldiers of the line went down before their whirling swords, like straw before the flames.

At that moment, through the smoke of the action there rushed an English officer towards the MacGregor's line. His sword was broken in his hand, and left him at the mercy of a gigantic Highlander, who pursued him with a tuagh, or Lochaber axe. He was bareheaded also, having lost his hat.

A stone caught the foot of this fugitive, who fell almost at the feet of Rob Roy. With a shout of triumph the fierce pursuer uplifted his axe, and was about to cleave the defenceless head of the Englishman, when the stroke was arrested by the interposed shield of MacGregor.

The man with the axe uttered a hoarse Gaelic oath, and turned furiously on the intercessor; but each drew back with an emotion of surprise that seemed quite mutual.

He was Duncan nan Creagh, the tall MacRae, from Kintail na Bogh, whom Rob believed he had killed on the hills of Glenorchy, and who, on finding himself now among the MacGregors, uttered a shout of "Righ Hamish gu bragh!" and rushed amid the smoke and carnage to rejoin the fierce MacRaes, who, sword in hand, with the *caber-feidh*, or banner of Seaforth, flying over them, flung themselves in

headlong charge upon the Swiss battalion of Brigadier Grant, and hewed a long and terrible pathway
through it.

Rob now lifted up the man he had saved, and to
his astonishment found him to be Captain Huske,
the same officer whom he had last met in Glendochart; so he sent him to the rear, a prisoner, in
charge of his son Coll, from whom the captain was
retaken a few minutes after by a detachment of
Captain MacDougal's dragoons.

This confused battle of Sheriffmuir, or Slia Thirra,
as the Celts name it, was claimed by both parties as
a victory ; but Mar found himself compelled to retire
towards Perth, and to Rob Roy was assigned the
onerous task of guiding his army through the deep
and treacherous Fords of Frew, when they crossed
the river Forth.

For a time after this battle Rob and his
MacGregors garrisoned the fine old royal palace
of Falkland, which lies at the foot of the Lomond
hills, and the memory of that occupation still
lingers in Fifeshire ; for they " harried the phari-
saical Whigs " to some purpose, laying the whole
country under military contribution for miles around
the palace, from which they retired at last with considerable booty, and after a sojourn of several weeks
of jollity and ease.

Their shoes being much worn by marching, " they
did not scruple to strip the feet of any civic and
clerical functionaries with whom they chanced to
meet, and whom they consoled with the jocular

assurance that his gracious majesty James VIII,
would be happy to afford them full compensation."

As the honour and advantage of the battle
remained with Argyle, and as Mar's unpaid army
began to disperse from want of food and subsistence,
the insurrection soon came to an end, and the
Government acted with a merciless barbarity upon
the fallen. Their severity was worthy of the orientals
alone, and in the hearts of the Highland youth a
hatred was instilled that found a terrible vent in the
future rising of 1745.

It was on the Lowland lords, however, that the
hands of the Ministry fell most heavily; for, by
retreating into their mountain fastnesses, the
Highlanders defied as yet all efforts at coercion.

The following story is told of Duncan-nan-Creagh
a short time after the battle of Sheriffmuir.

A tall and powerful Highlander, who had brought
a drove of cattle into the south Lowlands, sought a
night's shelter at the house of Captain MacDougal,
who, as we have stated, commanded a troop of horse
in that field.

The captain asked his Highland guest from what
part of the north he came?

"Kintail na Bogh," replied the other, with some
reserve.

"Know you a place called Corrie Choing?"

"I do, captain; but why do you ask?"

"I will tell you," replied the officer; "after the
battle, accompanied by two of the best men of my
troop, I overtook a strong and athletic Highlander,

who by the blood on his tartans and the white rose
in his bonnet, had evidently stood by King James
on that unhappy day. As we came up at a canter
he took off his plaid, folded it with great deliberation,
placed it on the ground, and then he stood upon it
to give him firmer footing. I was anxious to take
this man prisoner, so we three rode round him in a
circle, with our swords brandished; but one who
unfortunately and unwisely ventured within reach
of the clansman's sword, was cloven through his
grenadier cap and slain. He slew the other, on
which, sooth to say, I thought he had fairly earned
his life and liberty, and so left him to his fate,
simply asking him his name, and saying that he
was a brave fellow. 'I am from Corrie Choing,'
said he; 'but my name I may not tell you.' "

"I know him well, captain," said the drover;
"we call him Duncan Mhor nan Creagh."

"The wars are over now, thank Heaven, and I
wish him no harm," replied MacDougal, "for he is
a brave and resolute fellow."

"I shall be sure to tell him so," said the drover,
as he departed; but warily kept his own council,
for he was no other than the identical Big Duncan
of the Forays, from whom Rob Roy had saved
Captain Huske during the battle of Sheriffmuir.

CHAPTER XXII.

INVERSNAID GARRISONED.

AFTER the close of the whole insurrection, when the leaders of it were in their bloody graves or in hopeless exile, seeking in foreign camps and fields their bread at the point of the sword, the old rancorous sentiment against the Clan Alpine was still found to exist; for in the subsequent Act of Indemnity a free pardon was granted to all Jacobites, *" excepting persons of the name of MacGregor,* mentioned in an Act, made in Scotland in the first year of King Charles I., intituled 'Anent the Clan Gregor,' whatever name he or they may have, or do *assume;"* and hence especially among the proscribed appeared the now dreaded name of " Robert Campbell, *alias* MacGregor, *commonly called* Robert Roy."

This insulting mode of designating him, as if he had been a common thief in the " Hue and Cry," embittered yet more the soul of MacGregor; though he had been so long outlawed, and subjected to every severity and danger, this new act made little difference circumstantially to Rob, and doubtless he despised it. But the erection of a government fortress and barrack on *his own lands* of Inversnaid, for the direct purpose of overawing and subjugating his clan, and to lay him and it more completely at the mercy of the Whigs and Montrose, was more than he could suffer with patience.

His house of Auchinchisallan, in which he had resided in Breadalbane, had been wantonly burned, and his wife and children were once more driven to the caves and rocks for shelter; his cattle and crops were seized by a party of troops specially sent for those purposes by General Charles Lord Cadogan, an officer who had served as a brigadier under Marlborough, who had been taken prisoner at the siege of Messina, in 1706, and who was made Master-General of the Ordnance in 1722.

On MacGregor's lands he exercised great severity; and now, separated from his wife and children, the unfortunate Rob Roy, attended by his faithful henchman and foster-brother, Callam MacAleister, lurked in the mountains, and chiefly in the cavern near Loch Lomond, which still bears his name, and from whence he could see the flames of rapine and destruction, as the country was swept by fire and sword; and there he schemed out many a futile plan of vengeance on his oppressors.

Amid all this his heart bled for his children, who were growing up to desperate lives and wayward fortunes, the end of which he could not foresee. One thing, however, his own sense predicted : that the life of war and hazard he now lead could not last for ever, and that the erection of forts in the Highlands, and the entrance of war ships into the great salt lochs by which they were intersected, might ultimately curb the power of the Jacobite

clans, especially when the overwhelming strength of
the Campbells, the Grants, and other Whig clans,
was united to that of the Lowland invader; and
ultimately—but *not* in Rob's time—this prediction
of his soul came true.

And yet it was for his children, and the patrimony
which had been rent from them, that he maintained
a hopeless struggle with their oppressors. It has
been well observed by a modern writer, " that the
motives to exertion furnished by the possession of
children are as powerful as ever moved heart or
hand. The secret of many a struggle in life's battle
may be found at home. The man who has children
dependent upon him will and must struggle manfully
against the most adverse circumstances. The
thought that the joy of their innocent young lives
depends upon his courage, his perseverance, his
energy — this thought will enable him to work
wonders, and achieve what will appear impossi-
bilities to the man who has only his own selfish
needs and his own selfish ambition to urge him on."
And so, when poor MacGregor thought of the
future of his boys, his otherwise unflinching heart
was rent in twain.

Meanwhile, the erection of the government fortress at Inversnaid proceeded rapidly, though he
did all in his power to retard it; and he had the
mortification to see the stones of his own dwelling-
house and of the cottages of his tenantry used in
construction of the barrack and bastions.

A builder named Naysmith, from Edinburgh,

contracted to build this fort of Inversnaid; but his operations were frequently and roughly interrupted.

It was commenced during the winter season, and he and his workmen lodged in huts near the edifice.

One night, when the snow was falling heavily in great and feathery flakes, they were roused by some travellers noisily demanding shelter. On the door being opened, a number of fierce-looking MacGregors, with their plaids and bonnets coated with snow, rushed in, menaced the poor workmen with drawn swords, and reviled them bitterly.

Being defenceless and unarmed men, they were not slain by Rob Roy's followers, but they were driven half naked through the snow to a distance, when Greumoch and young Coll dismissed them, after exacting from them a solemn oath that they would never again enter the MacGregors' country.

Whether the same masons returned or not we have no means of knowing; but the fort was ultimately finished and garrisoned. "Mr. Naysmith," says Robert Chambers, "being held by Government to a contract which he could not fulfil, was seriously injured in his means by this affair; but its worst consequence was the effect of exposure on that dreadful winter night on his health. He sunk under his complaints, and died about eighteen months after."

When the fort was complete, the works were mounted with cannon, and the barrack within it was occupied by three companies of Lord Tyrawley's regiment, the South British Fusiliers, under Major (formerly Captain) Huske, with express orders to keep the MacGregors in check and to make *short work* with them on every occasion—orders not to be misconstrued.

During the progress of this—to Rob Roy—most obnoxious erection, he lurked with MacAleister in the cavern near Loch Lomond; the same place which, as we have said, sheltered the gallant King Robert I., after the battle of Dalree, where the famous Brooch of Lorn was torn from his shoulder. It is near Craigrostan and Inversnaid, on the eastern bank of the loch.

The entrance is near the edge of the water, and is partly concealed by great masses of rock, like a fallen Cyclopean wall, which have been shaken by the volcanic throes of nature from the crags above. Amid these masses, the wild foxglove, the purple heather, the green whin, and dense brushwood of every kind flourish, serving to conceal the access, which is every way one of peril and difficulty.

Here he was perfectly secure, though he could hear drums beating in Inversnaid; and sometimes he ventured at night to leave it, and visit his wife and children, who resided under Greumoch's care, in an obscure hut among the mountains of Breadalbane; and on these occasions he twice narrowly escaped being taken when returning to his retreat.

Once, when travelling with three followers, in a solitary and sequestered place near Loch Earn, a beautiful sheet of water, from the shore of which the mountains start in bold and rocky grandeur, he suddenly found himself face to face with seven horsemen, in red uniforms, with conical grenadier caps, on the blue flaps of which the "white horse" of Hanover was embroidered. In fact, they were seven horse grenadiers of Captain MacDougal's troop, which was then attached to the garrison of Inversnaid.

The tattered yet warlike aspect of MacGregor, the well-known red and black checks of his tartan, his powerful figure and ruddy-coloured beard, made them certain that he was Rob Roy, the outlaw, and with shouts of "MacGregor!—MacGregor Campbell!" some drew their swords, while others took pistols from their holsters and prepared for an attack.

Rob turned to seek safety in flight; but the soldiers fired, and his three companions fell mortally wounded. Infuriated by this, he sprang up the steep rocks, where their horses could not find footing, and taking the pistols from his belt, fired repeatedly, with calm and stern determination, sending shot after shot at his baffled pursuers, who remained on the narrow roadway by the loch side, trampling his dying clansmen under their horses' hoofs, and brandishing their swords while they menaced and reviled him.

So good was his aim that he killed three of the soldiers and wounded four of their horses. On this, the remainder galloped off, and left him to pursue, after nightfall, the secret way to his wild abode.

He reached it in safety, but by some means the

horse grenadiers, patrols of whom were constantly
abroad, succeeded in tracking him to its vicinity;
thus, a day or two after the last affair, when he and
MacAleister were issuing forth about dawn, in
search of such food as the mountains afforded, they
suddenly found themselves beset by a party, commanded by Captain MacDougal in person.

With a loud hurrah, the troopers, who were
about thirty in number, put spur to their horses,
and dashed in single file along the narrow footway on the eastern shore of Loch Lomond; but
one, who outrode all the rest, speedily came up
with Rob Roy.

"The thousand guineas are mine!" he shouted,
and raising himself in his stirrups, he dealt so furious
a blow with his long and ponderous cavalry sword at
MacGregor, that he beat down his guard, and would
inevitably have cleft him to the teeth by the next
stroke, but for a circular iron plate which he wore
within his bonnet. The blow, however, brought
him to the ground, and as he fell he exclaimed—

"To your gun, MacAleister!—to your gun, if
there is a shot in it!"

"A witch, and not your grandmother, wrought
your nightcap!" cried the astonished trooper, when
finding that his sword *rung* on MacGregor's head;
and he had his hilt drawn back to deal the fallen
man a deadly forward home thrust, when a ball
from the long Spanish musket of the faithful henchman pierced his heart. He fell from his saddle
lifeless and bleeding, and was dragged by his terri-

fied horse (for one foot hung in a stirrup) down the steep bank towards the water, where steed and corpse disappeared together.

MacAleister now assisted his foster-brother to rise, and escaping MacDougal and the rest of his troopers, they made a long detour, and reached their gloomy cavern unseen and in safety.

CHAPTER XXIII.

THE SNARE.

A NOBLE named the Duke of Athole, who was in close correspondence with the Government at Edinburgh, now conceived the hope of entrapping Rob Roy, and announced to the Secretary of State and other officials, that he had a sure plan for making him a prisoner.

As this peer was one of the leading Jacobites of the time, and as all his sons were involved in the various armed Risings for the House of Stuart, it is extremely difficult to conceive *why* he should have leagued himself with the oppressors of the hapless MacGregor, unless he had been influenced by the Duke of Montrose, or was inspired by the strange animosity which so many cherished against the Clan Alpine.

The duke contrived to send to Rob Roy a letter,

by a messenger, who found him either in or near his miserable hiding-place. This missive contained a pressing invitation to see him immediately at the castle of Blair, and offered horses for his conveyance there.

It was now the summer of 1717

Although Rob Roy had every reason to believe that Athole, from the similarity of their political views had no personal animosity to him, he would not fail to remember, that he had at one time leagued himself with the Whig faction, and had taken from the English ministry the sum of a thousand pounds for his signature to the treaty of Union, ten years ago, though he had *publicly* opposed it in all its stages in Parliament.

So MacGregor was too wary to trust himself in such slippery hands without some firm assurance of safety. He, therefore, wrote to the duke, delicately hinting the want of confidence he now felt in most men; the desperation of his circumstances, the condition of his homeless wife and children, and wishing to have his grace's commands in writing.

In reply, the wily duke " gave him the most solemn promises of protection, adding, that he only wished to have some private conversation with him on certain political points. This was followed by an emissary, who gave even more positive assurances that no evil was intended, and then handed him a *protection from Government.* On seeing this our hero consented, and fixed a time for being at the duke's residence."

Accompanied by MacAleister, he duly appeared on a day in July at the castle of Blair, in a chamber of which the duke had treacherously concealed an officer and sixty soldiers.

The castle is a baronial edifice of great extent and unknown antiquity; one portion of it is still named the Comyns Tower, from John of Strathbolgie, who built it, and it has stood many a siege in the stormy times of old. A forest of splendid trees and a vast expanse of beautiful scenery are around it.

The wandering life led by MacGregor had now imparted somewhat of wildness to the aspect and costume of his henchman and himself.

His eyes were sunken and had become keen and fierce, as those of one who in every sound, even to the rustle of a dry leaf, heard the tread of an enemy. Long untrimmed and unshorn, his hair and curly beard waved in masses about his weatherbeaten face. His red tartans, every thread of which had been spun by Helen's hands, her labour of love, were worn and frittered. His coat was made of coarse homespun black and white wool in its natural state, just as it came from the sheep's back, with two rows of large wooden buttons; and he wore a red woollen shirt, for the Highlanders still disdained linen and cotton as effeminate.

He had an eagle's feather and a sprig of pine in his bonnet; his target, battered and dinted by many a blade and bullet, was slung on his left shoulder, and he had as usual his sword, dirk, and pistols, when, all unconscious of the wicked snare that was laid for him, he and his follower presented themselves at the splendid residence of the Duke of Athole.

The latter, who had been made aware of his approach, received him, apparently, with great cordiality.

"I know not how to express the joy I feel in having so brave a gentleman in my house," said he, "but, as a first favour, I must beg of you to lay aside your sword and pistols."

"Wherefore, my lord?" asked Rob, who felt surprised at a request so unusual.

"The duchess is somewhat timid, and the sight of such things always alarms her."

"By my faith, Athole, had she seen her rooftree in flames, and as much of her own blood shed as the goodwife of Inversnaid has seen in *her* time, the sight of an armed man would not cause uneasiness," replied Rob, with a sigh of anger, as he unbuckled his sword-belt, took the dirk and pistols from his girdle, and said, "but where is your good lady, duke?"

"In the garden, where we shall join her."

"MacAleister, keep my claymore and tacks for me, and await me here," said Rob, handing the weapons to his henchman, through whose mind some vague suspicions floated, as he never once removed his keen glance from the face of the duke, on whom he gazed as if he would have read his soul. But now Rob and his host descended by a flight of steps into the garden of the castle.

The duchess, Katherine, who was a daughter of the Duke of Hamilton, came hurriedly forward to meet the famous outlaw, of whom she had heard so much, and to whom she frankly presented her hand to kiss,—for she was as yet ignorant of the vile plot her husband had framed.

She then presented to him her son, the little Lord Tullybardine, who eight-and-twenty years after was to unfurl the banner of Prince Charles Edward in Glenfinnan; and poor Rob, when he saw the rich dress of the fair-haired boy, thought with a sigh of his own sons, who were at times compelled to share the abode of the fox and the eagle.

" MacGregor," exclaimed the duchess, on seeing him without a sword; " MacGregor here, and *unarmed !* "

Rob discovered in a moment that he was the victim of some perfidy, for by this simple exclamation the duchess proved that her husband had been guilty of falsehood. He bestowed a glance of stern inquiry on the duke, who coloured deeply, and said with an air of manifest confusion—

" I thought your sword might prove troublesome if anything unpleasant occurred between us."

" Between friends—between a guest and a host —what could occur that would be unpleasant ? " replied MacGregor ; " Athole, I understand you not."

"You will understand this, *Mr.* MacGregor," said the duke, suddenly throwing aside all disguise, "that you have committed such wild work along the Highland border since the battle of Sheriffmuir, ay, since you harried the lands of Kippen, after the battle of Killycrankie, that I must detain you."

"Detain?" repeated Rob, with surprise and contempt.

"And send you to Edinburgh."

"Where I should swing on a gibbet, a holiday sight for the psalm-singing burgesses, even as Alaster of Glenstrae was swung after the field of Glenfruin! Am I then snared—betrayed?" exclaimed Rob, starting back, and looking round for the means of defence or escape; but the high walls of the garden were on three sides, and the towers of the castle closed in the fourth, and therein was his faithful henchman, whom he could not desert in peril, even could he have made an escape from the garden. "Dare you tell me, Duke of Athole," he resumed, "that you have betrayed me?"

"Phrase it as you please, I——"

"Has a man of your rank and name a soul so mean, so vile, that he will forfeit honour and faith to win the paltry reward offered for the head of a loyal and unfortunate gentleman, whom tyranny and oppression have covered with ruin, and driven to despair and shame?"

Deadly pale and terrified by this unexpected scene, the gentle duchess shrunk close to her husband, who when MacGregor made a forward stride, laid his hand on his sword.

" Sir," said he, " do you threaten me, in my own castle of Blair ? " ;

" Villain ! " exclaimed MacGregor, " you shall live to repent the deed of to-day."

Clenching his right hand, he would have struck the duke to the earth, but for a piteous shriek which burst from his lady. , At that moment the iron gate of the Comyns Tower was thrown furiously open, and an officer rushed forth, sword in hand, followed by sixty soldiers, who instantly surrounded MacGregor, and beat him down with the butt-ends of their muskets.

" Had you surrendered in proper time, Mr. Mac-Gregor *Campbell,*" said the duke, with ungenerous irony, " we had not been compelled to resort to these rough measures in capturing you."

Rob Roy laughed scornfully.

" You would have asked me to surrender, my lord duke ; but for a MacGregor to surrender is to die with ignominy; to resist to the end is to die with honour to ourselves and our forefathers. A hundred and twenty years of oppression have made us what we are now ; but a time may come when even the cunning Lowlander shall weep for the snare of to-day, and shall tremble at the vengeance of Clan Alpine ! "

" Zounds ! but you are a bold fellow to be a gentleman-drover—a seller of black cattle," said the duke, mockingly.

" Do not condescend to sneer at an unfortunate man, my lord ; it was honester to sell Scottish cattle than our good old Scottish kingdom. I have sold many a thousand head of stots and stirks to the English ; but I would rather have died—yea, upon a common gibbet—than have sold the free land of my forefathers, as Esau sold his birthright for a mess of pottage—even as you and others sold yours on that black Beltane day, in 1707 ! "

" Tie this fellow with cords, and away with him," said the duke, rendered furious by this taunt.

He was then secured with ropes, and dragged from the castle to the adjacent village, where he was thrust into a cottage and kept under a strong escort till his captor made further arrangements.

Bound and manacled like the fugitive bankrupt, the rebel and outlaw they had made him, and which they so ungenerously assumed him to be, Mac-Gregor for a time felt all the bitterness and despair that could sting a spirit so generous, so proud and untameable, when reflecting on the perfidious stroke of fortune which thus placed him so completely at the mercy of his tormentors.

He thought of the joy and triumph of Montrose and Killearn, of Carden, Luss, Aberuchail, and others, whom his sword had so long kept at bay ; he thought of the grief of his homeless wife and children, whom that sword had been so often drawn to feed and to defend. He thought of the shameful and ignominious death which awaited him as surely as the breath of Heaven was in his nostrils; he thought of his landless, nameless, broken and degraded clan, left without a head to direct, or a leader to avenge them, and he well-nigh wept in his agony of soul!

MacAleister, on beholding him dragged across the lawn, surrounded by a company of soldiers, uttered a shout of grief and rage, as he sprang from one of the windows of the castle.

Some there were who rashly made an effort to stop him, but with his sword in one hand and his dirk in the other he dashed them aside like children, and escaping a few shots that were fired after him, fled with the speed of a roebuck towards the river Tilt, into which he plunged and disappeared.

Some averred that he was drowned, as the stream was swollen by a summer flood; but it was otherwise, for he reached in safety the hut where Helen MacGregor resided, and related what had happened,

" A Dhia ! " she exclaimed, as she threw up her hands in despair; not Fingal's self could save him now ! "

" The Red MacGregor is not out of the land of the heather yet," said MacAleister, hopefully, as he prepared to return to watch over, and, if possible, to succour him.

But Helen experienced all the bitterness of a sorrow that was *without hope.*

CHAPTER XXIV.

WILL HE ESCAPE?

THE Duke of Athole immediately wrote to Lieutenant-General Carpenter, who had succeeded John, Duke of Argyle and Greenwich, as Commander-in-Chief in Scotland (the general was also Governor of Minorca), informing him that he had " captured Robert MacGregor Campbell, the famous outlaw and rebel, for whose apprehension a large sum had been so long offered by the authorities."

He requested the general to send from Edinburgh a body of troops to escort the prisoner to that city, and, in compliance with his wish, a troop of Lord Polwarth's Scottish Light Horse (now the 7th Hussars), marched so far as Kinross.

Meanwhile, the unfortunate MacGregor was kept a close prisoner, manacled with cords, and guarded day and night by the vassals of the duke, and a party of Captain MacDougal's Horse Grenadiers, whom he had obtained from the officer commanding in Perth.

In a short time it was known all over Scotland that Rob Roy was a captive; but the *mode* of his capture, and the foul treachery which characterized it, covered Athole with disgrace, though he seems to have felt no small vanity at the success of his snare, if we may judge from a letter which he wrote to John, Duke of Roxburgh, who was Secretary of State for North Britain, minutely detailing the affair.

Panting for freedom and for vengeance, both of which were justly his, Rob Roy was kept under the military escort at a place called Logierait, which lies eight miles north of Dunkeld; there he had been conveyed after his capture in the castle of Blair.

It was a dark and boisterous night when the troops began their march from the latter place, with the prisoner still bound and tied to a horse; a horse grenadier with his unslung carbine riding on each side of him. The clouds were driven in black masses along the summits of Ben-ghlo and Cairn-na-Gabar (or the mountain of the goats), and the roaring wind rolled over the thick old forests of Blair Athole, bowing the trees till their masses seemed to heave like the waves of the sea, in the fitful gleams of the moon. On halting at Logierait, the duke ordered MacGregor to be kept there securely, until a properly-mounted escort of his own people was in readiness to convey him to Edinburgh. The duke was resolved that the whole merit of the capture should remain with himself, and that even the king's troops should not share it.

But this vanity proved in the end his own defeat.

Rob Roy, on finding himself in one of the miserable cottages of the village, began to hope that he might perhaps achieve an escape. As a preliminary, he begged the sergeant who commanded the troopers, to undo the cords which bound his hands, that he might write a farewell letter to his unhappy wife, who had then found shelter in the little farmhouse of Portnellan, at the head of Loch Katrine.

The sergeant was a humane man; he said something about his own wife and little ones who were far away in old Ireland, and he did as Rob requested, though in defiance of express orders.

Then, as he had been liberal in supplying the soldiers with whisky and ale, they became friendly with MacGregor, and so, after a time, the letter was written; but there was a difficulty in procuring a messenger to Loch Katrine, as several MacGregors had located themselves thereabout, and reprisals were dreaded.

The stormy night wore on, and ere long all the soldiers were sleeping, save one, who stood with his loaded carbine at the door of the cottage.

To MacGregor it seemed as if this man pitied him, as he had been more gentle than his comrades, and had ministered to his comfort, so far as he dared, since the time of his betrayal at Blair.

Being strong, active, and wiry as a mountain stag, to rush on this trooper and wrench away his carbine would have been an easy task to Mac-Gregor, but the key of the cottage door hung at the waist-belt of the sleeping sergeant; thus the preliminary scuffle would only serve to rouse the whole party, and ensure his being shot down by some of them.

As these ideas occurred to the captive, he surveyed the sentinel, whose gaze was never turned from him. With a swarthy, almost olive-tinted face, and deep, dark eyes, he was a stout and handsome young man; and his profusely-braided uniform, with its heavy red cuffs, his Horse Grenadier cap, and tasselled boots, became him well. He had his right hand on the lock of his carbine, the barrel of which rested in the hollow of his left arm.

"How goes the night?" asked MacGregor.

"Twelve has just struck on the kirk clock without," replied the soldier ; and the night is wild and eerie yet. You can hear the sough of the wind among the trees, and the roar of the Tay, too."

"You are, I think, a south-country man, by your accent," said MacGregor.

"Yes," replied the trooper, drily, as he was loth to become too familiar with a prisoner of a character so formidable, and, moreover, the sergeant might be awake.

"Take another taste of the whisky, man : there is a drop in the quaich yet. What part of the south are you from?"

The trooper drained the little wooden cup, and replied—

"I come from Moffatdale ; my auld mother bydes in a bit thatched housie at Cragieburnwood. Weary fall the day I ever left it to become a soldier!"

"Moffatdale," said Rob, ponderingly; "many a good drove of short-legged Argyleshires I have had driven through it to the southern markets at Car-

lisle and Penrith.   I know well the place, the
Hartfell——"

"And Queensbury Hill, Loch Skene, and the
Greymare's Tail, and Yarrow wi' a' its dowie
dens!" added the soldier, with kindling eyes.

"Once when there I fought some militiamen, and
gave them good cause to remember Rob Roy;
though perhaps the loons knew not my name."

"When was this?" asked the soldier, earnestly.

"A year or so after the Union.   It was in a
summer gloaming, when I was riding northward
near Moffat village, I heard the cries of a woman in
anguish.   They came from a deep, dark hollow called
the Gartpool Linn——"

"Weel ken I the place," said the soldier.

"A true Highlander has ever his sword at the
service of a friend, or the defenceless.   I rode into
the dark dingle, and found some rascally militiamen,
with a queen's officer, about to hang some unfortunate gipsies; but, by my faith! I gave them their
kail through the reek.   I threw one half of them
into the water, drove off the rest, and passed two
feet of my claymore through the body of the officer,
who must have been a tough fellow, for he seemed
never a bit the worse when I saw him last at the
field of Sheriffmuir.   I cut down the poor gipsies,
who hung on the lower branch of a tree, but they
were dead——"

"All?"

"All, except one—a boy about the age of Coll—
my own boy Coll, whom I may never see again; in

this world, at least," added MacGregor, with a burst of emotion.

The soldier, who had listened to this anecdote with deep interest, said,—

"You did more, MacGregor; you gave some money to the poor harmless lassie that lay at the foot of the tree—money to comfort her ere you went away."

"Yes, perhaps I did; but how know you that?"

"She was *my* sister, and I am the half-hanged gipsy lad whom you saved, MacGregor."

"You!" exclaimed the other, with astonishment in his tone.

"Yes," said the soldier, giving his hand to the outlaw; "I enlisted in Polwarth's Light Horse after that, and have smelt powder at Ramillies, at Oudenarde, and Malplacquet. Then I became a Horse Grenadier. Oh! MacGregor, what can I do to serve and thank you for the brave deed of that doleful summer evening?"

"Get me a messenger," said MacGregor, huskily; "one who will take this letter to my poor forlorn wife."

"I shall," replied the soldier, in a whisper, as he glanced uneasily at his sleeping comrades; "and I shall do more; the best horse in the troop shall be at your service before the day dawns if another cannot be had!"

"Say you so?" exclaimed MacGregor, whose heart leaped with joy.

"Yes, so sure as my name is Willie Gemmil, even if I should be shot for it at the drumhead."

"I thank you, — I thank you! my wife, my bairns!" said Rob, in a broken voice. "You know, soldier, what I have been—think of what *I am.* I have much of goodness, of kindness, of charity, of love in my heart; yet men decm me a savage, and seek to make me one. It may be that in my desperation and fury, when fired by the sense of unmerited wrong, I have done severe things; but the memory of the station I have lost, and of the success I once hoped to achieve, add deeper bitterness to my fallen fortunes now. 'Tis well that old Donald of Glengyle is in his grave, and knows not the fate of his son!"

When day broke, Gemmil was relieved from his post, and exerted himself to procure a messenger, with a fleet and active horse.

On the man coming to the door of the cottage, having been instructed by the gipsy trooper what to do, he dismounted at the moment that Rob Roy, with the sergeant's permission, came forth to give the letter and some special message to Helen MacGregor.

Rob's emotion was great on recognizing in the messenger who had volunteered so readily, his foster-brother MacAleister, who had been hovering about Logierait in the hope of achieving something; but beyond a keen, quick glance nothing passed between them ; but that glance contained a volume.

The eyes of the whole troop were upon Rob, yet

he sprang past them, leaped into the empty saddle of the messenger's horse, and urged it at full speed towards the bank of the Tay.

"Boot and saddle! To horse and after him!" exclaimed the sergeant, while a scattered volley of carbine bullets whistled after MacGregor; but long before the troop horses were bitted and saddled, he had plunged into the foaming river, crossed it, and disappeared.

The vexation and chagrin of the Duke of Athole were extreme, when about an hour after this occurrence he arrived with a band of his own retainers, all well mounted and armed with swords and musketoons, to escort the prisoner to Edinburgh, and found no trace of him but the letter he had written to Helen, and the cords with which he had been so ignominiously bound.

For a time the fortification and garrison of Inversnaid were a complete check upon the projects of Rob Roy; but he resolved ere long to capture the works and expel the soldiers.

Though of small value in some respects, his lands had been sufficient, in those frugal days, for the maintenance of his family and dependants; and, as his ancestral rocks and hills, he loved them dearly. "It is felt as a strange and uncouth association (to quote the "Domestic Annals of Scotland"), that Steele, of *Tatler* and *Spectator* memory—kindhearted, thoughtless Dicky Steele — should have been one of the persons who administered in the affairs of the cateran of Craigrostan. In the final

report of the Commissioners (for forfeited estates)
we have the pitiful account of *the public ruin of
poor Rob,* Inversnaid being described as of the
yearly value of £53. 16s. 8½d., and the total sum
realized from it, of purchase-money and interest,
£958. 18s. There is much possible reason to believe
that it would have been a much more advantageous,
as well as humane arrangement, for the public to
have allowed these twelve miles of Highland
mountains to remain in the hands of their former
owner."

In the close of the year he went with Greumoch,
MacAleister, and a few other followers to the ducal
castle of Inverary, and there affected to submit to
the Government, by delivering some forty or fifty
swords and pistols to his remote kinsman, Colonel
Patrick Campbell, of Finab ; from whom he obtained
a signed protection ; after this act, which was per-
formed merely *to gain time,* he could not be molested
by the troops or civil authorities.

But he returned to Breadalbane more than ever
determined to exert every energy in storming the
fortress of Inversnaid, in expelling the garrison,
and resolved to spend the last of his life in punishing
Montrose, Athole, Killearn, and all who had ever
wronged or injured him.

We shall soon see the sequel to these bold
projects.

CHAPTER XXV.

LITTLE RONALD.

ABOUT this time there occurred two circumstances, which—more than any outrage that had preceded them — impelled Rob to attack the Sassenach invaders, for so he deemed them at Inversnaid.

Near Eas-teivil, or the Fall of the Tummel, in the face of a tremendous rock, is a cavern to which there is a narrow path, accessible only to one person at a time. Therein several fugitive MacGregors were surprised by some of Huske's soldiers, who had been conducted there by a spy named MacLaren. One-half were shot down or bayonneted. The others fought their way out, but fell over the rock, and clung to the trees which grew from its face.

There they swung in blind desperation above the foaming stream, "upon which," says the "Statistical Reporter," "the pursuers cut off their arms, and precipitated them to the bottom," to be swept away by the rushing water.

These tidings filled Rob Roy with a glow of fury, which the second event was in no way calculated to cool.

It chanced that on a day in spring, his second son, Ronald, a boy in his fourteenth year, despite the intreaties of his mother, and the injunctions of his father, strolled over the hills with his fishing-rod, along the banks of Loch Arclet, and actually fished within sight of Inversnaid.

Little Ronald was brave as a lion. Once he had climbed the giddiest of the rocks above Loch Lomond, with his dirk in his teeth, to destroy the nest of a gigantic iolar or mountain eagle, which preyed on the lambs of a poor widow who was his foster-mother.

He was generous, too, as he was brave, for the boy once nearly perished in the deep drift of a corrie, when searching amid the winter snow for the lost sheep of a poor herdsman who was sick. Every way in spirit Ronald was his father's son !

On this day in spring, when his fish-basket was pretty well filled with spotted trout, and the long mountain-shadows cast by the setting sun began to remind him of the distance that lay between Loch Arclet and the secluded little farm of Portnellan, he was preparing to quit his sport, when three red-coats suddenly appeared on the narrow footway, so Ronald turned to fly.

That he strove to avoid them in those days need not excite wonder ; for such were the atrocities of the British and Hessian troops in the Highlands, and so much was their uniform abhorred for gene-rations after, that many a Highlander, who in manhood has led his company or regiment to the storming of Badajoz and the fields of Vittoria and Waterloo, when a boy was wont to fly to the woods for concealment, when by chance he saw a redcoat on the roads that led to the chain of forts in the Great Glen of Caledonia.

A pistol-shot fired by one of these strangers now made Ronald pause, as it struck a rock before him, and turning, with a flushed brow and an agitated heart, he found himself confronted by Major Huske and two soldiers, with whom he had been shooting, scouting, or rambling by the side of Loch Arclet.

Enraged to find himself thus molested, on the land which Ronald knew to be his father's heritage, he laid his hand on his dirk and boldly confronted the major, whose large, square, red-skirted coat, three-cornered hat, and Ramillies wig, were all fraught with terrors, which the boy sought to conceal, for he felt that it would ill become his father's son to quail beneath a Saxon eye.

"Will you sell your fish, my little man?" asked the major; but Ronald knew as little of English as the major did of Gaelic so a soldier had to act as interpreter for them.

"No," replied Ronald, sullenly.

"Then as we want some at the garrison, we shall be compelled to appropriate what you have," said Huske, peeping into the basket; "I warrant the money offered will not be allowed to lie on the heather."

"Take the fish if you want them, and let me be gone," replied Ronald, throwing his basket down.

"Whither go you?" asked Huske, suspiciously.

"To my home."

"Where is it?"

"Among the mountains—where you would not be wise to follow," replied the boy, boldly.

The soldier perhaps interpreted this with some awkwardness or severity, for Huske exclaimed furiously—

"'Sdeath! you young rascal; do you speak thus to me?"

"And why not, when I am a son of the Red MacGregor?" was the rash boy's response.

"Zounds! I thought as much," exclaimed Huske, with a malevolent gleam in his eyes; "Come, my lad, don't let us quarrel about a few fish. I have a particular desire to see your worthy father—he is a fine fellow, and a good judge of other men's cattle. We want some of the latter for the garrison. Can you tell me where he is?"

"Yes," said Ronald, with knitted brows and clenched teeth.

"Where, my boy?"

"Where you had better not seek him."

"Pshaw! will not this bribe you?" said Huske, slipping three guineas from his purse into Ronald's hand.

Though nurtured amid civil war and sore adversity, the poor boy knew well the value of the bribe so infamously offered by Huske, who had never forgotten nor forgiven his meetings with Rob Roy in Moffatdale and elsewhere. Ronald drew himself proudly up, and said—

"You ask me—you, a soldier—to betray my father?"

"Nay, nay; to discover——"

"To betray—Saxon captain, or Saxon dog, mince the words as you will!"

"A mutinous cur; but I'll tame him yet," muttered the major.

"You shall never get my father, alive at least; for he is strong and brave as Cuchullin!"

"Some other Highland savage, I suppose; but, egad, we shall see."

"Sir," said the soldier who acted as interpreter, "would it not be a good plan to let the young cub loose, and watch him well? in the end he would be sure to lead us to the old wolf's den."

"He would scramble up rocks where none but a cat or a monkey could follow, or leave us all floundering to the neck in some treacherous bog. No, no, I know better than that. Offer him three guineas more."

The soldier did so.

"You might as well ask me to blow the fire with my mouth full of meal," was Ronald's contemptuous reply; "for I would rather die than betray any man —to a base Saxon churl least of all!"

The soldier clenched his hand, but paused.

"Threaten if you will; but *strike not!*" said Ronald, with his right hand on his dirk.

"You little villain, would you dare to draw on us?" thundered Major Huske.

"Yes, even if you stood at the head of all your

men, and dared to lay a hand on me," replied Ronald, bursting into tears of passion and fury, as he flung the guineas full into Huske's face.

Filled with rage by this insult, the latter rushed upon the brave boy and wrenched his dirk away. Ronald made a desperate resistance, he struggled kicked, bit, and fought; but he was soon dragged into the fort by the soldiers, who cast him, handcuffed, into a dark stone cell.

Huske, a brutal officer of the old Dutch or Revolution school, proposed to tie a cord round the poor boy's head, and twist it with a pistol-barrel or drumstick, until agony compelled him to furnish all the details required about his father's movements; but the officer next in command, Captain Henry Clifford, of the South British Fusiliers,* a humane English gentleman, opposed the cruel idea so vigorously that Huske abandoned it; so Ronald was closely watched, and fed on bread and water.

He was threatened with being flogged at the halberts, or with being hung on a tree; but nothing would make him tell aught to his father's enemies. Yet, though he kept a brave front to "the Saxons," as he named them, in the fulness of his heart and the solitude of his cell, he wept for his parents, and repeatedly offered up the prayers his mother taught him, and repeated to himself the twenty-second Psalm, " Shi Dhia fhein 'm buachalich" (the Lord is my shepherd).

* Now

Oina speedily informed the family at Portnellan of all this. She had now grown to womanhood, and was the wife of Alaster Roy. As a dealer in eggs, butter, and milk, she frequented the fort, and there learned the story of the young angler's capture.

This unwarrantable action filled MacGregor with just indignation, and Helen with lively fears, lest her golden-haired Ronald might be impressed for a sailor or soldier, or perhaps sold to the Dutch planters for a slave; and Rob swore upon the bare blade of his sword to raze Inversnaid to the ground, and to give Huske's flesh to the eagles of Ben Lomond ere the sun of the next Beltane day had risen, while his mother—an aged woman now—vowed that she too would march to the rescue, though armed only with her spindle and scissors.

CHAPTER XXVI.

PAUL CRUBACH.

BEFORE collecting his followers, or making preparations to storm Inversnaid, and expel the royal troops from his patrimony, Rob Roy resolved to make himself well acquainted with the strength and resources of the garrison, and with the number of men and cannon at Major Huske's disposal; and for this service he availed himself of Oina, who brought him daily intelligence of the enemy.

Moreover, he had another very efficient spy in the person of Paul Crubach, whose grotesque figure and quaint conduct made him a welcome visitor to the soldiers, who jested and made fun with him, as a half-witted being; but as usual with such characters in Scotland, there was a "method in the madness" of Paul Crubach.

One night as he sat by the fireside, in the little farmhouse of Portnellan, where Ronald's absence formed a source of perpetual grief, he urged that before attacking Inversnaid the oracle of the "House of Invocation" should be consulted; but Rob Roy though brave as man could be, shrunk from seeking intercourse with the world of spirits.

"Are you afraid?" exclaimed Paul Crubach, striking his cross-staff fiercely on the floor with indignation.

"Afraid, Paul—yes, of the devil."

"Then I shall face the King of the Cats for you, and from him I shall extort the knowledge whether ever again *the three glens* shall be ours."

The eyes of MacGregor sparkled.

"The old inheritance of Clan Alpine!" said he; "yes; Glenlyon, Glendochart, and Glenorchy, shall again be ours, Paul, but first I must root out and raze this nest of Saxon hornets at Inversnaid!"

"And set free my red-cheeked Ronald," added Helen, weeping with sorrow and anger, as she twirled her spindle on the clay floor.

"But look before you leap, MacGregor; before marching learn what the oracle may tell," urged the old man; "but I shall learn for you, if I have not, as in past times, a vision before the hour, when, as the bard of Cona says, ' the hunter awakes from his noon-day slumber, and hears in his vision the spirits of the hill.' "

Rob shuddered as Paul spoke, for a strange wild glare flashed in the eyes of this old man, who was supposed to be a seer, possessing the gift of the second sight.

"If the time serves, Paul," resumed MacGregor, who wished to change the subject, "I will inscribe on the rocks of Craigrostan and Inversnaid, in Gaelic letters, my indisputable right thereto, in defiance of the elector and his redcoats."

"Ah! thou art right," said Paul, grinding his teeth and brandishing his cross-staff; "do so, even as MacMillan of South Knapdale, and the

MacMurachies of Terdigan and Kilberrie, had *their* charters carved upon the rocks of their land."

"But alas, Paul, that time may never, never come," said Helen, with a sad smile.

"And little would such charters avail me, good wife, if the good claymore fails," said Rob, with irony in his eye and tone.

"Then," observed Greumoch, who sat in a corner smoking his pipe and oiling his gun, "we have the fair sleek skins of the Saxons whereon to write the story of our wrongs with a pen of pointed steel."

"Enough of this," said Paul Crubach, rising and drawing a deerskin over his shoulders; "the sooner my task begins 'twill be the sooner ended."

"Whither go you, Paul, and at this hour?" asked Rob, attempting to detain his strange guest.

"To consult the *Tighghairm*. Meet me at sun-set on the second day from this, at the Ladders, above Loch Katrine, and you will there learn what the future has in store for us; whether we shall be the victors at Inversnaid, whether your boy shall be freed, and whether we shall again possess the three glens, which are the heritage of Clan Alpine, or be vanquished and destroyed."

And before MacGregor, Helen, or Greumoch could interpose, Paul had snatched his cross-staff, and, with his long white hair streaming behind him in elf-locks, had rushed forth into the darkness.

MacGregor, whose intercourse with Englishmen and Lowlanders had made him somewhat more a man of the world than his followers, was nevertheless too strongly imbued with the old superstitions and native predilections of his race and country not to await with considerable interest, though mingled with doubt, the result of those spells which all in the district believed the half-witted Paul Crubach was capable of weaving, or the visions with which he was supposed to be visited.

Accordingly, about the sunset of the second day, MacGregor, well armed as usual, repaired alone to the appointed place of tryst.

The Ladders was the name of a dangerous and difficult track, which then formed the only access to Loch Katrine from Callendar.

He entered the narrow pass, which is half a mile in length. There the rocks are stupendous in height, in some places seeming to impend over the head of the wayfarer; in others, aged weeping birches hang their drooping foliage over the basaltic cliffs from which they spring, adding a wild beauty to the rugged gorge.

Across the summits of this pass, which is a portion of the famous Trossachs, the dying sunlight shone in red and uncertain gleams, through stormy clouds of dusky and saffron tints, for all the preceding night loud peals of thunder had shaken the mountains, and even yet the atmosphere was close and sulphurous.

At last Rob reached the Ladders, which consisted

of steps roughly hewn out of the solid rock. By means of these, and ropes suspended from the trees, to be grasped by the hand, the bold and hardy natives of this part of the Highlands were wont to traverse the pass, which, in time of war, one swordsman could defend against a thousand.

Rob slung his target on his shoulder, grasped the ropes, and from step to step swung himself lightly up the beetling rocks until he reached the summit, from whence he could see, far down below, Loch Katrine, a lovely sheet of water ten miles in length, gleaming redly in the last light of the sun, whose rays lingered yet on the vast peak of Benvenue, and on the beautiful hills of Arroquhar, that closed the view to the west.

In the loch is an islet, wherein, during the invasion of Scotland by Oliver Cromwell, the Clan Gregor had placed all their aged men, their women and children, for security. On finding that the only boat remaining was moored at the islet, an English soldier swam across to seize it, but was stabbed to the heart by Iole MacGregor, the grandmother of Rob's foster-brother, Callam MacAleister.

The scenery was alike wild and grand, and the great masses of lurid and dun-coloured thunderclouds that overhung the darkening hills added to its effect.

With his keen and glittering eyes fixed on the place where the sun had set, Paul Crubach sat on a fragment of volcanic rock. He seemed wan, pale, and weary; his masses of tangled hair and his

primitive garb of deerskin seemed to have been
scorched by fire, and his bare legs and arms were
covered with scars and bruises.

Propping himself on his cross-staff, he arose with
apparent difficulty on the approach of MacGregor,
who said, with anxiety,—

"In Heaven's name, what has happened—what
have you done, Paul?"

"I have opened the House of Invocation. I
have consulted the oracle of the *Tighghairm*," said
he, solemnly.

"Did it speak?" asked Rob, with growing
wonder.

"Listen; I passed the night in the Coir nan
Uriskin."

"In the cave of the wild shaggy men!"
exclaimed the other, starting with more of actual
fear than astonishment in his manner.

"Yea, even there," replied Paul, closing his eyes
for a moment, and sighing deeply.

"What did you see—what did you hear?"

"Listen, and I shall tell you what happened."

CHAPTER XXVII.

THE HOUSE OF INVOCATION.

PAUL related that after sunset on the preceding evening he had sought that remarkable cavern or den, which lies at the base of Benvenue.

It is a deep and circular hollow in the side of the mountain, about six hundred yards wide at the top, but narrows steeply towards the bottom, on all sides surrounded by stupendous masses of shattered rock, covered so thickly with wild birches that their interlaced branches almost intercept the sunlight even at noon.

For ages, local superstition has made this place the abode of the Urisks, wild shaggy men, or lubber-fiends, who were fashioned like the ancient satyrs, being half-men and half-goats ; thus their very name was fraught with many indescribable terrors, and hence the spot was avoided by the most hardy huntsmen, even at mid-day.

There Paul had repaired as the night was closing in, carrying with him, instead of his cross-staff, the blade of an ancient sword without a hilt, and a black cat securely tied in a bag.

Selecting the very centre of the coir, or hollow, he drew a circle three times round him with the sword-blade, and collecting a quantity of dry branches, dead leaves, and moss, he added some pieces of coffin-boards, brought from his remarkable hut in Strathfillan, and lighted a fire. Amid the growing flames he thrust the sword-blade firmly into the earth, with the point uppermost.

Then he drew from the bag the fated cat, the paws of which were securely tied with a cord. As the increasing flames rose fast, he thrust the poor animal upon the upright sword, impaling it alive, the supposed necessity of the ordeal rendering Paul completely callous and heedless of the cruelty he was perpetrating.

Then the shrill cries of the tortured cat woke a thousand echoes among the rocks of that ghastly hollow, while it spat and bit at the steel on which its blood was dripping to hiss on the fire below. Its jaws were distended, and its protruding eyes glared like opals in the light; its ears were laid flat, and every hair was bristling with fear and agony, till scorched off by the rising flames.

Their lurid light cast strange and fantastic gleams on the rocks of that solemn hollow; and when in the moaning night wind the birches waved their drooping branches to and fro, the whole place seemed to fill with moving figures of quaint and unearthly aspect.

As the yells of the tortured cat woke them up, sharp-nosed foxes peeped forth from their holes with glittering eyes, fleet squirrels scampered up the trees, and the birds screamed and whirred in flocks out of the hollow; but fast and furiously there gathered from all quarters cats, wild and domestic; over the bushes and rocks they came swarming, as if to the rescue, with open mouths, protruding eyes, extended claws, and backs erect; but they were compelled to pause, being unable to enter the charmed circle, or it might be perhaps that the glare of the fire terrified or bewildered them.

Cats in countless numbers—black, white, grey, and brindled—covered all the rocks of the Coir nan Uriskin, according to Paul, denouncing in fury the torment of their companion, till their spitting and hissing sounded like the rush of a waterfall; for though many of these sudden visitors were of the common size and kind, many more were the wild cats of the mountains, which are four times larger than the domestic, with yellow coats, black streaks, thick flat tails, and are armed with claws and teeth well calculated to inspire terror.

Then as the branches of the trees waved to and fro, their shadows on the weather-beaten rocks seemed more distinctly to assume the strange form, the quaint and savage faces of the terrible Urisks, that glimmered and jabbered at these unhallowed proceedings.   But the resolute Paul continued to mutter,—

> See not this !
> Hear not that !
> Round with the spit,
> And turn the cat !

So he never looked about him nor quailed in his

grim work, for he knew that greater terrors would yet surround him ere the fiend he was summoning would appear. For if the *Cluasa-leabhra* came to the rescue of his tortured subject—this terrible king of the cats, distinguished from all others of the mountain by his tiger-like proportions and wondrous strength—Paul knew that *then* would be the critical moment of his fate; for if his heart failed him on hearing the yell of this half-cat, half-demon, he must be overborne by the whole living mass, which now covered the sides of the Coir nan Uriskin; his body would be rent into a thousand pieces, and the *future* of Clan Alpine would never be learned !

The midnight air was growing dense and sulphurous; gleams of lightning began to play about the bleak summit of Benvenue, and the deep thunder grumbled in the distance. Drops of hot rain were falling heavily too; but Paul felt them not, for his heart leaped within him as he shouted,—

" Wretch, come forth ! He is coming !—he is coming ! "

The poor cat impaled upon the sword-blade was expiring now; half-roasted alive, its eyeballs yet protruded from their sockets; surcharged with blood, they had become red as rubies, and its mouth opened and shut spasmodically.

White as milk or thistle-down, Paul's long and tangled hair glittered in the wavering fire-light and in the livid gleams that shot athwart the sky;

but still he tossed his skeleton arms aloft, and whirled the dying cat upon the sword-blade with a piece of burning brand.

In their sunken sockets Paul's eyeballs blazed like burning coals, for every moment he expected to see the trembling earth open, and the unchained fiend appear before him; but the rocks of the Coir nan Uriskin trembled by no demoniac spell, but with the boom of the pealing thunder alone.

Suddenly there was a splitting roar and a dreadful crash; a blinding sheet of livid flame filled the whole hollow; for a moment the wet rocks seemed to sparkle like masses of crystal, and the trees were seen to toss and twist wildly upward their rending branches in the blast. Then all became darkness and all silence, save when the thunder of the midnight storm grumbled in the distance far away.

A thunderbolt had struck the rocks of the hollow; Paul became senseless, and remembered no more till morning dawned, when he found himself lying near a thunder-riven rock in the Coir nan Uriskin amid the ashes of his extinguished fire, and close by him the charred remains of his victim still impaled by the sword-blade.

The adventures of the night—how much of these were true and how much were *fancy* the reader may easily determine—had sorely exhausted the strength of this strange old man, to whose narrative Rob Roy listened with astonishment, not unmingled with alarm, for the scene of his spells was fraught with innumerable terrors.

"Thus, MacGregor, I have sinned and perilled my soul for nothing," groaned Paul, closing his eyes, as if in exhaustion; "I have invoked in vain, and in vain has the terrible ordeal of the *Tigh-ghairm* been undergone ! "

"If all this be true, Paul, you were near rousing the devil to little purpose. For had he told you that we would be victorious, we would fight; if defeated and dispersed, *still* would we fight, till the last of us was gathered to his fathers. So for true tidings of the enemy I would rather trust to the lass Oina than to your devilish cantrips."

"You would trust in a woman?" said Paul, disdainfully.

"She can reckon every redcoat in Inversnaid as well as you or I could do, Paul."

"What said St. Colme of Iona? 'Where there is a cow there will be a woman, and where there is a woman there will be *mischief;* so neither one nor the other ever set foot on the Isle of the Waves in *his* time."

"An ungallant speech," said Rob, laughing.

"But a true one. Pause and consider well, for a son of Fortune waits and attains his end in peace; but the luckless hastens on unadvisedly, and evil befalls him."

"Dioul ! " said the other, with knitted brow; "I am no son of Fortune, but an outlawed son of Alpine ! I thank you for your advice, Paul; but return to Portnellan, and get food to restore your wasted strength. I will trust to the kind God above us," he added, uncovering his head, and looking upward, "to Him and to my father's sword, rather than to a voice from hell! To-night I cross the hills to Inversnaid, where my poor boy Ronald and my patrimony are alike kept from me by these Saxon intruders. Coll, Greumoch, Mac-Aleister, and the rest are to follow me with five hundred men. We shall gather at the burn foot, where it flows into Loch Lomond, on the third night from this. Sharp war brings sure peace; and ere the sun of the next day shines upon the mountains, I shall cock my bonnet on the ruins of Inversnaid, or lie low on the heather as death can lay me!"

With these words Rob and Paul Crubach parted.

The latter turned away with tottering steps to seek the farmhouse of Portnellan, where Helen MacGregor, with her boys, Hamish and Duncan, were to wait the issue of the attack upon the king's fort and barrack; while Rob threw his target on his shoulder, and lithely and agilely descended the precipitous ladder in the rocks, and alone, as night was closing, sought the road to Callendar.

CHAPTER XXVIII.

ROB ROY'S CAVE.

THE Red MacGregor knew well that the destruction of Inversnaid and the dispersion of its garrison would render him popular even with his enemies; for that fort had been built to overawe the Buchanans, the Colquhouns of Luss, and the Stewarts of Ardvoirlich, as well as the MacGregors; yet none but the latter had the daring to attempt its capture.

It was always garrisoned by a strong party from the castle of Dumbarton, relieved at regular intervals.

Full of thought and of the bold deed he had in contemplation, MacGregor travelled alone by the northern base of Benvenue, from whence, across the waters of Loch Katrine, he could see the lights glittering in the windows of the thatched farm-house, where his family resided, at Portnellan, near where the western end of that lovely sheet of water flows into Glengyle, and with a prayer on his lips for their protection, and a sigh of hope for the future, he drew tighter his girdle, secured his belted plaid upon his breast by his brooch, and crossed the rugged mountain slope with long strides unerringly in the dark, for the night was moonless, and after a journey of ten or twelve miles, he reached his old lurking-place, the cavern, on the banks of Loch Lomond.

From this place he could overlook the lands that were once his own, and where whilom he had been able to count the grey smoke of a hundred cottages rising in the clear air of an autumn evening, and knew that in these humble abodes all loved him with a love that went beyond the grave; but the times were changed, and with a sigh of bitterness he entered the cavern.

He looked carefully to the flints and priming of his pistols, and casting himself on a bed of dry soft heather, prepared for him in a hollow of the rocks by the careful hands of Oina, he placed his drawn sword beside him, and addressed himself to sleep, as he expected a visit from her in the morning when she could leave the fort, where she had been latterly engaged as the servant of an officer's wife.

Hour after hour passed, and MacGregor heard no sound but the night wind as it swept the bleak mountain side, and tossed the wild whins and brakens that fringed the mouth of his dark hiding-place.

Sleep was stealing gradually over him when some strange dark objects appeared at the cavern mouth. Starting, he snatched up his sword and pistols; but paused, for the figures had short horns, floating beards, and red glaring eyes that peered in at him from behind the ledges of rock.

On the first alarm he thought that soldiers had tracked him hither; then the diablerie of Paul's recent proceedings, and his strange narrative of the night he had passed in the den of the Urisks, flashed upon Rob's memory, and made his flesh creep; for now, head after head, with horns and beard and red glancing eyes, came along the lower edge of the cavern floor, appearing darkly and indistinctly against the dim light without.

MacGregor levelled a pistol and fired; then there was a rush of many feet down the slope, and on springing to the cavern mouth, he found that he had been scared by a herd of poor mountain goats, which he saw now leaping from rock to rock in terror and dismay.

Then Rob laughed aloud at the excitement or overstrained fancy which had caused such unusual emotions of alarm; and he thought of the good King Robert I., who had been similarly startled in the same place. For we are told, that after his defeat by the rebellious Western Highlanders at Dalree in Strath-fillan, he fled down the glen, crossed the Falloch, and alone and unattended reached Loch Lomond side, and at Inversnaid took shelter in this same cavern. There he slept in his armour on the bare rocks, with his sword drawn by his side—the sword that was never to be sheathed till Scotland were freed alike from Western rebels and English invaders.

In the mirk midnight, the war-worn king awoke, and was at first astonished, and then amused, to find the cave full of wild mountain goats, whose lair it was; and tradition adds, that Bruce found himself so comfortable among them, that when peace was proclaimed and the Parliament met, he passed " a law whereby all goats should be grass mail (or rent) free."

In that cave King Robert passed the night, and in the morning there came to him Sir Maurice of Buchanan, who conducted him to Malcolm Earl of Lennox.

On the same rock where, perhaps, the Bruce's head was pillowed, Rob Roy dropped into a profound sleep, and the morning sun was shining brightly on the woods of silver birch and sombre pine, and on the green isles of Loch Lomond, when he awoke to find Oina seated near him, with a little basket by her side, and a red plaid drawn over her head, patiently watching him, and waiting the moment when he would be stirring. In one hand she had a hunting-bottle of usquebaugh, and in the other a little quaich formed of juniper and birch staves alternately, smoothly polished, and hooped with silver.

The little girl, with the thick brown tresses described in the first chapter of our story, was now a tall matron, with her dark hair gathered under a curchie. Her brow was thoughtful and severe, for many a time since the day on which her boy companion, Colin Bane, had been slain by Duncan nan Creagh, had she looked death in the face amid flashing swords and flaming rafters; and she was now, as stated, the wife of Alaster Roy MacGregor.

" You have come at last, Oina," said Rob Roy.

" Say not that as a taunt," said she, " for I could

not leave the fort of Inversnaid before the gates were opened at daybreak."

" I did not say it tauntingly, Oina," replied Rob, patting her shoulder; " but what of my poor boy Ronald ? "

" He is still in a cell, where I cannot have speech with him."

" A cell! How his free Highland soul must abhor such confinement! Patience yet awhile, my boy, for the blades are on the grindstone that ere long shall free you. But do they keep surer watch than usual at Inversnaid ? "

" I cannot say; but more of the red soldiers arrived yesterday."

" More? " repeated Rob, starting.

" Yes."

" How many ? "

" Forty at least; they came by a boat up Loch Lomond from Dumbarton."

" How many are in the fort now? "

" I have reckoned four companies of eighty men each."

" Three hundred and twenty muskets."

" Nay, for twenty of these have halberts."

" True—the sergeants."

" Then there are six *tairneanach* " (thunder-mouths).

" At the gate. I have marked them from the hill; they are six-pound cannon, I believe; but let us once pass the barrier and they will be useless. I have but five hundred claymores, yet I will make an attempt, if it should cost me my life and the lives of all who adhere to me," said Rob Roy, firmly.

" At what hour will you advance?"

" To-morrow night at twelve."

" Good.   I shall endeavour to dispose of the sentinel at the gate."

" With the dirk?   Nay, I like not that, Oina," said Rob Roy.

" Nay, with *this*," she replied, laughing, as she took the hunting-bottle of whisky from the basket in which she had brought a breakfast for MacGregor.

" To-morrow night we muster at the burn foot, near Inversnaid.   At twelve the attack will commence—twelve remember, Oina; and if the sentinel be not silenced by you, we must e'en trust to the sledge-hammer first and the steel blade after."

When Oina left him to return to the fort the hours passed slowly and anxiously with MacGregor, who in his hiding-place could hear the drums when they were beaten at daybreak, sunset, and tattoo, in the barrack at Inversnaid; and he prayed that the time might come when that sound, which was rendered, by association, so hateful to a Highland ear, would be hushed among his native hills for ever.

Whether victorious or not, Rob Roy could scarcely hope that an act so daring as an attack on a royal garrison would pass unpunished; but he heeded not.   By that deed he resolved to make a terrible protest against the usurpation of his land, and the erection of such a building in the country of the MacGregors.

CHAPTER XXIX.

THE STORMING OF INVERSNAID.

THE eventful night proved dark and cloudy. The month was April, but already the young buds had burst, and were in full leaf in the wild woods that bordered Loch Lomond, when Rob clambered out of the deep rocky fissure which formed the approach to his cavern, and sought the place of tryst.

Sweeping down glen and corrie, the night wind came in squally gusts to furrow up the waters of the Loch. About the bare summits of the mighty mountains which overlooked it, the red sheet-lightning gleamed at times, giving a weird aspect to the black and silent scenery, as rock, hill, and tree came forth for a moment in dark outlines upon the lurid background, and then vanished into obscurity.

No sound broke the solemn stillness save those gusts of wind, or the rushing cascade of the mountain burn that brawled from Inversnaid over rocks and stones towards the loch, while the MacGregors arriving in parties of ten, twenty—even forty— from the banks of Loch Arclet, from Glengyle, Glenstrae, and the braes of Balquhidder, mustered at the appointed place, every man armed with sword and dirk, target and pistol.

In addition to these (the invariable weapons of the Highlander) many had long muskets with bayonets, taken from the troops, and the terrible *tuagh*, or pole-axe, and each wore a sprig of pine in his bonnet.

A wild and warlike yet resolute band, they were anxious for the conflict, as they had the traditionary and actual wrongs of their race to avenge — the violation of their clan territory; and, moreover, many of them had suffered by the spoliation or appropriation of their cattle and sheep, which had been taken or shot by the king's garrison; for, as stated elsewhere, cattle were then the whole wealth of our mountaineers. Forty head were a woman's dowry; the rents were paid, daughters were portioned, and sons provided for in life by herds and flocks.

With MacAleister, Greumoch, Alaster Roy, Rob found his eldest son Coll already there. There, too, came even old Paul Crubach, armed with the hiltless sword on which he had impaled the unfortunate cat; and on reckoning his force, Rob found that it consisted of five hundred and two claymores, all men resolute and true as the steel of which their weapons were made.

The milky light of the stars glimmered at times through the flying clouds, on their swords and round shields studded with polished nails and bosses of brass and steel, as they sat or stood in picturesque groups, muttering and whispering, and chewing the *muilcionn*, as the Highlanders name the spignel, which they were wont to chew like liquorice or quids of tobacco, in winter and spring.

Measures for the attack were soon resolved on by a force alike destitute of cannon, petards, or scaling-ladders. They were simply these: To advance to the gate in the ancient and classic form of a wedge, led by Rob Roy; and if Oina had failed to remove or overcome the sentinel, to trust to the sledge-hammer first and the sword-blade after.

Those nearest in blood, highest in rank in the clan, and the best armed, were to keep close by Rob in the conflict; so Coll, MacAleister, and Greumoch were immediately in his rear, as the march was begun in silence up the side of the stream, towards the point of attack.

The cuarans, or shoes of untanned deerskin, then worn by the Highlanders, strapped sandalwise over the instep and ankles, enabled this mass of men to advance over the rocky and rough ground as silently and noiselessly as if they trod on the soft heather, or on "the down of Cana," the cotton grass of which Ossian sang, and which whitens the Highland mosses in spring, when the sheep crop it, before it bursts into flower.

After a march of something less than a mile, before them, on an eminence, rose the strong walls and black outline of the fort and barrack they were about to assail.

Halting his men at some distance, MacGregor crept forward softly and drew near the arched gate, on each side of which three pieces of cannon frowned through embrasures of stone.

He listened intently for the step of the sentinel

within, but heard only the wind, as it moaned past the mouths of the cannon.

He uttered a shrill whistle like that of a curlew, a signal he had agreed on with Oina, and her expected response, three knocks on the gate, made his heart leap, for he now knew that the sentinel had fallen into a snare, that she had succeeded in intoxicating him, and that the outer barrier at least was open. Hastening back to his men, he exclaimed,—

" Come on, my lads, and follow me; the path is clear ! "

He drew his sword, and a gleam of light seemed to pass over all the dusky mass as every man followed his example, and rushing on like a living flood, they flung themselves against the gate, within which the sentinel was lying in his box quite intoxicated.

With shouts of " Dhia agus ar duthaich ! Righ Hamish gu bragh ! " (" God and our country ! King James for ever ! ") the MacGregors burst into the fort ; but, unknown to them, there was an inner gate of iron, which secured the passage to the barracks. This, Captain Clifford, the officer commanding the main guard, instantly shut and secured ; and through the bars of it his men opened a fire of musketry, that in five minutes brought the whole garrison under arms.

Swinging ponderous sledge-hammers, Rob Roy, MacAleister, and others, strove in vain to beat or break down the malleable iron bars of this unex-

pected barrier, through which the musketry flashed
incessantly, and many of their men were falling
killed or wounded, while others returned the fire
with their long guns, which they discharged
through the barrier right into the faces of the
redcoats.

The outworks of Inversnaid were completely in
possession of the MacGregors, but the inner wall,
by its height, defied their efforts, and Rob knew
that from it and the barrack windows ere long there
would be opened a fire of musketry, which would
decimate and destroy his men, unless the heart of
the place was entered, while consternation existed
in the garrison.

Already the windows were full of lights, as the
soldiers were dressing and arming in haste. Sharply
and rapidly the long roll was beaten on the drum, and
scores of voices were heard in clamour and confusion within, while without rang the wild cheers of
his men and the pipes of Alpine, who played,—

> Oh that I had *three* hands,—
> One for the sword and two for the pipe !

The red explosion of muskets and pistols echoed
on both sides of the barrier, which Captain Clifford,
a resolute officer, who shared with his men a hatred
and fear of the Celts, defended with resolution;
expecting only extermination if taken, the King's
Fusiliers acted with great vigour and courage.

From an angle of the inner wall, which his men

were now rapidly lining, Major Huske shot off a number of lighted shells or bombs from a little brass howitzer. These soared through the air, forming long and dazzling arcs of light, which enabled his Fusiliers to see the number and disposition of the attacking force, and to direct their fire upon the tumultuous mass of men wedged below the walls, where the long blades of their brandished swords seemed to flash sharply up from a sea of blue bonnets, red tartans, and round targets.

The soldiers, in their square-skirted red coats, white cross-belts, and three-cornered hats, were rapidly lining all the walls, firing at random as they came upon the platforms, till Huske lighted three *cercles goudronnes,* by the blaze of which they directed their aim.

These are old gunmatches, pieces of rope dipped in pitch and tar, made up in the form of a circle, to be placed upon ramparts during a night attack.

The clear light they cast upon the strife, together with the sharp and destructive explosion of three or four well directed hand-grenades, were causing great consternation among the MacGregors, some twenty or thirty of whom had fallen killed or wounded when the bewildering cry of *" fire ! fire ! "* in the heart of the garrison, produced a panic among the soldiers, and a red blaze was seen to start above the roof of the barracks. In fact, Oina, to create a diversion, and distract the attention of the defenders, had thrown a lighted candle into the lofts, where the hay and straw for the officers' horses were stored.

A part of the wall was thus left undefended by Huske drawing off his men to extinguish the flames. At this part, the faithful and devoted Oina threw down a ladder, up which the Highlanders scrambled with the activity of wild cats; but at the same moment a stray bullet pierced her head, and she fell lifeless across the wall with her arms and her long dark hair spread over it.

Rob Roy was the first man in!

As he placed a foot upon the parapet, he stumbled and fell; but his figure and red beard had been recognized by the light of the blazing *cercles goudronnes*.

"The red MacGregor! down with him," exclaimed an officer; "at him, my lads, with your bayonets breast high!"

Four soldiers rushed forward, and Rob's life had likely ended there, had not Eoin Raibaich (John the Grizzled) a MacPherson who bore his standard (for the Clan Vurich were the hereditary banner-bearers of Clan Alpine), devotedly flung himself before him; and after thrusting the point of the standard pole into the heart of one soldier, received the bayonet of a second on his target, and those of the other two in his own gallant breast.

"Righ Hamish gu bragh!" he exclaimed, and expired, as Greumoch snatched the banner from his hand. Then Rob Roy leaped down into the heart of the place, and with shouts of triumph and fury, his men spread over the whole barrack.

Paul Crubach was seen hobbling hither and thither, yelling like a fiend; his cross-staff uplifted in one hand, his rusty sword-blade in the other, and his long white hair streaming behind, and glittering like hoar frost in the blaze of the burning haylofts, and the flashing of the musketry.

Captain Clifford finding the rear turned, and the foe in the heart of the garrison, opened the inner gate, and at the head of the main guard forced a passage through and escaped.

By this avenue the whole garrison also escaped or were expelled, being driven forth at the point of the sword. Many cast aside their muskets and belts, and fled down the glen of Inversnaid, they knew not whither; but had they been pursued in the old Highland fashion, not one could have escaped; however, Rob was merciful, and would not permit a man to follow the fugitives.

Greumoch in the *mêlée* caught Major Huske by his queue at the moment he was rushing sword in hand through the gate of the fort. The Celt was about to hew the Saxon down, when the wig of the latter came off, so he escaped bareheaded, while Greumoch fell heavily on his face.

"Oich," muttered he; "prutt-trutt! he has a sliddery grip that takes an eel by the tail."

MacAleister soon discovered the cell wherein Ronald was confined, and he rushed forth to embrace his father ere the fray was well over.

Rob's plaid was torn to pieces by bayonet thrusts and musket balls, and he had a severe wound in his left shoulder, where a captain, named Dorrington, stabbed him through the gate with his spontoon, a pike then carried by all officers.

Save about fifteen or twenty soldiers who lay killed or wounded (chiefly near the iron gate), not one of the garrison remained in Inversnaid; but the barrack-yard was strewed with muskets, swords, cartridge-boxes, blankets, haversacks, hats, and wigs; and there also lay two drums, for the fugitives in their panic and desire to escape abandoned everything, even to their regimental colour, for a standard of the South British Fusiliers was found in Major Huske's quarters by young Coll MacGregor, having the English rose embroidered upon it, together with the white horse of Hanover, and the motto, *Nec aspera terant.*

" Carry this to the farm of Portnellan, my boys," said Rob to his sons, " and give it to your mother as a trophy of this night's work. She has wept and wearied long for you, Ronald."

As there was no time to be lost, he gave orders to destroy the fort utterly. The wounded were carefully removed, and the slain MacGregors he sent by a boat for interment on Inchcailloch, beside the ruined church, which had been disused since 1621.

Among these was Oina, whom her husband had rolled in his plaid, as the only shroud and coffin he had time to procure her.

The whole of the plunder found in the barracks and stores—arms, powder, clothing, food, and money—Rob Roy, with his characteristic gene. rosity, gave to his poor and faithful followers, which completely consoled them for many a stab, slash, and bruise received in the attack.

To himself he reserved only the captured standard and a little child—a boy of about three years of age—who was found asleep peacefully in his bed amid all the horrid din and hurly-burly of the night assault and capture.

On inquiring among the wounded soldiers whose boy this was, Rob was informed that he was the only son of Major Huske; so he gave the little fellow in care of his foster-brother, MacAleister, saying—

"Well, major, turn about is fair play. You took my son—I now take yours. Carry him to Port-nellan, Callam, and give him to Helen. Tell her (but it is needless) to keep the little Saxon tenderly, as if he were our own, till such time as we can restore him to his father."

So MacAleister wrapped his plaid about the child, who screamed with terror on seeing the Highlanders; for it was a common belief then in England, and for long after, that they were wont to eat children, like the ogres of the fairy tales.

Rob next ordered the cannon to be spiked and the barracks to be set on fire.

"Alpine, strike up the *Brattach Ghael!*" said he to the piper, who at once began the "White

Banner," a famous pibroch of the Jacobite clans.
" By the deed of to-night I shall teach these robber
Whigs and truckling Lowlanders to consider well
ere again they build a fort on our land ; this will
be the worst twist in their cow's-horn ! "

Rob now gave orders to retire, with the wounded
slung in plaids over the shoulders of their comrades,
who applied handfuls of nettles to stop the bleeding
of cuts and stabs ; and the retreating MacGregors
saw the flames of the burning barrack and fort
rising like a pyramid of fire above the walls, as the
daylight stole down the vast steeps of Ben Lomond
into its solemn glens and rocky corries.

The blaze was yet shining across the grey
morning sky, when they retreated to their fastnesses at the head of Loch Katrine, by the wild
way of Loch Arclet, whither MacGregor believed
the bravest men in the castles of Stirling or Dumbarton dared not follow him !

CHAPTER XXX.

THE FIGHT AT ABERFOYLE.

THE little boy found at Inversnaid was kindly and tenderly received by Helen MacGregor, who made him share the heather-couch of her youngest son, Duncan, a hardy little Highland colt, who was about the same age as the yellow-haired Saxon. The arrival of the latter created great speculation in the small clachan or farm-town of Portnellan; but the poor boy, accustomed to other sights and sounds than those around him now, was scared and terrified by the aspect of the Highlanders, and mourned for his father and for the soldiers among whom he had been reared, and clung to the skirts of Helen MacGregor as his only protectress.

However, as children so young have but shallow griefs and short memories, a few days found him quite reconciled to his fortune, to little Duncan as a bedfellow and playmate; and he learned to sup his porridge with a horn spoon from a large wooden trencher, and to make a companion of the stag-hounds, collies, and otter-terriers, that shared the fireside and sitting-room of the family of Portnellan.

"Alas!" said Helen, one evening, as she sat with the little stranger on her knee; "this fair boy is too sweet, too good and beautiful to find a proper place on earth."

"How—what mean ye, goodwife?" asked Rob, with displeasure.

"Such children never live to comb grey hairs."

"Say not so, Helen," said Rob, impressed by her manner.

"I would the youngling was with his own people. I judge of their sufferings by what I myself have suffered," said Helen, with a sigh.

"True, Helen," said Rob Roy, sternly, as he sat at the table oiling the locks of his pistols; "but little cared they for our heartaches when Ronald was their prisoner—fettered like a felon in the port of Inversnaid, because he fished on the patrimony of his father, and scorned to betray him for gold!"

"To seek the major at Dumbarton——"

"To seek Major Huske anywhere would be to seek death, even for him who took the child to him. A dab MacAleister gave him with his dirk is not likely to have improved the major's temper; so let us bide our time, Helen. Our Highland air but ill suits Saxon lungs, yet the blue-eyed boy thrives bravely, and our little Duncan loves him well. They share their bannocks and cheese, their brochan and brose, like sons of the same mother."

"Yet I would the child were with *his*," said Helen, earnestly.

"She is, I hope, in heaven," said Rob, looking upward.

" Dead ! " exclaimed Helen ; " mean you that she is dead ? "

" Ay, Helen, even so. She was killed by a cannon-ball at the siege of Landau, in the Lowlands of Holland ; and the poor child, then at her breast, was covered with her blood. Thus, poor Oina, who heard a soldier say so, told me."

Helen's eyes filled with tears, as she kissed and caressed the motherless boy, who, while creeping close to her, always viewed her husband's red flowing beard, glaring tartans, and glittering weapons (which he could scarcely lay aside for a moment, even by his own hearthstone) with an undisguised fear and mistrust that frequently made Rob and his henchman laugh heartily.

Helen dressed little Harry Huske in a home-made kilt and short coat, which she adorned with buttons formed of those remarkable pebbles which are found on the isle of Iona. Her own hardy boys never wore shoes except in winter, and then she fashioned for them soft warm *cuarans* of the red-deer's hide, to protect their feet from the snow ; but to little Harry, having been more gently nurtured, she gave every luxury their circumstances would admit, and nightly she sang him to sleep with her harp, and the plaintive old song of MacGregor na Ruara.

Assisted and protected by Sir Humphry Colquhoun, James Grant of Pluscardine, and others, Major Huske, though severely wounded, with all his half-disarmed fugitives, reached the castle of Dumbarton, which is more than twenty miles from

Inversnaid, and from thence in a few days, by order
of Lieutenant-General Carpenter, commander-in-
chief in Scotland, a company of grenadiers, and
three of the line, were ordered to penetrate into
the district of the MacGregors, to punish them,
and, if possible, to capture Rob Roy.

This party, notice of whose march was speedily
brought to Portnellan by Coll MacGregor and
Greumoch, who had been scouting among the hills
of Buchanan, was commanded by Captain Clifford,
whose residence at Inversnaid had rendered him
pretty conversant with the country. The tidings
filled Helen and her household with something very
like dismay; but her husband fearlessly prepared
for the emergency, and resolved to meet the
invaders in one of those narrow passes which then
formed the only avenues to the Highlands—avenues
which no foreign sword had ever been able to
open up.

Clifford's detachment consisted of picked men of
the South British Fusiliers, all burning to avenge
the late affair at Inversnaid and the loss of their
regimental colour. As incentives to them, the price
of Rob Roy's head, the entire spoil — cattle, arms,
and goods of his adherents — were given in pro-
spective; thus, they commenced the expedition with
great alacrity; and the noon of the third day after
quitting Dumbarton saw them crossing the mountains near Gartmore House, and approaching the
pass of Aberfoyle, intending by that circuitous
route to penetrate towards Loch Ard and the Tros-

sachs, and then fall suddenly in the night on Rob
Roy's quarters.

They required no guide, as Captain Clifford
alleged that he had shot and fished over all the
district, and knew it very well.

Brightly shone the steel bayonets and polished
musket-barrels in the setting sun of the May
evening, and the redcoats looked gay and gallant,
while chatting and singing, for no fife was blown
nor drum beaten when the strong detachment of
Captain Clifford entered the valley of Aberfoyle;
but little knew he what awaited him between the
Trossachs and Loch Katrine !

Clifford, a brave, handsome officer, rode at the
head of the Grenadiers, mounted on a fine white
charger. He was a good horseman, and sat well in
his saddle. They seemed intended for each other,
steed and rider; both seemed to have high spirit
and good blood in them; and, in sooth, the steep
and rugged mountain path they had to traverse put
both to the test.

He had a red feather in his cocked hat, and the
snow-white curls of his regimental Ramillies wig
flowed over the low cut collar of his wide-skirted
scarlet coat. He wore fine lace ruffles, and long
black riding-boots.

The Grenadiers had all conical caps of blue
cloth, shaped like episcopal mitres, but with scarlet
flaps in front, whereon was worked in worsted
the white horse of Hanover. Their wide skirts
and loose sleeves were all looped up, and they

marched with their pouches open and fuses in their
hands.

The rest had their bayonets fixed and arms
loaded.

Ere long the silence of the vast solitude on which
they were entering — the utter absence of all
appearance of life or inhabitants — made Captain
Clifford begin to dread a surprise. Anon, even
the voices of his men died away; they began to
speak in whispers, and as the purple shadows
deepened amid that tremendous mountain scenery,
they kept closer in their ranks, and looked anxiously
about them, and at the narrow pass in front.

The arms taken at Inversnaid had, more than
ever, completely equipped the Clan Gregor; so
now, in the gloomy gorge of Aberfoyle, one of the
greatest barriers between the Gael and the Lowlander, were posted in ambush one hundred and
sixty marksmen armed with muskets. Under
Alaster Roy and Coll, eighty manned one side of
the pass, and as many under Greumoch were on
the other.

There, too, was little Ronald, crouching among
the thick heather, armed with a long horse-pistol,
and intent on deadly mischief, if he could see Major
Huske, whom he vowed should pay dear for his
basket of trout.

Well did Rob and his men know that, if con-
quered, death and decimation awaited them,
together with the utter ruin — it might be the
extirpation — of their families : for the terrible

massacre at Glencoe was still fresh in all their memories.

Moreover, they remembered that this spot was one of good augury; for there, in the days of their grandsires, a fierce encounter took place with a body of Cromwell's soldiers, who were cut to pieces, and some of whom were buried in a grave which yet remains by the wayside.

Under Rob Roy in person, the main body of his men lay concealed right in front of the marching soldiers.

Sombre twilight was stealing now across the deeper glens, but a bright glory of sunshine yet lighted the vast mountain cones that towered above the valley.

Clifford and his officers frequently uttered exclamations expressive of admiration, for the vale of Aberfoyle, with its splintered rocks, abrupt precipices, and richly-wooded hills, is singularly beautiful; but when Loch Ard began to open its sheet of water on their view, gleaming like a golden shield in the last light of the western sky, the scene became more lovely still.

The dusky *iolar* was seen winging his way to his eyry in the craggy steeps; and the sweet notes of the *druidhu,* or Alpine blackbird, rang loudly from the hazel woods; while the wild goat, perched on a sharp pinnacle, with his long beard floating on the wind, looked down on the marching troops.

Above hills covered with oak and birch, that waved in the evening breeze like ostrich plumes, above even the saffron clouds, Ben Lomond towered into the grey mist; and far across the placid lake fell its shadow with that of the isle that holds the ruined tower of Murdoch, Duke of Albany; while far in the distance rose the Alps of Arroquhar, with their summits hid in mist, or capped still with the last year's snow.

Such was the scene that opened beyond the dark and narrow defile on which the soldiers were entering.

"A sergeant and three men to the front—double quick!" cried Captain Clifford, as certain undefinable suspicions crossed his mind on seeing that some large boulder-stones had been dislodged from the rocks above, and were hurled down on the narrow pathway, as if to form a barricade. "Grenadiers," he added, "blow your fuses; be ready to throw your grenades, and fall on at a moment's notice."

Still nothing was seen, though five hundred men and more were crouching within musket range— crouching amid the long green braken, the thick purple heather, and the wild bloom which grew so luxuriantly that the crows and magpies built their nests in it; but the tartans of the Highlanders blended with the colours of Nature so admirably that they were still unseen, when at last the whole detachment, officers and men, were *between* the muzzles of the musketeers who lay in ambush on both sides of that narrow and gloomy gorge, and already the sergeant and his three advanced files were clambering over the boulders and stones that lay beyond the ambush.

Before MacGregor's horn could give the signal, his son Ronald, unable longer to restrain his anger and enthusiasm, fired his pistol, and the ball struck Clifford's holsters.

Then red fire flashed fiercely from both sides of the dusky hollow, as a hundred and sixty muskets poured their adverse volleys on the unfortunate soldiers, who in a moment were panic-stricken, thrown into confusion — a huddled mass — above their dead and dying.

Springing from amid the grey rocks, the MacGregors, with a simultaneous shout, flung down their plaids and muskets, drew their claymores, and amid the white curling smoke, rushed downward to the charge.

"Steady, men, steady!" cried Captain Clifford, loudly and rapidly. "Grenadiers to the centre! Keep shoulder to shoulder, and face outwards— close up in your ranks, and bayonet them as they come on! Be firm, my Royal Fusiliers!"

"Firm, in the king's name, and we shall yet bear back these Highland savages!" added Captain Dorrington, a brave officer who had served in the war of the Spanish succession.

Leaping over bank, bush, and rock, with heads stooped behind their targets in the usual Celtic fashion, their bodies bent, and sword and dirk in hand, down came the MacGregors, in front and on both flanks, like a herd of wild cats, all yelling, " Ard choille ! ard choille ! Dhia agus ar duthaich ! "

A confused volley was fired by the soldiers; but almost before the bayonets could be brought from the "present" to the "charge," the swordsmen were among them. Stooping *below* the charged bayonets, they tossed them upward by the target, dirking the front rank men with the left hand, while stabbing or hewing down the rear rank men with the right; thus, as usual in all Highland onsets, the whole body of soldiers was broken, trod underfoot, and dispersed in a moment!

These were the whole tactics of the Scottish Highlanders. Hence their clan battles, no matter how many swordsmen might be engaged, seldom lasted more than five minutes. It was usually an instantaneous charge—a rout—a killing, and all was over !

Captain Dorrington rushed sword in hand upon Greumoch, who, by a single blow with his Lochaber axe, clove him literally through hat and wig to the teeth; then, by the hook of the same weapon, he dragged Captain Clifford from his saddle, and would have slain him had not Rob Roy strode across the fallen officer, and by receiving the blow on his own target, saved him.

Several soldiers, who had burst out of the press, leaped behind rocks and stones, from whence they opened a desultory fire ; but they were soon pursued, and cut down or pistolled.

The whole detachment would have been destroyed

in a few minutes, had not Rob Roy, towering over
the throng, shouted in English, and with a voice
that rose above the shrieks and shouts, the clash of
weapons, and explosion of firearms, which woke a
thousand echoes in the narrow pass, the overhanging
rocks and mountains,—

"Surrender, yield—lay down your arms! on
your lives lay them down, and I promise you all
quarter,—I, the Red MacGregor!"

On hearing this, his own men partly drew back,
and many a claymore was withdrawn from a thrust,
or lowered from a cut, and the firing instantly
ceased.

"You hear what I have said, Captain Clifford,"
exclaimed Rob Roy; "to resist now is to court
death. I know you are too brave a soldier to deem
rashness is valour."

"Unfix your bayonets, my lads, and ground
your arms. Grenadiers, extinguish your matches,"
cried Captain Clifford, sullenly. "Our time for
sure vengeance shall come anon. But what manner of man are *you*, sir," he added, turning fiercely
to Rob Roy, "who dare thus attack the king's
troops on the open highway?"

"The pass of Aberfoyle, which leads to the
country of Clan Alpine, is *not* an open highway,
as you, captain, have found to your cost; and as
for me, I am the man your king and laws have
made me," replied MacGregor, sternly.

"Sir, is not our king yours?"

"Nay, sir. You serve the Elector of Hanover.

Our king is far away in France, beyond the sea; but we are his true liege men, nevertheless. We have no time to spend in talking, captain. The night darkens fast, and the sooner your men with the wounded get out of the Highland bounds the better. Do not be cast down, my friends," said he, still speaking English to the prisoners, who were now huddled together in a crowd, and surrounded by the armed MacGregors; "you are not the first men who have come into the Highlands to shear, and have gone home closely shorn."

"But your terms : our fate, Mr. Rob Roy Campbell?" began Clifford, in a blundering way.

"'Sdeath and fury!" exclaimed Rob; "call me Campbell again, and I shall cleave you to the belt!"

"Excuse me; but I do not understand all this," said the officer; "are you not named MacGregor Campbell?"

"Yes; by tyrannical acts of Parliament, which I treat with the scorn they merit."

"Well, sir; your terms?"

"Are these,—Surrender your arms and ammunition; leave the Highland border, and begone to England or the Lowlands; let us see you no more in the country of the Clan Gregor."

"The Lowlands," said Clifford, haughtily; "sir, we are quartered in the castle of Dumbarton."

"Where you are quartered, captain, is nothing to me."

"There will be a bloody reckoning for this," said

Clifford through his clenched teeth, as he gazed sadly on the mangled body of his poor friend and comrade, Captain Dorrington. "Chief, have you no fear for the future?"

"I fear nothing," replied Rob, haughtily; "moreover I am no chief, but a simple Highland gentleman, whom wrong and tyranny have driven to desperation. You have yet to learn, sir, that though the king may create a titled noble, Heaven alone can make a Highland chief."

The English officer shrugged his shoulders, and gave a disdainful smile, for to his ears this sounded like mere rhodomontade.

"To you, Captain Clifford," resumed Rob Roy, "I return your sword. The arms of your men I retain for the service of King James and the protection of my own people. I restore you all to liberty; but bear this message to the Saxon Governor of Dumbarton, to General Carpenter, or whoever sent you hither, that of the next band which on a hostile errand enters the country of Rob Roy, not one shall return alive if I can help it—*not one*, by the blessed God of my forefathers, and by St. Colme of Iona, for they shall be cut off root and branch, and the eagle of the hill shall alone tell their fate." He pressed his bare dirk to his lips as he spoke, and many of his men followed the example. "Go, sir; and may we never meet again. My foster-brother, with a hundred of my men, shall escort you so far as Bucklyvie to assist in bearing your wounded. After reaching that place you will be safe from all molestation. Farewell. Strike up, Alpine ! " he said to the piper, while saluting the captain with one hand and sheathing his sword with the other.

Then, as the disarmed band of soldiers, after getting, by Rob's orders, a good dram of whisky each, carrying or supporting their wounded, and escorted by MacAleister with a hundred picked men, proceeded in the shadowy gloaming down the dark and rugged pass of Aberfoyle, Alpine's great warpipe woke its many echoes with the triumphant pibroch of "Glenfruin."

Only two MacGregors were killed, so instantaneous had been their onset; but ten redcoats lay dead in the pass; and these the MacGregors buried with reverence by the wayside, where their tomb may yet be seen.

Encouraged by this victory to attempt greater enterprises, MacGregor now resolved to break down into the Lowlands, to carry off the spoil of his enemies; and remembering that it was about the time when the rents of his great enemy the Duke of Montrose were collected, he conceived the idea of visiting the chamberlain on the rent-day—of putting the whole money in his own pocket, and, to punish his grace for old scores, to carry off the obnoxious Killcarn bodily into the mountains.

"As the runnels from a hundred hills unite in one, and form a mighty stream," said he, in a stirring address to his followers, "so must all the branches of our outraged people now converge in one. From Glengyle and Glenstrae, from Menteith and Balquhidder, let us muster and march—march down on those sons of little men, the Lowlanders; and they shall shrink before us like dry leaves beneath the lightning! Our forefathers sleep on Inchcailloch; but we, alas! must find our graves on the mountain side, where nothing shall mark them to future times but a grey cairn or a greener spot amid the purple heather."

"Down on the mongrel bodachs—down on the Whigamores!" responded his followers, brandishing their swords with almost savage glee; for to the Highlander then the single word *Whig* expressed the acme of anything that was sordid, mean, and treacherous to king and country.

CHAPTER XXXI.

ROB SEIZES THE RENTS OF MONTROSE.

It was about the middle of summer in the year 1717, when Rob Roy, leaving the main body of his followers, uhder his son Coll, posted among the hills of Buchanan, where they had collected a great herd of cattle, the spoil of their hereditary enemies, set forth with twenty men and his favourite piper, Alpine, on a visit to Killearn.

MacAleister and Greumoch were, of course, among these chosen twenty, who were literally his *Leine a chrios*—the select men of his followers, meaning in English his " shirt of mail," or children of the belt—men at all times ready to support, obey, defend, or die for him.

Fearing that Killearn might obtain tidings of his approach, and take to flight with his grace of Montrose's money, Rob marched towards his residence with great secrecy and rapidity ; and avoiding the highways passed through woods and defiles, and about twelve in the forenoon presented himself suddenly at the Place of Killearn, as Grahame's mansion is still named.

It stands a mile and a half south of the village of Killearn, at the western extremity of Strathblane, in Stirlingshire, and having been built in 1688, it was then surrounded by clumps of wood and plantations.

Here MacGregor was informed by the terrified household that the laird was at the Inn of Chapel-erroch, where the tenantry of the duke had been summoned to pay their rents; so he departed at once, with a threat, that if they deceived him, he would return and burn the house to the ground.

He soon reached the inn, which stands half-way between Buchanan House (the duke's residence) and the village of Drymen; and close by it he placed his men in a copsewood.

Killearn, with many of the duke's tenants, was in the dining-room, and he had already given receipts for a large sum of money, when the sound of a bagpipe was heard approaching. The air played, "Up wi' the Campbells and down wi' the Grahames," betokening something hostile, they hurried to the windows, and great was the consternation of Killearn when he beheld Rob Roy, but alone, or preceded only by the piper, Alpine, advancing straight to the door of the inn.

Though in terror that his own life might be the forfeit of the proceedings instituted against Rob nine years before, he sought to preserve his master's property, and gathering up his rent-rolls, receipts, and the bags containing the money, he flung them into a loft above the room.

At that moment the door was thrown open, and with a respect that was in no way assumed, the landlord ushered in Rob Roy, fully armed, with a smile on his lip and irony in his clear grey eye, while Alpine remained as a sentinel at the entrance of the inn.

"God save all here!" said MacGregor, bowing.

"A hundred thousand welcomes!" replied Killearn, whose dapper little figure trembled in his buckled shoes, and he nervously fingered the breeches bible that was always in one of the large flapped pockets of his square-skirted black velvet coat. He trembled so much that the powder of his wig floated like a cloud about his head, as it was shaken from the curls.

On this occasion, Rob wore a short green jacket profusely laced with silver; a long red waistcoat, and scarlet woollen shirt open at the neck; a belted plaid, and pair of deerskin hose and cuarans elaborately cut and tied with thongs. His sporau was ornamented with silver and closed by a curious lock, which concealed two pistol barrels that were always loaded, and would infallibly blow to pieces the hands of any person attempting to open it while ignorant of its secret springs. (This singular clasp is now preserved in the Museum of Antiquities at Edinburgh.) In his bonnet was a long eagle's feather, a tuft of pine, and the proscribed white cockade.

His lawless and predatory life had imparted a wild expression to his eye and a boldness to his bearing that impressed all present; but one of the duke's farmers, named MacLaren, gathering courage, pushed a bottle of wine and another of whisky towards him, saying, with affected confidence,—

"You will drink with us, MacGregor?"

"That will I do, blithely," replied Rob, as he filled up a silver quaich with whisky, and drank it off, previously giving the old Highland toast,—

"The Hills, the Glens, and *the People!*"

He then laid his sword and pistols on the table, and presenting his little crooked snuff-mull to go round the company, in token of amity, he said,—

"Keep your seats gentlemen, pray; do not let me interrupt you," and proceeded to partake of the cold roasted meat, the bread, cheese, and wine which had been provided as a repast for the tenants, about thirty of whom were in the room.

While Rob was eating, the spirits of the party rose, and the bottle went cheerfully round till he called to the piper, who stood outside the inn near the open windows,—

"Alpine, strike up *Glenfruin.*"

On hearing this order, which seemed the forerunner of mischief, the chamberlain and tenants exchanged glances of uneasiness, which in no way subsided when Rob stuck his pistols in his belt and snatched his sword, as his henchman and other followers burst into the room, with claymores drawn, and ranged themselves at the door and windows, precluding all chances of escape.

"Now, Killearn," said Rob, for the first time addressing his enemy; "you will perhaps have the kindness to inform me how you have come on with your collection of his grace's rents ?"

Hesitation and fear made the factor silent.

" Speak!" exclaimed Rob, impatiently.

"I have got nothing yet," stammered Killearn.

"How! nothing from all this goodly company?" asked Rob, with a deepening frown.

"I have not yet begun to collect."

" Come, come, chamberlain; I know you of old, and so your tricks and falsehoods will not pass with me. I must reckon with you fairly by the book. Produce at once your ledger!"

Killearn, with the perspiration oozing on his temples, still hesitated and began to protest; but Rob laid his watch on the table, and cocking one of his steel pistols, said, with assumed calmness,—

" Killearn, I give you but three minutes to reflect and to obey me."

In terror of death the chamberlain grew deadly pale and looked sick at heart, while a glassy stare dimmed both his eyes, which wandered from the dial of the watch to the muzzle of the pistol, and then to the blank faces of the shrinking farmers, who were seated at the table as if rooted to their chairs.

" One minute has already passed," said Rob, as he began to hum an air, a sure sign that further mischief was not far off; so Killearn, seeing the utter futility of resistance, produced his rental-book and bags of money.

" Now, Killearn, this is acting like a sensible

man," said Rob Roy as he uncocked the pistol and placed the watch in his pocket ; " so help yourself and take a dram, while I examine your accounts."

———◦◇◦———

CHAPTER XXXII.

KILLEARN CARRIED OFF.

ROB ROY turned over leaf after leaf of the ledger, examined the whole of the rental, drew from the farmers those sums which the chamberlain had not yet received, and, pocketing a total of £3,227. 2s. 8d. (Scots), with great formality granted receipts in full.

" I will have a due count and reckoning," said he, " with the Duke of Montrose, when his grace repays me the sum of 3,400 merks Scots——"

" For what ?" asked Killearn, gathering courage.

" Dare *you* ask me for what ? For the havoc made on my property by the troops whom Lord Cadogan sent to Craigrostan, and to burn my dwelling-house at Auchinchisallan ; to say nothing of the heirship of my lands at Inversnaid. When all these damages have been repaired and repaid, I will then consider the *older* · scores (anent our unlucky cattle speculation) that exist between your master and me."

" Suppose all this were done," said Killearn,

"would you give up your predatory habits, which keep the whole Highland border in hot water; and would you teach your people those of industry?"

"Killearn, as for predatory habits, think you a Highlander ever felt his conscience prick him for taking *spreaths* of cattle from his natural foemen the Lowlanders? And as for habits of industry, a kilted duinewassal at a shop-counter, or seated at the loom, would be like an eagle in a cage, or a red-deer yoked to a plough," said Rob, with an angry laugh.

"How will this wild life of yours end, Mac-Gregor?"

"*Not* where you anxiously wish it may end—on the gallows-tree; but it shall end when our wrongs are righted."

"At civil law you have——"

"What!" interrupted MacGregor, with a fierce and hollow laugh, "would you have me, upon whose head a price has been set for these nine years past, sneak into the Lawyers' Court at Dunedin, among truculent Whigs and psalm-singing pharisees, to crave and beg the restoration of my patrimony? The hills, with all their woods and waters, were given to the Gael in the days of old, to be their dwelling-place and inheritance, and none but He hath a right to deprive us of them."

"Then we part in peace, MacGregor?" urged Killearn.

"Part—far from it, my good chamberlain," said Rob.

" How ? " asked Killearn, uneasily.

" I must have the pleasure of your company with me into the Highlands."

Killearn again grew deadly pale, and faltered out,—

" For what purpose ? "

" To be kept as a hostage until Montrose pays me the sum of 3,400 merks which he is justly owing me."

" If he refuses ? "

" Then, I will hang you, John Grahame of Killearn, on the highest tree that grows by the banks of Loch Katrine ! Away with him, Greumoch. Good night, gentlemen all. Alpine, strike up ; the *glomain* grows apace, and we must begone to the mountains with speed."

In less than an hour after this the unfortunate factor found himself on the march with Rob Roy's men among the hills of Buchanan, from whence the whole clan, with their spoil, departed under cloud of night, by Auchintroig and. Gartmore, and through the pass of Aberfoyle towards the Trossachs.

In irony the piper played before him all the way, till, at a place near Loch Ard, Alpine suddenly stopped as they passed a green knoll.

" Why do you pause ? " asked MacGregor.

Alpine pointed to the green knoll. It was a haunt of the fairies, who had decoyed therein his own grandfather, also a piper (for he played the clan into the action at Glenfruin), and he was seen no more till on a Halloween night, about fifty years after. His son, then an aged man, on passing, saw the hillock open like a chamber, and his father, still young and beardless, playing vigorously to hundreds of quaint little dancers in green doublets and conical hats.

On finding himself conveyed into that Highland wilderness, whither few Lowlanders dared to venture in those days, all hope for the future died away in the heart of the unhappy Grahame of Killearn.

Chance of escape he had none. He was secured by a rope round his waist, and this was tied to the girdle of Greumoch MacGregor, who, regardless of the failing strength and weak limbs of the dapper little chamberlain, marched sullenly on, with his poleaxe on his shoulder, a short tobacco-pipe in his mouth, and his vast plaid floating behind him, dragging his prisoner over rocks and stones, up steep ascents and down foaming watercourses, without pity or remorse, and without giving him time either to breathe or implore rest and pity.

With growing terror Grahame remembered his treatment of the wife of MacGregor, when he pillaged Inversnaid, though under colour and authority of the civil law; he knew that it was by his counsels that the powerful Duke of Montrose had ruined poor Rob, and driven him to the hill-side as an outlaw and reiver; and he gave himself up for utterly lost when the wild pass of Aberfoyle closed upon the rear of the marching band, and the vast spoil of cattle they had collected at the point of the sword.

——◆◆——

CHAPTER XXXIII.

KILLEARN'S FATE.

Rob Roy conveyed his prisoner to the head of Loch Katrine, and by the time he arrived there, exhausted by toil, by the rough nature of the steep paths he had been forced to traverse with such unwonted celerity, and moreover being in constant fear of a dreadful death by hanging on a tree, being drowned like a cur with a stone at his neck, or being shot by a platoon of MacGregors, the unhappy Killearn was in a deplorable plight, and had long since become quite passive in the hands of his captors.

By order of Rob Roy, Greumoch placed him in a boat, and rowed him to an island in the loch, now well known to tourists as "Ellen's Isle;" it was covered with the richest copsewood, and there, in a hut with Greumoch and another equally grim Celt to watch him, Killearn remained in captivity, during which nothing was known of his fate in the Lowlands, until he was permitted to write to the duke.

This letter, which he was compelled to date from Chapelerroch, lest the real place of his detention should become known, acquainted the duke that he was the helpless prisoner of Rob Roy, who was resolved to detain him until a ransom of 3,400 merks Scots was paid for the damage by Lord Cadogan's troops at Craigrostan and Auchinchisallan; adding, moreover, that he would receive " *hard usage* if any military party was sent after him."

In breathless suspense poor Mr. Grahame waited for a reply, but the duke was in London, the means and the mode of postal transmission were slow in those days, and no answer came to his prayer.

Greumoch frequently terrified him by saying he should be cut joint from joint and sent to London in a hamper, packed in heather, like a haunch of venison for the duke's table.

After being detained a considerable time, one day, when hope of release was becoming more and more faint, Killearn saw a boat pulled by eight sturdy rowers in MacGregor tartan, the chief colours of which are red, green, and black, coming down the loch from Glengyle.

It reached the island, and a tall, armed Highlander, in whom he recognized Rob Roy, leaped ashore, and advanced towards the hut, followed by several of his men.

Killearn, believing that his last hour had arrived, and that they had come to execute him, drew forth his breeches bible with trembling hands, and so much did his tongue fail him that he could scarcely reply to Rob's courteous but ironical salute.

" Killearn," said he, " I am come to set you at

liberty. Montrose, your master, has proved as treacherous to you as he has been to me. Little recks he whether I hang you on one of those trees, or give you a swim in the loch with a stone at your neck! You are free; and this you must admit is very different treatment to that which *I* should experience if our circumstances were reversed, and I were *your* prisoner, as now you are *mine*. Return, with this advice from me. Collect no more the rents of that land from whence I took you, as I mean to be factor there myself in future."

"You, MacGregor?"

"I—and what matter is there for wonder? All that country which Montrose and more than he brink and boast as their own, is but a portion of the heritage of Clan Alpine. By false attainder and studied legal villanies we have lost it; thus whatever is possessed by the Grahames, the Murrays, and the Drummonds is ours, and ours it shall be with the help of God and our good claymores!"

He then restored to the bewildered Killearn all his papers, receipts, and rental-book, and sent him under an escort homeward through the pass of Aberfoyle as far as the hills of Buchanan.

On this man, who had so greatly aided in his ruin, and who had so grossly insulted his wife, he thus " took no personal satisfaction," says a writer, " which certainly shows the mildness of his character, when we consider the habits and mode of thinking of the Highlanders of his day."

In accordance with his threat he now proceeded

to summon the whole heritors and farmers of the western district of Stirlingshire, to meet him in the old church of Drymen, there to pay the black-mail which for some time past they had neglected to send to his nephew Glengyle.

On the appointed day he marched there with five hundred men fully armed, and took possession of the ancient church, which, as tradition avers, the Wizard Napier (whose castle is close by) removed from another place to its present site.

The land here belonged chiefly to the Grahames of Montrose and Gartmore, yet such was the terror of MacGregor's name, that all the farmers attended and duly paid the usual tribute—all at least save one, who was bold enough to decline compliance; in consequence of which his lands were instantly swept of everything that could be carried off, or driven into the mountains.

Immediately on his return from London the Duke of Montrose applied to the Scottish Commander-in-Chief, Lieutenant-General Carpenter, for a sufficient body of troops to repress, if not totally root out, the MacGregors, who were now feasting in ease, triumph, and jollity on the plunder of his estates, in their fastnesses at the head of Loch Katrine.

Rob Roy gave a grand entertainment in the old Highland fashion at Portnellan, and the joviality was great, for the formerly poor and penniless members of the clan he had enriched by the spoil of their oppressors.

On this occasion deer and beeves were roasted

whole, and laid on hurdles or spars placed athwart
the trunks of trees, so arranged as to form a rustic
table, at which hundreds could seat themselves. For
a hall they had the open valley, bordered by the
great mountains that look down on Glengyle,
canopied by the mists and clouds of heaven; in the
distance the blue water and the wooded isles
of Loch Katrine, all reddening in the setting
sun, and overshadowed by the vast summit of
Benvenue.

Alpine and other pipers played, nor were harpers
from the Western Isles wanting to make music
there, and plenteous libations of whisky (that never
paid duty to the king), of claret landed by French
smugglers, and of Helen's home-brewed ale went
round in stoups and quaichs and luggies.

There on Rob's right hand sat his aged mother,
with the little English boy, Harry Huske, upon her
knee, for the child was alternately the plaything
and pet of her and of her daughter-in-law, Helen
MacGregor.

After this great open-air banquet reels were
danced on the smooth turf, and torches of blazing
pine were tied to poles when the light of the long,
clear midsummer night began to fail.

But lo! a sudden gathering of dark clouds, and
the playing of green lightning about the summit of
Benvenue, announced a coming storm, warning all
to separate and seek shelter ere midnight came.
Many supposed the sudden storm which so rapidly
followed this entertainment was ominous of coming

evil; but a few hours after it was discovered to have been the means, perhaps, of saving Rob Roy and all his followers from death or capture.

CHAPTER XXXIV.

GREUMOCH TAKEN.

On the evening of the rustic banquet, in compliance with the request of the Duke of Montrose, three bodies of troops were on their march, by three different routes, to surprise the whole of the MacGregors.

One party of the 15th Foot (then as we have said called Harrison's Regiment) advanced from Glasgow; another of the South British Fusiliers, under Major Huske, came from Stirling, accompanied by the ungrateful Grahame of Killearn as Sheriff Depute of Dumbartonshire; and a third party consisting of the Scots Royals (or 1st Regiment of the Line) advanced from Finlarig.

But their marching was slow and devious, for the country was strange, especially to the English troops, none of whom could be quartered in Scotland prior to the Union in 1707. The Highlands were then without roads, and the Government possessed " no correct map of those unexplored regions which," as a recent writer says, " were almost as little known south of the Tweed—or we may rather say, *south of the Tay*—as the African deserts, or the interior of North America."

Hence, a night march among those pathless mountains was an arduous task in these times; and on this occasion the rain descended in blinding torrents; the water-courses became white cascades; mere runnels were swollen to streams, and streams became dark impassable floods. The guides led the troops astray, either wilfully or by mischance; so that all arrived too late at the passes, and ere the storm was fairly over, Rob Roy (whom they had hoped to pounce upon when in bed) had intelligence of his unwelcome visitors, and got all his men under arms.

Some firing took place about daybreak, and the king's troops retreated, after the loss of only one man, a grenadier, who was shot by Coll Mac-Gregor from the summit of a rock; but in retiring the Scots Royals captured and carried off Rob's right-hand man and long tried follower, poor Greumoch MacGregor, who was immediately transmitted to the Tolbooth of Creiff.*

Greumoch had been taken when lurking in the clachan of Aberfoyle, a circle consisting of ten

* "Feb.—, 1717, Gremoch Gregorach, airt and part with Rob Roy *alias* MacGregor, in seizing of —— Grahame of Killearn; robbing him, carrying him away, and detaining him a prisoner several days. A party ordered to be sent by Brigadier Preston to guard him from Crieff Gaol to Edinburgh."—*Records of the Tolbooth of Edinburgh.*

large stones, a druidical temple, situated on rising ground near the Parish manse.

On tidings reaching Edinburgh that this important outlaw had been captured, Brigadier George Preston, of Valleyfield, governor of the castle, despatched a sergeant and six troopers of Campbell's Dragoons (the Scots Greys) to Creiff, where they received Greumoch, with strict orders to watch him by day and night until delivered to the civil authorities, and safely lodged in the heart of Mid-lothian. Being the first of Rob's men who had fallen into their hands, and moreover being that bold outlaw's chief follower and kinsman, it was resolved by rope, by axe, and knife to make a terrible example of him by a public execution—to have him hanged, drawn, and quartered.

But in all these barbarities they were nearly anticipated by the burghers of Crieff, who hated the Celts for repeatedly burning their town, and a mob followed the captive, shouting,—

"The wuddy—the wuddy! a tow—a tow! let him fynd the wecht o' himsel by the craig!" (which meant in English—" The gallows—the gallows! a rope—a rope! let him feel the weight of himself by the neck!")

So cried the Lowlanders, as Greumoch was conducted by the troopers, not, as the mob expected, to the fatal circle at the Gallow-hill, where the Stewards of Strathearn held their courts of old, but away on the road that led to the south.

Bound upon a horse, the sergeant marched his

prisoner through the long and lovely valley of the Earn; with carbines loaded, a trooper rode on each side of him, with orders to shoot him down if he attempted to escape.

A village near Dunblane formed their first halting place. There one of the troopers, who seemed less rough than his comrades, gave Greumoch a dram, on which the sergeant said,—

"Come, Highlander, I'll teach you a toast."

"Will you?" asked Greumoch, sullenly.

"Yes—you dour-looking Redshank."

"Well—my glass is full."

"Here's to the health of King George—and to the confusion of his enemies, including Rob Roy, the Pope, the Devil, and the Pretender!"

On hearing this offensive speech, Greumoch dashed the glass and its fiery contents full into the eyes of the sergeant and half-blinded him.

Inspired with rage, the non-commissioned officer ordered his men to secure the prisoner beyond all chance of escape during the night. The dragoons selected a heavy old-fashioned chair, in which they placed Greumoch, and tied thereto his hands, arms, and legs, lacing about him some twenty yards of rope, the knots of which were tied behind; and now, deeming him secure beyond all hope of flight, they stabled their horses, threw off their accoutrements, applied themselves to the whisky-bottle, and after making very merry, retired to rest in the outer room.

When all was dark and still, and poor Greumoch's

hands and limbs were fast becoming swollen, benumbed, and stiff—all but powerless, in consequence of the cruel manner in which the soldiers had bound him—he remembered having seen a knife on the table, where the sergeant had left it by chance.

Could he but reach that knife ! But, tied as he was, of what use could it be ? Yet there occurred to him an idea, which he resolved at once to put in practice.

By vigorous, yet almost noiseless, efforts with his feet, he dragged the chair across the room towards the table. At last he reached it, and, after being so frequently baffled that he was about to relinquish the attempt in despair, he contrived to take up the knife in his mouth, and to grasp the handle firmly with his teeth.

Then, by turning his head on each side alternately, he applied the edge so successfully to the cords which crossed his shoulders, that he soon severed them. By this process he gradually got one hand loose; but for many minutes it hung powerless by his side. However, anon he grasped the knife with it, and in a short time was free; but on rising from the chair, so much were his limbs benumbed, that he staggered like a tipsy man, and overturned both chair and table. Heavily they fell with a crash on the floor !

Greumoch rushed to the window, opened it, and leaped into the dark and silent street of the village; but at the same moment, from another window of the house, two carbines flashed, and the balls whizzed past as the troopers fired at him in their shirts.

"You are only dragoons," shouted Greumoch, in Gaelic; "and dragoons never hit anything; so fire away!"

Then with a derisive laugh he disappeared in the darkness.

———◦—

CHAPTER XXXV.

ROB'S NARROW ESCAPE.

THE Duke of Montrose began to despair of ever capturing Rob Roy or of conquering his men; but he distributed among his tenantry a great number of muskets, bayonets, and swords, with plenty of ammunition, that they might be able to defend themselves if attacked; but all these military stores fell into the hands of the enemy, for Rob, Mac-Aleister, Greumoch, Coll, and other MacGregors, by a systematic series of attacks or visits in the night, disarmed all the tenants in succession; so the duke gained nothing by the arrangement.

Another insurrection for the House of Stuart was expected in the Highlands; and as the Mac-Gregors, by their conflicts, raids, and depredations, had collected a great quantity of weapons, more than were requisite for their personal equipment, Rob Roy had all these carefully oiled, packed in well-greased cowhides, and buried in secret places, where perhaps many of them remain undiscovered to this day.

The MacGregors daily became more daring, and sometimes drove away the cattle from the parks, beneath the very windows of Buchanan House, where the duke resided. The practice of "lifting," as it was termed, the cattle of a hostile clan was then, and for many years after, common in the Highlands; and as the feud between Rob and his grace was of the most bitter nature, he carried the system to the utmost extent.

The duke's rental was principally payable in kind. Thus Killearn had established large granaries for storing up corn, meal, butter, cheese, &c., at a place called Moulin and elsewhere, which he deemed secure. Yet at all these storehouses Rob Roy appeared regularly, when least expected, and demanded supplies of grain, meal, or cheese for the use of his family, his followers, or for the poor people of the district, who were all devoted to him, for he was deemed the friend and father, protector and champion, of all who were necessitous, unfortunate, or oppressed.

For the quantities thus taken he regularly gave signed receipts, which stated that he took these goods as a return in some part for the property of which the duke had so unjustly deprived him; and at times he frequently compelled the Montrose tenantry to convey the goods thus appropriated to his house at Portnellan, or wherever they were required.

In his desperation, Montrose resolved to attempt the capture of Rob in person, and applied to the

Privy Council for authority to raise a body of horse and foot militia among his own dependants, supposing probably that they would be better suited to a warfare among the mountains than the troops of the line.

It is said that the duke had such a dread of the greater or more active enmity of Rob Roy that, singularly enough, "*his name* was intentionally omitted, and the act was expressed in general terms, as being one to repress sorners, robbers, and broken men—to raise the hue-and-cry after them, to recover goods stolen by them, and to seize their persons."

In consequence of the state of society which then existed in the Highlands, where the people dwelt in tribes or communities and in sequestered glens, which were separated by great mountain ridges, by pathless forests, while deep defiles or narrow passes formed the only access to the country, sudden raids and onslaughts, if vigorously conducted, could be easily made, with great peril, however, and with certain subsequent vengeance.

The two bodies of horse and foot now mustered and armed by Montrose were composed of men entirely devoted to him, and more or less antagonistic to the MacGregors, at whose hands they had all suffered severely. They wore the duke's livery—blue coats faced with red, with trews of the Grahame tartan, and each wore in his bonnet a laurel leaf. There was not a man among them but had something to revenge, in the shape of a farm burned, a kinsman slain, or a herd carried off; so the measures now put in force against him compelled Rob Roy to be more than ever wary, for although hitherto most fortunate in all his achievements and escapes, he could not hope to be always so.

Selecting a time when many of the MacGregors were absent at distant fairs, on a dusky evening in the November of 1717, it was resolved to beat up Rob's quarters.

Assisted by a few of the horse grenadiers of MacDougal (now a lieutenant-colonel), the duke's militia, led by a gentleman named Colonel Grahame, a brave and determined fellow, who had served under Charles XII. in his war with Russia, passed rapidly and unseen through the pass of Aberfoyle, and about midnight reached the house and clachan of Portnellan, at the head of Loch Katrine.

There was no moon, and all was dark and still; not even a dog barked, when the house, which was thatched with heather, was completely surrounded on all sides by men with muskets loaded and bayonets fixed. The dragoons were led by the only unwilling member of the expedition—Willie Gemmil, now a sergeant.

The cottages wherein MacAleister, Greumoch, and others dwelt, adjoined the house of Rob, and formed a kind of small square, in the centre of which was a patch of ground, cultivated as a kitchen garden, and common to the whole community.

These cottages were built as such edifices are still

constructed in the Highlands. The smoothed face
of a rock made the floor; several large boulders of
black whin formed the corners of the gables, and a
few courses of turf plastered with clay made up the
walls. On the rough pine *cabers* of the roof
lay the thatch, composed of fern with its root
ends outwards, and tied with ropes of twisted
heather.

As these humble edifices burned like a heap of
straw, Colonel Grahame said,—

" Fire all these thatched roofs at once, and smoke
the rascals out like foxes. Then shoot down every
one who comes forth ! "

" Nay, nay, colonel," said an old officer, a quartermaster named James Stewart; " under favour,
sir, I will have no hand in such butcherly work.
Our orders are——"

" To seize or destroy Rob Roy at all hazards ! "

" Yes; but we have not King William's sign-
manual in our pockets to make another Glencoe
at the head of Loch Katrine," retorted the quartermaster.

" Sirrah—do you dispute my orders ? " began
the colonel, furiously, when Sergeant Gemmil approached and said,—

" Please your honours, to fire the cottages would
rouse the whole country on us, as if the fiery cross
went through it; and we should all be cut to pieces,
horse and man, before we could escape by Aberfoyle,
or the pass of Loch Ard."

" Egad, you are right, sergeant; so let us beat

up this rogue's quarters more quietly," replied Grahame.

Though the house was humble, being merely a cottage with stone walls, the door was strong; but it was soon dashed open by a musket butt; then all shrunk back, with their bayonets at the charge, expecting MacGregor, like a baited lion, to spring forth upon them sword in hand, for all dreaded the length and strength of his arm; but instead there appeared only three women trembling in their night-dresses.

One of these, an aged woman, was Rob's mother; the others were Helen MacGregor and her foster-sister, who, when she married, had come with her from her father's house of Comar, which stood on the eastern slope of Ben Lomond.

On Colonel Grahame imperiously demanding "where Robert MacGregor Campbell was?" they assured him that he and all his followers were absent; and that if this was doubted, the house might be searched.

"Absent—where?" said Grahame, biting his long leather gauntlet with undisguised vexation.

Ere the ladies could speak, a scout or spy named MacLaren—the same person whom Rob had met at the inn of Chapelerroch—arrived, breathlessly, to inform the colonel that on the preceding evening he had seen MacGregor with a chosen party of his men at a change-house, or wayside tavern, near Crianlarich in Strathfillan.

" You are sure of this ? " said the colonel, sternly and suspiciously.

" Sure as that I now address you, sir."

" If this be true, you shall have ten guineas; but woe to you, rascal, if you deceive us! Sergeant Gemmil, look to this fellow, and if he attempts to give us the slip before we reach Strathfillan shoot him down."

Leaving the farmhouse untouched, for to fire it would have defeated the object in view, the colonel's party, guided by the spy, proceeded up Glengyle, from thence across the Braes of Balquhidder, and just as day began to brighten the mountain peaks, they found themselves at the lonely change-house of Crianlarich, which stood in a sequestered and pastoral part of Strathfillan.

Rob Roy, as the spy informed them, was then in the house; but his men, to the number of twenty, occupied a barn which adjoined it. In that place they feared no surprise, and kept no watch; thus, Colonel Grahame, when he dismounted and approached the barn, on peeping through one of the air openings in the wall, saw the MacGregors lying asleep on some bundles of straw, with their swords, shields, and muskets beside them.

" You are right, fellow," said he to MacLaren, to whom he gave at once the promised guineas. " There are twenty rogues asleep here, and we shall cut them off to a man; but the master thief must be taken before we rouse his followers. Then I shall hang the keeper of this tavern, and burn it down, without studying the scruples of our quartermaster," he added, with a dark frown at Mr. Stewart.

A dismounted trooper applied the heel of his heavy jackboot to the door of the house, and with a single kick made it fly open.

Softly though the troop had approached the dwelling, by riding on the grass or heather, Rob had heard them, and was up, clad, and armed, with his target braced upon his left arm, at the moment the door was broken open.

He put forth his bonnet upon the point of a stick, and in the grey twilight of the morning twenty muskets were discharged at it. Then, before the soldiers could reload, he sprang upon them with a shout, and cut down two. The noise of the volley having brought all his men to their feet, they rushed from the barn and assailed the Grahames in the rear, driving them and the horse grenadiers pell-mell round the house, and severely wounding several of them.

"To the hills! to the hills! and follow me!" shouted Rob, as he slung his shield on his back, and dashed off at his utmost speed towards the mountains.

Under a fire of muskets and carbines, he and his men crossed unhurt a torrent that foamed through the valley, and seeking a path, where few infantry and certainly no cavalry could follow, they began a leisurely retreat up the mountains towards the head of Loch Lomond.

Exasperated by this sudden and unlooked-for

escape, Colonel Grahame ordered the horse to make a detour, and the infantry to follow in direct pursuit.

Then began a desultory skirmish, in which the MacGregors had all the advantage ; for their tartans blended with the dun-coloured heather and green ferns, while the militia were fatally conspicuous in their blue uniforms. Thus, several were shot, and MacAleister threw the spy, MacLaren, into a mill-race, near the House of Comar, where he was swept away and drowned.

After this, " the Grahames thought proper to withdraw," and thus ended another attempt to capture Rob Roy.

To avenge this defeat, and the capture of his factor, it is related in the " Domestic Annals of Scotland," that the Duke of Montrose got all his farmers in the Lennox armed and mounted, for the purpose of attacking Rob; but Glune-dhu, the nephew of the latter, with the MacGregors of Glengyle, attacked his grace's men, and surrounded and disarmed them. Of this encounter we are unable to furnish the details; but, unfortunately for our hero, the *next* attempt had a very different result.

CHAPTER XXXVI.

A WEIRD STORY.

IN tracing the history of Rob Roy, we now come to one of those dark and supernatural events which, according to Highland tradition, were then a portion of the everyday life of the Scottish mountaineers, and were the result of local influences, and by their minds being deeply imbued in early youth by poetry and music, by legends anterior even to the songs of Ossian, and by the solemn scenery of the vast solitudes which formed their home.

The strange event referred to, occurred in the Tower of Glengyle. Another version of it has been given by a celebrated essayist on the superstitions of the Highlanders, but without stating the locality, or who were the actors therein.

Some days after baffling Colonel Grahame's party at Crianlarich—and while Montrose was planning a raid, to be led by himself in person into the mountains, for the purpose of capturing Rob Roy—the latter, with MacAleister, was hunting in the old Royal forest of Glenfinglas, and among the hills that look down on Glenlochy, a long and narrow vale in Breadalbane, where, in his father's time, Duncan of the Heads resided, and where the ruins of his house are still to be traced among the heather.

Rob and his foster-brother had urged the sport in the good old Highland fashion, for then the clansman would pursue the antlered stag for days, sleeping by night in his tartan plaid on the bleak mountain side; or propped on the beetling rock, with his long gaff, heedless alike of death or danger, would catch the scaly salmon in the leap between the sky and the foaming cascade; but, as a recent author says, "nothing short of starvation would make him take part in the brutal German battues which now prevail in the Highlands."

When on hunting expeditions, Rob always gave the salmon taken, the venison stalked, or the capercailzie and ptarmigan shot by his long Spanish gun, to the poor, or to the aged who were no longer able to hunt for themselves; and often he shared their huts, however humble; for north of the Highland border Rob Roy was everywhere welcome among the people.

The short autumn day was closing; the mountains were growing dark; the eagle and hawk had gone to their eyry in the rocks of Benvenue, though the wild grey geese were still floating on the bosom of Loch Voil, when Rob and MacAleister took their way across the hills to return home; but a storm came on as they descended Glengyle, so instead of progressing towards Loch Katrine, MacGregor repaired to the residence of his nephew, who, in conformity to the oppressive laws passed against the clan, was compelled to name himself Gregor MacGregor *Grahame*, yet is better known as Glune-dhu, and captain of the castle of Doune under Prince Charles Edward.

On reaching the tower, Rob found that his nephew, the laird, with all his followers, was absent on a hunting-match with the Earl of Breadalbane; but the old housekeeper and butler made him welcome. The two hunters had brought more than enough with them to sup the whole household, for Rob had two bunches of blackcock and curlew at his sword-belt, and MacAleister carried a small red deer slung over his shoulder.

A blazing fire of bog-pine and fir-cones was made in the arched fireplace of the old hall, and there the hunters prepared to pass the night comfortably, after the toil of their late hunting expedition.

Supper over, a jorum of hot whisky-toddy was brewed in an antique punchbowl; the iron gates of the tower were secured for the night; the old servants retired to their beds, and Rob and Mac-Aleister sat by the ruddy hearth, talking of their late wanderings, of tidings they expected to hear from Seaforth about a rising in the Western Isles; and without any intention of passing the remainder of the night elsewhere than by that jovial fire, and wrapped in their ample plaids.

Their late arduous wanderings in the keen cold mountain air, with the warmth of the glowing fire and the steaming punch, combined to make Rob drowsy, and ere long he dozed off into a sound sleep; but MacAleister, as he afterwards related, felt in no way able to follow his leader's example, though particularly anxious to do so. He became acutely wakeful, for a strange and unwonted anxiety weighed upon his mind, and at times a shudder passed over his frame—a *grue*, as the Lowlanders term it—a supposed sign that an unseen spirit hovers near you, or that some one is treading on the ground which is to form your grave, however far away that ground may be.

His eyes wandered over the old and faded family portraits which adorned the hall; he sought to shun them; but they seemed to exercise a strange fascination over him, which compelled him to look at them again and again, till they grew, to his alarm, almost instinct with life.

There was Alaster of Glenstrae, who led the clan to battle at Glenfruin, and who died on the gibbet at Edinburgh, looking grimly out of his iron helmet. There, too, was Colonel Donald MacGregor, in his wig and breastplate, looking as fierce as when he slew Duncan nan Cean, or carried terror among the Westland Whigs when the Highland host came down in the days of the Covenanters.

There were others in laced coats and tartan plaids, but all armed to the teeth — worthies who had departed this life with a foot of cold steel in their bodies, leaving more quarrels and broadswords than silver or gold behind them; and as he turned from one pale face to another, while the candles burned down and the fire waxed low on the hearth, Mac-Aleister began to feel how,

> By dim lights seen, the portraits of the dead
> Have something ghastly, desolate, and dread!

Add to all this the wavering gleams of the fire, the weird shadows they cast across the ancient hall, and the solemn sough of the midnight wind without, as it swept down Glengyle and moaned through the machicolated battlements of the old tower, shaking its grated windows, and waving too and fro the russet-coloured tapestry that overhung the doorway, driving out the brown moths to flutter about the fading lights.

Meanwhile Rob Roy slept heavily.

By Highland superstition it had long been understood, that when two persons were left thus, they should either both sleep at the same time or keep each other awake; for if one slept, the other was left to the mercy of the spirits of the air.

MacAleister called to MacGregor, but received no answer, and in the vaulted hall the hollow echoes of his own voice affrighted even his bold spirit. Then as a sudden and heavy chill fell over his sturdy frame, and a sickly and deadly fear stole into his heart, he strove to rise and grasp his foster-brother, but found himself frozen, riveted, chained, as it were, to his seat by a power or will superior to his own!

At that moment the arras which closed the lower end of the hall, and which had been violently shaken from time to time by the stormy gusts of wind, was suddenly parted, and there entered two tall and grim-looking gillies, in the Highland dress, and fully armed, bearing lighted candles in antique silver branches.

Other figures, misty, wavering, and indistinct, appeared beyond; but in the gillies MacAleister, with horror in his soul, recognized two MacGregors whom he had seen slain in his boyhood, and whom he had actually assisted to bury near the ruined church on Incheailloch.

Behind the bearers of the candles came a bearded piper, with his pipe on his shoulder, the drones decorated by long tartan streamers; the bag was distended, and he fingered the notes of the chanter rapidly, while his pale face seemed swollen by the exertion of playing; but neither from the instrument nor the tread of his feet came the slightest sound, as he passed like a shadow slowly round the hall, without looking on either side, though his glazed eyes shone with a blue weird gleam in the light of the fire; and then the henchman discovered, by a peculiar mole and a wound on the right cheek, that this was the phantom of Alpine's grandsire, who played the clan to Glenfruin, and was said to have been spirited away by the *Dosine Shie*, or fairies.

Then followed many ladies and gentlemen of the House of Glengyle, who had been in their graves for years, with grey visages, wan, ghastly, and solemn, and wearing costumes quaint in fashion and

long since obsolete, or to be seen only in such portraits as those which hung around the hall.

Spellbound, incapable of motion, and while his
leader slept soundly, MacAleister saw all these
phantoms take seats at the table beside them ; the
ladies spreading out and gracefully disposing the
ample flounces of their great tub-fardingales, as if
in life ; the gentlemen adjusting the curls of their
cavalier locks, or great perukes ; others shook out
the folds of their belted plaids, or ran their wan and
wasted fingers through their long wavy beards, as
they seemed to converse with each other, to assent
or dissent, and sometimes frown—conversed, but
without a sound, for the pinched blue features of
their long and awfully solemn faces moved spasmodically, and their gestures varied, as if they talked,
but not a voice or a word reached the ear of the
terrified MacAleister.

At last one who closely resembled the portrait of
Alaster of Glenstrae, for his helmet was crested by
the entire wing of a golden eagle, and whose neck
was moreover distorted as if by strangulation (for
Glenstrae had been ignominiously hanged), produced a pack of cards, and then all proceeded
to play.

The cards were scarcely dealt, when MacAleister
saw the figure of Oina—of his daughter—she who
had perished at Inversnaid, with her dark hair dishevelled and floating about her shoulders, wearing
the very plaid in which her husband buried her,
hovering at the back of those unearthly visitors ;

and with deadly fear he perceived that she was regarding him with a sad yet tender smile in her black lack-lustre eyes.

It was remarkable that Oina's form was more palpable than the rest, for some who had died ages ago were transparent, so that he saw other objects through them.

After a time the players relinquished the cards, and some betook them to what the Highlanders called *palmermore* (the tables), which requires three on each side, who throw the dice alternately; but though shaken violently, neither boxes nor dice emitted the slightest sound.

Now a muffled figure glided to the side of Oina.

On her regards being again turned to her father, this muffled figure threw off a wet and dripping plaid, and lo! MacLaren, the spy, whom he had drowned in the millrace at Comar, stood before him, with a malignant and demoniac grin on his cold and damp visage.

He drew near and breathed on the face of Mac-Aleister, and so cold was that breath, so icy and chill, that it seemed to freeze the marrow in his bones.

At that moment a cock crew, and with a shriek the spellbound man started to his feet, to find the fire extinguished, the candles burned out in their sockets, MacGregor still muffled in his plaid and fast asleep in a chair beside him, while grey dawn stole through the grated windows of the gloomy castle hall.

CHAPTER XXXVII.

THE HAUNTED WELL.

ROB ROY was instantly roused by MacAleister, who, in an excess of terror, related the vision of the past night, and begged that they might retire from Glengyle at once, as his soul was filled with dismay.

Rob, though deeming the whole affair a dream, as it was no doubt, felt somewhat disturbed by the story; for MacAleister maintained that it was a warning of his last hour being at hand; and still on his pale, blanched face he seemed to feel the icy breath of the phantom MacLaren.

Rob was too deeply imbued with the superstition of his time and country not to feel unpleasantly impressed by the whole affair, and fearing that something might be wrong at Portnellan, or that his presence there might be necessary, he and his follower set forth at once from the tower of Glengyle.

They proceeded quickly down the valley, passing through a dense old wood, which had grown there for ages.

In this wood was a clear and silvery fountain, which flowed into a tributary of Loch Katrine, and near it stood a little stone cross, covered with green moss and grey lichens. It had a great reputation for sanctity, and though frequently removed and

cast elsewhere by the Presbyterians, by some means
it always found its way back to the well, which was
said to have been haunted of old by a beautiful
fairy, with long flowing golden hair and shining
garments—a water spirit like the Undine of the
German romance.

Seeking the old fountain, Rob took a long draught
of its pure cool stream, and drew aside a little way
while MacAleister took off his bonnet and proceeded to say a prayer, for the adventure of the
past night pressed heavy on his heart: but he had
only uttered a single sentence, when he started back
in terror, exclaiming that the pale grey face of Mac-
Laren appeared under the water of the well, with
the old malignant smile on his lips and in his eyes.

"Your dreams have bewildered you, Callam,"
said Rob Roy; "take courage — anon you will
forget them."

But he had scarcely spoken, when there was a
shout that woke every echo in the wood, and
bursting through the trees and bushes about
twenty dismounted troopers fell upon them, sword
and carbine in hand.

MacGregor's claymore flashed from its sheath in
a moment; and opposing his shield to them, he was
about to break through and escape, when six levelled
their carbines, and Colonel Grahame called upon him
to "surrender, or he would be shot down without
mercy!"

"I know how to die, but not how to yield,"
replied MacGregor, proudly.

"Then die in your obstinacy!" exclaimed the colonel; "fire!"

But the troopers paused, on which the faithful MacAleister exclaimed to his foster-brother in Gaelic.

"Let them fire at *me*, and when their guns are empty do thou break through, thou who wert nursed at my mother's breast—and God speed!"

With these words MacAleister threw himself, sword in hand, upon the troopers, who fired their carbines, and, pierced by four bullets, the devoted foster-brother of Rob Roy fell dead on the grass!

The heart of the latter was wrung within him on witnessing this sad catastrophe, and instead of flinging himself with fury on the soldiers and breaking away, as his foster-brother had expected, and had exhorted him to do, he stood for a minute with irresolution, gazing at the corpse, from which the blood was yet welling, with rage and sadness on his face and in his soul.

That minute of irresolution and grief lost all!

From every quarter of the wood, soldiers whom the firing had summoned, came hurrying in, and hemmed round on every side by swords, by levelled bayonets, halberts, and clubbed carbines, Rob Roy was beaten to the ground, and when well-nigh senseless was disarmed and bound with strong ropes, as if he had been a madman or a wild animal.

Then, on being dragged to his feet, he found himself the prisoner of the Duke of Montrose, who surveyed him with a fierce and exulting expression in his proud and haughty face.

"Oh!" exclaimed MacGregor, with a groan, "oh, eternal infamy! a prisoner, and Montrose—*to thee!*"

———◦◆◦———

CHAPTER XXXVIII.

ROB ROY TAKEN.

THE duke wore a blue coat, faced and cuffed with scarlet, richly braided on the breast with broad bars of gold lace. Save at the throat, it was unbuttoned, and thus displayed a cuirass and gorget, both of the finest steel, which he wore in lieu of a vest, and over which fell the ends of his long cravat of Mochlin lace. He had on a three-cornered hat, a flowing white periwig, and black jackboots with gold spurs; and a sword and a brace of silver-mounted pistols hung at his waistbelt.

By his side were Colonel Grahame, Quartermaster Stewart, and others; for his grace had come hastily into the mountains with three hundred men, to reinforce the party from which Rob had escaped so successfully at Crianlarich.

"At last, MacGregor Campbell," said the duke, through his clenched teeth, while his eyes sparkled with triumph and resentment; "AT LAST you are in my power, and your doom hangs upon my lips!"

MacGregor uttered a scornful laugh, and though his hands were bound behind him, he drew his sturdy figure proudly up to its full height and measured the duke with a provoking glance of profound disdain—viewing him deliberately from head to foot.

"Now, my bold reiver, what have you to say?"

"For myself, my lord duke?"

"Yes," said Montrose, fiercely.

"Simply, that by fraud and force you have won a poor victory over a single man. *Use* that victory as you please, Montrose, but *abuse* it not."

"Nay, nay, I shall use it justly, as I am entitled to do; for you know that you have long been a doomed felon, on whose head a price has been set."

"By whom?" asked MacGregor, disdainfully.

"The king and government."

"A German usurper and Scottish traitors like yourself!" replied the other furiously.

"Ha!—it matters not how you name them; you are nevertheless a foredoomed felon, and as such shall you die!"

"And who caused me to be stigmatized as such —who but you? Silence! Duke of Montrose, and lead me where you will; but be silent, I say. Honour is like fine steel—breathe upon it and the surface becomes stained. Sorely have you striven to

stain the honour of Rob Roy; but you have striven
in vain; for Rob will be remembered among these
green mountains and in the hearts of the Gael—
look down, O Heaven, and bless them!—when you,
duke so venal and corrupt, will be remembered
only as the enemy and oppressor of him you would
destroy."

"Egad, I like your spirit, MacGregor!" said
Colonel Grahame, as he sheathed his sword with an
emphatic jerk.

"My spirit may break, Colonel Grahame, but
never shall it bend," replied Rob Roy; "I may have
my faults like other men, but if the best of us had
these written on his forehead, he would, as the saw
hath it, pull his bonnet well over his eyes. Till
your chief made himself my enemy, I was a quiet, a
peaceful, and a God-fearing man; but he made
desolate my hearth and home; he seized my patrimony, and cast me forth into the world a broken
man, an outlaw, and a beggar, with a price upon
my head, to be hunted like a wild beast by soldiers
and militia, horse and foot—I, a Highland gentleman, whose lineage was equal, if not superior to his
own. But as Fingal said to Swaran, 'The desert
is enough for me, with all its deer and echoing
woods!' so I took my target and claymore, and
retired to the steep mountain and the wild forest,
with my good wife and my little ones. Since then,
all we have endured has been enough to summon
all the spirits of the Clan Alpine who have
suffered and died since the field of Glenfruin,

back from blessed heaven to the vengeance of earth ! ''

" Let their spirits come," said the duke, with fierce irony ; " see if they will avail much, when you swing by the neck in the Broad Wynd of Stirling, even as Alaster of Glenstrae swung after his fine day's work at Glenfruin."

" We are not yet in the Broad Wynd of Stirling," said Rob, confidently; " but set me free for five minutes — put my broadsword in my hand, and here, on this plot of grass, will I fight you face to face and foot to foot—ay, with three of your best men, if you choose."

" I do not fight with felons," replied Montrose, loftily.

" Will you not meet me like a brave,—I cannot call you an honest, man ? "

" I do not fight with felons," was again the cutting reply.

MacGregor crimsoned with passion, and exclaimed hoarsely,—" Woe to you, dastard duke ! Alas, that I should ever speak thus to one who bears the good name that was borne by the Great Marquis, the gallant Dundee !"

" Enough of this," said the duke, also becoming red and husky with passion. " To horse, gentle-men, and away for Stirling. Colonel Grahame, bind the villain to one in whom you can place implicit trust, and let him be well watched. The man who permits him to escape, I will pistol with my own hand !"

MacGregor was secured to a horse behind a trooper, whose waistbelt was passed through the belt from which his sword and pistols were taken; his hands were also tied behind, so that it was impossible for him either to slip or leap off; and in this ignominious fashion, escorted by nearly four hundred of the duke's local militia, horse and foot, he was carried away a prisoner.

As they departed from the Haunted Well, he gazed sadly at the stiffened corpse of his faithful friend and foster-brother, Callam, son of the arrow-maker,—one who had never failed him in many an hour of peril, and whose remains were left where he fell, and where a cairn now marks his grave.

The captors had to travel with great secrecy, lest the country people should rise to the rescue of Rob Roy; but with all their speed the journey of twenty miles towards the banks of the Forth occupied the whole day, so rough and roadless was the district through which they marched, down by Glenfinglas and Bochastle, through the pass of Leney and by the beautiful Braes of Callender; and many a wistful glance their unfortunate prisoner cast back to the mountains; for they looked down on his secluded home, where his wife and children dwelt, and where ere long they would be bewailing him in hopeless sorrow.

CHAPTER XXXIX.

THE FORDS OF FREW.

In his exultation at having personally made captive a prisoner so important to the State, and for whose seizure a reward had been so long offered, as a rebel, traitor, outlaw, and robber, the Duke of Montrose ordered his trumpets to play and his kettledrummers to beat, when the smoke, the steep ridge, the castled rock, and grey old walls of Stirling appeared in the distance rising amid the green and lovely valley of the Forth.

MacGregor gazed sullenly and fiercely at the distant fortress, wherein, for a brief time, he would be a prisoner, if he could not escape by the way.

They had now crossed Lanrick Mead and the green Braes of Doune, and before them lay the long snaky windings of the Forth, which the duke ordered his troopers to pass by the Fords of Frew— those deep and treacherous fords which Rob knew so well that, as history tells us, and as already related, he guided the army of Mar through them after the battle of Sheriffmuir.

As they drew near the river, the duke, for the greater security of his prisoner, ordered him to be bound anew with a horse-girth to Quartermaster James Stewart, one of the most powerful and resolute of his followers, adding, as he saw the buckle secured under his own eye,—

"And you shall keep him company thus until we have him in the care of the captain of Stirling Castle, or the goodman of the Tolbooth."

Stewart evinced some repugnance to this mode of conducting the prisoner, for the latter and he were old acquaintances, who had frequently trafficked in cattle in more peaceful and happy times.

Rob submitted in silence to this new arrangement; again the brass trumpets sounded shrilly, and the kettledrums rang, as the horse began their march towards the fords; but Rob heeded little this display of pride and triumph, for all his thoughts were elsewhere, — at the fireside of Portnellan, with his aged mother, his wife, and children.

Again a prisoner! Oh, how his brave heart yearned for them, and trembled for their future, all the more that now the faithful and unflinching MacAleister was gone.

Coll was now a man, strong, brave, and active; but had he sufficient skill or strategy to maintain with success the desperate career which his father might bequeath to him from the scaffold at Stirling?

And then there were Duncan and Hamish, with little Ronald, who was always in scrapes and turmoils, and exhibited more scars and bruises than even Greumoch, or the most veteran of the clan, what might their fate — their future be?

Their ruddy sunburnt faces, their hearty boyish voices, all came vividly to memory with the terrible question,—How were their lives to end?

By a tender succession of links in his boys, he had beheld a future life *beyond* his own; for by the natural course of events they were to see what he could never hope to see, or feel, or share in—the coming time, which they were to enjoy (or endure) when his strong hand was lying in the grave, when his sword had returned to the anvil, and when on earth he could avail them no more. But what an heritage of danger had he to bequeath them!

Then the future plans of the Jacobites (with whose success he identified the restoration of his people to their own name, and of his patrimony to himself) came before him, for he was deeply involved in their intrigues; and about the very time of this most unexpected capture he was to have met a messenger from the Marquis of Seaforth, as that noble was styled by the loyalists in Scotland— a messenger who was to precede an invasion of the Highlands from Spain.

Twilight stole over the scenery. The eagle had gone to its eyry in the rocks; the lazy cormorant and the long-legged heron had forsaken the shore, and all was silent, or nearly so, for no sound broke the stillness now, save the tramp of the horses, or at times a loud shriek that rung upon the wind, and wailed away in the distance.

It was the melancholy cry of the night-owl.

Darkness had set in when the leading files of the duke's column began with great deliberation and care to cross the Forth at Frew. Recent rains had swollen the river, which made a brawling sound at the fords, though it usually rolls silently and even somewhat sluggishly through its lovely valley, a winding course of ninety miles towards the sea.

While the centre and rear of the horsemen were halted by the margin of the river, the others crossed, half-fording and half-swimming, and thereafter scrambling up the rugged bank on the opposite side, Rob Roy began to converse in low tones with the quartermaster, James Stewart.

The grandson of the latter was some years ago an innkeeper at Loch Katrine, and a guide to tourists; and it was to his relation of this adventure that Sir Walter Scott was indebted for one of the most stirring passages in his novel, wherein, however, he designates the trooper to whom Rob was bound "Evan of the Brigglands."

Taking advantage of the darkness, the splashing, the shouting, and noise as the troopers crossed cautiously by two at a time, Rob implored Stewart, "by all the ties of old acquaintance, of common humanity, and good neighbourhood, to give him some chance of escape from an assured doom—a death of ignominy."

For some time Stewart heard him unmoved, till MacGregor began to remind him that a day of terrible vengeance would assuredly come anon, as he would leave to his sons and followers the task of destroying all who were in any way accessory to his capture and execution.

Stewart knew too well what the MacGregors were capable of attempting and performing, to hear this without alarm, or to consider it an empty threat; and to some emotions of compassion for Rob as an old friend, and a sorely wronged and oppressed man, were now added those of fear for himself and his possessions.

He made no reply; but when the voice of the duke was heard, as he called from the opposite bank to bring over the prisoner, the quartermaster guided his horse down the bank, and entered the dark stream, which, with a loud rushing sound, was flowing rapidly past.

Overhead the stars shone clearly and coldly, yet the river and its wooded banks were involved in gloom and obscurity; and when in the middle of the stream, the quartermaster reined in his horse, as if uncertain of its footing.

At that moment MacGregor felt the girth which secured them together relaxed, as the buckle was parted, and the cord which bound his wrists was cut, by the friendly hand of Stewart.

" 'Tis well," he whispered, as he pressed the latter's hand; " you will never repent the deed of to-night—never, if you live for a thousand years ! "

Slipping over the crupper of the horse, he dived into the river, and swam under its surface for some yards, till he could emerge with safety under the shade of a clump of willows, where he crept ashore, quietly and unseen, exactly as described in the splendid novel which bears his name.

On Stewart ascending the opposite bank, where the horsemen were getting into their ranks, and forming in order under Colonel Grahame, the duke instantly missed Rob Roy.

" Villain ! " he exclaimed, " where is your prisoner ? "

Stewart began to falter out something by way of explanation or excuse, when the duke, blind with rage and fury, drew a long horse-pistol from his holsters, and dealt him a blow on the head with the steel butt—a blow from the effects of which his descendant (the innkeeper) said he never recovered.

Carbines were now discharged up and down the stream, flashing in the darkness and waking the echoes of the rocks. A close search was made on both banks by troopers on horse and foot, but vainly, till day broke, for no trace could be discerned of the fugitive, who knew the country better than his pursuers, and by that time had reached in safety the hill of Vaigh-mhor, amid the rocks of which is a secret cavern, the haunt of outlaws and robbers so lately as 1750.

There he lurked in safety until nightfall, after

which he proceeded with all speed back to the banks of Loch Katrine, and reached his household at Portnellan, where his family were in despair, and where Greumoch, his future henchman, was arraying five hundred men, for the purpose of falling down into Stirlingshire to rescue or revenge him.

But now a messenger arrived who warned them that their swords were required for another purpose, a third rising in the Highlands for King James VIII., as he was named by the Scottish cavaliers.

CHAPTER XL.

SEAFORTH'S MESSENGER.

THE preceding chapters of our story will in some degree have illustrated to the reader the peculiar character, habits, and manner of the Scottish Highlanders, and have shown how different they were in many respects from their Lowland countrymen.

"The ideas and employments which their seclusion from the world rendered habitual," says General Stewart of Garth, "the familiar contemplation of the most sublime objects of nature—the habit of concentrating their affections within the narrow precincts of their own glens, or the limited circle of their own kinsmen—and the necessity of union and self-dependence in all difficulties and dangers, combined to form a peculiar and original character. A certain romantic sentiment, the offspring of deep and cherished feeling, strong attachment to country and kindred, and a consequent disdain of submission to strangers, formed the character of independence; while an habitual contempt of danger was nourished by their solitary musings, of which the honour of their clan, and a long descent from brave and warlike ancestors, formed the theme.

" Thus their exercises, their amusements, their mode of subsistence, their motives of action, their prejudices and their superstitions became characteristic, permanent, and peculiar. Firmness and decision, fertility in resources, ardour in friendship, and a generous enthusiasm were the result of such modes of life and such habits of thought. Feeling themselves separated by nature from the rest of mankind, and distinguished by their language, their habits, their manners, and their dress, they considered themselves the original possessors of the country, and regarded the Saxons of the Lowlands as strangers and intruders."

But to resume :—

The messenger who reached Portnellan was no other than Sir James Livingstone, whom Rob had encountered after the devastation of Kippen, and who had now changed sides and become a Jacobite in sheer disgust of the atrocities of the Ministry after the battle of Sheriffmuir.

From Seaforth, chief of the MacKenzies, he bore a letter to Rob Roy, stating that he intended to rise in arms for the king, and desired the aid and assistance of the Clan Alpine, when and where the bearer would inform him, as it was dangerous to commit his plans to paper.

The writer was William MacKenzie, Earl of Seaforth, whose father had been created a marquis by the exiled king.

" So, MacGregor, I have come at a fortunate time," said Sir James, as they walked in conference together by the shore of Loch Katrine; "your men I see are all in arms——"

"And prepared to do all that men can do," replied Rob; "but the Lowlands are full of troops, close up to the Highland border; now ships of war come at times even into the salt lochs of the Campbells, and so the Highlands are scarcely what they were when we were boys, Sir James."

"True; but one good battle may alter all that; and remember, Rob, that the Grampians are still the *Dorsum Britanniœ.*"

"The what?" said MacGregor, with perplexity.

"The Backbone of Britain, as they were called of old by a Scottish Kuldee."

"Seaforth refers me to you for information; where is he now?"

"At Madrid,"

"Madrid—oich; that is a long way from the Braes of Balquhidder!" said Rob, with fresh perplexity.

"At Madrid," repeated Livingstone, "where his Majesty James VIII. has been received with all the honours due to the King of Great Britain by Philip V., who is too good a monarch not to remember the claim of King James to our throne—a claim derived from Scripture, which says, 'The right of the first-born is his.'"

"But what help does the Spanish king offer the Blue Bonnets if they rise in arms?"

"Six thousand Spanish soldiers of the line, with

twelve thousand stands of arms, are to be embarked on board of ten ships of war, under the command of the Irish Duke of Ormond."

"A brave man!" exclaimed Rob; "but where are these ships and Spaniards?"

"At San Sebastian and elsewhere. This armament will sail in the early part of next year for the Western Isles, and will probably arrive while yet the Highland passes are blocked up by snow. Seaforth doubts not that you will join him, and if possible make short work with the Munroes, the Rosses, and other Whig clans, who will be sure to break into Kintail on the first tidings that the Spanish keels have passed through the Sound of Slate. With these Spanish soldiers, and with these twelve thousand stands of arms, when distributed among the loyal clans, and with the aid expected from the Welsh and Irish, we may well hope, Rob, to crush both the English and the Lowlanders; and by this day twelvemonth we may see every head wearing its own bonnet, and the elector at home in Hernhausen."

All this sounded very well to Rob, who seldom required a great incentive to attempt anything desperate, especially against Highland Whigs, such as the Rosses, Munroes, or Grants; so he pledged himself "to meet the Marquis of Seaforth in Kintail in the spring of the following year, with at least four hundred good claymores;" and after spending a few days at Portnellan, Sir James Livingstone

T

departed to visit some other Jacobite gentlemen, and seek their aid.

The Highland winter had now set in with its usual severity; the snow, which drifted deep in the passes, rendered Rob safe from all attacks at that time; so the days were occupied peacefully by his people in attending to their cattle, hunting deer, and collecting fuel: the evenings were spent with the harp and pipe, with sword play, or practice with the target and claymore, in dancing and athletic exercises; till the spring days came, and the ice began to melt in the deep lochs, and the snow to dissolve in runnels of water down the steep slopes of the mountains.

"The three Faoilteach have been as bad as the worst days of winter," said Rob, as he looked over the vast extent of hill and glen that lay round his home; "so, please God, we shall have fair spring weather, Helen, to meet Lord Seaforth in Kintail na Bogh."

It is a belief in the Highlands that if the *faoilteach*, three days which January borrowed from February by the bribe of three young lambs, prove fair and pleasant, there will be bad and stormy weather throughout the ensuing year.

"I would you were safely back from Kintail," said Helen; "for danger, it may be death, are before you, Rob. Does not Paul Crubach say that he has had visions of grey warriors riding along the steepest cliffs of Craigrostan and Benvenue, where mortal horseman never rode, nor living horse could keep its footing?"

"Likely enough, good wife; for poor Paul sees that which others never see," said Rob, laughing.

And now on the 1st day of April, 1719, came a messenger from Sir James Livingstone, to state that the Spanish fleet had sailed for the Hebrides, and directing Rob to march for Glensheil with all the loyal and discontented Highlanders he could collect, and to halt near the head of Loch Hourn, till the Spaniards arrived.

"These Spaniards come from a land of wine and oranges," said Helen; "how will our long kail and oat cakes agree with their dainty stomachs?"

"Better than English bullets, Helen," said Rob.

When he departed with his followers from Port-nellan he took with him the little English boy, Harry Huske, for he doubted not that after falling down into the Lowlands, or even before that time came to pass, there would be many encounters with the Government troops, and an opportunity must occur for restoring him to his father the major.

Helen MacGregor had become deeply attached to the child, who had many pretty and winning ways; thus she wept bitterly when he was taken from her, and is said to have repeated the ominous words of her former prediction, " that the boy was too fair and beautiful to find a place on earth."

Secretly though the messengers of Livingstone were despatched, the Government were on the alert, and had their troops in the field nearly as soon as the Jacobites, for so great was the terror in England of this Spanish invasion, that aid was sought as usual from Holland; and already six thousand Dutch infantry, with a great body of British troops, were on the march for Scotland.

At that period, the fighting force of the Highlands consisted of at least fifty thousand men; but so divided were the clans among themselves, that seldom more than five thousand men at a time came forth in any of the insurrections for the House of Stuart.

CHAPTER XLI.

ROB'S MARCH TO GLENSHEIL.

ON this occasion Rob Roy had four hundred men with him, having left the rest at home under Coll and Red Alaster MacGregor, with orders to keep the pass of Loch Ard against any soldiers whom General Carpenter might send by that route to plunder or destroy.

It was on a lovely day in April when the Mac-Gregors, after a march of more than eighty miles north-west across the mountains from Loch Katrine, guided by a wandering harper named Gillian Ross, from the Isle of the Pigmies, after skirting the vast waste of the braes of Rannoch and the hills of Glenorchy—by ascending the Devil's Staircase, and from thence, passing by the base of the snow-clad Ben Nevis, whose summit was hidden in masses of grey vapour, by Corpach (or the vale of the corpses), by Glen Arkaig and the head of Loch Hourn, halted on the hills of Glensheil, in sight of the dim and distant peaks of the Isle of Skye, and the waves of the Atlantic.

Along the base of the dark mountains which there start abruptly, like masses of blue rock, from the deep salt lochs of the west, wreaths of grey smoke were curling on the wind. These were from the fires of the busy burners of kelp—a manufacture the abolition of which, by the Parliament of 1823, brought ruin and famine upon the poor peasantry of Argyle and Ross.

The weather was mild and warm, though tempered by the breeze from the ocean. The MacGregors encamped on the sheltered side of a mountain slope; a stray cow or so, and the deer of the glens, supplied them with food, which they cooked in the old Scottish fashion, by boiling the flesh in its own skin, or broiling it in fires formed of roots from a morass, or dry branches from the nearest forest.

Every man carried his own oatmeal and hunting-bottle of usquebaugh; and other incumbrance or baggage they had none, save their arms and ammunition.

Little Harry Huske had become hardy now, and slept as snugly in the neuk of Rob's or Greumoch's plaid, as when at home in Portnellan, though he sometimes wept for his mother, as he had learned to call Helen MacGregor.

The third day had been passed on the mountains thus, when a gentleman in tartan trews, with a laced coat and periwig, was seen approaching the camp, mounted on a strong Highland garron.

He and his followers (he had four armed men with him, clad in Highland dresses of the MacKenzie tartan) wore in their bonnets the white cockade, the forbidden badge of the House of Stuart; consequently they were received with acclamations by the MacGregors, though one of the visitors was no other than the redoubtable Duncan nan Creagh, now somewhat bent and older than when we first introduced him to the reader, but active, fierce, and resolute as ever.

On this occasion he acted as guide to Sir James Livingstone, the mounted man in trews.

"Welcome, Sir James," said Rob Roy; "I trust you bring us good tidings of the king and his adherents."

"Would to heaven I could do so," replied the baronet, with unconcealed dejection.

"How?" asked the other, with alarm.

"The fleet, with all the Spanish troops and munitions of war, set sail from San Sebastian for Scotland; but Heaven itself seems against this most unlucky House of Stuart."

"Sir James Livingstone!"

"It is so; for Fortune and the elements are alike their enemies!" exclaimed the other, bitterly.

"Speak quickly, Sir James," said MacGregor, stamping his foot on the heather; "I am in no mode either for parables or riddles, after marching all this distance, and leaving my family and my country all but open to the enemy; and I know the tricks that Montrose and Killearn are capable of playing me. The fleet, you say, has sailed?"

"But encountered a dreadful gale off Cape Finisterre——"

"I know not where that may be."

"'Tis a headland off the coast of Brittany—where, it matters not; but the storm lasted two entire days, and drove the armament back, dismasted and battered, to the Spanish coast, thus disconcerting all the plans of the Duke of Ormond and the friendly schemes of Philip V."

"Then we have marched here in vain!"

Sir James nodded his head sadly in assent.

"Has not a single vessel reached the Western Isles?"

"Yes; two frigates — only two — under the Spanish flag are now anchored at Stornoway, in the Lewis, where they have landed the Marquis of Tullybardine——"

"Tullybardine!" repeated Rob, with knitted brow. "I remember him, a fair-haired youth, at the castle of Blair, when his father, Duke John of Athole, laid a black snare for me."

"Think not of that now, MacGregor," said Livingstone, earnestly; "he is young and brave, and steadfast to our king."

"Who more?"

"The Lords Seaforth and Marischal, with some arms."

"How many?"

"Two thousand stands of muskets, and five thousand pistols. And there are three hundred Spanish soldiers."

"Any money?" asked Rob, quickly.

"Yes, some treasure in care of Don José de Santarem, a Knight of Malta."

"Dioul!" said Rob, waving his bonnet; "matters are not so bad after all. We are in for it now, and must play out the game. We cannot disperse without fighting somebody, were it but to save from distress the strangers who have come so far to serve our exiled king."

"Yes," added Sir James, bitterly; "and we have to save our own necks from the gallows."

"Are we to seize birlinns, and cross to the Lewis ? "

"No. In a few days Seaforth will unfurl the Caberfeidh,* and come hither with all his men; and to you his wishes are, that you shall keep the pass of Strachells against all who approach it from the east or south until he arrives in Glensheil. The Rosses and Munroes are already in arms for the elector."

"Let us cut the traitors to pieces," said Rob, " and then the loyal and the timid alike will join us from all quarters."

In obedience to his instructions, Rob marched to the narrow pass which is in the highest part of the disrict of Glensheil, or *sheilig* (the Vale of Hunting), that lies between the great forests of Seaforth and Glengarry; but so long were the delays that the

* A famous banner of the MacKenzies.

snow had disappeared from the loftiest mountains, and the swallow and cuckoo had come to the woods of evergreen pine and feathery birch, ere the Spanish soldiers with the MacKenzies and the wild MacRaes reached the camp of the MacGregors.

Leaving Stornoway, in the Isle of Lewis, they crossed to the mainland, and fortifying the mouth of Loch Duich, took possession of Eilan Donan, a castle of the MacKenzies, and placed cannon on it.

Meanwhile, General Joseph Wightman, an active and resolute officer, was pushing on through the mountains from Inverness with a mixed force, consisting of several companies of the 11th, 14th, and 15th Regiments (then known respectively as Montague's Devonshire, Clayton's Bedfordshire, and Harrison's Yorkshire), and two thousand Dutch auxiliaries, with whom also came the Rosses, the Munroes, and other clans who adhered to the House of Guelph.

Huske was the brigade-major.

CHAPTER XLII.

A STRANGE MEETING.

MARCHING with all speed by paths that were wild and rugged, the old Fingalian war-paths, or tracks by which the cattle were driven, on the 9th of June the troops of General Wightman came within ten miles of the camp of Seaforth, when a halt was ordered just as the sun was setting amid that solemn scenery, where a deep and secluded arm of the sea penetrates among the hills of Glensheil.

"Major Huske," said General Wightman, as the wearied troops piled their arms, posted sentinels, and prepared to cook some venison which had been shot for them by the Munroes of Culcairn, "with an officer and a hundred men of Montague's as an advanced guard, or rather as an outlying picket, you will march one mile further on, and see them properly posted. Reconnoitre well before you halt, and if aught can be seen of the enemy send back a messenger to me."

"For further instructions?"

"Yes. Look well about you; for the notorious and desperate outlaw, Robert MacGregor, or Campbell, who has been in arms against the Government ever since the Revolution, is among these rebels, and may give us more trouble with twelve men than Lord Seaforth could with so many hundreds."

" Rob Roy ! " exclaimed Huske, starting.

" Egad, yes ; Rob himself," said the general, dismounting. " You seem surprised, major. Did he give you so great a fright when he beat up your quarters at Inversnaid ? "

" Do not mistake me, General Wightman," replied Huske, with an air of severity. " It was but the start of an almost savage joy which I experienced, on hearing that I was to have again opposed to me the man to whom I owe the infliction of a terrible grief—the loss of my son Harry, my poor little motherless boy ! "

" Oh, your son—yes," said the general, in an altered voice ; " I heard that he perished unhappily—in the daring night attack on Inversnaid."

" Yes ; and I would rather that he had perished when his mother did at Landau, than in the hands of those half-naked Highland savages,"

" Landau !   Zounds, major, I remember that unfortunate affair too, for my tent was near yours, on the left of the lines.   You remember our brigade was posted near the river Zurich ? "

" But if I am spared to meet these MacGregors again I may teach this Rob Roy to feel something of the torture I now feel ; for two of his sons, I have been told, are among his followers, and if one of them fall into my hands again——"

"Well, do as you please, major, with Rob Roy and his sons; but beware of ambuscades like that into which he lured Clifford and poor Dorrington, at Aberfoyle. And now move to the front, if you please. Keep the picket under arms, and throw out a line of double sentinels towards the pass in the mountains."

In obedience to this order Major Huske marched a hundred men of Montague's Regiment to the distance of one mile from the main body, and halting them among some wild whins for conceal-ment, with orders to remain accoutred, threw forward a chain of sentinels, whom he posted in person, in such places as he thought they could best observe the approach of the enemy, and communicate with each other, or with the picket in their rear.

After this, as the night was clear and beautiful, he walked a little way beyond them, to reconnoitre and observe the country.

The scenery was wild in the extreme. On one side of a narrow inlet rose a tall cliff, where the black iolar built his nest; at its base lay the still water of the sea, where, in moonshine and sunshine alike, the round black heads of the sea-dogs (whom the Celts supposed to be fairies) were visible, as they swam to and fro, fixing their dark and melan-choly eyes on the twinkling stars or the passing boats.

On the other side of the inlet rose an ancient

barrow or burial mound, from which, as the peasantry averred, strange gleams of lustre came at
night, with sweet melodious sounds.

The place was said to be enchanted, for any
person who sat thereon and spoke aloud heard
whatever they said repeated thrice. Then it was
the fairies or the devil who replied; now it is only
the echo—the son of the lonely rock.

Huske was now nearly half a mile from his
sentinels; but in the clear summer twilight he
could see their figures distinctly, with their dark
grey coats and white leggings; and then he thought
of returning, when an armed Highlander, who had
been crouching among the heather, rose up suddenly as an apparition, to bar his way.

His round shield was braced upon his left arm,
and his drawn claymore was glittering in his right
hand.

Major Huske laid his hand on his sword, and
stepping forward a pace or two resolutely, found
himself face to face with—Rob Roy!

CHAPTER XLIII.

MAJOR HUSKE'S REVENGE.

FOR a moment Rob, who had been scouting or reconnoitring in person by the Earl of Seaforth's request, surveyed the major with evident doubt and irresolution expressed in his sunburnt face, for this was the hour when, as the Celts suppose, the spirits of evil are abroad, and when wraiths and demons of the air may assume the forms of human beings at will; while, on the other hand, Huske, to whom no such absurd idea occurred, and who had just reason to respect and fear Rob's personal strength, thrust his cocked-hat firmly upon his head, and surveyed his foe, with fury and hatred sparkling in his sombre eyes.

"So, villain!" he exclaimed, "we are fated to meet again!"

"Beware how we part, if this is to be the style of our conversation!" replied MacGregor, sternly.

"Fellow, are you so ignorant, or so stupid, as to be unaware that by uttering a shout or firing this pistol I can have you surrounded, and hanged or shot, in three minutes?"

"Then, beware, Major Huske, how you fire the shot or utter the shout; for ere you finished either, my father's sword would clatter in your breast-bone," replied the other, quietly.

" Defend yourself, then, traitor though you be ! "
said Huske, drawing a pistol from his girdle and
cocking it.

" I am no traitor," retorted MacGregor, proudly,
" for I never owned as king the German prince you
serve, but am the liegeman of James VIII., whose
enemies may God confound ! Moreover, I have no
wish to encounter you again, Major Huske — at
least, until this child, which has been long my
peculiar care, is in a place of safety." As he spoke
he pointed to a boy, who was no other than little
Harry, the child taken at Inversnaid, and who was
sound asleep on the soft heather, with Rob's tartan
plaid wrapped round him.

" Right," said Huske, hoarsely ; " my time for
retribution has come ; this child shall go before the
Highland dog his father ! "

Levelling his pistol in an instant, and before
MacGregor could interpose, the major shot the
sleeping child through the body. There was a
convulsive gasp, a shudder under the tartan plaid,
and all was over ! " Unfortunate wretch—oh, mis-
taken coward ! " exclaimed Rob Roy, in a piercing
voice. " Major Huske, by Heaven and St. Mary,
you have destroyed *your own son !*"

" How—how ? " cried Huske, wildly ; for the
solemn and excited manner of MacGregor impressed him with a terrible conviction of truth ;
" my son, say you—my son ?"

" I have spoken but too truly," said the Highlander, while, heedless of what Huske might do with sword or pistol, he knelt, with a sob in his throat, and unfolding the bloody plaid, showed to the horror-stricken officer the dead body of a little golden-haired boy, whose features he could not fail to recognize.

He covered his face with his hands, exclaiming—

"Oh, MacGregor, what dreadful deed is this I have done?"

There was a long pause, and then Rob said—

"My people found your son asleep in his little bed at Inversnaid, and carefully preserved him until such time as he could be restored to you, his father, or friends. Hunted and proscribed as we are, treated by such as you like wolves or other wild beasts, a hundred difficulties were in the way of having the child thus restored; and the poor little fellow learned to love us, to be the playmate of my children, the sharer of our humble hearth and frugal board, while my good and gentle wife, who knew that the boy was motherless, nurtured him tenderly. Being certain that you would be with the army sent against Seaforth and the Spaniards, I brought hither the child that we might restore him, in the hope that for the good deed we had done you might allow, as we say in Scotland, bygones between us to be bygones; but, alas! this is the restoration that Helen's heart foreboded!"

"How, Macgregor?"

"When she predicted so often that the child was

U

too sweet in temper and too fair in form to find a place on earth; and now, woe worth the hour! he has been sent by his father's hand to Heaven, from whence he came!"

When MacGregor ceased, Huske had cast himself on his knees among the heather, cowering down, in wretchedness, with his face buried in his hands, and sobbing heavily; while the former covered up the little body, tenderly and gently, in his plaid, lest the sight of its blood should too much shock the murderer.

"Go, Major Huske,—return to your men," said he, laying a hand kindly on the shoulder of the officer; "my hand can never inflict on you a deeper wound than your own has done. From my soul I pity you! When seeking to wrong me—wrong me cruelly and foully—you have destroyed your fair little boy, whom I was learning to love as if he had been my own; but," added Rob, taking off his bonnet and pointing upward, "his pure spirit is among the flowers that the angels will gather at the foot of His throne who is above us."

"Oh, MacGregor," groaned Huske, "end, I pray you, my existence!"

"That I may not do; and I pray you to avoid me when next we meet."

"Where?" asked Huske, incoherently.

"Where the angel of death is hovering—on the hills of Glensheil," replied Rob Roy, as he sprang up some rocks that were close by and disappeared;

for at that moment an officer named Captain Dawnes, who had heard the explosion of the pistol, came hurriedly up with some twenty men of the picket, all with their bayonets fixed.

CHAPTER XLIV.

THE BATTLE OF GLENSHEIL.

By sunrise on the 10th of June, the shrill pipes playing "Tulloch Ard" (the gathering and war-cry of the MacKenzies) rang in Glensheil, the dwelling place of the wild MacRaes, as the British redcoats, and the Dutch in yellow uniforms, were seen to enter that beautiful valley, which is fifteen miles in length, forming line by regiments as they advanced into the open space.

The Marquises of Seaforth and Tullybardine, as the loyalists termed both, with Rob Roy, took up a position at the narrow pass of Strachells, the highest part of Glensheil. With them was an expatriated chieftain, Campbell of Glendaruail—a place which means the Vale of Red Blood, where Magnus, King of Norway, perished with his army in defeat.

The first troops that appeared were Harrison's

u 2

Foot, a wing of the 15th Regiment, which thirty years before fought against Viscount Dundee at the battle of Killycrankie. They had philemot yellow facings, and coats elaborately laced with white braid.

On their left were some of the clans who were adverse to the House of Stuart, the Munroes in gay scarlet tartans, the Rosses, Sutherlands, and others, whose appearance in the ranks of the enemy filled the insurgent Highlanders with rage; and in front of the Rosses marched a tall grey-bearded harper, playing on his harp. This was Gillian Ross, who had guided the MacGregors to Glensheil; and Rob Roy vowed, if he came within arm's length of him, to " tear his chords asunder."

The other corps came up in succession, and gradually formed across the valley, the Grenadiers marching in front of the line, with their pouches open and fuses lighted.

General Wightman, a Dutch colonel named Van Rasmusson, and Major Huske alone were mounted.

Seaforth's men, including the MacRaes, under Duncan nan Creagh, were about a thousand strong, and all armed in the usual Highland fashion. On their left were six companies of Spanish Infantry under Colonel Don Alonzo de Santarem, and his brother Don José, a Knight of Malta. A quarter of a mile eastward on their left flank were posted the MacGregors under Rob Roy, whose orders were to make an attack upon the enemy in flank.

On perceiving how the insurgents were posted, and that they had formed a breastwork (which still remains) to protect the pass, Wightman sent forward a line of skirmishers, who were completely exposed to the long muskets and deadly aim of the Highland marksmen. Thus, during the sharp-shooting only one MacKenzie fell, while Huske's horse was shot under him, and many soldiers of the line were killed and wounded.

Here the clan of Munro, becoming impatient, made a rush forward, but were driven back by the MacKenzies and Spaniards, and their leader, George Munro of Culcairn, fell severely wounded. As the Spaniards continued to fire at or over him, while he lay on the ground, he said to his servant, who was also his foster-brother, and who lingered affectionately beside him,—

" Retire; leave me to my fate; but say to my father that I died here with honour, and as became the race we spring from."

"Never," replied the other, bursting into tears; "how can you suppose that I would forsake you now? No, no, George Munro; I will save you if I can, or remain and die with you!"

He then spread himself and his plaid over the body of Culcairn, to interrupt the balls of the Spaniards, and received several severe wounds before they were both rescued and dragged off the field by a sergeant of the Munroes, who had sworn upon his dirk—the Holy Iron—to accomplish the deliverance of his leader.

Prior to this, the MacGregors had been—*repulsed!*

"Rob Roy," says the new statistical account of Scotland, "acted with more zeal than judgment by attacking the *rear* of the enemy, before their front became engaged."

On seeing the steady array of red and yellow uniforms advancing, the impetuosity of his men could no longer be restrained by the same rules of discipline which ordered Don Alonzo and his six companies of Spaniards.

"Strike up, Alpine!" cried Rob to his piper; "fall on, my lads, and cleave them down as a boy would cleave the thistles!"

Then in the usual Highland fashion, the whole tribe came down like a living flood upon the foe, with their uplifted swords flashing in the sunshine. An officer thus describes the *fine* motions of a Highlander when charging:—"His first motion when descending to battle was to place his bonnet firmly on his head by an emphatic *scrug;* his second, to cast off his plaid; his third, to incline his body horizontally forward, cover it with his target, rush to within fifty paces of the enemy's line, discharge and drop his fusee or rifle; his fourth, to dart within twelve paces, discharge and fling his iron-stocked pistols at the foeman's head; his fifth, to draw claymore and at him!"

The MacGregors wheeled round in a half circle, fired their muskets and pistols, and then fell on the rear of the Dutch and 15th, who faced about and received them on their bayonets, while some companies of the second line opened an oblique fire which drove them back in rout and confusion; not, however, until Rob had actually his hand upon a regimental colour, after which, closing up hand to hand with the Dutch colonel, Van Rasmusson, he unhorsed and slew him. Dawnes, a captain of the 15th, came rushing to the rescue of the Dutchman; but a pistol-shot broke the blade of his sword near the hilt just as Rob was closing on him.

"Pass on," said MacGregor, nobly, as he saluted with his sword the defenceless officer, who almost immediately after was killed by a stray bullet.

Driven up the hill in confusion and rage, the MacGregors now joined the MacKenzies and Mac-Raes in defence of the pass; but previous to this, a young clansman named Eoin MacPhadrig (John, son of Patrick MacGregor) rushed back furiously among the Dutch like a tiger, and slew five of them before he was bayoneted and killed. With a thousand reverberations the steep hills echoed the reports of the firearms, the cries of the wounded, and the cheers of the combatants, as the lines drew closer.

General Wightman now recalled his skirmishers, and ordered the Grenadiers to advance. They did so, blowing their matches and throwing their hand-grenades as fast as possible. By the bursting of these, several Highlanders were wounded, and Lord Seaforth fell severely injured by a splinter, while to add still more to the confusion and sufferings of the wounded, the heather, which was dry as tinder, soft, and deeply rooted, caught fire by these explosions, and now sheets of flame rolled up the mountain sides, with clouds of murky smoke.

Under cover of this the British and Dutch infantry made no less than *three* desperate attacks upon the insurgents, but were repulsed, and, after a three hours' engagement, these combined forces had to retire, leaving the Highlanders in complete possession of the pass, where, according to Wightman's despatch, lay one hundred and forty-two of his soldiers, killed and wounded.*

Next day, seeing the utter futility of further resistance, Don Alonzo, whose Spaniards were naturally cold and indifferent to the cause, and who had suffered in the conflict, surrendered the survivors, two hundred and seventy-four in number, to Major Huske, as prisoners of war.

On this the MacKenzies and MacRaes dispersed to places where none could follow them ; and Wightman began his retreat for Edinburgh, a march of more than a hundred and fifty miles.

The Marquis of Tullybardine, the Earls Marischal and Seaforth, and Sir James Livingstone, after long

* Captain Dawnes and two lieutenants of the 15th were killed ; Captains Moore and Heighington of the 14th were wounded ; Culcairn's thigh was broken.

concealment, and though £2,000 were offered for each of their heads, escaped and reached the Continent in safety; and thus ended, says Salmon, "this mighty Spanish invasion, which had so much alarmed the three kingdoms." Traces of this conflict are still to be seen. Gun-barrels and bullets are found in the valley, and especially behind the manse of Glensheil, where the Spaniards, before surrendering, blew up their magazine; and there is yet shown the green grave of the Dutch colonel, Van Rasmusson, who fell by the hand of Rob Roy, near the small cascade which flows into the glen.

CHAPTER XLV.

THE KNIGHT OF MALTA.

ROB ROY and his followers being now left to themselves by the sudden dispersion of the MacKenzies and MacRaes, while the Rosses, Munroes, and others were still in arms against them, and while General Wightman's troops, though retreating, covered the main roads that led to the Perthshire highlands, were thus compelled to linger near the shore of Loch Duich and in the castle of Eilan Donan for a few days ere they could set out on their return home.

In the historical account of Rob Roy and his clan, we are told briefly, that after Glensheil, "he and his party plundered a Spanish ship, after it had been in possession of the English, which so enriched him that he went to the braes of Balquhidder, and began farming."

The details of this affair are as follows :—

On the night after the battle, Rob, on learning that Duncan nan Creagh and other MacRaes were wandering over the field, dirking and plundering the wounded, went there to drive them off, and to save as many as possible of the poor fellows.

The early June morning dawned brightly in the dewy glen, which was dotted thickly with red and yellow coats, among whom lay nearly thirty Spaniards; and Rob saw with regret the body of Captain Dawnes; it presented a deplorable spectacle, for both his eyes were shot out, and his face was a mass of blood.

Near him was a Spanish officer, seated half upright against a large stone; his dark-olive face was pale, ghastly, and sorrowful. As Rob approached, he raised his head, and opened his black and now lacklustre eyes with a vacant stare, as if the poor fellow sought to assure himself that blindness and death had not yet come upon him. His uniform was blue, richly laced with silver, and on his left breast was the gold and eight-pointed cross of Malta. He had received two bullet wounds in the body, and appeared to be sinking fast.

As Rob Roy, like most of the loyal Highlanders, was perhaps more a Catholic than a Protestant, the cross upon the breast of the dying Spaniard excited his interest, and stooping down, he asked in English if he could assist him.

"*Aqua—aqua!*" (water—water!) muttered the sufferer, hoarsely, and then added in good English, "Water, for the love of Heaven!"

"Run to the linn, Greumoch, and fill your quaich," said Rob, raising the sufferer against his knee; "our forefathers lie under the shadow of the old cross on Inchcailloch, and they died believing in it as the sign of redemption unto men, so it would ill become us to neglect the stranger, who, with the cross on his breast, dies here for King James VIII. Quick, Greumoch, dash in some whisky too—it comes not amiss to the Saxons, and won't to the Spaniards!"

As soon as it was brought, he applied the quaich of cool spring water and usquebaugh to the parched lips of the wounded officer, whose tongue seemed to have become baked and hard by loss of blood and a night of agony.

Rob now proposed to have his wounds looked to and the blood stanched; but there were no surgeons near, and the Spaniard shook his head sadly, as if to indicate that their efforts were useless, and his eyes dilated wildly when Greumoch approached him with a bunch of wild nettles, the old Highland panacea for all manner of cuts, stabs, and slashes.

Then the Spanish cavalier smiled sadly, for he knew that he was mortally wounded, and felt death in his heart.

"What is your name—your rank?" asked Rob, kindly.

"I am Don José de Santarem, a Knight of Malta."

"A relation of the Spanish colonel?"

"I am his brother; but Alonzo has left me to my fate."

"Upbraid him not," said Rob; "he has been sorely pressed by the men of Culcairn and Morar Chattu, and is far down the glen by this time."

Had Rob said that he was "sorely pressed by the Medes and Persians," it would have been quite as intelligible to the Spaniard, who said,—"Senor Escosse, could you get me a priest?"

"A priest!" reiterated Rob, with perplexity.

"That I may confess me before I die."

MacGregor shook his head. "The priests are all banished or in their graves," said he; "the faith of our forefathers is proscribed here now—even as the Clan Alpine are proscribed by the Parliament and paper courts of the Lowlanders."

"No priests?" sighed the Spaniard, with a start.

"Not one," said Rob, on which Greumoch, who knew a little English, whispered,—

"Maybe Paul Crubach might do—he was mighty near being a priest once."

"No—no," said Rob. "Yet there is the parish minister of Glensheil."

But the Spaniard shook his head with disdain, and the blood spirted anew from his wounds.

"My forefathers lie buried in the chapel of our old castle at Quebara, in Alava—each under marble, with helmet, sword, and gloves of steel above his tomb; but I, a brother of St. John of Malta, must lie here among heretics, and, it may be, in earth that is unconsecrated otherwise than by the blessed dew of heaven!"

"Nay," said Rob, earnestly; "this shall not be! You are dying, my brave man—I can see death in your face, for I have seen it in the faces of too many not to know it now; but I swear that you shall lie in consecrated earth."

"Swear this to me!" gasped the Spaniard, writhing his body towards the speaker, whose hand he grasped convulsively.

"I swear it!" said Rob, pressing his dirk to his lips.

"You vow on your steel, as we do in my country," said the Spaniard, while his eyes sparkled with an unwonted light; "listen to me—I will reward you, if I can."

"I seek no reward," said Rob Roy; "you are a Spaniard who came hither to fight for our king, and against those lumbering louts, the Dutch, who came from King William's country—bodachs, who know not a stag's horn from a steer's stump, as the saying is."

"Alas! (*ay de mi!*) how little I thought to die in this wild land," said the Spaniard, closing his eyes, while his voice became more and more husky; "but draw nearer; keep your oath, and I shall reward you. I had charge of our treasure chest; it contains three thousand pistoles of Madrid and Malaga."

"And where is this chest?" whispered Rob, very naturally becoming more interested.

"It is on board a small galley or launch—which —which lies wedged——"

"Where—where?" asked MacGregor; for the Spaniard's voice and powers were failing fast.

" Wedged among the rocks, near where we formed a battery—"

" At'the mouth of Loch Duich ? "

"I know not how you name it—but 'tis there —there ! "

" Good ; speak on."

" Three British ships of war are hovering off the coast, and that treasure will become their prize, if you do not anticipate them. The pistoles are—are —are in a coffer marked with the cross of Malta." After this, the poor Spaniard relinquished his English, which was very broken, and began to talk and pray incoherently in Spanish and Latin, till gradually he became insensible, and in less than an hour had ceased to exist.

Rob Roy kept his word, and as soon as Don José was dead, he wrapped him up in a plaid, and conveyed him, with Alpine playing a lament in front, to Killduich, and there buried him at the east end of that ancient church, in a grave over which he placed a rough wooden cross, and above which all his followers fired thrice their muskets and pistols in the air.

That the Colonel Don Alonzo de Santarem did not endeavour to secure the military chest before surrendering to General Wightman, was probably because he was menaced by the Clans of Ross and Munro, who hovered between him and the sea, and by threatening his little camp, ultimately enforced his capitulation.

Rob now instantly seized boats, and with half his followers departed in search of what he termed, "the Spaniard's legacy;" while Greumoch, with the rest, occupied the castle of Eilan Donan, to await his return. It was evening now. After a long and careful search—a search which a dense fog impeded — in a sequestered creek of Loch Duich, the MacGregors found the craft they sought, partly jammed upon a reef. She appeared to be the large, half-decked launch of one of the Spanish frigates, both of which had now put to sea and disappeared. She lay in a deep chasm of the wild rocks, at the base of a steep mountain, the sides of which had been bared and rent by the *scriddans* of a thousand years—for so the natives term those water-torrents which at times hurl down gravel and massive stones, in vast heaps, to desolate the fields, the shore, or whatever may lie at the foot of these rugged hills in Kintail and Glensheil.

Here dense green ivy covered the brows of the chasm that beetled over the sea, and under it the hawks, the wild pigeons, and the sea-birds built their nests. Lower down were holes and fissures, in which the crabs and lobsters lurked, till the countrywomen came in boats to drag them out with old corn sickles, or other iron instruments, and by their songs and voices to scare the sea-dogs from the ledges, where they lay basking in the sunshine.

The launch was mounted with pateraroes, but

how she came to be in such a situation we have no means of knowing; her crew, which consisted of some thirty Spanish seamen, though all well armed, jumped out of her, and fled up the rocks on the appearance of the MacGregors, as they knew not whether they were friends or foes, and were scared by their singular costume and bare limbs.

This craft, which was undoubtedly the launch of one of the frigates (that is, a boat of the largest size, for carrying great weight), had a kind of half-deck forward; and under the hatch of this, which was well secured by locks, bars, and iron bands, Rob had no doubt the money lay. Just as he and a number of his followers sprang on board, a shout from some of them who were higher up on the rocks drew his attention to seaward.

The fog had risen now, like the lower end of a thick grey curtain, showing the offing of Loch Alsh sparkling in silver ripples under the rising moon, and there, creeping along the shore, were three British frigates—doubtless the three of which the dying Spaniard had spoken—under easy sail, with their topsails, white as snow, glittering in the silvery sheen, though darkness yet obscured their lower sails and hulls.

Right before the wind they had been standing up Loch Alsh, and slightly altering their course, were now penetrating that branch of it which is named Loch Duich.

x

CHAPTER XLVI.

EILAN DONAN.

SAILING up Loch Duich, favoured by the fog, they had approached unseen to within a mile of where the Spanish launch lay in the creek, and midway between were three large armed boats, full of seamen and marines, pulling in shoreward with long and easy strokes. Up, up went the fog from the bosom of the brightening lake,—up the steep slopes of the dark mountains; and now the full splendour of the moon shone along the deep and narrow arm of the Atlantic, showing the bayonets, cutlasses, and broad-bladed oars, as they flashed and glittered in her silver rays. These vessels were the *Mermaid*, the *Dover*, and the *Stirling Castle*, three thirty-gun ships or fourth-rates. The latter was one of the old Scottish fleet amalgamated with the English at the union, when Scotland had a complete set of frigates named after her royal palaces and castles.

The sudden appearance and close proximity of their approaching foes somewhat disconcerted even the MacGregors; but Rob, who was full of strategy, formed his plans in a moment.

"Dioul!" said he; "to have this prize—the

Spaniard's legacy—torn out of our teeth at this moment will never do! We must draw the attention of these Sassenachs to another point."

"How—how?" asked his followers.

"By firing on them."

"But they are beyond range!"

"Never mind," said Rob; "they will soon be within it."

"Your plan—your plan?" asked some, with anxiety.

He sent twenty of his best marksmen with all speed to a point of rock about a quarter of a mile above where the launch lay, with orders to lure the enemy along the shore.

"Away, lads," said he, "and join us at Eilan Donan."

Running with the speed of hares, the MacGregors scampered over the rocks, loading their long Spanish guns as they went, and on gaining the place indicated, crouched among the whins and heather, from whence they opened a fire on the boats, which were barely yet within range of the firearms then in use. Flash, flash, flash, went the muskets redly out of the dark obscurity along the rocky shore, and a thousand echoes repeated the reports.

The challenge was soon accepted. A cheer rang across the shining lake from the man-of-war boats, and with fresh energy the oarsmen bent them to the task of rowing. Ere long the marines and small-arm men began to reply with their muskets; but they never hit one of the MacGregors, who were protected and concealed by bushes, boulder-stones, and ridges of rock; while the crowded boats presented a large mark for their muskets, which they could level steadily over the objects which protected them.

Leaping from rock to rock and from bush to bush, stooping down to reload, and starting up to fire, the MacGregors lured the boats' crews for nearly two miles up the loch in search of a landing-place, and then left them; for the whole twenty marksmen, with a shout of defiance and derision, plunged down a dark ravine, and took their way leisurely to Eilan Donan, without one of them being injured, while, on the other side, several unfortunate fellows were killed and wounded in the baffled boats of the frigates.

In the meantime Rob Roy was not idle on board the launch.

The hatch of the foredeck was soon burst open, and the black coffer described by the knight of Malta as being the military chest of the Spanish expedition — at least, of that portion which his brother commanded—was found. It was speedily forced, and there, in canvas bags, were found the heavy gold pistoles of Madrid and Malaga, each of which was worth sixteen shillings and ninepence sterling.

While the firing between the marksmen and the boats' crews was proceeding briskly, but receding up the loch, and while the frigates with their starboard tacks on board, crept closer and closer in shore, till Rob could hear the voice of the leadsman in the forechains of each as they sounded constantly in these, to them, almost unknown waters, he and his men were filling their dorlachs, or haversacks, with the treasure, after which they eat and drank all the provisions and liquors found in the launch, chiefly a bag of biscuits and a keg of brandy.

Then, to prevent the boat from becoming a prize to any of the king's ships, he ordered her to be set on fire, which was speedily done by thrusting bundles of dry branches and tarred rope under the foredeck, where her sails were stowed, and then applying a light.

The launch burned rapidly. The glare of the conflagration and explosion of the pateraroes as they became heated, soon attracted the attention of the boats' crews, and brought them down the loch, pulling with all their speed; but ere they reached the creek there remained only a heap of charred and smouldering wood, with the brass swivels or pateraroes, lying among it. By this time Rob Roy and his men had crossed the intervening hills, and were far on their way to Lord Seaforth's castle of Eilan Donan.

They soon reached this fine old fortress, which had been built by Alexander III. to protect Loch Duich from the Danes, and of which he made Colin Fitzgerald (a brave Irishman, who served under his banner at the victory of Largs) the first constable,

in the year 1263. It consisted of a square keep, the
walls of which measured four feet thick. It was
surrounded by an outer rampart, and by water at
full tide. Eilan Donan was a place of great strength,
and the keep was lofty and spacious. The oldest
parishioner (in 1793) remembered to have seen
Duncan nan Creagh and other Kintail men under
arms on its leaden roof, and dancing there merrily,
ere they marched to the battle of Sheriffmuir, from
whence few of them ever returned.

Here Rob Roy and the MacGregors took up their
quarters. Roaring fires were lighted in the great
kitchen, and a couple of deer were soon roasting
and sputtering on the spits, while ale and usquebaugh went joyously round in quaichs, cups, and
long blackjacks in the hall, where the spoil—the
treasure of the Spanish launch—was fairly portioned
out, every man sharing alike, while a large sum was
put aside for old and poor folks at home, not forgetting even Paul Crubach.

In the midst of all this the boom of a distant
cannon was heard; another and another followed;
and then a tremendous crash, as a 24-pound shot
passed through the windows of the hall and tore
down a mass of masonry opposite.

All rushed to the windows or to the roof, and lo!
with their broadsides to the shore, there lay two of
the frigates, the *Mermaid*, under Commander Samuel
Goodiere, and the *Dover*, under Nicolas Robertson,
with their foreyards backed, and opened ports, from

which the red flashes of the ordnance broke incessantly, as they commenced a vigorous cannonade on Eilan Donan, which they had special orders to destroy, as a stronghold of the house of Seaforth.

"This is no place for us now, lads," said Rob, "so, ho for the march home. We have many a step between this and Balquhidder, so the sooner we depart the better."

Dislodged thus unexpectedly from Eilan Donan, to reach the mainland Rob and his hardy followers forded that portion of the isthmus which lay under water when the tide was at half ebb, and just as the clear summer twilight was brightening into day, they retired among the mountains that look down on the Sheil.

For some hours they could hear the din of the cannonade against Eilan Donan, which was so completely battered and destroyed, that little or nothing remains of it now, save its foundations, and a well in which, a few years ago, a quantity of plate and firearms was discovered. Several of the cannonballs fired on this occasion have been found from time to time by the country people, who used them as weights for the sale of butter and cheese.

Not content with the demolition of the castle, the commanders of the frigates landed their crews, and with great wantonness burned the old church of Killduich to the ground, and pillaged the poor peasantry.

This severity was not unrequitted by fate; for we learn from Shomberg's "Naval Chronology," that Captain Nicolas Robertson was soon after tried by a court-martial for keeping false musters and defrauding the Government, in whose cause he was so zealous when in the Highland lochs; and on the 4th April, 1740, Samuel Goodiere, then a captain, was hanged for the murder of his own brother on board H.M.S. *Ruby* in the Bristol Channel.

CHAPTER XLVII.

THE HARPER'S RANSOM.

TOWARDS the evening of the next day the Mac-
Gregors, on their homeward march, found themselves in the country of the Camerons, at the head
of Loch Arkeig, a long and narrow sheet of water,
lying between rugged mountains, and stretching
far away towards Glen Mhor n'Albyn, or the great
valley of Caledonia, which runs diagonally across
the kingdom from the German Sea to the Atlantic.
They bivouacked at the head of the loch, lighted a
fire, and having no enemies in the neighbourhood,
prepared to pass the night pleasantly, wrapped in
their plaids, on the soft blooming heather; but first
Rob Roy placed two sentinels on the drove road
that led to and from their halting-place, that perfect
security might not be neglected.

The summer night was clear and warm, and every
star shone brightly amid the blue ether; all was
stillness and deep silence, save where a mountain
stream, a tributary of Loch Arkeig, swept down,
now over falls and stony rapids, or among bold
impending rocks spotted with lichens and tufted
with broom, and now among pale hazel groves and
black clumps of red-stemmed pine.

The MacGregors had scarcely been here two

hours, and, weary with their march and lulled by
the hum of the hurrying stream, most of them were
fast asleep, when Rob heard his sentinels in violent
altercation with a stranger; and as the Gaelic
language is deficient neither in expletives nor male-
dictions, they were plentifully used on this occasion.
On sending Greumoch to ascertain the cause of all
this, he soon returned, with his drawn dirk gleaming in one hand, while by the other he dragged
forward a harper, in whom, by the firelight, Rob
immediately recognized Gillian Ross the Islesman,
who had acted as their guide to Glensheil.

He was a man well up in years; his hair and
flowing beard were snowy white; but his cheek was
ruddy, and his eyes had a merry twinkle which
showed that as a son of song he had led a jovial
life and a roving one, though among turbulent
clans, in a wild country and in perilous times.

His kilt and plaid were of the Ross tartan, which
is gaily striped with red, green, and blue; and his
clairsach or little Scottish harp was slung on his
back by a belt, and covered with a case of tarpaulin
or tarred canvas—probably a piece of a boat-sail.
He carried a blackthorn stick, and as his occupation
was a peaceful one, he had no weapon save a dirk,
which, like the mouth-piece of his sporan, was gaily
adorned with silver. " A spy, a spy ! " cried the
MacGregors, starting up and crowding about him
with ominous expressions in their weatherbeaten
faces.

" What is the meaning of this, thou son of the son of Alpine? " he boldly demanded of Rob, in his figurative Gaelic; " the children of the Gael should not draw their swords on each other, and still less on a son of song."

"Yet, son of song," replied Rob, drily, "you played those Rosses and Munroes, and the men of Morar Chattu, into battle against us near Dounan Diarmed* in Glenshiel—the tomb of one whom Ossian loved. Eh, what say you to that?"

" There have been cold steel and hot blood between our people," began the harper in a gentler tone.

" True; but that was in the times of old; and now the righteous cause of our king should make even the false Whigs true, and every clan unite in one."

" Even the Grahames with the Clan Alpine? " said the harper, with a cunning smile.

"Yes—even the Grahames with the Clan Alpine!" repeated Rob, stamping his foot on the heather. "I could find in my heart forgiveness for them all, would they but join the king."

" When that day comes, the lamb shall share the lair of the lion, and the cushat-dove shall seek the nest of gled and iolar," replied the harper, still smiling.

* A warrior of Fingal, whose grave lies near the manse of Glensheil. Morar Chattu is the Celtic name of the Earls of Sutherland.

" Whence come you, and where is your home ?"

" The Isle of the Pigmies, in the west—far away amid the sea," replied the harper with a sigh ; " and would, MacGregor, I were there now, where its black rocks are covered with sheets of snowy foam, where the wild sea-birds wheel and scream above the breakers, and where the level sunshine and the rolling sea go far together into its gloomy caves and weedy chasms."

The harper referred to one of the Western Isles, a little solitary place, where stand the ruins of a chapel, and where it was believed a dwarfish race were buried of old; " for many strangers digging deep into the earth have found, and do *yet* find," says Buchanan, " little round skulls and the bones of small human bodies, that do not in the least differ from the ancient reports concerning pigmies."

" I am grieved, harper, that you should die so far from your kindred and their burial-place," said Rob, gravely.

" *Die !* wherefore should I die ?" asked the harper, starting, while his countenance fell.

" Oogh ay ! " exclaimed several MacGregors, who were yawning and crowding round; " just let the bodach be hanged at once, and then we shall go to sleep again."

" Or would you prefer to be drowned ?" said Greumoch ; " Loch Arkeig is close by, and the water there is warm and deep."

"Neither is my wish," said the harper, fiercely; "I am a guiltless man, and demand my freedom!"

"Why were you in the ranks of the king's rebels at Glensheil?" asked Rob, sternly.

"I was *not* in their ranks!"

"You played them into battle."

"But I fought not—nor was I even girded with a sword."

"By my father's soul, that mattered little! A minstrel—a harper—should not play the traitor like a glaiket gilly."

"I went but to sing of the fight, that the story of it might go down to future times, even as the battles of our forefathers have come down by the songs of the bards to us. I went but as Ian Lom went with Montrose to Inverlochy. Had he fought there and fallen, who would have told us how he,

The bard of their battles, ascended the height
Where dark Inverlochy o'ershadowed the fight,
And saw the Clan Donnell resistless in might!"

"Have you so committed to song our victory at Glensheil?" asked MacGregor, with a sharp glance; but the harper hung his head. "Ha! then what sought you *here* to-night?"

"Was it to spy upon us?" added several MacGregors, with scowling brows; "answer, Islesman, while your skin is whole!"

"By the Black Stones of Iona, I swear that I

knew not you were in the land of Lochiel!" said
the harper, earnestly; "and beware how you spill
my blood, for my mother was one of the Camerons,
the sons of the Soldier of Ovi. I was peacefully
pursuing my way to the fair of Kill-chuimin."

"It may be so," said Rob Roy; "for that fair is
almost at hand. Tie him to a tree; in the morning,
I will speak with him again."

The harper submitted in silence, and was bound
to a tree, when a plaid was thrown over him and his
harp, as a protection from the dew; and Greumoch,
with a true Highland grin or grimace, gave him a
dram, saying, "As it is the last you are likely to
get, drain the quaich."

By dawn the MacGregors were all afoot again;
they wiped and rubbed their weapons to preserve
them from rust; shook the crystal dew from their
kilts and plaids; then the pipes struck up a quick
step, and they proceeded on their homeward way,
taking with them the harper, concerning whom Rob
Roy had given no instructions, for he was loth to
punish him, though deeming that he deserved to
be so.

For two days he conveyed him thus a prisoner,
telling him that if he was actually going to the fair
of Kill-chuimin (or the burial-place of the Cumins,
as the Highlanders called Fort Augustus) his time
would not be lost, as their way lay so far together.

Towards the evening of the second day, they
halted on a wild moorland waste, called Blair na

Carrahan, or the moor of the circles, for there amid the vast expanse of purple heather were several large Druidical rings, wherein, it was confidently affirmed, the fairies always danced on the Eve of St. John; but more especially around a large obelisk which stood in the centre of one, and was covered with Runic figures.

When they halted in this desolate place, the harper became alarmed, and begged so earnestly to be released, that Rob said,—

"You must ransom yourself—— "

"Ransom !—do you speak of ransom to one who has not in the world a coin the size of a herring scale ? "

"Ransom yourself by a song or a story, I was about to say. If either meet with the general approval of my kinsmen, you shall be free—free as the winds that shake the harebells and the broom on the braes of Balquhidder; but fail us in song or story, and by the Grey Stone in Glenfruin, you shall hang—hang like the false cullion I deem you ! "

Gillian Ross made a double Highland bow; the cord was taken from his wrists, and slung with a noose of very unpleasant aspect over the Druid monolith, for thereon he was to hang, if he failed to win the general applause.

The poor harper eyed it wistfully, and then seated himself on the green grass in the centre of the fairy circle, around which the MacGregors were lounging, with their arms beside them. He uncased his harp, and after running his fingers rapidly through the strings, suddenly seemed to change his intention to sing, and said he would tell them a story. A murmur of assent responded.

On that vast purple moorland, bounded in the distance by the countless dark-blue mountain peaks of Argyle, a picturesque group they formed, those weather-beaten clansmen, in their garish tartans, with their polished weapons, their round targets, and bare legs stretched upon the heather. Then there was also the green fairy circle, in the centre of which rose the grey old obelisk, and at its base reclined the bearded harper on his harp. The sun as he set beyond the western peaks crimsoned like a sheet of wine the heather of the Blair na Carrahan, and tipped with ruddy light the harper's silver beard and the glittering strings of his harp, as he told the following story, which we render here, not in his poetical and somewhat inflated Gaelic, but in our own way.

CHAPTER XLVIII.

MORRAR NA SHEAN, OR THE LORD OF THE VENISON.

FAR away in the north of Caithness stands the castle of Braal, on an eminence above the river Thurso. It is a vast square tower, with walls of great thickness, having the narrow stairs which lead to its various stories formed in the heart of them. A deep fosse lies on its north side, and the remains of various other ditches and outworks are traceable around it.

In the days of William I. of Scotland, surnamed *the Lion*, because he first put that emblem on his banners and seals, this castle was one of the many residences of Harold Earl of Caithness and Count of Orkney, Lord of Kirkwall, Braal, and Lochmore, who was otherwise named Morrar na Shean, or Lord of the Venison, from his passionate love of hunting and all rural sports.

Yet his character was cruel, fierce, morose, and savage; and he loved hunting chiefly because it was a means of indulging in bloodshed, slaughter, and destruction.

He brained with his axe every hound which proved faulty; and on more than one occasion, huntsmen who had erred, violated the rules of the chase, or otherwise incurred his displeasure, were tied to trees and left to be devoured by wolves. One, named Magnus of Stancland, he chained to a low rock in the sea, and left there to perish miserably by drowning as the tide rose.

Harold was a handsome and stately man, of great stature and strength. His fair hair and beard were curly and flowing; but his eyes were keen and wicked in expression, and his brows were ever knitted as if in perpetual defiance or wrath, unless at times when, gorged with food or flushed with wine, he joined in the chorus of the harpers who sang his praises at his banquets and festivals.

He could bend a stronger bow than three men could bend together. He was wont to twirl three sharp swords at once, catching each by its hilt in turn; and he could walk lightly and agilely along the oars of his great birlinn, or galley, when it was being propelled by the rowers, most of whom were Finns or Wends, whom he had captured in the Baltic and chained to its benches as slaves.

Though he gave vast sums towards the completion of the cathedral church of St. Magnus, which had been founded at Kirkwall by his predecessor, Count Rognwald of Orkney, in 1138, he was averred to be at heart an infidel; and Adam Bishop of Caithness, an amiable and gentle prelate, who frequently reproved his excesses, once said to him,—

"Earl Harold, are you a heathen or a believer?

Do you hope for the Valhalla of Odin or the Heaven of the Christians?"

" I believe in my strong arm and sharp sword," said he, haughtily. " Am I a woman or a boy, that thou, a mitred monk, shouldst question me thus? Moreover, remember that I would rather be addressed as Morrar na Shean—Lord of the Venison—than as lord of all our uncounted isles."

And from that time he hated the old bishop in his heart; so much so, that John of Harpidale, one of his chief followers, proposed to have the prelate boiled alive in the great hunting cauldron, and given in broth to their hounds.

The earl's galley had thirty benches of rowers; its prow was adorned by the head of a horse, richly gilded, and its sides and stern shone with gilding and plates of burnished brass; its sails were purple, and along its sides hung the shields of John of Harpidale, Thorolf Starkadder, and others, who were his vassals. In its prow sat twenty bearded harpers, with their harps, and to their songs the long sweeps of the rowers kept time.

Wolves are said to have followed this great war-galley along the shore, and screaming eagles, carrion crows, and other birds ventured out to sea in expectation of the banquet that awaited them; for in his quarrels and feuds with his island neighbours, Morrar na Shean carried havoc and dismay wherever he went, and frequently appropriated, without inquiry, the ships that sailed between the Baltic coasts, the Elbe, and Flanders.

Then when his galley, with its purple sails shining in the sun, and its long red streamers floating on the wind, was seen cleaving with gilded prow the stormy seas that roll round the Orcades and Thule, it spread terror, for the simple people of the isles believed it had been built by the gnomes who abode in the sea-riven caves of Cape Wrath, and that they had constructed it with such powerful spells, that whenever the sails were spread, they directed its course wherever the earl wished, without an order being issued.

On the 16th of April, 1150, the festival of St. Magnus the Martyr, John of Harpidale and Thorolf Starkadder, on feeling some unpleasant twinges of temporary compunction for their misdeeds, urged the earl to visit either Rome or Kirkwall; for so great was the sanctity of the Patron of the Isles, that the Orcadians were long wont to decide by a throw of the dice whether they should pay their devotions at the shrine of St. Peter or the Martyr of Orkney.

But Morrar na Shean laughed at them, and swore with a great oath that he would visit neither, as he had merrier work to do. Then, collecting a great train of followers, he sailed away north, up the Cattegat, to the assistance of the King of Denmark, Waldemar the Great, who had recently repaired the wall of Gotrick, subdued the pagans of Rugen, and called himself lord of all the countries northward of the Elbe.

Earl Harold was long gone, and silence and emptiness reigned in the hall and chambers of Braal; but there were peace and repose in Caithness and the Isles. The red deer roamed on the hills, unscared by the bay of hound or the blast of horn; without fear, the fishers put forth to cast their nets in Scapa Flow and the Sound of Yell, to hunt the huge whale in the sandy bays, or the tusky walrus on the seaweedy rocks; and the white-haired Bishop of Caithness began to hope that they had all seen the last of the terrible Morrar na Shean.

But lo ! one day, when the dark scud was driving fast across the northern sky, when the boiling foam rose high on every storm-beat cape and bluff, when the wild sea-fowl were flying far inland, and the hissing waves rolled white as snow over the Skerries of the Pentland Firth and the black Boars of Dungisbay Head, the well-known purple sails of the great birlinn were seen, as she came flying through the mist and spray, with her long sweeps flashing and the sheen of helmets and bucklers glittering above her bulwarks in the partial gleams of a stormy setting sun.

Then fast went the news over continent and isle that Morrar na Shean had come again, and that he had brought with him, out of the distant north, the Princess Gunhilda as his wife—the only daughter

of Waldemar, the Danish king; so many who
feared more than they loved him, crowded to see
the dame who was now to be the lady of Braal and
mother of the future Earls of Caithness and Counts
of Orkney.

With the wiry tinkle of harps, the blare of brass
trumpets and of hunting-horns, the voices of the
rowers mingling with the regular plash of the long
sweeps to which they were chained, the great galley
came into the Bay of Inver-thorsa (or the mouth of
the great river of Thor), whence Thurso takes its
name; and all the people of Caithness were crowding on the shore, as thickly as the gulls and
cormorants that cluster on the rocky Clett, which
guards the entrance of the haven.

As she stepped ashore, the grace and beauty of
the Danish princess charmed all; but she seemed
pale and sad, for she had espoused the warlike
Harold in obedience only to her father's will. Yet
they seemed a stately pair.

She wore a blue silk tunic, a long flowing mantle
of fine white cloth, adorned by ribands and tassels
of gold; a veil of rich lace flowed from under the
half-diadem which she wore above her golden
tresses in virtue of her rank as a king's daughter
and an earl's wife; and she had massive bracelets
and armlets of gold.

The fierce Harold wore his lurich, or shirt of
mail, that reached to his knees, which were bare.
It was formed of fine rings of the brightest steel.

He had long sandal-like boots of thick leather, studded with gilt knobs; and a golden serpent surmounted his helmet, which was of polished steel. His mantle was of purple silk, and hung from his shoulders by two sparkling brooches.

Massive bracelets of gold and silver were on his wrists. He carried a sword, a spear, a round shield of steel burnished like a mirror, and wore at his right side a mattacuslash, or long Scottish arm-pit dagger.

John of Harpidale, Thorolf Starkadder, and others, all similarly armed, leaped noisily ashore, with helmets and hauberks ringing, and brandished their swords in token of greeting to the people, and to express joy on treading their native soil again.

And now the gathered multitude divided like the waves of the sea to make way for an aged man who approached with a gilded pastoral staff in his hand, but whose garments were humble as those of a cowled friar. He was Adam, Bishop of Caithness, and lately Abbot of Melrose, who, preceded by his crossbearer, and followed by many ecclesiastics of his diocese, came to bless the newly-married pair.

The countess, though the daughter of a powerful king, knelt reverently and humbly to receive the old man's benison; but not so the haughty earl, who had sworn never to bow his head to mortal man, so he passed proudly on, and repaired to his castle of Braal.

On the very day after his arrival, he quitted the countess, and, accompanied by John of Harpidale, by Thorolf Starkadder, and other favourite companions, departed on one of his great hunting expeditions.

There were with him more than five hundred huntsmen, armed with bows, arrows, knives, and spears; and they had with them at least two hundred of the strong, wiry, rough-haired Scottish hounds, to scour the hills for game.

For many days the sport was carried over hill and through valley; and every night the hunters formed a camp. A fire was lighted of fuel piled up as high a house, and often the houses of the poor were unroofed for the purpose.

The glare of this great fire was visible at midnight from the mountains of Pomona and the Pentland Skerries far away out in the lonely ocean. Around it were scores of pots and kettles boiling salmon and chickens; and thereat were heathcocks, capercailzie, ptarmigan, venison, boars' hams, and partridges, being baked, broiled, roasted, or stewed; while ale, usquebaugh, and wines from Burgundy and the Flemings of Ostende were drunk by the roystering huntsmen, who often danced hand in hand round the vast roaring pyramid of flame, as their pagan sires were wont to do at the Baal-tein feasts of old, and if one by chance fell in, the fun was all the greater.

At times they would fill their cups to the brim,

and standing in a circle round Morrar na Shean, whose goblet was full of wine, of ale, and of usquebaugh mixed together, they shouted,—

" Oh ! Lord, let the world be turned upside down, that brave men may make bread out of it ! "

And then the cups were drained and, amid wild hurrahs, flung high into the air.

Morrar na Shean, though he lived in so early an age of Scottish history, was not without some skill in mechanics, for we are informed that " there was a chest or some kind of machine fixed in the mouth of the stream below the castle (of Lochmore), for catching salmon in their ingress into the loch, or their egress out of it, and that immediately on the fish being entangled in the machine, the capture was announced to the family by the ringing of a bell, which the struggles of the fish set in motion, by means of a fine cord, one end of which was attached to a bell in the middle of an upper room, and the other end to the machine in the stream below."   .

This was an ingenious fish-trap; but while the Lord of the Venison pursued his more furious sports and drunken orgies, the poor Princess Gunhilda was left in utter loneliness at the castle of Braal ; and the long nights which her husband spent in roystering among his wild followers, were passed by her, often in tears, and at the deeply arched windows of the lofty hall or of her bower chamber, watching the merry dancers, the streamers of the northern lights, which made her think of her Danish home, of her mother's farewell kiss, of the castle of Axel-huis, and the green, waving woods of Zealand.

Harold was soon weary of his wife, for her extreme gentleness tired him, and he loved her not, though he longed for a son — a little Count of Orkney—to heir his vast possessions, and in whose baby face he might see his own ferocious visage reflected.

He prayed at holy wells, and, candle in hand, he went bare-foot in sackcloth garments, with ashes on his head, to every shrine of sanctity in the Northern Isles; he sent gifts to Adam the bishop, and offerings to the altar of St. Magnus at Kirkwall, with silver lamps, rich garments, candles of perfumed wax, and jars of oil and wine; seeking in return of the prebendaries only their prayers that he might have a son; but on the Yule-day of 1153, the countess had a *daughter*, whom she named after her mother the queen, Algiva.

Morrar na Shean was furious with disappointment; he reviled Bishop Adam, and threatened to burn his cathedral, where prayers had proved of so little avail. Then for days and nights he sat drinking with John of Harpidale and Thorolf Starkadder; and thereafter ordering his great galley to be got in readiness, they put to sea, and were driven by a storm so far as Rona, a lonely isle which lies far

amid the Atlantic sea, thirty leagues westward of
the Orcades. In Rona was a little chapel, dedicated
by a chief of the isles to St. Ronan, and it was said
to be guarded by an unseen spirit; for if any person
in the island died and a shovel was placed near the
altar overnight, a grave was found ready dug in the
morning.

The place was lonely and solemn, for no sound
was ever heard there but the sough of the gusty sea-
breeze, and the mournful moan of the white waves
as they clomb the echoing rocks.

Sad and soothing as was the scene, yet in sheer
despite at being driven so far away, Morrar and his
followers ravaged this poor place, destroyed the
chapel, and slew some of the people on the adjacent
island of Suliska. But the vengeance of Heaven
pursued them; for when returning, the great galley
struck upon the Clett, a rock four hundred feet in
height, near the entrance of Thurso Bay, and many
of her crew were drowned.

Prior to this, Morrar na Shean had ceased to
address Heaven, and now appealed to the idols of
his forefathers. He visited the Temple of the Moon
in Innistore, and at midnight, with strange barbaric
rites, on his bare knees, spilt some of his blood by
the self-inflicted stab of a dagger, on the central
stone of Power.

This was a great obelisk carved with serpents,
and the jormagundr or great sea-snake, the emblem
of eternity; and with many mystic emblems and

Runic inscriptions; and there between midnight and morn, he prayed for the assistance of the Moon, of Odin, and Thor. But all this mummery was vain ; for on his return he found that the countess had given birth to *a second daughter*, whom she had named Erica; and ın the blindness of his wrath the earl struck her with his hand clenched in his steel glove, and threatened to toss the child from the windows of Braal into the Thurso.

Again with John of Harpidale, with the long-bearded Thorolf, and other roysterers, he put to sea in the great galley, and sailed into the Baltic, where they aided King Waldemar in the destruction of the famous city of Iomsberg, the stronghold of the northern pirates, whom on his return the earl imitated, for he destroyed several towns on the shores of the Baltic, and robbed the churches of their holy vessels. Then the earl sought the aid of enchanters and wizards, and passed whole nights in dark caverns and pine forests, where Druid circles stood, hoping to see elves, demons, gnomes, or fairies, but sought in vain.

He next sailed to the Isle of Rugen, where the Wends were still, in the twelfth century, unbaptized pagans, who worshipped Svantavit, the God of Light, in their capital, Arcona, which is situated on a high rock above the waves of the Baltic.

Svantavit was a monstrous idol having four heads; but he was consulted as an oracle, and the captain of every merchant ship which made a good voyage was compelled to pay tribute to the priests of his temple.

In the hands of this idol was a cornucopia, which in the first month of every year was filled with precious wine; by looking into what remained of it at Yule-tide, the chief-priest could predict peace or war, dearth or plenty for the ensuing year; and this absurd paganism existed in Rugen until the middle of the thirteenth century. Ratzo, King of the Isle, was a famous but aged warrior, who had destroyed the flourishing city of Lubeck in 1134; so to him, and to the chief-priest, the earl appealed, and laid at the foot of their hideous idol in Arcona all the plunder of the Christian churches—chalices of gold, lamps of silver, croziers studded with precious stones, and altar-cloths covered with embroidery.

The priest accepted the plunder, ascended a ladder, and peeped into the horn in the hands of the idol, where, as he averred, he could see amid the wine the figure of a little boy, with an earl's coronet on his head, and a sword in each hand. So Morrar na Shean with joy spread his purple sails upon the northern sea, and came home to find that the countess had brought into the world *a third daughter*, whom she named Thora. The earl was ready to expire with passion.

" Let us return to Arcona ! " said Thorolf Stark-adder.

" For what purpose, fool ? " asked the earl, gruffly.

" To destroy the temple of Svantavit, hang the false priest, and burn his idol."

" Nay," said Morrar na Shean, grinding his teeth. " I shall take other vengeance upon fate, for fate has conspired against me."

" How—how? " asked his followers.

" Anon, ye shall hear ! "

" Shall we not *see* ? " asked Thorolf, grimly, for he was a lover of mischief and cruelty.

" No," replied Morrar, briefly, as he gnawed his yellow moustaches in wrath.

CHAPTER XLIX.

GUILT AND REMORSE OF MORRAR NA SHEAN.

ONE evening, when twilight was closing on the land and sea; when the clouds were gathering in heavy masses that portended a storm, and when the Thurso ran hoarsely and rapidly over its stony bed beneath the castle wall, Harold commanded the countess to assume her hood and cloak, and to accompany him. "Whither?" she asked, timidly, for his manner was strange, and he was sorely flushed with wine.

"Whither, matters not; but you shall learn when we reach the place."

"Do we go on foot?" she inquired, trembling, for there was a wild glare in his eyes that terrified her.

"Yes."

"Alone—unattended?"

"Yes," he repeated, hoarsely.

Then the heart of the countess sank; but she was compelled to obey. Her husband grasped her hand, and together they quitted the castle of Braal by a private postern at the foot of a long and secret stair.

Gunhilda was silent; she pressed her ivory

crucifix to her breast with her left hand, for it
was the parting gift of Absalon, Archbishop of
Denmark; her right was firmly grasped by her
husband, and she felt that *his* hand was cold—yea,
cold as ice !

She had heard of his proceedings on the shores
of the Baltic, and how he had publicly worshipped
the God of the Wends at Rugen; her soul became
a prey to grief and horror, and beneath her veil
her tears flowed hot and fast.

He led her along the banks of the Thurso for
more than a mile, by a dark and lonely path. No
one was near them; the hour was late, the place
was solitary, and the countess gazed anxiously
about her for succour, if required; but the pastoral
hills were desolate. Even the sheep were in their
folds, and there came no sound to her ear, save the
rush of the dark and hurrying stream.

It was a night in the pleasant month of June,
and in that part of Scotland at this season there
is scarcely any darkness, the reflection of the sun
on the Atlantic being so distinctly visible for the
brief time that he is below the horizon, that
one may read the smallest print even at midnight.

As they drew near a little chapel which stood
upon a rock above the river, and was dedicated to
St. Monina, the countess gathered courage, and
said,—" Unless you say, my lord, for what purpose
you have brought me hither in this secret manner,

and at this unwonted hour, I go not one step further with you!"

"Listen," said he, drawing his long arm-pit dagger, while a cruel and wild glare came into his fierce blue eyes; "I have brought you hither to slay you!"

"Oh, my soul foreboded as much!" said Gunhilda, in a breathless voice; "to slay me—for what? What crime have I committed?"

"None; yet I will not have a wife who is to be the mother of baby-faced girls, whose husbands, if they get them, will rend and divide my heritage among them. I must have a son to heir me, as Earl of Caithness, Count of Orkney, Lord of Braal and Lochmore, and to transmit my name to future times; but thou——"

"I am the daughter of a king!" said the countess, haughtily.

"A king who is too far away to help you," said Harold, with a mocking smile.

"But not too far away to avenge me!"

"Let him do so, if he will!" replied the barbarous earl, as he grasped her wrists and dragged her shrieking, and on her knees, towards the rocks which overhung the stream.

"Oh!" she exclaimed, "my three helpless daughters—your children—think of them with pity, if not with pity for me!"

"My daughters—name them not," said he, hoarsely, "lest I have them drowned in boiling

z

water, even as Halli and Leckner were in the days of old!"

"I am not prepared to die!" she exclaimed in a piercing voice; "my sins of omission are many; oh, have mercy on me!"

"Thou art better prepared than I," said Morrar na Shean.

"At least let me say one prayer in yonder chapel ere you slay me—in pity for my sins and soul, permit me this."

"Go, then," said Morrar, grimly; "but return quickly, lest I drag you from its altar."

With tottering steps Gunhilda hurried into the little chapel; but ere three minutes had elapsed, the inexorable Morrar cried, sternly,—"Come forth!" There was no response.

"Come forth, Gunhilda, or by the Demon of the Wends I will drag thee out!"

"I come—I come," replied a voice within the vaulted oratory, from the arched windows of which a sudden light gleamed forth.

"'Tis well," said Morrar, "for my patience is nearly exhausted;" and the countess, with her head bent, and muffled in her veil, approached him from tho arched doorway, through which a broad and rosy flake of light was streaming.

Seizing her again by the arm, he dragged her to the edge of tho beetling rocks, where he meant to stab and toss her into the eddying stream, which was rushing in full flood towards the sea; but, marvellous to relate! as he tore the veil asunder, he beheld, not Gunhilda, but a strange woman whose face was of wondrous beauty, and whose head was encircled by a shining light. Then he knew in his heart that the spirit of St. Monina stood before him! The dagger fell from his hand; he closed his eyes with awe and dismay, and when he looked again the figure had melted into thin air and disappeared.

Appalled by this incident, he rushed away to the wildest part of the hills, and on being joined by Thorolf and John of Harpidale, he put to sea as usual in his galley, and departed no one knew whither.

The countess was found by her attendants in a deep but soft slumber, before the little altar of the river chapel; but immediately on her return to Braal, she took her three daughters, Algiva, Erica, and Thora, to Bishop Adam of Caithness, and besought him to conceal and protect them; and leaving them with tears and prayers, she returned to the home of her terrible husband, giving out that the children were dead.

Meanwhile the bishop, with all speed, despatched them to the court of King William the Lion, and consigned the three helpless girls to the care of the Queen Ermengarde de Beaumont.

The vision he had beheld on that night by the river Thurso long filled with terror the soul of Morrar na Shean; but after a time the impression

became fainter, and gradually he came to the conclusion that the whole affair must have been a
dream, originating most probably in his wine-cup.

He was long of returning to Braal, and solaced
himself by ravaging Heligoland and plundering
several of its towns, the sites of which have long
since been covered by the encroaching sea. He
then visited Shetland, carrying havoc and dismay
wherever he appeared, and returning by Orkney,
committed a crowning act of impiety at Kirkwall.
There was preserved there a silver bowl, in which
St. Magnus had baptized the earliest Christians of
the Orcades. It was of great size, curiously carved,
and was carefully preserved in the cathedral.*

Accompanied by his two inseparable comrades
and mentors to mischief, he entered that stately
Gothic church, which is one of the finest in Scotland,
seized the great bowl, and filled it with wine, which
he solemnly consecrated to Odin. Then, ascending
the steps of the High Altar, he quaffed it to the
dregs, after exclaiming,—

"I worship thee, Odin, and I am a heathen! A
heathen will I die, if thou givest me but a son to
heir my lands, my isles, and to send down my name
to the days of other years."

For these proceedings they were all excommuni-
cated by the Bishop of Caithness, and while they

---

* "It so far exceeds other bowls in size," says Buchanan, in
his "History of Scotland," "that it seems to be a relic of the
feasts of the Lapithœ."

laughed to scorn the prelate and his solemn ana-
thema, they swore by the blades of their swords
and the shoulders of their horses (the old oath of
the northern pagans) to have a terrible revenge
upon him.

With this intention, after six years' absence, they
returned home, and again the great war-galley,
with all its purple sails spread, was seen to
stand round the rocky bluff named the Clett,
and come to anchor in Scrabster Roads, on the
western side of Thurso Bay. On landing, the earl
repaired straight to the episcopal palace, with all
his followers, " to punish," as he said, " the bishop
with the serpent's tongue." On seeing them
approach, the old man came forth to meet them;
and on beholding his serene and reverend aspect,
John of Harpidale, Thorolf Starkadder, and other
grim outlaws, were somewhat abashed and appalled,
and leaned irresolutely on their drawn swords.

" After a six years' absence, come you here, Lord
Harold, instead of visiting your lady at Braal? "
asked the bishop, with an air of surprise that was
not unmingled with alarm.

" The countess?—you speak not of my daughters."

" Alas! they are here no longer," said the bishop,
evasively.

" Dead? " asked the earl, with a cold smile.

" To you and all of us."

" 'Tis well," said Harold, grinding his teeth;
" but I came not hither to speak of them! "

"Of what then?" asked Bishop Adam, with anxiety.

"Of thyself, who hast dared to pour empty anathemas on me, for merely drinking a bowl of wine in my own town of Kirkwall."

"Silence, thou blasphemous lord, who desecrated the altar of God by the praises of a heathen idol! I think of the coming time when thou shalt die!"

"And what then?" asked Morrar, with a fierce and mocking laugh.

"In all thy vast possessions, who shall mourn thee?"

"The greyhounds in my hall, and the birds of prey, for whom I have prepared many a banquet: yea, the black wolf and the yellow-footed eagle too shall mourn for Morrar na Shean. Priest, I have come to punish your insolence. Seize and drag him forth, Thorolf Starkadder!"

In a moment the mailed hands of Thorolf were wreathed in the white hair and reverend beard of the old bishop, who was roughly dragged through his own gate, and beaten to the earth beneath a shower of blows dealt by clenched hands and the heavy iron hilts of swords and daggers. Breathlessly, and on his knees, he implored mercy, beseeching them not to peril their souls by murder, and a sin so foul as sacrilege, by imbruing their hands in the blood of a priest; but the fury of cruelty and destruction was in their hearts. Thorolf, with his dagger, destroyed the eyesight of the poor old man; and John of Harpidale cut out his tongue.

Then procuring the large cauldron in which food was usually prepared for the staghounds of Morrar, they actually cast the blind and bleeding bishop into it, and boiled him alive.*

On hearing of these proceedings, the Countess Gunhilda fled in horror to the cathedral of Kirkwall, and took refuge with William Bishop of Orkney, with whom she resided for several years, while her daughters, under other names than their own, were growing up to womanhood at the court of Queen Ermengarde, and while her husband, the Lord of the Venison, spent his days in hunting and his nights in drinking, carousing, fighting, and outrage, with his inseparable ruffians, John of Harpidale and Thorolf Starkadder.

It was long before King William, who resided at the palace of Scone, heard the correct details of these outrages, and then his soul was filled with sorrow and indignation, for he was a gentle, wise, and valiant king.

He resolved to punish the wicked Earl of Caithness, and for this purpose two earls, named Roland and Gillechrist, were sent against him with a body of troops.

---

* The scene of this terrible outrage is still shown near the Manse of Halkirk.

Roland was the son of Uchtred, a brave lord of Galloway, who had recently defeated the King of England at Carlisle, when preparing to invade his province; and he had become the husband of Algiva, the eldest daughter of Morrar na Shean.

Gillechrist had wedded Erica, the second daughter. He was Earl of Angus, and from this marriage are descended the clan and surname of Ogilvie. By a singular coincidence these two peers were now marching against their father-in-law, with orders to subject him to the same death as that by which the unhappy bishop died.

Morrar na Shean met them in a battle which was long and bloody, though his people were cold in his cause. The men whom he had drawn from his county of Orkney and the town of Thurso ultimately gave way; and four hundred were instantly hanged on the field.

The castle of Braal, to which the survivors fled, was attacked, entered by the secret postern, and stormed. Therein, after a terrible conflict, were taken John of Harpidale and Thorolf Starkadder, who were put to dreadful deaths, and then the fortress was burned to the ground.

It was supposed that Morrar na Shean had perished in the flames; but he had escaped by the postern—the same postern through which he had led the countess to die—and reached his castle of Lochmore, a secluded tower of great strength, which is situated at the end of a loch, and overhangs the current of the Dirlet out of it. There the river is narrow, deep, and rapid.

This tower was then remote and little known, so there for years did Morrar live, secluded, forgotten, and abandoned by all; and then, as time crept on, he became a prey to remorse and horror.

Terrific visions and appalling spectres were said to haunt him, and the unquiet souls of Thorolf, of John of Harpidale, and others who had died in his service, were averred to wander at night through the silent chambers of Lochmore, and their wailing voices were heard to rise from the lake in the moonshine, and to mingle with the roar of the Dirlet beneath the castle-wall. At last no one would remain in such a dwelling-place, and the wretched Morrar na Shean was left entirely alone.

Then a sore illness came upon him with his growing years; and sick, despairing, and sad at heart, the earl lay on what he feared was his bed of death.

None were near him now: even the last of his hounds had gone to seek another, a merrier, or it might be kinder master; and he wept the salt, bitter tears of age, of sorrow, and repentance,—of an age that was lonely and unfriended—of sorrow for his lost wife and children—of repentance for a wasted life, and for his many unatoned-for crimes and sacrileges.

He found himself abandoned on earth, and feared that he would be excluded from Heaven. He was

wifeless, childless, friendless, and alone — alone
with only memory and the terrors of death and
superstition!

He saw the clear, bright stars in the northern
sky sparkling through the gloomy windows of
Lochmore. He heard the hoarse brawl of the
Dirlet beneath the castle wall; but he shut out
the sound, for it made him think of that terrible
night when the swollen Thurso was rushing over its
stony bed, and Gunhilda was saved from his dagger
by the vision of St. Monina; and again he seemed
to see that pale, beautiful, and miraculous face
shining amid its halo, in the twilight before him.

The perspiration burst upon his wrinkled brow;
he called wildly for lights, but no one heard him
now; and the echoes of his own voice appalled him.
He trembled to be in the dark and alone; and yet
there was no darkness, for it was the clear twilight
of the northern summer, when the sun scarcely dips
beneath the horizon.

"Old, old! childless and alone!" moaned the
earl, crushed beneath the weight of sad thoughts
and unavailing sorrow, as he covered his grey head
beneath the coverlet, and sobbed heavily.

"Harold—husband," said a gentle voice, that
thrilled through him, and tremblingly he started and
looked up.

Lo! in the clear light of the midsummer night,
there stood by his bedside the Countess Gunhilda,
as he had last seen her, so fair and stately, with

her Danish tunic of blue silk, her flowing mantle, and long lace veil, that fell over her shoulders from under her half-diadem, the gems of which sparkled in the light of the stars.

Beside her, but a little way behind, stood three tall and handsome girls, each of whom wore riding-hoods edged with pearls and long white veils, which they held upraised, as they surveyed him with sad and earnest eyes.

Believing that he saw but disembodied souls, the upbraiding spirits of his wife and their three daughters—for midsummer night is the time when demons, ghosts, and fairies are all supposed to be abroad,—the lonely earl uttered a cry of wild despair and fainted.

Yet they were no spirits whom he had seen, but the Countess Gunhilda and his three daughters, who, having heard of his sad and repentant condition, had hastened to visit and console him, and arrived thus in the night.

And with Thora, the youngest and the fairest, had come her husband—for she, too, was wedded to William Sinclair, Lord of Roslin ; and thus from her descended the future Earls of Orkney, who were also Dukes of Oldenburg.

On returning to consciousness Morrar na Shean came to a new life of joy and happiness. With these came a more sincere repentance. He spent the remaining years of his life in endeavouring to atone for the atrocities of his youth, and died at a good old age when Alexander II. was King of Scotland—passing peacefully away, while the faces of his children and grandchildren were bowed in prayer around him.

Such is the story of Morrar na Shean, the Lord of the Venison.

CHAPTER L.

THE RUINED HOUSE IN GLENSTRAE.

AFTER the conclusion of his tale, Rob gave the harper a piece of Spanish gold, and permitted him to pursue his own way. The MacGregors saw him no more; he was killed three years after, in the September of 1722, when, by some of the Mac-Kenzies, a party of the king's troops under a captain MacNeil were lured into an ambush, and so severely handled that they were compelled to retire to Inverness in great disorder.

The day after Gillian left them saw the Mac-Gregors traversing Glenstrae, a wild and romantic valley which opens at the northern base of Stronmiolchoin, a lonely mountain that forms the eastern boundary of Glenorchy.

All these were possessions of which the clan had been deprived; and there every hill and rock, every thicket and ruin, was connected with some tradition of the past and of Clan Alpine.

The glen was desolate and lonely; for it had long since been swept of its people by the hostile tribes who had leagued against them.

" Seid svas do piob, vich Alpine ! " (" Strike up your pipe, son of Alpine ! ") said Rob Roy, as they approached a mass of ruined walls which rose on a gentle eminence in the glen. " Here, to-day, let us remember the true and faithful dead, who bequeathed to us the task of avenging them ! "

Then in the still and silent valley the wild lament of the MacGregors rang mournfully and shrill, as Rob and his men, with their swords drawn, advanced slowly to the ruins *deisail*-wise—by the way of the sun's course,—and marched thrice round them, and then departed, but with many a frowning glance and backward look.

This was the ruined residence of the chief, Alaster Roy of Glenstrae, before the clan had been broken up and suppressed. It had been destroyed amid the events subsequent to the battle of Glenfruin. At the time of which we write a portion of the walls were standing ; *now* their foundations can scarcely be discerned above the blooming heather.

With these old ruins is connected a tradition of the clan which exhibits some of the strongest traits of the old Highland character.

Alaster Roy MacGregor of Glenstrae had but one son, a brave and handsome youth, named Evan, to whom he was deeply attached, and whom, as the future heir of all his possessions, he trained up with peculiar care, leaving nothing undone to make him perfect as a soldier and huntsman.

One day when Evan was deerstalking among the mountains he met the young Laird of Lamond, who, with two attendants, was travelling from Cowal towards the king's castle of Inverlochy, and they dined together at a little inn or changehouse, near the Blackmount at the mouth of Glencoe.

After dinner a dispute occurred; hot words ensued, for both were passionate and fiery in spirit; and, drawing his dirk, young Lamond killed Evan MacGregor by a single blow, and he fell across the table at which they had been seated.

Horrified at what he had done, Lamond leaped from a window and fled, but was pursued by Dugald Ciar Mhor and other MacGregors, who first made short work with his two attendants.

The flight and pursuit were maintained on foot; and with Lamond, who knew that he would be instantly sacrificed if taken, fear added wings to his speed, so that ultimately he outstripped the friends of him he had slain.

Ignorant of whither he went, as night was closing he found himself in a lonely glen, where at the base of a mountain stood a tower, at the gate of which he breathlessly demanded shelter, succour, and rest.

On being admitted, he asked what place this was?

" Stronmiolchoin — the house of Glenstrae ! " replied the wondering gateward.

" The dwelling of Alaster Roy ? "

"Yes."

" Then I am lost — utterly lost ! " exclaimed

the unhappy Lamond, as he sank exhausted on a seat.

"Lost! how — what mean you?" asked the laird of Glenstrae, coming hurriedly forward. "Who are you?"

"The son of Lamond of that Ilk."

"By whom are you pursued, that my house will fail to afford you succour?" asked Glenstrae.

"I am pursued by MacGregors," replied the sinking fugitive, "and I beseech you, by all the claims of hospitality and compassion, and by your authority, to save me from them."

"You are safe," said Alaster, kissing the blade of his dirk; "but what have you done—whom have you slain?"

"Whom?" reiterated Lamond, in a hollow voice.

"Yes; there is blood upon your hands, and on the hilt of your dirk."

"Alas!" said Lamond, and paused.

"Speak! for you are safe in the house of Glenstrae, whatever you have done," said the chief impetuously; but the unhappy fugitive clasped his hands, for a din of voices rang at the tower gate, and Dugald Ciar Mhor, with other pursuers, came rushing in, bearing with them the body of Evan, and after informing the unfortunate father of what had occurred, they loudly demanded that the assassin should be surrendered unto them.

"I have passed my word to protect him, and I must respect it, even in this moment of agony!" replied Glenstrae, while the tears rolled over his face; "never shall it be said that a MacGregor broke his word, even to an enemy!"

In their rage and sorrow for what had occurred, his wife and daughter besought him to yield the fugitive to the clansmen, that they might put him to death; but Glenstrae stood over him with his sword drawn, and said,—

"Let no man here dare to lay a hand upon him! MacGregor has promised him safety, and by the soul of my only and beloved son, whom he has slain, he shall be safe while under the roof of Glenstrae—safe as if beneath his own!"

And before the interment of Evan, when the sorrow and the angry passions of the assembled clan would be roused to their full height, the chief, with a chosen party, escorted young Lamond far across the mountains, and almost to within sight of his home in Cowal.

"Farewell, Lamond," said he, gravely and sternly; "on your own land you are now safe. Farther I will not and cannot protect you. Avoid my people, lest your father may have to endure the sorrow that wrings this heart of mine; and may God forgive you the woe you have brought on the house of Glenstrae!"

In a few years after this, the Field of Glenfruin was fought; the castle of Stronmiolchoin was

2 A

destroyed, and Alaster of Glenstrae, then an aged man, and all his people were proscribed fugitives.

Homeless, nameless, and a wanderer, with the severe parliamentary acts of James VI. hanging over his head, the laird of Glenstrae had to lurk in the caves and woods among the glens that had once been his own, till he was captured by Sir James Campbell of Ardkinlass, from whom he made an escape, and fled to Cowal, a peninsula of Argyle, that stretches far into the Firth of Clyde.

Here the young laird of Lamond found the poor old man, and received and protected him in his house, with many other fugitives of the Clan Gregor, saving them from Archibald Earl of Argyle and other powerful enemies.

To the earl, Glenstrae at last yielded himself, on the solemn promise that he should be sent out of Scottish ground—a promise which was truly but fearfully kept!

He was marched as far as the English side of Berwick, under an escort of the Scottish Horse Guard, commanded by David Murray, Lord Scone, and then brought back to Edinburgh, where, with eighteen devoted men of his surname, he was hanged on the 20th of January, 1604.

"Being a chief," says Birrel, "he was hanged his own height above the rest of his friends."

It was the memory of severities such as these, together with their local position, that fostered a

spirit of resentment and ferocious resistance to all
civil law in the tribe of MacGregor.

"When I asked a very learned minister in the
Highlands," says Dr. Johnson, "which he considered the most savage clans, *those,* said he, *which
live next the Lowlands.*"

This was the mere force of circumstances and
position; and hence the most warlike and predatory
of the Lowland clans were those of the borders
adjoining England.

CHAPTER LI,

HE FIGHTS THE LAIRD OF BARRA.

" Rob Roy had two especial qualities," says the
" New Picture of Scotland " (published in 1807):
" he spent his revenue generously, and was a true
friend to the widow and the orphan."

On his return to Portnellan, he now hoped
that, by the treasure which he had judiciously
distributed among his people, they might, if the
persecution of them ceased, stock their little farms
and take to cattle-dealing, that they might all
live in ease and comfort, and that his sons might
learn some of the arts of peace without forgetting
those of war.

Soon after his return from Glensheil, Rob heard
that Grahame of Killearn, who always treated the
tenantry of Montrose with great severity, had
sequestrated, or distrained, the cows and furniture
of a poor woman who lived near the Highland
border.

As she was a widow, and more especially as she
was the widow of Eoin Raibach, who had fallen at
the storming of Inversnaid, he immediately visited

her cottage, and she burst into tears when she beheld him, exclaiming,—

"MacGregor, *mo comraich ort!*" (my protection is thee.)

"And never was that appeal made to me in vain by the poor," replied Rob; "I shall be your buckler and your sword of vengeance if requisite, widow. How much do you owe Killearn?"

"Three hundred marks; for which he has seized upon my two cows, the food of my children—my spinning-wheel, which gives them clothing—our beds and everything."

"When comes he here?" asked Rob, grimly.

"To-morrow; to-morrow will see us desolate and forlorn."

"Not so, widow. Here are the three hundred marks; pay the greedy vulture, and be sure that you get a receipt duly signed."

Duly as the morrow came, the legal messengers of Killearn arrived, with carts to convey away the chattels of the widow, who paid them, and received a receipt; but about a mile distant from her house, they were met by Rob Roy, who, with a cocked pistol in his hand, forced them to hand over the money to him. He then gave them a severe beating with a heavy stick, advised them to choose another trade than the law, and returned the three hundred marks to the widow.

We are told that, under circumstances nearly similar, he relieved a tenant on the Montrose lands who was three years in arrear of rent. When the poor farmer offered to repay Rob's loan, the latter replied,—

"No, no; I will get it back from Grahame of Killearn—yes, every farthing, by Patrick of the Holy Crook! so keep the money, farmer."

MacGregor now leased some pasture-lands further among the mountains, in that place with which his name is much associated, the braes of Balquhidder, a name which signifies the dwelling-place where five glens open.

He occupied the farmhouse of Inverlochluvig, at the head of the braes, where there was excellent pasture for black-cattle and sheep; and there was born, in 1724, his youngest son, Robin Oig, whose stirring story and sad fate created a deep interest in future years.

Like all his brothers, young Robin was baptized in water brought by Paul Crubach from the holy well of St. Fillan; and during the ceremony was held over his father's broadsword, for it was a Highland superstition that the voices of children who died without receiving this warlike consecration were heard faintly wailing in the woods and other lonely places at night.

Robin grew a sturdy but wild young Highlander; and afterwards bore that sword with honour in the ranks of the 42nd Regiment.

At Muirlaggan, in Balquhidder, Rob built a comfortable house for his mother, then a very aged woman; and he began to hope that the government troops, the civil authorities, Athole, Montrose, and Killearn, had forgotten him, and that he would be permitted to spend a few years of his life in peace; but he hoped in vain!

To the land he now leased or occupied in Balquhidder he had an hereditary claim, as a descendant of Dugald Ciar Mhor; but the MacLarens of Invernentie had some similar right, and ere long this proved the cause of much strife and bloodshed.

With great generosity Rob offered a portion of his share of the Spanish treasure to redeem another bond which a neighbouring proprietor held over the lands of his nephew, MacGregor of Glengyle.

Hamish MacLaren of Invernentie had lent a sum of money to Glengyle, and by the tenor of the bond, the lands so held, or named therein, " if the money was not repaid within ten years, were to be *forfeited to the lender*, though the sum was less than half their value."

Knowing well that the utmost advantage would be taken of this unjust contract, Rob Roy gave his nephew money sufficient to repay Invernentie.

As the bond had but a few months now to run, Glengyle, with gratitude and joy, hastened to his creditor and offered the money so generously lent by his uncle.

Hamish MacLaren was a man of rough and forbidding exterior, with a low forehead and black

eyebrows that were thick, shaggy, and joined in
one.   His face was one of the lowest of the Celtic
type, and consequently expressed intense cunning,
falsehood, and cruelty.   He received Glengyle coldly
—all the more so, perhaps, because he was a near
kinsman of that MacLaren whom MacAleister had
flung into the millrace at Comar.

"I cannot take the money," said he, bluntly.

"How—wherefore?" asked the other, with surprise.

"Because I cannot find our bond."

"It must and shall be found!" said Glengyle,
impetuously.

"Must and *shall!*"

"Yes; there are but three months to run."

"Only three months?" repeated the other, with
affected surprise.

"Yes—we have no time to lose."

"After the date at which the bond expires your
lands will be forfeited to me."

"How can you prove that if the bond be lost?"

"Ha, ha! it is recorded in the books of the
sheriff of the county.   My friend Killearn looked
to that."

"Here is your money—principal and interest,"
said Glengyle, crimsoned with fury; "bond or no
bond, take it and give me a receipt in full, or woe
unto you, Invernentie!"

But MacLaren was too wary either to accede or
to lose his temper.   By an exertion of cunning

and flattery, he contrived to cajole Glengyle, who promised to wait until the actual bond could be found; and for the three following months MacLaren kept sedulously out of his way, avoiding all visits, and receiving all messages and letters with studied silence; and on the very day on which the stated time expired, he took legal means to get himself *infeft* in the lands which he alleged to be forfeited. At the same time, through Grahame of Killearn, he served notices upon young MacGregor to remove from these lands, with his family, tenants, and cattle, within eight days.

These proceedings were rendered darker by the circumstance that Glengyle was labouring under a severe illness, which made him totally incapable of defending himself.

Rob Roy was filled with rage on hearing of these lawless proceedings against his nephew; for to him they seemed but a repetition of those severities to which he had been subjected by Montrose.

"Greumoch," said he, "we cannot suffer Glengyle to be treated thus; get our lads together, and we shall teach Invernentie a lesson he is not likely to forget."

The *lads* were soon collected, and at the head of two hundred of them Rob marched into Strathfillan, whither, he heard, MacLaren of Invernentie had gone to attend a fair which is usually held there on the 3rd of July.

He traversed the vast extent of the fair—for the strath was covered with great herds of cattle—searching in vain for Invernentie, until he ascertained that, having sold all his stock, he had taken his way homeward through Glendochart.

In those days nothing was paid for pasturing cattle; but as roads were made, fields inclosed, and grass became valuable, the armed drovers were forced to bargain for it in their routes to those fairs, and more especially to Falkirk and Carlisle—innovations which they bitterly hated.

A rapid march over the hills brought Rob and his men upon the homeward path, at a point where it is joined by the road from Tyndrum, some time before Invernentie could possibly have passed. Rob was assured of this, and ere long he saw a party of armed men, some of whom were mounted, coming along that beautiful valley which the Dochart traverses in its course to the Tay.

That the men on foot were well equipped was evident, for the long barrels of their Spanish muskets glittered in the sunshine, which streamed athwart the winding valley, bathing in gold and purple light the hills on one side, and casting into deep-blue shadow those on the other.

The travellers, who were about twenty in number, on seeing the MacGregors posted on the highway, began to prepare for service, by loading their muskets; the footmen unslung their targets; the horsemen loosened their swords in the sheaths, and looked to the priming of their pistols, as they all came briskly up ; and on Rob Roy stepping forward to meet them, he found among the mounted men the identical laird of Invernentie whom he sought, with Campbell of Aberuchail, Stirling of Carden, and another gentleman whom he did not recognize, but who was followed closely by several well-armed gillies on foot.

"What does this meeting bode, MacGregor ? " asked the baronet of Aberuchail; "peace or war ? "

"That is as may be," replied Rob ; "my present business is with Hamish MacLaren of Invernentie."

The latter smiled grimly, and under his black brows his keen, fierce, hazel eyes glared forth like those of a polecat, as he said,—

"You must first speak with one who has travelled a long way to see you, and who moreover is a friend of mine."

"A bad recommendation; but to whom do you refer ? " asked MacGregor.

"He refers to *me*," said the strange traveller. "I have indeed come a long way to see you, Mac-Gregor, and we meet most opportunely."

Rob surveyed the speaker with some surprise. He was a man of great stature and apparent strength, handsome, athletic, and in the prime of life. His sword, pistols, dirk, and powder-horn were richly mounted with silver; he had *three* feathers in his bonnet, indicating that he was a chief; but MacGregor recognized neither his badge nor his tartan.

"And who may you be, sir, that have been so desirous to see me?" he asked, haughtily.

"I am Roderick MacNeil of Barra," replied the other, on which Rob saluted him by uncovering his head; for the MacNeils of Barra were an old family in the Western Isles, famous for their antiquity—which dated back to the days of the first Scottish settlers—for their valour, and for their vanity : thus one of them, named Rory the Turbulent, who lived in the days of James VI., in the vastness of his Highland bombast, had a herald who proclaimed, in Gaelic, daily, from the summit of his castle,—

"Hear ye people, and listen all ye nations! MacNeil of Barra having finished his dinner, all the kings and princes of the earth have liberty to dine."

The chief who now confronted Rob Roy was considered one of the best swordsmen in Scotland; and certainly he was the first in his native Hebrides. He was possessed of a high spirit, with a romantic love of adventure. He had heard of Rob Roy's skill in the use of his weapons and his renown in arms ; so he determined with his own hands to put his skill and valour to the test.

"And so," said he, while surveying him from head to foot, "you are Rob Roy MacGregor, whom I have so long wished to meet."

" For what purpose ? " asked the other, haughtily; "I never saw you before, MacNeil, and by your bearing I care little if I never see you again."

"I have heard much of your fame, MacGregor, and I have come hither—I, Roderick MacNeil of Barra—to prove myself a better swordsman than you ! "

At these words he leaped from his horse, tossed the bridle to one of his gillies, and drew his sword and dirk.

" Roderick MacNeil," said Rob, calmly, " I have no doubt of your being what you assert—the Chief of Barra, and of a noble and ancient lineage ; a better swordsman, and it may be a better man, than I ; but I have no wish to prove it. My business is with Invernentie here, and I never fight a man without a reason. With you I have no quarrel; so keep your sword for the service of Scotland and her king."

" I do so keep my sword; but you must fight me, nevertheless," said the other, imperiously.

" Fie, sir ! " replied Rob, whose temper was rising ; " this is a bad trade you have taken to."

" Trade ? "

" Dioul, yes !—molesting honest people on the open highway."

" Truly the taunt comes well from you—*you*, who have kept the whole Highland border in hot water since Dundee fell at Rin Ruari ! "

On the face of MacLaren of Invernentie there was a malicious smile, which compelled Rob to seem calm ; for he feared that if he fell in this impending conflict, his nephew's interest would infallibly suffer by the wiles and roguery of Invernentie and Killearn, especially if aided by the bad influence of Athole and Montrose.

"Barra," said he, "I never draw my sword without a just cause of quarrel. Go your way in peace, and leave me to pursue mine."

Then Barra is recorded to have taunted him by saying,—

"*You are afraid—your valour is in words.*"

"You shall have more than words," replied MacGregor, furiously, as he unsheathed his sword. "You have come a long way to see me, and shall not go back without having done a portion of your errand. My hand is strong."

"And *my* sword sharp and sure."

"Neither sharper nor surer than mine, Barra," replied Rob Roy.

"That we shall see, MacGregor Campbell."

"And deeply shall you *feel*," said Rob, more than ever enraged at being named Campbell. "Greumoch," he added, "stand by the side of Invernentie, and if he attempts either escape or foul play, slice him down with your axe. And now, Barra, have at you ! "

While all who were on the pathway which traversed the glen assembled in a large and excited

circle around them, the two combatants engaged
with great fury, and not a sound was heard but the
clash of their blades and their deep breathing.
Both were brave to the utmost, and both were
equally skilled in the use of their weapons; but
while sentiments of mere family pride .and military
bravado animated Barra, MacGregor was inspired by
just indignation at being thus baited and molested
by a total stranger, and forced into an unexpected
duel, at a time so critical to the interests of his
household and his nephew, who by illness was
unable to protect himself.

Both were so exceedingly well matched in
strength and skill, that for more than twenty
minutes neither had in any way the advantage of
the other, till Barra made a feint, and then a fierce
thrust at Rob's bare throat; but he parried it by
a circular whirl of his claymore, which nearly
wrenched the other's weapon away.

During a second thrust Rob caught the blade of
Barra in the iron loops of his basket-hilt, but being
a younger man, the latter bounded agilely back,
and released his sword in time to save it, ere
Rob could snap the blade, or lock in and use
his dirk.

After a time Barra's sword shook in his hand and
bent—it was soon full of deep notches; and fatigue
rendered his arm weary. He was compelled to give
ground step by step, till at last MacGregor tossed
aside his shield, and throwing all his strength into

one tremendous double-handed stroke, beat down his guard, snapped his blade like a withered reed, and gave him a wound so severe that he "nearly cut off his sword-arm, which confined him to the village of Killearn for three months."

"When next we meet," cried Barra, as he fell into the arms of Stirling of Carden, "*our parting shall be different !*"

But, fortunately, they never chanced to meet again.

CHAPTER LII.

INVERNENTIE PUNISHED.

GREAT was the exultation of the MacGregors, and with wild halloos of triumph they crowded about their leader, who, with his characteristic generosity, was one of the first to proffer assistance to the wounded chief.

As the parties separated, Invernentie was whipping up his Highland garron, preparatory to taking a speedy leave, when Greumoch inserted the hook of his Lochaber axe in the collar of his coat, and roughly tumbled him on the roadway.

Enraged by such treatment, MacLaren drew his dirk, and was rushing on his captor, when the latter charged the pikehead of the axe full at his breast, and would have killed him without mercy, but for the interference of Campbell of Aberuchail and Rob Roy, who desired his followers to seize and convey him to a small inn which stood at the head of the strath; and there, as night was closing, MacLaren found himself abandoned by his companions, helpless, and a prisoner of the easily exasperated MacGregors, all somewhat excitable Celts,

whose patience
Was apt to wear out on trifling occasions.

2 B

Hamish MacLaren, a dark, fierce, and resolute fellow, asked Rob Roy, sternly, "for what purpose he had been separated from his friends, disarmed, and brought as a prisoner to this solitary house?"

"Because, in the first place," said Rob, calmly, "I wish to speak with you; and, in the second place, to punish you if you do not take my advice."

"In what matter—dioul!—in what matter?" demanded MacLaren, knitting his black brows till his gleaming eyes were almost hidden by them.

"The matter of the bond——"

"Which I hold over the lands of Grahame of Glengyle?"

"No; I know nothing of *that* document," replied Rob, twirling one of his pistols ominously round his forefinger by the trigger guard.

"Then to what do you refer?"

"To the bond which you allege to hold over the lands of my sick nephew, Gregor *MacGregor* of Glengyle."

"Well—well?"

"Hamish MacLaren of Invernentie," said Rob, making a great effort to appear calm, "I have here the money to release this bond."

"But I decline it—the time has expired," said MacLaren, doggedly.

"It may have expired *now*," said Rob Roy;

"but it had not expired when, more than three months ago, Glengyle offered you the money, principal and interest."

"I told him——"

" A falsehood—a black lie, Invernentie! You told him the bond was lost, when it was, and still is, in your charter-box; and now I swear, by the Grey Stone of MacGregor, that until you produce that bond, we part not company, in life at least!"

MacLaren's breast swelled with rage and spite. His face grew ashy white, and the veins of his forehead were swollen like whipcord, with the baffled avarice and passion he strove in vain to conceal.

" Allow me to return to Invernentie," said he, in a husky voice and with averted eyes, " and I shall send hither the bond, if I can find it."

" Nay, we part not company until it is produced *here;* and if that fails to be done, you shall go back to Invernentie heels foremost."

" How mean you? "

" In your coffin," replied MacGregor, with a dark and terrible frown.

Aware that he had to deal with one who did not stand on trifles, MacLaren, apprehensive for the result, agreed that two of his servants (who had ventured to the inn), accompanied by Coll and Greumoch, should go to the house of Invernentie and get the bond, while he remained as Rob's hostage in Strathfillan.

They were absent some time, as Invernentie (which means the conflux of dark waters) was several miles distant; but on the evening of the second day they returned with the bond, and placed it in the hands of MacLaren, who, without opening it, tossed it across the table to Rob Roy, saying, sullenly,—

"Here is your precious document, and now let me begone."

"Not quite so fast—tarry, I pray you," said Rob, as he read over the paper, examined it in every particular, tore it into minute fragments, and scattered them over the clay floor of the room.

"Now," he added, "here is the money of Glengyle."

"I shall record the discharge of the debt in the books of the sheriff," said MacLaren, rising and putting on his bonnet.

"You and the sheriff may do exactly as you please," said Rob; "in fact you have my full permission to hang yourselves, if it suits your fancy; but, in the meantime, give me a discharge in full for the money which you lent my nephew, Gregor *MacGregor* of Glengyle."

Invernentie, who had some other roguish scheme in his head, most unwillingly wrote and signed the required quittance, which Rob carefully read, folded, and put in his pocket, together *with the bay of money*, telling him that now he would not pay him a farthing—" that the sum lost was too small a fine for the outrage he had attempted to perpetrate in form of law, and that he might be thankful that he escaped with a sound skin."

They separated. MacLaren was choking with resentment, and vowed to have a terrible revenge; but Rob and his men merely laughed at him, as they marched off towards their new home on the bracs of Balouhidder.

CHAPTER LIII.

ATTACKED BY THE DUKE OF ATHOLE.

ROB having retired further north-west, was living in comparative peace and ease at Balquhidder, though ever armed, watchful, and on the alert; but now his old and wanton enemy, the Duke of Athole —an enemy despite the cavalier sentiments of Tulli-bardine and his other sons, and the sympathies of the gentle Duchess Katherine—during the middle of 1724, made no less than *three* vigorous attempts to capture him, for he was still outlawed, and the warrants for his apprehension were yet in full force against him, with ample rewards for those who could achieve this hitherto perilous and difficult task. Of Atholo's final attempts we shall briefly relate the success.

In retaliation for the trick so basely played him at tho castle of Blair, Rob had certainly more than once ravaged tho estates of the Duke of Athole, carried off the cattle, and put to the sword several Drummonds who resisted.

Though he had drawn these reprisals on him-self, Atholo could as little forgive such proceedings as his Grace of Montrose; and on his return from a visit to London he secretly despatched a party of Lord Polworth's Light Horse up the glens to

Balquhidder, at a time when most of the Mac-
Gregors were absent at fairs, or on the mountains
herding cattle.

MacLaren of Invernentie is said to have given
them exact information of Rob's movements, for
they came upon him most unexpectedly, during a
fine summer evening when he was superintending a
few of his people, who were cutting turf with the
ceaba, a long, narrow spade of peculiar form, used
by the Highlanders and Irish.   Suddenly there was
a cry of—

" The   Redcoats !   the   Redcoats ! "   and   the
women threw down their keallochs, or creels, as
a party of troopers, on light active horses, dashed
round the shoulder of a rocky ridge, and came
pellmell among them, with swords flashing in the
sunshine.

Rob had only three men with him, and save their
dirks, each was armed only with a turf-spade.
While he swung one of these implements aloft, to
use it like a poleaxe, resolved on making a desperate defence, its shaft was shattered in his hand, as
a trooper adroitly broke it by a pistol-shot, and
then spurred his horse right over him.

Rob lost his dirk, but plunged his skene-dhu
deep into the bowels of the animal, which reared
wildly and threw his rider head downward into the
soft bog, where his spurred jack-boots stood uppermost in the air.

Beaten down again under a shower of sword-blades and clubbed carbines, MacGregor was made prisoner. He was then mounted on a horse and carried off, amid the yells, screams, and lamentations of the women. He was threatened with instant death if he attempted to resist or escape; and, fortunately, on this occasion, they were without a rope to bind him; but the officer in command, an Irish captain, held a cocked pistol in his right hand, and rode by the side of the prisoner.

"Remember," said he, "that your *head* may be more easily carried than your body, if you prove troublesome. Forward—away for Stirling—away at full speed!" were the orders; and the Light Horse disappeared with MacGregor, while the turf-cutters flew to arms and to muster others for rescue and revenge.

This, however, was unnecessary; for, when passing through a glen or ravine which lies between the church of Balquhidder and Glendochart, at a place where, on the side of the former, the ground is steep and rugged, but on the latter has a long and gradual slope towards the Dochart, Rob suddenly wrenched away the Irishman's pistol, which exploded in the air, and slipping over his horse's crupper, sprang up the rocks, where not a single trooper could follow him.

Enraged by the sudden escape of his prisoner, the officer spurred his horse till the steel rowels tore the flesh; it bounded madly upward against the rocks, and fell back upon its haunches, half-stunning its rider; and to this day the place bears the name of *Shiam an Erinich*, or the "Irishman's Leap."

A few days after this, Rob escaped again by mere coolness and presence of mind, when in Glenalmond he encountered the same party of Polworth's Light Horse, who instantly knew and greeted him with a shout; while some drew their swords, others loaded their carbines, and all spurred their horses on. Rob was quite alone; he had been separated from his eldest son and followers, with twenty of whom he had been purchasing cattle at a neighbouring fair.

No succour was near. The place of this *rencontre* is a savage and solitary pass, overlooked by hills about fourteen hundred feet in height, the steep sides being pressed so close together as barely to leave space at the bottom for a narrow path and the brawling river's bed. On their sides some meagre shrubs sprout from the fissured rocks, beneath the shadow of which the Almond looks sombre, dark, and inky, save when churned into brown foam, as it thunders over a linn, or chafes on the obstructing boulders.

At the upper end of this lonely pass stands a grey and time-worn block of stone, eight feet in height, which marks the grave of the Scottish Homer—Ossian, the son of Fingal.

In the wildest and narrowest path of this mountain gorge, Rob suddenly found himself confronted, about nightfall, by the same Irish captain and his party of horse. In an angle of the narrow way, where an overhanging rock protected him on one side and the deep river's bed on the other, he stood facing them, sword in hand, and covered by his round shield; thus the troopers could see nothing beyond him.

As only one at a time could attack him, the leading trooper was somewhat impressed by the resolute expression of his well-bearded face, his stature, and firm posture of defence.

"I know whom you seek," said he, sternly; "but I swear that if you do not instantly depart, not one of you shall return alive! In less than half an hour my men will have possession of the bridge of Buchanty, and your retreat will be cut off."

On hearing this, the soldiers began to rein back their horses.

"Retire in time," resumed MacGregor, "and tell him who sent you that, if any more of his pigmy race come hither, by the bones of our dead, I will hang them up to feed the eagles!"

He then placed his horn to his mouth and blew a loud and ringing blast, to which hill and river echoed.

On this, believing that the whole clan were concealed among the rocks, from whence a fire would be opened upon them, the troopers seized by a panic, wheeled round their horses and retired at full gallop, while Rob ascended the cliffs, and leisurely pursued his way in another direction.

The government, in despair perhaps, were now ceasing to molest Rob Roy, and the last time troops were sent against him was the sudden despatch of a strong force of infantry from the castle of Stirling, under Colonel Grahame.

This party were seen on their march to Callendar by some MacGregors, who were driving a herd of cattle along the banks of the Forth, so Rob was immediately apprised of the unwelcome visitors. In an hour, the whole fighting men of the braes of Balquhidder were in arms, and had scouts posted at every pass and avenue; but as Rob had no wish to subject his people to severity on his own account— for it was *he* alone whom Grahame had orders to capture—he retired further off into the mountains, a precaution he would not have adopted in his younger and more fiery years.

The soldiers met with every opposition, and frequently with bloody resistance from the Mac-Gregors; and they had a four days' fruitless search, toiling, with knapsacks and accoutrements, cocked hats, pipe-clayed breeches, and long gaiters, up steep mountains, down ravines, where they floun-dered, and sunk knee-deep among wet heather, fern, and rushes; stumbling over precipices, and always misled by the guides, who took the bribes of the officers, and then vanished into the mist or a thicket, leaving them to shift for themselves, till the evening of the fourth day found Colonel Grahame and his detachment, starving, weary, and worn, occupying a deserted house on the verge of the Lowlands, near the hills of Buchanan.

The rain was falling in torrents, and no sentinels were posted without; so there Rob came upon them in the night, and, by throwing in combustibles, set the house on fire about their ears.

This immediately dislodged the enemy. As they rushed forth in disorder and dismay, many were severely injured by bruises and by the explosion of the ammunition in their pouches. Many lost their weapons, and " one man was killed by the accidental discharge of a musket. The military, thus thrown into confusion, broken down by fatigue, and almost famished by want of provisions, withdrew from the country of the MacGregors, happy that they had escaped so well."

This was—as we have stated—the *last* encounter of Rob Roy with the forces of the government.

CHAPTER LIV.

THE FINAL ATTEMPT OF ATHOLE.

It was the Lammas now of 1724, when the gool or wild marigold began to make its appearance among the little corn patches on the sunny side of the Highland hills; and in this month the mother of Rob Roy (a daughter of the house of Glenfalloch), then in extreme old age, being nearly a century old, expired at Muirlaggan, the house which he had built for her.

Though her passing away had been long expected, her death was accompanied by the omens and mysterious warnings then and still so universally believed in among the Highlanders. Rob's grey staghounds howled mournfully the livelong night, a sure sign that they had seen what the eyes of men could not—the shadow of Death enter the house of Muirlaggan; and Paul Crubach, now aged, half-blind, and bent with years, averred that on last Midsummer-eve he had beheld her figure pass before him into the churchyard of Balquhidder with a shroud *high* upon her breast, a certain token that her death was close at hand.

On the day preceding the funeral, and before the clan, tenants, and gillies assembled to drink the dredgie, he came close to the chair of Rob, who was seated at window, full of thought.

"Paul, you have been absent some days," said Rob kindly to the old man, "and at your years——"

"I have been on Inchcailloch, and there I spent three nights," said he, with unusual solemnity.

"Three dreary nights they must have been," said Rob, with a sad smile; "a ruined church for shelter and the graves of the dead below you."

"But I slept thereon, knowing that the dead would give me counsel just and true; and in my dreams there appeared unto me twice one whom I knew to be Dugald Ciar Mhor."

"How knew you this?"

"By his mouse-coloured hair and beard, and he told me—told me——"

"What — what?" asked Rob, impatiently; "oh, Paul — Paul — Dugald lies in his grave in Glenlyon."

"It matters not — he told us to *beware of Athole!*"

"Paul, is not this mockery, and at such a time? Beware of Athole? We have done little else for these twenty years past."

"Above the graves of the dead we get counsel just and true," repeated poor, old, half-witted Paul, ignorant that, sixteen centuries before, Pomponius Mela recorded a similar idea.

The escapes of Rob had been so numerous and

so desperate that they became a byeword—a joke in the Highlands, where the people were wont to say,—"You might as well attempt to say MacNab thrice with your mouth shut as attempt to catch Rob Roy;" and believing himself to be singularly favoured by fortune in that matter, he paid but little attention to the warning of Paul till about sunset, when his son Ronald came running in bareheaded and breathless from a cattle-fold to announce that a party of soldiers were rapidly approaching the house!

The natural grief which Rob was enduring for the death of his mother turned into exasperation. He now kept fewer men about him than had been his wont in other times, and it chanced that, though some hundreds would muster for the funeral on the morrow, there were not ten in the house at this desperate crisis!

He buckled on his sword, thrust his loaded pistols in his belt, threw his target on his arm, kissed Helen and the babe Robin at her breast, and was rushing from the house to seek shelter on the hills, when the Duke of Athole, with two hundred and fifty of his tenantry, all mounted and armed with sword, pistol, and musketoon, drew up before the door.

Keeping his hand on his sword, Rob saluted the duke, saying, with that suave irony which a Highlander can so well assume,—

"I am obliged to your grace for coming unasked

with such a goodly company to attend my mother's funeral. Glenfalloch and Breadalbane will alike deem it an honour which neither they nor I expected."

"I have not come here for any such purpose," replied Athole, haughtily, as he shook the long curls of his peruke, and kept his horse well in hand, while keenly eyeing every motion of MacGregor. "I have come but to crave the pleasure of your company so far as the Tolbooth of Perth, where we shall settle some old scores at leisure."

"Indeed!" said Rob, sternly. "Had I received sufficient notice of your grace's visit, we had met at the pass of Loch Ard, not at my own door, and I should have resorted to other means than temporising. Within that chamber, duke, lies my mother in her coffin — a woman old in years — yea, so old that she remembered the earliest days of Charles I., to whom your grandsire, Earl John of Athole, was a steadfast man and true; so, should I die for it here upon the threshold, I shall neither yield nor go to Perth your prisoner; for now in death, as in life, my place shall be by my mother's side!"

"Enough of this," said Athole, coarsely; "the funeral may go on very well without you."

Taken at vantage, however, Rob gradually perceived that he could gain nothing by resistance; and, as the duke dismounted, and stood by the bridle of his horse, he affected to comply with his wish. Then shrill screams and cries of lamentation rose from the women of the tribe, great numbers of whom had already assembled at Muirlaggan; and within the doorway of the house were seen the dark and scowling faces of men, with the gleam of arms, as swords and skenes were drawn and muskets loaded; for there Greumoch, Alaster Roy, and Rob's sons, Coll, Duncan, Hamish, and Ronald, prepared, like brave youths, to defend or die beside him.

A babel of hoarse and guttural Gaelic tongues rang on all sides, and many of the duke's yeomanry had unsheathed their swords and unslung their musketoons preparatory to carrying off the prisoner.

The voices of his sons, the lamentations of the women, thoughts of Helen with the babe at her breast, and his mother lying dead in her coffin, filled MacGregor's soul with desperation. Thrusting aside by main strength of arm half a dozen of the troopers who had begirt him, he drew forth his claymore, and called upon them all to stand back— back, upon their lives!

On this, snatching a pistol from his holsters, Athole fired it full at the head of Rob, who at the same moment fell to the ground. He had only slipped a foot, but on seeing him fall a mingled yell pierced the welkin, and before the smoke had cleared away, the duke found himself in the grasp of a woman.

This was a sister of Rob, who had married her cousin Glenfalloch. A strong and active woman, of a fiery and affectionate temper, on seeing her brother fall, she believed he was killed, and making a furious spring at Athole, clutched his throat with such energy that his grace was soon speechless. He reeled and staggered, while his followers, none of whom dared to use their pistol-butts or clenched hands to a lady, were unable to release him, till Rob seized his sister's wrist, and rescued him. On this the lady fainted.

This strange and unseemly scuffle fortunately caused some delay. For a time the duke was unable to mount his horse ; and ere he did so, the mustering MacGregors, summoned by Greumoch, Paul, and the shrieking women, from farm and clachan, came pouring in with brandished swords and axes in such numbers that Colonel Grahame, who was present, deeming discretion the better part of valour, seized the duke's horse by the bridle, and gave the order to retire as fast as possible.

Rob permitted Athole to do so unmolested, and now, for a time, the house of Muirlaggan, where the dead woman lay, presented that which was not uncommon then in the Highlands in cases of either sorrow or joy, a scene of fearful wrath and noisy uproar.

Had Athole come next day, he might have experienced a warmer reception ; for when Glengyle came in, more than seven hundred armed men, with twenty pipers, attended the funeral, and thus the old lady was born to her long home by her four grandsons ; for in the Highlands it was ever a boy's pride, and one of the tests of manhood, to be permitted to act as bearer of a coffin, perhaps for many miles over steep and rugged mountain-paths.

On this occasion, Paul Crubach stumbled and fell on his face as the funeral procession approached the church of Balquhidder, *deisail*-wise, and then the old superstition was whispered, that he who stumbled at a burial was certain to be the *next* whose coffin would be borne that way; and this was fully realized when poor old Paul was found dead in bed next morning.

The duke never again had an opportunity of molesting Rob Roy, as on the 14th November of this year his grace paid the debt of nature at his castle of Blair, in Athole.

CHAPTER LV

ROB ROY IN LONDON.

FROM this time forward the life of the Red Mac-Gregor was passed in ease and contentment ; around him his sons grew to manhood, brave, active, and hardy ; while the sons of those who had followed him to the battles of Sheriffmuir and Glensheil, to the storming of Inversnaid, the pass of Loch Ard, and to many a desperate conflict, became, under his care and advice, thriving cattle-dealers and industrious farmers.   Yet neither he nor they were permitted entirely to let their swords rest, or forget the warlike lessons of their forefathers, for the battle of Culloden had not yet been fought, and in disposition and character the secluded Highland clans were little different from what their ancestors were when they routed the Romans on the Grampians, and hemmed them within the wall of Agricola —as their songs have it, " forcing the King of the World to retire beyond his *gathered heaps.*"

In 1727, George II. was crowned, and six months after it was known in the Highlands that another " stranger filled the Stuarts' throne," and perhaps as many years elapsed before it was known in some of the Scottish isles, so dilatory was the transmission of news in the last century.

Even Montrose had now ceased to molest Rob Roy, who in his prosperity no longer " drew his grace's rents," but, extending his possessions beyond Balquhidder, leased some mountain-farms from the Duke of Argyle. On learning this, Montrose, in whose breast the old emotion of animosity still rankled, before the Lords of the Privy Council in London, accused his grace, who was the famous Field-Marshal John Duke of Argyle and Greenwich, of " fostering and protecting an outlaw."

" I do neither," replied he, angrily; " I only supply Rob Roy with the wood of the forest, the fish of the stream, the grass of the glen, and the deer of the hill—the common heritage of all Highlanders. But *you* have afforded him cattle, corn, and meal; moreover, we are informed that he is your grace's factor, and that on more than one occasion he has collected your rents, especially at Chapelerroch."

Montrose, who felt the taunt implied his own inability to defend himself, bit his lip in angry silence.

About this time Rob would seem to have visited England.

It is also said that he went so far south as London, as a *protégé* of the Duke of Argyle, who was then in the zenith of his military and political influence. The story adds, that the duke requested Rob, in his full Highland dress and arms, to promenade for some time before St. James's Palace, where the attention of George II. was drawn to him—his garb being somewhat unusual in such a locality, and more especially in those days.

Some time after, when Argyle attended a royal *levée*, the king observed that he had " lately seen a handsome Scots Highlander near the palace."

" He was Robert MacGregor," replied the duke; " the identical outlaw who has long kept the Highlands of Perthshire in a turmoil by his resistance and resentments."

At this reply the king was very much incensed; but be the story as it may, there appeared in London, about this time, a pretended memoir of Rob, under the flattering title of *The Highland Rogue.* " It is," says the great novelist, " a catch-penny publication, bearing in front the effigy of a species of ogre, with a beard a foot long, and therein his actions are as much exaggerated as his personal appearance."

It was during his absence in the south that Helen MacGregor enacted the only bold and masculine part she is known to have played on the stage of real life.

The proprietor of Achenriach, near the clachan of Campsie, having refused to pay his arrears of black-mail, Helen, as her two eldest sons were absent, being lieutenants in the Highland Watch under Glune Dhu, mounted on horseback, with a pair of loaded pistols at her saddlebow, and attended by Greumoch and twelve tall gillies fully armed, with targets on their backs and long muskets sloped on their shoulders, crossed the Campsie Fells, and presenting herself at the gate of Achenriach, demanded of the laird the tax which was due to her absent husband.

He speedily came forth with the money, saying, " Madam, I can refuse a lady nothing—neither would I have the hardihood to oppose *you.*"

In this district Rob's nephew levied black-mail till within little more than a hundred years ago.

CHAPTER LVI.

THE DUELS WITH INVERNAHYLE AND ARDSHEIL.

As time stole on and ripening age wrinkled the brow and whitened the beard of Rob Roy, he lived a quiet and inoffensive life. A change came gradually over him. Time with its mellowing influences rendered him less fierce, less irritable, and in the events that marked the close of his career he showed less inclination to meet half-way those who would seek a quarrel with him.

In the winter of 1727, while purchasing some cattle at the fair of Doune, he obtained among others a cow from a woman who offered it for sale.

On the following Sunday he happened to attend the parish church. The sermon of the minister was directed against the sin of covetousness, fraud, and roguery; and his text was the Eighth Commandment.

Emphatically and amply did the divine expatiate upon his subject; and with his eyes fixed resolutely on MacGregor, threw out so many offensive hints, which were evidently meant for *him*, that Rob soon found himself the centre of observation; and his heart swelled with rage, while he could not but admire the daring of the man who thus bearded one who might have fired both church and manse about his ears.

However, smothering his wrath, Rob waited quietly until the sermon was over and the congregation had dispersed. He then repaired to the manse, and requested to see the minister, who met him with a calm and unflinching front.

" Reverend sir," said he, " I was present, as you no doubt perceived, at sermon this morning, and heard your discourse, every word of which I understood, but should like to know what you *meant* by it. I am an old man now, and have lived a bold and perilous life, but I shall thank you to point out a single instance of fraud or roguery that has dishonoured it. If you cannot, as you have made me a spectacle to your parishioners, by the souls of those who died in Glenfruin ! I will compel you to retract your words in your own pulpit."

Unmoved by the stern bearing of Rob, whose right hand clutched his dirk, the minister replied,—

" I own, MacGregor, that I alluded to you."

" Dioul, to me ! " exclaimed Rob, furiously.

" To you. Did you not buy a cow from a poor widow at the fair of Doune—a cow at little more than half its value ? "

" Sir, I was ignorant that she was poor, that she was a widow, and considered her cow worth double what she asked for it ; but is my whole life to be slandered thus, and about a miserable cow ? "

" Her family are starving—that cow was the last of her herd, for the others all died of disease."

" If this be the case," said Rob, " I shall restore to her the cow with double the sum I paid for it; here," he added, laying the bank-notes on the table, " I leave the money with your reverence. I shall do more; she shall have eight cows, the best in my herd, and money to stock her farm anew, for never shall it be said that a widow appealed in vain to the sympathy of Rob Roy ! "

After this time he passed nearly seven years in perfect peace; but in 1734 he became embroiled with a very powerful enemy, Stewart of Appin.

The clan of MacLaren laid claim to the land of Invernentie in Balquhidder; to this the MacGregors also had a right, which they enforced by the blades of their swords, expelling therefrom Hamish Mac-Laren. A portion of Balquhidder was certainly the ancient patrimony of the Clan Laren, and their feud with the MacGregors was embittered by the memory that the latter, in 1604, had slain *forty-six* of their householders, with all their wives and chil-dren, as the criminal record has it.

In 1734, they appealed to Appin, chief of the Stewarts, a powerful tribe, which could always muster from seven to eight hundred swordsmen. General Stewart of Garth, so lately as 1821, reckoned the fighting force of this name at four thousand men.

The MacLarens assembled in great numbers;

Appin reinforced them with four hundred chosen men, and together they marched into Balquhidder, where Rob Roy with all his kindred was in arms to oppose them.

The summer sun shone brightly on the grey walls of the old kirk of Balquhidder, shaded by its dark yew-trees, and its quaint old burial-ground studded with mossy head-stones, when close by it the hostile clans approached each other in two lines, each man with his round shield braced upon his left arm, and his sword brandished in his right hand.

All the Stewarts had thistles in their bonnets; the MacLarens had laurel leaves, and their war-cry, "Craig Tuirc! Craig Tuirc!" was shouted fiercely by a hundred tongues, for they were eager to engage.

Conspicuous in front of the MacGregors stood Rob Roy, in his waving tartans; his once ruddy beard was now white with time, but his strong form was erect as ever. Anxious to avoid bloodshed, when the adverse clans were about a hundred yards apart he stepped resolutely forward, sheathed his sword and requested Stewart of Appin to meet him half-way. Stewart accordingly sheathed his weapon, and also stepped forward from his line.

"Appin," said Rob, "I am deeply grieved that those who bear the royal name should come as invaders into the land of Clan Alpine, whose race is also royal. Our forefathers were friends, and stood side by side in battle on the braes of Ran-

noch. The same inscription is on both our sword-
blades—see," he added, showing the favourite
legend, usually carved on all Scottish swords
between 1707 and 1746,—

" PROSPERITY TO SCOTLAND, AND NO UNION."

" I have come but to right my kinsman Invernentie, and restore to him the lands of which your
people have reft him," replied Appin.

"Those lands were ours of old, Appin. But
hearken ! we are all loyal men to *the king*, and it
were a pity we should weaken our mutual strength
by mortal conflict, so I shall consent that Hamish
MacLaren hold the lands of Invernentie at an easy
quit-rent."

" To that will I agree blythely," said Appin, who
was a tall, brave, and handsome man, dressed in
scarlet Stewart tartan, with a grass-green coat
covered with gold lace, and who had in his bonnet
a white rose, with the three feathers of his rank.

" 'Tis well—so there's my thumb on't," said
Rob, as they shook hands. "But now," he added,
" as we have here so many gallant men in arms, it
will be a shameful thing if we all separate 'thout a
trial of skill ; so I here take the liberty of inviting
any gentleman Stewart to exchange a few blows
with me for the honour of our respective clans."

On this, Appin's brother-in-law, Alaster of Invernahyle, sprang forward, exclaiming,—

" I accept the challenge ! "

" Good ; and we shall lower our swords when the first blood is drawn."

The pipers struck up on both sides, as the two combatants engaged with claymore, dirk, and target ; but in a few minutes the red blood spirted from the sword-arm of Rob Roy, who immediately lowered his blade, and said,—

" I congratulate you, Alaster of Invernahyle, on being one of the very few who have drawn blood from the veins of Rob Roy."

" Nay," said Stewart, as he offered his handkerchief to bind up the wound, " without the advantages which youth and its agility give me, I had come off with neither honour nor safety."

" I thank you, MacGregor," said Appin, " that your brave blood has alone been shed here to-day. Farewell !—we go back to the braes of Appin. If I survive you, this hand shall lay the first stone of your cairn and bid it speak to future times."

" To you, Appin, thanks ! you must indeed survive me. The Red MacGregor is *red* only in name now—his hair is white as the snows on Ben Lomond."

This was his *last* appearance in arms.

Some time after this, in a trial of strength with Stewart of Ardsheil, finding his eyesight dim, his sword-arm weak, and that he was compelled to give ground, his cheek—a wrinkled cheek now—flushed red with shame ; tears stood in his eyes, and he flung his old and faithful blade upon the heather.

"Never have I drawn thee without honour," he exclaimed; "but alas! never shall I draw thee more!"

Ardsheil, a generous and high-spirited gentleman, was deeply moved by the grief of the old warrior for his own decay of strength. Picking up the claymore, and presenting the hilt to Rob Roy, he politely raised his bonnet, and said,—

"Shame on me, shame that I should have drawn on years and bravery such as yours! But give me your hand, MacGregor—your hand, and henceforth let us be friends."

"Alas!" said Rob, sadly; "I am too old now to be your enemy!"

CHAPTER LVII.

THE CLOSING SCENE.

THE health and strength of Rob Roy decayed rapidly after this, and the winter of 1734, with its unusual severity, sorely affected his shattered form. Helpless as a child, he was confined to bed at last by extreme old age rather than illness, at his house of Inverlochluvig.

On an evening towards the end of December he sunk rapidly. Helen, then an aged woman, was his constant attendant, and he requested her to throw open the windows that he might take a last farewell of the sun, then setting in his ruddy splendour, and casting the purple shadows of Ben More far across the snowclad braes of Balquhidder.

In the clear, frosty atmosphere of the winter eve he could hear the cattle lowing in the fold, and the laughter of the children ringing merrily from the adjacent clachan, and both were music to the old man's ear.

" Death is at hand, Helen—close—close ! " said he, sadly, to his wife; " I may at times have been harsh—sharp with you."

" Oh, never—never to me, Rob," said she, sobbing heavily.

" If ever so, forgive me ! "

" Forgive you, my poor old Rob ! " she exclaimed, and threw her arms around him.

" I have never asked forgiveness save from those I loved, and most of them have gone before us, Helen. The hands of my forefathers beckon me; I can see their dim forms amid the blue mist on the hill! Has the sun set, Helen ? "

" No—why ? "

" It is growing so dark—so very dark—open the window !"

" It *is* open," said Helen, in a broken voice.

" Oh that I could but have again the sweet perfume of the yellow broom and purple heather-bell; or hear the hum of the mountain-bee and the voice of the cushat-dove ! But who comes ? " he added, as a step approached softly.

'Twas old Alpine, who entered to say that MacLaren of Invernentie had called to inquire for him.

Then there came over Rob Roy something of the same impulse which, according to the English legend, animated the brave freebooter Robin Hood, when he was propped up on his death-bed, to shoot a last clothyard shaft with his trusty yew.

" MacLaren ! " he exclaimed, rallying all his failing powers, while his sunken eyes flashed with light; " raise me up, Helen ! Coll ! Hamish ! Robin Oig ! bring me my bonnet and plaid, my pistols, dirk, and claymore, and *then* admit him ; for never shall it be said that a foeman saw Rob Roy defence-less and unarmed!"

His commands were immediately obeyed. Mac-Laren entered and paid his compliments by inquiring after the health of his formidable neighbour, who maintained a cold and haughty civility during their brief conference.

After MacLaren's departure Rob still sat up in bed, with his plaid about him, and his sword in his hand, and he muttered scraps of Ossian with his prayers.

"The winds shall whistle in my grey hair and not awake me. The sons of future years shall pass away—another race shall rise, for the people are like the waves of ocean: like the leaves of woody Morven, they pass away in the rustling blast, and *other* leaves lift their green heads on high.* Now, Helen—wife," he added, "all is over! Strike up, Alpine, *Ha til mi tulidh!* (We return no more!)"

Old and blind almost, like his dying leader, Alpine, while the hot tears streamed over his withered cheeks, played that solemn dirge, and ere it was over Rob Roy had passed away, and Helen MacGregor and her five sons were on their knees around a breathless corpse.

He expired on the 28th of December, 1734, in about the eightieth year of his age, and

* Berrathon.

his demise is recorded thus simply in the *Caledonian Mercury* newspaper of 9th January following :—

" *On Sunday se'nnight died at Balquhidder, in Perthshire, the famous Highland partizan,* ROB ROY."

*   *   *   *   *

His funeral was the last in Perthshire at which a piper was employed, according to General Stewart.

Helen did not survive him long.

The future of their sons—that future which had filled the soul of poor Rob Roy with so many fears and anxieties—was varied, and the fate of two was dark and tragic.

History tells us that Hamish commanded the MacGregors in the army of Prince Charles, and that he had his leg broken by a cannon-ball at the battle of Gladsmuir. He escaped from the Castle of Edinburgh with characteristic daring, and fled to France, where a free pardon was offered him if he would betray another fugitive, named Allan Breac Stewart; but he declined, saying,—

" I was born a Highland gentleman, and can never accept that which would make me the disgrace of my family and the scoff of my country."

Shortly afterwards he died of *starvation* in the streets of Paris, when George III. was king.

In his thirteenth year Robin Oig shot MacLaren of Invernentie dead between the stilts of his plough, for insulting his mother; and the gun with which he perpetrated this terrible act is now at Abbotsford. He fled, became a soldier in the 42nd Regiment, and fought gallantly at Fontenoy, where he was wounded and taken prisoner by the French; but five years after the battle, by an overstrained power of the officers of the Crown, he died on the scaffold at Edinburgh. For the others, I must refer my readers to Burke's "Landed Gentry."

"Happily, now-a-days," says a recent writer, "the Celt and the Sassenach — Scotsman and Englishman—fight side by side, under one standard. *How* the brave soldiers of the Highlands fight has been shown in many a glorious struggle—at Talavera, Salamanca, and Waterloo; nor will history forget *the thin red line* of Balaclava, or the shrill pibroch of Havelock's small but gallant force, which came like home-music to the ears and hearts of those who defended Lucknow!"

*   *   *   *   *

At the east end of the old church of Balquhidder, within an enclosure formed by the foundations of the more ancient Catholic place of worship, lies the grave of Rob Roy.

It is covered by a rough stone of hard mica, on

which a number of emblems are rudely sculptured. Among these the figure of a Highlander and a large broadsword can be distinctly traced.

Under this stone, in February, 1754, were also interred the remains of his son, Robin Oig.

Such is the story of ROB ROY the Outlaw.

THE END.

WYMAN AND SONS, PRINTERS, GREAT QUEEN STREET, LONDON.

GEORGE ROUTLEDGE AND SONS.

LITTLE LAYS FOR LITTLE FOLK. Selected by John G. Watts. Illustrated on every page in the highest style of Art. Imp. 8vo. cloth elegant, gilt edges, 5s.

ORIGINAL POEMS. By Emily and Jane Taylor. Numerously illustrated in the highest style of Art. Imp. 8vo. cloth elegant, gilt edges, 5s.

PLEASURES OF OLD AGE. From the French of Emile Souvestre. Post 8vo. cloth, gilt edges, 4s.

THE JOURNAL OF A LONDON PLAY-GOER. By Professor Morley. Fcp. 8vo. cloth, 5s.

MERRY CONCEITS AND WHIMSICAL RHYMES. By Charles H. Ross. With Thirty Humourous Illustrations printed in Colours. Small 4to. fancy boards, 1s.

LITTLE LADDERS FOR LEARNING. With 750 Illustrations. Crown 8vo. cloth, 3s. 6d.

PETER'S ADVENTURES. By J. Greenwood. With Thirty-six Comic Illustrations by Griset. 4to boards, 3s. 6d.

THE QUEENS OF SOCIETY. By Grace and Philip Wharton. With 16 Illustrations by Doyle, &c. Post 8vo. cloth, 5s.

THE WITS AND BEAUX OF SOCIETY. By Grace and Philip Wharton. With 16 Illustrations. Post 8vo. cloth, 5s.

A THOUSAND AND ONE GEMS OF ENGLISH POETRY. Selected and arranged by Charles Mackay, with Illustrations. Crown 8vo. cloth, 3s. 6d.

BARFORD BRIDGE; or, Schoolboy Trials.
By Rev. H. C. ADAMS, Author of "Cherry Stones," &c. With Illustrations. Fcp. 8vo. cloth, 5s.

THE EARTH AND ITS INHABITANTS.
By MARGARET E. DARTON. A new and revised edition. Crown 8vo. cloth, 3s. 6d.

THE CHILD'S COLOURED GIFT BOOK.
With 100 Illustrations, printed in colours by LEIGHTON BROTHERS. 16mo. cloth, 5s.

THE CHILD'S COLOURED SCRIPTURE
BOOK. With 100 Illustrations, printed in colours by LEIGHTON BROTHERS. 16mo. cloth, gilt, 5s.

Author's Editions.

THE COMPLETE POETICAL WORKS OF
LONGFELLOW. With 170 Illustrations by JOHN GILBERT. Printed on toned paper by CLAY. 4to. cloth elegant, gilt edges, 21s.

THE RED LINE EDITION OF LONG-
FELLOW'S COMPLETE POETICAL WORKS. With Fifty Illustrations by JOHN GILBERT. 8vo. cloth elegant, gilt edges, 10s. 6d. Also the crown 8vo. edition, cloth gilt, 5s. And the following cheaper editions : Fcap. 8vo. cloth elegant, gilt edges, 3s. 6d. ; fcap. 8vo. cloth, 2s. 6d. ; 16mo. sewed, 1s.

THE PROSE WORKS OF LONGFELLOW.
With Illustrations by JOHN GILBERT. Crown 8vo. cloth, 5s.

THE DIVINE COMEDY OF DANTE ALI-
GHIERI. Translated by HENRY WADSWORTH LONGFELLOW. On thick post 8vo. cloth, 7s. 6d.

"We know of no translation in English in which the beautiful and profound thoughts of Dante are rendered with a more conscientious, loving regard than this very literal version of Professor Longfellow."—
The Athenæum.

THE POULTRY BOOK. By W. B. TEGETMEIER.

With 30 full page Illustrations by HARRISON WEIR, printed in Colours, and numerous Woodcuts. Royal 8vo. cloth elegant, gilt edges, 18s.

THE FAMILY DOCTOR: a Dictionary of

Domestic Medicine and Surgery, especially adapted for Family use. By a Dispensary Surgeon. With numerous Illustrations. 800 pages, crown 8vo. cloth, 3s. 6d.

JOHNNY JORDAN AND HIS DOG. By the

Author of "Ernie Elton." With Illustrations. Fcap. 8vo. cloth, 3s. 6d.

WILL ADAMS, the First Englishman in Japan:

A Romantic Biography. By WILLIAM DALTON. With Illustrations. Post 8vo. cloth, gilt edges, 3s. 6d.

THE BIBLE HISTORY OF THE HOLY

LAND. By Dr. KITTO. Illustrated with numerous Illustrations and Maps. Royal 8vo. cloth, gilt edges, 7s. 6d.

ONCE UPON A TIME. By CHARLES KNIGHT.

A new and enlarged edition. Crown 8vo. cloth, gilt edges, 5s.

WATCH THE END. By THOMAS MILLER.

With Forty Illustrations. Post 8vo. cloth, 5s.

A PICTURE HISTORY OF ENGLAND, from

the Invasion of Julius Cæsar to the Present Time. Written for the use of the Young by Dr. DULCKEN. With Eighty Engravings from the designs of A. W. BAYES. 4to. cloth, 5s.

THE WHITE BRUNSWICKERS; or, Remi-

niscences of Schoolboy Life. By the Rev. H. C. ADAMS, Author of "Cherry Stones," &c. With Illustrations. Fcap. 8vo. cloth, 5s.

MEN I HAVE KNOWN. By WILLIAM JERDAN.

Illustrated with Facsimile Autographs. Post 8vo. cloth. 10s. 6d.

GRISET'S GROTESQUES ; or, Jokes drawn on
Wood. With Rhymes by TOM HOOD. One Hundredquaint Designs by ERNEST GRISET. Engraved by the Brothers DALZIEL. 4to. cloth elegant, gilt edges, 3s. 6d.

SUMMER TIME IN THE COUNTRY. By
ROBERT ARIS WILLMOTT. Numerously Illustrated by BIRKET FOSTER. Impl. 8vo. cloth elegant, gilt edges, 7s. 6d.

THE TRAVELLER: a Poem. By OLIVER
GOLDSMITH. Illustrated with etchings on steel, by BIRKET FOSTER. Cloth, elegant, gilt edges, 7s. 6d.

THE NATURAL HISTORY OF MAN : ASIA,
AMERICA, AUSTRALASIA, ETC. Being an Account of the Uncivilised Races of Man. By the Rev. J. G. WOOD, M.A., F.L.S. With numerous Illustrations by ANGAS, DANBY, WOLF, ZWECKER, and others. Engraved by the Brothers DALZIEL. Royal 8vo. cloth, 20s.

THE WORKS OF PRESCOTT, 5 vols., post
8vo. in a beautiful fancy binding, 25s.

THE MICROSCOPE : its History, Construction,
and Application. Being a familiar Introduction to the use of the Instrument, and the study of Microscopical Science. By JABEZ HOGG, F.L.S. F.R.M.S. With upwards of Five Hundred Engravings and Coloured Illustrations by TUFFEN WEST. Seventh edition, crown 8vo. cloth, 7s. 6d.

HOUSEHOLD STORIES, Collected by the
Brothers GRIMM. Now translated, with 240 Illustrations by E. H. WEHNERT. Crown 8vo. cloth, gilt edges, 7s. 6d.

STORIES FOR THE HOUSEHOLD. By
HANS CHRISTIAN ANDERSEN. Translated by Dr. DULCKEN. With Two Hundred and Forty Illustrations, engraved by the Brothers DALZIEL. Crown 8vo. cloth, gilt edges, 7s. 6d.

NOVELS AT ONE SHILLING.

By CAPTAIN MARRYAT.

Peter Simple.
The King's Own.
Midshipman Easy.
Rattlin the Reefer.
Pacha of Many Tales.
Newton Forster.

Jacob Faithful.
The Dog-Fiend.
Japhet in Search of a Father.
The Poacher.
The Phantom Ship.

Percival Keene.
Valerie.
Frank Mildmay.
Olla Podrida.
Monsieur Violet.

By W. H. AINSWORTH.

Windsor Castle.
Tower of London.
The Miser's Daughter.
Rookwood.
Old St. Paul's.
Crichton.

Guy Fawkes.
The Spendthrift.
James the Second.
Star Chamber.
Flitch of Bacon.
Lancashire Witches.

Mervyn Clitheroe.
Ovingdean Grange.
St. James's.
Auriol.
Jack Sheppard.

By J. FENIMORE COOPER.

The Pilot.
Last of the Mohicans.
The Pioneers.
The Red Rover.
The Spy.
Lionel Lincoln.
The Deerslayer.
The Pathfinder.
The Bravo.

The Waterwitch.
Two Admirals.
Satanstoe.
Afloat and Ashore.
Wyandotté.
Eve Effingham.
Miles Wallingford.
The Headsman.
The Prairie.

Homeward Bound.
The Borderers.
The Sea Lions.
Heidenmauer.
Precaution.
Oak Openings.
Mark's Reef.
Ned Myers.

By ALEXANDRE DUMAS.

Three Musketeers.
Twenty Years After.
Doctor Basilius.
The Twin Captains.
Captain Paul.
Memoirs of a Physician. 2 vols. (1s. each).
The Chevalier de Maison Rouge.
Queen's Necklace.

Countess de Charny.
Monte Cristo. 2 vols. (1s. each).
Nanon.
The Two Dianas.
The Black Tulip.
Forty-Five Guardsmen.
Taking of the Bastile. 2 vols. (1s. each).
Chicot the Jester.

The Conspirators.
Ascanio.   [Savoy.
Page of the Duke of
Isabel of Bavaria.
Beau Tancrede.
Regent's Daughter.
Pauline.
Catherine Blum.
Ingénue.
Russian Gipsy.
Watchmaker.

By MRS. GORE.

The Ambassador's Wife.

By JANE AUSTEN.

Northanger Abbey.
Emma.

Pride and Prejudice.
Sense and Sensibility.

Mansfield Park.

By MARIA EDGEWORTH.

Ennui. | Vivian. | The Absentee. | Manœuvring.

Published by George Routledge and Sons.

4

www.ingramcontent.com/pod-product-compliance
Lightning Source LLC
Chambersburg PA
CBHW021343110726
47900CB00005B/1581